"You look so beautiful, Kiley."

He stepped just inside the door to take her in his arms and give her a soft, lingering kiss. "I'll be the envy of every man at the ball."

"I was just thinking something very similar about you and the women attending the ball," she said, smiling.

"Is the pony princess okay with staying at your folks'?" he asked, as he helped her with her evening wrap.

Nodding, Kiley picked up her sequined clutch. "I don't know who was more excited about her spending the night with them, Emmie or my parents. She has them wrapped around her little finger."

Josh laughed as he placed his hand to her elbow and guided her out to his car. "She has that effect on just about everyone. She's an adorable little girl."

"Thank you," Kiley said, wondering when and how she was going to tell him that Emmie was his daughter.

Texas Cattleman's
gul novel:

Love and scandal meet in Royal, Texas!

HAPPENED
ONE NIGHT

BY
KATHIE DeNOSKY

Published in Great Britain 2013
by Mills & Boon, an imprint of Harlequin (UK) Limited,
Eton House, 18-24 Paradise Road, Richmond, Surrey TW9 1SR

© Harlequin Books S.A. 2013

Special thanks and acknowledgement to Kathie DeNosky for her contribution
to the Texas Cattleman's Club: The Missing Mogul miniseries.

ISBN: 978 0 263 90493 2

51-1213

Harlequin (UK) policy is to use papers that are natural, renewable and
recyclable products and made from wood grown in sustainable forests. The
logging and manufacturing processes conform to the legal environmental
regulations of the country of origin.

Printed and bound in Spain
by Blackprint CPI, Barcelona

H

IT HAPPENED
ONE NIGHT

BY
KATHIE DeNOSKY

79 788 283 6

Published in Great Britain 2013
by Mills & Boon, an imprint of Harlequin (UK) Limited,
Eton House, 18-24 Paradise Road, Richmond, Surrey TW9 1SR

© Harlequin Books S.A. 2013

Special thanks and acknowledgement to Kathie DeNosky for her contribution to the Texas Cattleman's Club: The Missing Mogul miniseries.

ISBN: 978 0 263 90493 2

51-1213

Harlequin (UK) policy is to use papers that are natural, renewable and recyclable products and made from wood grown in sustainable forests. The logging and manufacturing processes conform to the legal environmental regulations of the country of origin.

Printed and bound in Spain
by Blackprint CPI, Barcelona

Kathie DeNosky lives in her native southern Illinois on the land her family settled in 1839. She writes highly sensual stories with a generous amount of humor; her books have appeared on the *USA TODAY* bestseller list and received numerous awards, including two National Readers' Choice Awards. Kathie enjoys going to rodeos, traveling to research settings for her books and listening to country music. Readers may contact her by emailing kathie@kathiedenosky.com. They can also visit her website, www.kathiedenosky.com, or find her on Facebook, www.facebook.com/Kathie-DeNosky-Author/278166445536145.

This book is dedicated to the authors
of the Texas Cattleman's Club: The Missing Mogul.
Working with you all was a real pleasure.

Prologue

When Josh Gordon let himself into his girlfriend's apartment, he wanted two things—to make love to Lori and get some much-needed sleep. He'd spent a long day preparing job bids for Gordon Construction and an even longer evening wining and dining a potential client, who couldn't seem to make up his mind whether to give the contract for his new office building to the construction business Josh and his twin brother, Sam, co-owned or to one of their competitors.

Josh wasn't overly proud or happy about it, but they'd had enough to drink to float a fleet of ships before the man finally gave the nod to Gordon Construction. That's why Josh had made the decision to spend the night with Lori. The wine had dulled his normally sharp senses and he didn't think his being behind the steering wheel of a car was in anyone's best interest.

Since she had given him a key to her apartment a few weeks back and it was only a couple of blocks from the restaurant, walking to Lori's place had seemed wiser than trying to drive the five miles to his ranch outside of town. Besides, he hadn't seen her in a few days and missed losing himself in her soft charms.

The fact that their relationship was more of a physical connection than it was an emotional attachment should have bothered him. But neither he nor Lori wanted anything more, and he couldn't see any harm in two consenting adults spending their time enjoying each other for as long as the attraction lasted.

As he made his way across the dark living room and headed down the hall toward her bedroom, he decided not to turn on a lamp. The headache that had developed during the last few rounds of drinks already had his head feeling like his brain had outgrown his skull. The harsh glare of a light certainly wouldn't make it feel any better.

Loosening his tie, he removed his suit jacket as he quietly opened the bedroom door and, stripping off the rest of his clothes, climbed into bed with the feminine form he could just make out beneath the covers. Without thinking twice he took her in his arms and teased her lips with his to wake her.

He thought he heard her murmur something a moment before she began to kiss him back, but Josh didn't give her a chance to say more. He was too captivated by her. Lori had never tasted as sweet and the scent of whatever new shampoo she had used caused him to ache with the urgent need to sink himself deep inside of her.

When she ran her hands over his shoulders, then

tangled her fingers in the hair at the nape of his neck as she kissed him with a passion that robbed him of breath, a shaft of longing coursed through him. She needed him as badly as he needed her. He didn't hesitate to slide his hand down her side to her knee, then, catching the hem of her nightshirt, he brought it up to her waist. Never breaking the kiss, he made quick work of removing the scrap of silk and lace covering her feminine secrets and nudged her knees apart.

His heart felt like it might jump right out of his chest when he rose over her and she reached to guide him to her. Her desire for him to join their bodies was as strong as his and, giving them what they both wanted, he entered her in one smooth stroke.

Setting an urgent pace, he marveled at how much tighter she felt, how her body seemed to cling to his. But the white-hot haze of passion was stronger than his ability to reason and he dismissed his confusion as a result of too much wine.

When she clenched her tiny feminine muscles, he knew she was poised on the edge, and deepening his strokes, Josh pushed them both over the edge. As he emptied himself deep inside of her, her moan indicated that she was experiencing the same mind-blowing pleasure that pulsed through him, and feeling drained of energy, he collapsed on top of her.

"Oh, Mark, that was incredible."

Josh went completely still as his mind tried to process what he had heard. The woman he had just made love with had called him Mark. If that wasn't enough to send a cold sense of dread knifing through him, the fact that it wasn't Lori's voice sure as hell was.

What had he done? Where was Lori? And who was the woman he had just made love with?

Sobering faster than he could blink, Josh levered himself to her side, then quickly sat up on the side of the bed to reach for his discarded clothes. "I…um… oh, hell. I'm really sorry. I thought…you were Lori."

The woman was silent for a moment before she gasped and he heard her jump to her feet on the other side of the bed. "Oh, dear God! No, this can't be… We didn't… You must be—"

"Josh," he finished for her, since she seemed to be having problems conveying her thoughts.

He kept his back to her as he pulled on his pants and shirt. Not that she could see in the dark any more than he could. But all things considered, it just seemed like the right thing to do.

"I really am sorry." He knew his apologies weren't nearly adequate enough for the circumstances, but then he wasn't sure anything he could say or do would make the situation any less humiliating for either of them. "I swear to God, I thought you were Lori."

"I'm her…sister," the woman said, sounding like she might be recovering her ability to speak in a complete sentence.

He knew Lori had a sister, but since their relationship was mostly physical, he and Lori hadn't delved too deeply into the details of each other's lives. And if she had mentioned her sister by name, he'd be damned if he could think of it now.

"I'd give anything if this hadn't—"

"Please, don't," she said, cutting him off. "Just leave…Josh."

He hesitated, then, deciding that it was probably

the best—the only—thing he could do, he walked to the front door and let himself out of the apartment. He had no sooner pulled the door shut than he heard her set the dead bolt and slide the chain into place.

His heart stalled for a moment, then began to beat double time. He had been just drunk enough and she apparently had been sleepy enough for both of them to forget the use of a condom. It was something he had never forgotten before and he couldn't believe that he'd done so this time.

Completely sober now, he shook his head as he walked the short distance to his Mercedes still sitting in the restaurant's parking lot. He was going to drive home and when he woke up in the morning, he hoped to discover that he'd dreamed the entire incident.

But as he got into the car and started the engine, he knew as surely as the sun rose in the east each morning that wasn't going to be the case. Nothing was going to change the fact that he had done the unthinkable. He had made love to his girlfriend's sister—the most exciting, responsive woman he had ever met. And what was even worse, he had no clue what she looked like and didn't even know her name.

One

Three years later

Standing in the hallway outside the meeting rooms at the Texas Cattleman's Club, Kiley Roberts sighed heavily. If she hadn't had enough problems dealing with the vandalism of the club's new day care center a few months ago, now she was about to face the funding committee to ask for an increase in funds to run it. Unfortunately, from everything she had heard, she was facing an uphill battle. Several of the committeemen had been extremely vocal about not seeing the need to provide child care for club members, and among them was the chairman of the funding committee, Josh Gordon.

They had never been formally introduced and she didn't even know if he knew who she was. But she knew him and just the thought of having to deal with the man made her cringe with embarrassment.

Every detail of what happened that night three years ago had played through her mind since discovering that Josh was a member of the club. But when she learned he was chairman of the funding committee—the very committee that controlled the money to run the day care center—she felt as if she'd been kicked in the stomach. Being the center's director, she had to go to the committee for approval on everything outside of the budget they had set for it. That meant she would frequently have to deal with him.

She took a deep fortifying breath. How could fate be so cruel?

If she hadn't been half-asleep and wanting so badly to believe that Mark—her then-boyfriend and now ex-husband—had followed her to her sister's apartment to apologize for the argument they'd had, the incident three years ago would have never taken place. She would have realized right away that Josh wasn't Mark and stopped him before things went too far.

Kiley shook her head at her own foolishness. She should have known when Josh kissed her with such passion that the man in bed with her wasn't Mark. The only thing Mark had ever been passionate about was himself.

Sighing, she straightened her shoulders. There was nothing she could do about it now, and there was no sense in dwelling on something she couldn't change. She just wished anyone other than Josh Gordon was heading up the funding committee. Aside from the humiliating incident, he had broken her sister's heart when he abruptly ended things between them a month or so after that fateful night, and Kiley simply didn't trust him.

When the door to the meeting room opened, interrupting her tumultuous thoughts, a man she assumed to be one of the members motioned toward her. "Ms. Roberts, the committee is ready to hear from you now."

Nodding, Kiley took a deep breath and forced her feet to move forward when what she really wanted to do was turn around and head in the opposite direction. "Thank you."

As she walked toward the long table at the head of the room where Josh sat with three men and a woman, she focused on them instead of Josh. The only two she recognized were Beau Hacket and Paul Windsor. Great. They seemed to be the unofficial leaders of those opposed to the day care center and it was just her luck that they both happened to be on the funding committee. Kiley's only hope was to appeal to the lone female member and the man sitting next to her.

"Good afternoon," she said, forcing herself to give them all a cheerful smile when she was feeling anything but optimistic.

"What can we do for you today…" Josh glanced at the papers on the table in front of him as if checking for her name "…Ms. Roberts?"

When their gazes finally met, she felt a little better. She had been hired by the club's personnel director and had managed to avoid coming face-to-face with Josh in the short time she had been working at the Texas Cattleman's Club. But now, she realized her nervousness had been unfounded. Apparently Lori had never mentioned her by name and thanks to the blackout curtains her sister preferred, neither of them had been able to see the other that night. Deciding he was either a good enough actor to deserve an Academy Award or he had no idea who she was, her confidence returned.

"As the director, I'm here to ask the committee to consider appropriating additional funds for the day care center," she stated, surprised her voice sounded strong and steady in spite of her earlier case of jangled nerves.

"What for?" Beau Hacket demanded. "We've already budgeted more than is necessary to babysit a bunch of little kids."

"I can't believe you just said that," the middle-aged woman seated to Josh's right said, glaring at Beau.

Kiley watched Josh give the man a disapproving glare before he turned his attention back to her. "What do you think you need the additional funds for, Ms. Roberts?"

"The club members' response to the day care center has been so positive, we have more children than we first anticipated," she answered, already knowing from the negative expression on his face how Beau Hacket would be voting on the matter.

"All you're doing is watching a handful of little kids for a couple of hours," Beau spoke up. "I don't see where you need more money for that. Sit them down with a crayon and a piece of paper and they'll be happy."

"Beau."

There was a warning in Josh's tone, but Kiley knew it was more a rule of order than any kind of support for her. Josh Gordon had been almost as vocal in his objections to the day care center as Beau Hacket and Paul Windsor had. Since the club started admitting female members a few years ago, the TCC had experienced quite a few growing pains as it made changes to accommodate the needs of women in its ranks, the most recent change being the addition of the day care center.

Focusing her attention on the others seated at the conference table and off the committee chairman, she decided it was time to set them straight. "I think some of you have a few misconceptions about the day care center. Yes, we do provide a safe environment for the members to leave their children while they attend meetings or events at the clubhouse, but we're more than just a babysitting service. Some of the members depend on us for early childhood education, as well."

"My granddaughter is one of your students and in the short time she's been attending, we've all been amazed at how much she's learned," the woman seated beside Josh said, smiling.

"Why can't they teach their own kids how to finger-paint at home?" Beau demanded, his disapproval evident in the tone of his voice as he glared at her.

"I'm trained in early childhood education," Kiley explained, hoping to convince the man of the importance of day care, but knowing she probably wouldn't. "The center's programs are age appropriate and structured so that the children are engaged in learning activities for their level of development." When the committee members frowned in obvious confusion, she rushed on to keep one of them from cutting her off. "For example, the toddlers learn how to interact and share with other children, as well as begin to develop friendships and basic social skills. The preschool class learns to recognize and print the letters of the alphabet, as well as their names. And in addition to teaching them how to count, my assistant and I play learning games with both groups designed to pique their interest in things like science and nature." She shook her head. "The list is endless and I could stay here all day outlining the importance of early childhood education and the benefits to a child."

When Kiley stopped to take a breath, the woman on the committee nodded. "My granddaughter has not only learned a lot, she's conquered some of her shyness and has become more outgoing, as well."

Appreciative of the woman's support, Kiley smiled. At least she had one advocate on the committee.

Josh glanced down at the papers on the table in front of him. "You're not asking for more space, just additional money for the center?"

"No, the size of the room isn't a problem. We have enough room for the children we have now, as well as many more." She could tell he wasn't paying much attention to what she had to say and would probably like to deny her outright. But protocol called for the committee to hear her out, discuss her request, then take a vote on the issue. "All I'm asking for is additional money for the day-to-day operation of the center."

"Since you don't have utilities or rent to worry about, what specifically would the funds be used for?" Paul Windsor asked, giving her a charming smile. A ladies' man if there ever was one, the older gentleman's flirtatious smile didn't fool Kiley one bit. He was just as opposed to the day care center as Beau Hacket.

"Some of the children are with us for the entire day, instead of a half day or just a few hours, Mr. Windsor," she answered, relieved she wasn't having to focus on Josh, even though she didn't like Paul Windsor. "We need the extra money for the materials for their activities, as well as the additional lunches and snacks. We also need to hire an extra worker for the infants we occasionally have when their mothers have a tennis match or engage in some of the other activities here at the clubhouse."

"We wouldn't have this problem if we hadn't let women into the club," Beau muttered as he sat back in his chair to glare at her.

"What was that, Beau?" the woman demanded, looking as if she was ready to do battle.

Beau shook his head as he belligerently folded his arms across his barrel chest. "I didn't say a damned thing, Nadine."

Kiley wasn't the least bit surprised at the man's comment or the woman's reaction. Beau Hacket was one of the men still resentful of women being permitted membership into the prestigious club, and the female members had quickly learned to stand up to the "good old boy network" and demand the respect they deserved.

"Is there anything else you'd like to add?" Josh asked, clearly ready to dismiss her and move on to the discussion phase.

"No, I believe I've adequately outlined the purpose of the day care center and the reasons we need the extra funds," she said, knowing in her heart that her plea had fallen on deaf ears—at least where the male members of the committee were concerned.

He nodded. "I think we have more than enough information to consider your request. Thank you for your time and detailed explanation, Ms. Roberts."

Looking up at her, he smiled and Kiley felt as if

the floor moved beneath her feet. His bright blue eyes and engaging smile sent a shiver of awareness coursing from the top of her head to the soles of her feet and, as much as she would have liked to forget, she couldn't stop thinking about what happened that night three years ago.

"I'll drop by the center later this afternoon to let you know the outcome of our vote," Josh finished, oblivious to her reaction.

Feeling as if having to listen to her had been an inconvenience for them, Kiley nodded and walked from the meeting room. There was nothing left for her to do now but await the committee's decision. She wished she felt more positive about the results of their vote. Unfortunately, with three of the center's biggest opponents on the committee, a favorable outcome was highly unlikely.

But as much as she feared hearing their decision, Kiley dreaded having to see Josh again even more. Why couldn't he send one of the other members to let her know what had been decided? Didn't she already have enough on her plate without having to worry about seeing him again?

She had a two-year-old daughter to care for and a house that seemed to be in constant need of one repair or another, and, if the additional money for the day care didn't come through, the center might have to close due to a clause in the club's amended bylaws assuring that no member's child would be turned away, and she would be out of a job. And even if he didn't know who she was, she certainly didn't need the added stress of being reminded of the most embarrassing incident of her entire life.

* * *

As Josh walked down the hall toward the day care center, he couldn't for the life of him figure out why he felt as though he knew Kiley Roberts. He didn't think they had met before she walked into the meeting room earlier in the afternoon. If they had, he knew for certain he would have remembered her. A woman that attractive would be damned near impossible to forget.

Normally he preferred his women tall, willowy and with an air of mystery about them. But Kiley made petite and curvy look good—real good. With her chin-length, dark blond hair and the prettiest brown eyes he had ever seen, she looked soft, sexy and very approachable.

He frowned as he tried to remember if he'd even seen her before this afternoon. She might have been at Beau Hacket's barbecue a few months back. It seemed that Hacket had invited the entire membership of the Texas Cattleman's Club, as well as most of the residents of Royal. Or more likely he'd seen her somewhere around the clubhouse, maybe in the restaurant or the bar. But he couldn't shake the feeling that there was more to it than that.

When he reached the door to the old billiard room—now renovated to house the day care center—he shrugged. It really didn't matter. Once he gave her the news that she wouldn't be getting any more money from the club, he would go straight to the top of her Grinch list and that would be the end of that.

Looking through the window in the door, he noticed that the room looked much nicer now than it had a couple of months ago when vandals broke in and tore up the place. They still hadn't caught who was behind the destruction or their motive for doing it, but Josh felt sure the culprits would eventually be caught and dealt with accordingly. Royal, Texas, wasn't that big of a town, and many of its residents were members of the TCC. It was just a matter of time before someone remembered seeing or hearing something that would lead the authorities to make an arrest.

He would hate to be in the vandals' shoes when that happened, he thought as he opened the day care center's door. Whether the place was wanted by all of the members or not, nobody came in and destroyed any part of their clubhouse without the entire membership taking great exception to it.

"I'll be right with you, Mr. Gordon," Kiley said from across the room.

"Take your time," he said, looking around. Several children sat in pint-size chairs at tables that were just as small. He couldn't imagine ever being little enough to fit into furniture that size.

As he watched, Russ and Winnie Bartlett's youngest little girl got out of her chair and walked over to hold up a paper with crayon scribbles for Kiley's inspection. She acted as if the kid had just drawn the *Mona Lisa,* causing the toddler to beam with pride.

Josh had never taken much to little kids. For one thing, he had never been around them and didn't have a clue how to relate to them. But he found himself smiling as he watched Kiley talk to the child as she pinned the drawing to a bulletin board. Only a coldhearted bastard would ignore the fact that she had just made the little girl's day.

"Carrie, could you take over for me for a few minutes?" she asked a young woman Josh assumed to be

the day care worker Kiley had hired not long after
the center opened. When the woman nodded, Kiley
walked over to him and motioned toward a door on the
far side of the room. "Why don't we go into my office?
Otherwise, I can't guarantee we won't be interrupted."

As he followed her to her office, he found himself
fascinated by the slight sway of her hips. He had to
force himself to keep his eyes trained on her slender
shoulders. But that only drew his attention to the exposed skin between the collar of her red sweater and
the bottom of her short blond hair—a spot that looked
extremely kissable.

His heart thumped hard against his rib cage and
heat began to fill his lower belly. What the hell was
wrong with him? Had it been that long since he and
his last girlfriend parted ways?

"Please have a seat, Mr. Gordon," Kiley said, walking behind the small desk to sit down in an old wooden
chair.

He recognized both the desk and the chair as having
been in the storage room for as long as he had been a
member of the club and probably for decades before
that. If circumstances had been different, he might
have felt guilty about the funding committee insisting
her office be furnished with the club's castoffs. But
considering none of the members on the panel, with
maybe the exception of Nadine Capshaw, expected
the center to remain open past spring, it had been decided that the used furniture would be good enough.

"Call me Josh," he said, sitting in a metal folding
chair across the desk from her.

"I assume you've come to tell me the funding
committee's decision on my request…Josh?" she

asked, sounding as if she already knew the outcome of the vote.

There was something about the sound of her voice saying his name that caused him to frown. "Before we get into the committee's decision, could I ask you something?"

"I...uh, suppose so." He could tell by the hesitation in her voice and her wary expression that she didn't trust him.

"Do we know each other?" he asked, realizing immediately from the slight widening of her expressive brown eyes that they did.

"No," she said a little too quickly.

"Are you sure?" he pressed, determined to find out what she knew that he didn't.

"Well, we...um, don't know each other formally," she said, suddenly taking great interest in her tightly clasped hands resting on top of the desk.

She was hiding something, and he intended to find out what it was. "So we have met?" he continued.

"In a way...I guess you could say that." Her knuckles had turned white from her tight grip and he knew whatever she hid was extremely stressful for her. "It was quite by accident."

Every hair follicle on his head felt as if it stood straight up, and he suddenly wasn't so sure he wanted to know what she obviously didn't want to tell him. "Where would that have been?" he heard himself ask in spite of his reservations.

Getting up, she closed her office door, then slowly lowered herself into the chair when she returned to the desk. "You used to date my sister."

A cold, clammy feeling snaked its way up his spine. "I did?"

When she finally raised her head to meet his gaze head-on, a knot the size of his fist began to twist his gut. "I'm Lori Miller's sister. Her *only* sister."

Josh opened his mouth, then snapped it shut. For the first time in his adult life, he couldn't think of a thing to say. But his unusual reaction to her suddenly started to make sense. From the moment she'd walked into the meeting room to plead her case to the funding committee, he had been fighting to keep his libido under control. Now he knew why. He might not have realized who she was, but apparently his body had. The chemistry between them that night three years ago had been undeniable and it appeared that it was just as powerful now. Unless he missed his guess, her nervousness had just as much to do with the magnetic pull between them as it did with her reluctance to admit what had taken place.

As he stared at her, it occurred to him why Kiley seemed familiar to him. Although it had been too dark to tell what she looked like that night, he could see the resemblance between her and her sister now. Kiley had the same extraordinary brown eyes and flawless alabaster skin that Lori had. But that seemed to be where the similarities between the two women ended. While Lori was considerably taller and had auburn hair, Kiley was shorter and had dark blond hair that looked so silky it practically begged a man to tangle his fingers in it as he made love to her. When his lower body began to tighten, he swallowed hard and tried to think of something—anything—to get his mind back on track.

"Your last name is different," he stated the obvious.

She straightened her shoulders and took a deep breath. "I was married briefly."

"But not anymore?" he couldn't stop himself from asking.

"No."

He swallowed hard as a thought suddenly occurred to him. "You weren't married—"

"No. Not then."

Relieved that he hadn't crossed that particular line, Josh released the breath he hadn't been aware of holding. "That's good."

"Look, I'm not any happier than you are about having to work with you on the day care center's funding," she said, her cheeks coloring a pretty pink. "But this isn't the time or the place to get into what happened that night. I think it would be for the best if we forgot the incident ever happened and concentrate on my request for the day care center and the committee's decision not to give me the extra money I need to keep it running."

He knew she was right. A day care center full of little kids certainly wasn't the place to talk over his mistakenly making love to her. And she had a valid point about forgetting that night. It would definitely be the prudent thing to do. But some perverse part of him resented her wanting to dismiss what had arguably been the most exciting night of his life. He'd never been with a woman, either before or since, as responsive and passionate as Kiley had been.

"I agree," he finally said. "We can take a trip down memory lane another time." He could tell his choice of words and the fact that he thought they should revisit the past wasn't what she wanted to hear.

She folded her arms beneath her breasts, causing his mouth to go dry. "Mr. Gordon—"

"I prefer you call me Josh," he reminded her.

"Josh, I think you'd better—"

"I have good news and bad news," he said, thinking quickly. If her body language was any indication, she was about two seconds away from throwing him out of her office.

Whether it was due to the lingering guilt he still harbored over his part in the incident or the distrust he detected in her big brown eyes, he wasn't sure. But he suddenly felt the need to prove to her that she had the wrong opinion of him.

"I'm going to give you a month's worth of the funding you requested in order for you to convince me that the day care center is worthwhile and a needed addition to the services the club provides to the TCC membership," he stated, before she could interrupt.

She frowned. "That isn't what the committee decided, is it?"

"Not exactly," he said honestly. "The committee voted four to one to deny you the extra money. But after seeing the way you were with the Bartletts' little girl, you've got my attention. I'll be checking in periodically to see for myself that the money was needed and put to good use."

If anything, she looked even more skeptical. "What happens at the end of that time?"

"If I determine that you do need the additional funding, at our meeting just before Christmas I'll give my personal recommendation to the committee that we add the amount you asked for to your yearly budget," he finished.

"If my request was turned down, where is this money going to come from?" she asked, looking more suspicious by the second.

"You let me worry about that," he said, rising to his feet. "I'll see that the appropriate amount is added to the day care's account as of this afternoon. It should be accessible for whatever you need by tomorrow morning."

Before she could question him further, he opened her office door and left to go to the TCC's main office to make arrangements for the funding to be put into the day care's account. He was going to be taking the money out of his own pocket to subsidize the center for the next month, but it would be worth it. For one thing, he wanted to prove to her that he wasn't the nefarious SOB she apparently thought him to be. And for another, it was the only thing he could think of that might come close to atoning for his role in what happened three years ago.

Two

Kiley spent most of the next day jumping every time the door to the day care center opened. True to his word, Josh had added money to the center's account and she did appreciate that. But it was his promised visits to observe how she ran things and to see what the funds were being used for that had her nerves stretched to the breaking point. She didn't want to see him again or have to jump through hoops to get the money the center needed. Besides, every time she looked into his blue eyes, it reminded her that they shared a very intimate secret—one that, try as she might, she couldn't forget.

"The children have put away the toys and I've finished reading them a story. Would you like for me to take them outside to the play area for a bit before we start practicing their songs?" Carrie Kramer asked, walking over to where Kiley had finished putting stars by the names of the children who had remembered to wash their hands before their afternoon snack.

"That would be great." Kiley smiled at the young woman she'd hired to be her assistant after meeting her at the Royal Diner. "While they expend some of their excess energy outside, I'll get things ready for us to practice their songs before they go home."

As she watched Carrie help the children get their coats on and form a single line by the exit to the play yard, Kiley turned to go into her office for the things they would be using for the holiday program they were putting on for the parents the week before Christmas. Gathering the props, she decided she would have to make two trips as she turned to retrace her steps back into the main room. Distracted as she tried to remember everything they would need, she ran headlong into Josh standing just inside the doorway to her office.

"Oh, my dear heavens!" The giant jingle bells in the box she carried jangled loudly as she struggled to hang on to it.

Placing his hands on her shoulders to steady her, he frowned. "I didn't mean to frighten you. I called your name when I found the other room empty."

The warmth of his hands seemed to burn through her pink silk blouse. Kiley quickly took a step back. "I must not have heard it over the sound of these bells."

"Let me help you with these," he said, taking the box from her. "Where are the kids?"

"My assistant took them outside for playtime before we start practicing for their Christmas program," she said, picking up her CD player and several large plastic candy canes.

Their arms brushed as she walked past him, and an awareness she hadn't felt in a very long time caused her heart to skip several beats. She did her best to ignore it.

"I intended to stop by earlier in the day, but I got tied up at one of our construction sites and it took longer than I anticipated," he said, following her over to the brightly colored carpet where the children gathered for story time. "I wasn't sure anyone would still be here. When do the kids go home?"

"Normally, all of the children get picked up by five-thirty," she answered, setting the candy canes and the CD player on a small table. "But Gil Addison sometimes gets detained by club business and runs a few minutes late picking up his son, Cade." A single father, the current president of the TCC had been one of the first to enroll his four-year-old son in the preschool class. Unlike the members of the funding committee, Gil seemed extremely enthusiastic about having the center at the clubhouse. "No matter what time it is, I stay until every child is safely in the care of their parents or someone they've designated to pick up the child."

"So this isn't just a nine-to-five job, then?" he asked, placing the box on the carpet.

"Not hardly." Shaking her head, she removed a disc from its case to put in the player. "I have to be here at seven each morning to get things ready for the children's arrival."

"When is that?" he asked, his brow furrowing.

"A couple of them get here a few minutes after I do, but they're all here between eight and eight-thirty," she said, wondering why he was so interested in the hours the day care center operated. "Why do you ask?"

He ran his hand through his short, light brown hair. "I realize you're working on contract with the club and aren't paid overtime, no matter how many hours you work, but doesn't that make for a pretty long day?"

She couldn't help but smile. Being able to be with her daughter while she did her job was well worth any extra time she had to put in at the center. "I don't mind. This is my dream job."

"I guess if that's what makes you happy," he said, looking as if he couldn't understand anyone feeling that way about working those kinds of hours with a group of small children.

When the children began filing into the room from outside, Kiley breathed a sigh of relief. It wasn't that she was afraid of Josh. But being alone with him made her feel jumpy and she welcomed the distraction of a roomful of toddlers and preschoolers. She wasn't at all happy about the effect he had on her and refused to think about why he made her feel that way. She was almost certain she wouldn't like the answer.

"After you've hung up your coats, I want you all to come over to the carpet and sit down, please," she announced to the children. "We're going to practice our songs for your Christmas program before you go home this afternoon."

Her daughter ran over to wrap her arms around one of Kiley's legs, then looked up at her and giggled. "Me sing."

"That's right, Emmie," Kiley said, stroking her daughter's dark blond hair as she smiled down at the only good to come out of her brief marriage. "Can you go over and sit with Elaina and Bobby so we can get started, please?"

Emmie nodded, then hurried over to join her two friends where they sat with the rest of the toddlers.

"Miss Kiley, Jimmy Joe Harper pulled my hair," Sarah Bartlett accused, glaring at the little boy seated beside her.

"Jimmy Joe, did you pull Sarah's hair again?" Even before he nodded, one look at the impish grin on the child's face told Kiley that he had. "I'm sorry, but I told you that if you pulled Sarah's pigtails again you'd have to sit in the 'time out' corner for five minutes."

Without further instruction, the child obediently got to his feet and walked over to sit in a chair by himself in the far corner of the room. When she noticed Josh glancing from her to Jimmy Joe in the "time out" corner, Kiley raised an eyebrow. "Is there something wrong?"

"You didn't even have to tell him to go over there," he said, sounding as if he couldn't quite believe a child would willingly accept his punishment. "And he didn't protest at all."

"Jimmy Joe is no stranger to the 'time out' corner," Kiley answered, smiling fondly at the adorable red-haired little boy. "He loves aggravating Sarah."

Josh looked confused. "Why?"

"Because he likes her." Kiley turned to her assistant. "Could you please pass out the bells and candy canes, Carrie?"

"I see," Josh said as a slow grin curved the corners of his mouth. "In other words, he's teasing her to keep her attention focused on him."

"Something…like that," Kiley said, her breath

catching at how handsome Josh looked when he smiled.

As her assistant finished handing each child an oversize bell or a giant plastic candy cane, Kiley queued up the music on her CD player and purposely avoided looking at Josh. He made her nervous and she wished he would leave. But it appeared as if he intended to stay for a while.

Deciding that as long as he was there, he might as well participate, she picked up one of the bells and shoved it into his hand. "I assume you know the words to 'Jingle Bells'?"

He looked surprised, then determined as he shook his head. "Yes, I'm familiar with the song, but I'm afraid I can't stay. I promised a friend I would stop by his place this afternoon and I'm already running late."

"That's a shame," she lied. She had accomplished what she set out to do. He was going to leave. She couldn't help but smile. "Maybe another time."

"Yeah, maybe," he said, sounding doubtful. He reached out and, taking her hand in his, placed the bell in the center of her palm, then gently folded her fingers around it with his other hand. "Will you be free tomorrow evening?"

Startled by his unexpected question and the warmth of his hands holding hers, she stared at him a moment before she managed to find her voice. "Wh-why?"

"I'd like to discuss a couple of things with you," he said evasively. He gave her a smile that made her insides flutter. "Unfortunately, I don't have time to talk to you about it now. I'll come by here around five-thirty on Friday evening and we'll have dinner in the club's restaurant. They have an excellent menu and we'll be able to talk without interruption."

Kiley opened her mouth to refuse, but when he tenderly caressed her hand with his, she forgot anything she was about to say. As she watched him walk across the room to the door, she shook her head in an effort to regain her equilibrium.

What was Josh up to? And what did he think they needed to discuss? She had been quite clear when she spoke to the funding committee about the use of the extra money for the day care center. Surely he couldn't want to talk about what happened that night....

"Miss Kiley, can I go back to the carpet now?" Jimmy Joe asked from the "time out" corner.

"'May I go back to the carpet,'" Kiley automatically corrected.

"May I?" the little boy asked, flashing his charming grin.

"Yes, you may," she said, deciding that she could give more thought to Josh and his dinner invitation after the children had gone home for the day.

Kiley went through the motions of rehearsing the Christmas show the children would put on for their parents in a few weeks. But her mind kept straying back to Josh and his ridiculous invitation. Even if she were willing to go to dinner with him—which she wasn't—she didn't think he would be all that enthusiastic about dining with a two-year-old.

It wasn't that Emmie wasn't well-behaved. She was. But by the end of the day, she was tired and wanted nothing more than dinner, a bath and to go to bed. Besides, there was absolutely nothing Kiley felt the need to discuss with Josh. Now or in the foreseeable future.

* * *

As Josh drove his Mercedes through the gates of Pine Valley, the exclusive golf course community where several of the TCC members had built mansions, he couldn't help but wonder what he'd been thinking when he asked Kiley to dinner. Why couldn't he just drop what had happened that night three years ago?

He knew that would be the smartest thing to do and what Kiley wanted. But for reasons he didn't want to delve into, some perverse part of him wanted her to admit that, although the circumstances that brought them together that night might have been an unfortunate accident, their lovemaking had been nothing short of amazing.

"You've lost your mind, Gordon," he muttered as he steered his car onto Alex Santiago's private drive.

Doing his best to forget the matter, he parked in front of the palatial home, got out of the car and climbed the steps to the front door. Before he could ring the doorbell, the door opened.

"Hello, Señor Gordon," a round-faced older woman with kind brown eyes said, stepping back for Josh to enter. "Señor Alex is in the sunroom."

"How's he feeling today, Maria?" Josh asked as the housekeeper whom Alex's fiancée, Cara Windsor, had recently hired led the way toward the back of the elegant home.

Maria stopped, then, turning to face him, gave Josh a worried look. "Señor Alex still has headaches and can't remember anything before he was found."

"I'm sure it's just a matter of time before he recovers his memory." Josh wasn't entirely sure who he was trying to reassure—the housekeeper or himself.

Alex had been missing for several months before being found, suffering a head injury, in the back of a truck with a group of migrant farm workers smuggled across the border from Mexico. No one seemed to know how he wound up across the border or how he got into the back of the truck with the workers, and he couldn't tell the authorities anything. There was strong evidence that he had been beaten several times and one theory was that he had been kidnapped. But no matter what had happened, Alex still had amnesia. It had only been recently that he'd been released from Royal Memorial Hospital. With Cara's encouragement, Alex's friends from the TCC had been taking turns dropping by to check on his progress. No one had said as much, but Josh knew they all hoped to help him recover his memory so they could find whoever had done this to him.

"How are you feeling today, Alex?" he asked, walking into the sunroom where his friend sat reading a book.

Alex smiled and slowly rose to his feet to extend his hand. "Josh, isn't it?"

Nodding, Josh shook Alex's hand. The man's grip was firm and Josh took that as a good sign that his friend was regaining some of his strength. But he was still cautious about making sure he called his friends by the correct name, which indicated his memory wasn't much better.

"I wanted to stop by and let you know that we're all hoping to see you and Cara at the Christmas Ball." Before his disappearance in the summer, Alex had been on the planning committee for the annual holiday gala. Josh hoped that referring to the event might spark a memory.

"Yes, Cara and I discussed it and we're hoping that being at the Texas Cattleman's Club with all of my acquaintances will help me remember something," Alex answered. He sighed heavily. "It's damned irritating not being able to remember anything about my life before waking up in the back of that truck."

"I'm sure there will be a break in the case soon," Josh said, hoping he was right. "The Royal Police Department's detective unit is one of the best in the entire state and they're letting Britt Collins, the state investigator, take the lead. With her FBI training and specialty in kidnapping cases, they'll have whoever did this to you behind bars in no time."

"I was told this morning they intend to send my picture to the national television networks in an attempt to find anyone who might have seen who I was with while I was missing. It might also help locate any family I have," Alex added. "Apparently none of them live close by, because there haven't been any family members respond to the local news reports about me."

Josh smiled. "I'm sure the news of all this going national will help to escalate the investigation."

As they continued to discuss Alex's frustration with his lack of memory and the possibility of the police turning up something that would give them a clue who had beaten him, Josh's mind kept straying back to Kiley and his invitation to dinner the following evening. It suddenly occurred to him that she hadn't said no.

Of course, she hadn't exactly accepted his invitation either. But he decided not to give that a second

thought. As far as he was concerned they were having dinner tomorrow evening and he fully intended to
discuss that night three years ago. He needed for her
to understand that he wasn't in the habit of making
love to a woman he didn't know, then leaving her like
some kind of thief in the night. He also wanted her to
admit that she had played a part in the incident when
she had been so receptive to him. Then, as far as he
was concerned, the matter would be closed for good.

Satisfied that he had a viable plan, he filled Alex
in on things that were going on at the clubhouse. "The
day care center is open and has quite a few kids attending."

"I am sure the female members are happy about
that," Alex said, smiling. "But Cara tells me her father
and a few others are less supportive."

Josh nodded. "I wasn't entirely sure it's needed, but
after the director's request for more money to operate
the center I'm taking the time to learn more about it
before I make up my mind."

"It is always good to keep an open mind and get the
facts before one passes judgment," Alex said, nodding.

As Josh listened to Alex, he appreciated the wisdom
in his friend's quietly spoken observation. "Thanks
for the advice. I'll be sure to do just that." Rising to
leave, he shook Alex's hand. "You know if you need
anything, all you have to do is give me a call."

"I appreciate that, Josh," Alex said, following him
to the front door. "I will certainly keep that in mind."

As Josh descended the front steps, he noticed a car
coming up the long drive. When it pulled to a stop behind his and the driver got out, he recognized Alex's
former housekeeper, Mia Hughes.

She waved. "Hi, Josh. How is Alex doing today?"

"He's frustrated with his lack of memory, but that's to be expected." He smiled. "I hear that congratulations are in order."

The pretty young woman beamed. "You heard about my engagement to Dave Firestone?"

"Yes." He laughed. "News like that travels through the TCC like a flash fire through a wood pile."

She laughed. "Thank you, Josh. I've never been happier."

"If the smile on Firestone's face these days is any indication, I'd say he's just as happy," Josh said.

"It was nice seeing you again, Josh," Mia said as she started up the steps to the front door.

Josh nodded. "I'll see you in a few weeks at the Christmas Ball."

Getting into the car, he drove away from the Santiago mansion feeling pretty good about the day. He had successfully straightened out a problem with the work crew on one of the Gordon Construction job sites, had a nice visit with his friend and had set up dinner with Kiley Roberts for tomorrow evening.

"A very good day," he said aloud as he drove across town to his ranch just outside Royal.

The next afternoon, Kiley tried to remain focused and not think about Josh stopping by, expecting her to go to dinner with him. But try as she might, every time the door opened, she looked up expectantly. So far, it had been parents arriving to pick up their children, but she knew it was just a matter of time before she looked up to find Josh entering the day care center.

Of course, she had no intention of going anywhere

with him. But how could she anticipate and dread him stopping by all at the same time?

"Kiley, would you mind if I leave now?" Carrie asked, looking hopeful. "There are only two more children to be picked up by their parents and I have an appointment at the hair salon in fifteen minutes."

"Do you have a date with Ron tonight?" Kiley asked. From the time the young woman started working for her, Carrie had chattered nonstop about her boyfriend and Kiley expected any day to hear that they had become engaged.

Her assistant nodded. "He's taking me out to dinner and then we're going to see the new Channing Tatum movie."

"You can only leave early on one condition."

"What's that?" her assistant asked cautiously.

Kiley grinned. "You have to tell me all about the movie and how many times Channing takes his shirt off."

Carrie laughed as she grabbed her coat and purse from the closet by the door. "I can do that."

"Have a nice evening, and I'll see you tomorrow morning, Carrie."

As her assistant rushed out the door to get her hair done for her date, Kiley's heart skipped a beat when Josh walked in. Dressed in a black suit, pale blue shirt and navy tie, he looked more handsome than any man had the right to look outside the pages of *GQ*.

"Instead of making a reservation for us in the restaurant here at the club, I thought we might try that new place on the west side of town," Josh said, flashing her a smile that sent goose bumps shimmering up her arms. "Have all of the kids gone home?"

"Not yet." She collected the Santa Claus faces made of construction paper and cotton balls that the pre-school class had made during their craft time. "But I'm afraid I won't be able to…" She let her voice trail off when Russ and Winnie Bartlett entered the day care center to pick up their two little girls.

While Josh shook hands with Russ and talked about the upcoming meeting of the general membership, Kiley and Winnie chatted about the children's holi-day program.

"It's all Sarah can talk about," Winnie said, smiling at her little girl. As she helped her youngest daughter into her jacket, she laughed and smoothed her toddler's straight dark hair. "And Elaina tells me she's going to be one of the 'kidney' canes."

Grinning, Kiley nodded. "She calls them 'kidney' canes and Emmie calls them 'kitty' canes."

"Isn't it fun deciphering what a two-year-old means as they learn new words?" Winnie asked.

"Oh, yes." When Emmie toddled over to give Elaina a goodbye hug, Kiley smiled fondly at her beautiful little girl. "At times it feels like they speak a foreign language."

After the Bartletts bid them a good evening, Kiley and Emmie were left alone with Josh. Turning toward her office to retrieve her purse, Kiley heard Emmie start chattering about her toy ponies. Glancing over her shoulder, she almost laughed out loud at Josh's perplexed expression.

"Me pony," Emmie said, reaching up to wrap her little hand around one of Josh's fingers to tug him in the direction of the play area.

"What does she want?" Josh asked, sounding a little

alarmed. He might have been bewildered about what Emmie wanted, but to his credit, he followed her over to the toy box on the other side of the room.

"She wants to show you her favorite toys," Kiley said, quickly grabbing her things and switching off the office light.

"That's nice." Josh smiled when Emmie held up a purple pony with a flowing white mane and tail. "How much longer before one of her parents arrives to get her?"

"Emmie goes home with me," Kiley said, taking their coats from the closet. "She's my daughter."

"I didn't realize you had a child," he said, glancing down at Emmie digging through the toys to find more ponies.

When he looked back at her, Kiley could tell by his expression that Josh realized her going to dinner with him wasn't going to happen. But as they continued to stare at each other, a mischievous spark lit his brilliant blue eyes.

"So you like ponies and horses, Emmie?" he asked.

Emmie vigorously nodded her little blond head. "Yes."

Squatting down to her level, he handed the toy pony back to her. "I like horses, too. I have several of them at my ranch."

Emmie's little face lit up. "Me wanna see."

"I think that can be arranged," Josh said, giving Kiley a triumphant grin.

Kiley didn't like the idea in the least. "I don't think that would be—"

"Why don't you ask your mother to bring you over to my ranch on Saturday afternoon so I can show you my horses?" he asked before Kiley could stop him from making the offer.

"Pease, Mommy?" Emmie asked, skipping over to her. "Pease. Wanna see ponies. Wanna see ponies."

Kiley was fit to be tied. Josh had deliberately manipulated the situation and now her daughter looked so hopeful, she hated to refuse. But on the other hand, she didn't want to spend more time with Josh than she had to. Nor was she overly happy about his taking control of the situation.

"Is this retaliation for not going to dinner with you?" she asked, delaying her answer. A thought suddenly occurred to her. "You aren't going to let this influence your decision about the funding for the day care center, are you?"

"Not at all." A frown creased his forehead as he rose to his full height and walked over to her and Emmie. "I just thought your little girl might like to see a real horse."

"You knew she would," Kiley accused.

"Not really," Josh said, rocking back on his heels. "I don't know enough about little kids to know whether she would or not."

She wasn't buying his innocent expression for a minute. "This is punishment for not going to dinner with you and we both know it."

"Oh, I wouldn't go so far as to call it that." Standing closer than she was comfortable with, he leaned over to whisper, "And no. I won't let this influence my recommendation to the funding committee. Although you could have told me sooner that dinner wasn't really an option."

"You didn't give me a chance yesterday afternoon,"

she said defensively. "And you didn't come by the center earlier for me to tell you."

"We both know you could have called my office or left a message for me here at the clubhouse," he reminded, his voice so intimate it sent a tiny shiver of awareness straight up her spine. "So what do you say?" he asked, smiling. "You just said yourself that Emmie would like seeing the horses."

The woodsy scent of his cologne and the fact that he stood so close were playing havoc with her equilibrium. Taking a step away from him, she looked down at Emmie. Her daughter looked so excited and happy, how could Kiley possibly disappoint her?

"Oh, all right," she finally conceded. "But we'll only stop by for a few minutes."

"Good." Josh gave her directions to his ranch just outside of town. "I'll expect you and Emmie around one." Bending down, he smiled at her daughter. "I'll see you in a few days, Emmie." Straightening, he lightly touched her cheek with his index finger. "Have a nice evening, Kiley."

As she watched him stroll to the door, a shiver coursed through her at his light touch and the sound of his rich baritone saying her name. She shook her head to clear it.

"This is ridiculous," she muttered as she put Emmie's coat on her, then stuffed her arms into the sleeves of her own.

Josh Gordon was the very last man she should be shivering over. He couldn't be trusted. He might have given her a month's worth of extra funds for the day care center, but that didn't fool her for a second. She had overheard enough comments from some of the other members to know that he would like to see it fail—almost as much as Beau Hacket and Paul Windsor did.

So what was he up to? And why?

Three

When Josh entered the bar, he looked around to see if any of his friends had stopped by for happy hour since it appeared he was going to be spending his evening hanging out with the guys. Not exactly what he had planned. He had intended to have an early dinner with Kiley at the exclusive new restaurant across town, lay to rest what happened that night three years ago and convince her that he fully intended to give her day care center a fair evaluation.

Why her opinion of him mattered was still a mystery to him. He had never before cared one way or the other what others thought of him. As long as he based his decisions on what he knew was right, he could sleep at night. But for some reason it bothered him that Kiley obviously had such little faith in his integrity. Why would she think he would stoop so low as to let her not going to dinner with him influence his recommendations to the funding committee? More importantly, why couldn't he just let it go?

Normally once he discovered a woman had a child, his interest in her took a nosedive and he moved on. But for some strange reason, Kiley and her daughter piqued his curiosity. Why would any man in his right mind willingly walk away from either of them?

"Hey, Josh," someone called, drawing him out of his introspection.

Spotting the current TCC president, Gil Addison, seated on the far side of the room, Josh threaded his way through the crowd. "I didn't expect to see you here, Gil," he said when he reached the table.

"Cade was invited to have dinner with one of his friends from the day care center." Gil shrugged. "I was just trying to decide whether to go home and raid the refrigerator or stay here and order something."

"Mind if I join you?" Josh asked. "My plans for dinner fell through at the last minute."

Grinning, Gil motioned toward the empty chair across from him. "Have a seat. I can't remember how long it's been since I had a meal that wasn't business-related or kid-dominated."

"You've had a pretty full plate since becoming president," Josh agreed, pulling out the chair to sit down.

A single father, Gil Addison was totally devoted to his small son, and he wasn't often seen having a beer with other members in the club's bar just for fun. It was nice to see his friend enjoying a little downtime for a change.

"Hi, I'm Ginny. I'll be your server tonight. What can I get for you two?" a tall, dark-haired waitress asked, placing cocktail napkins in front of them in anticipation of a drink order. "We have a steak and fries plate that's out of this world, it's so good."

"I'll have that and a beer," Josh spoke up.

"Might as well double that order," Gil added.

"Great choice," Ginny said, jotting their orders on a pad of paper. "I'll be right back with your beer."

While they waited on Ginny to return with their drinks, Josh and Gil talked about how the club membership had grown with the addition of women to its roster.

"I know some of the older members have a problem with it," Gil said, shrugging. "But the Texas Cattleman's Club needs to be progressive in its thinking and recognize that this isn't the same club Tex Langley founded around the turn of the last century. The 'good old boy network' was fine a hundred-plus years ago, but it just isn't practical in today's world."

"I have to admit, I've had my share of misgivings about women belonging to the club," Josh said honestly. "But after working with Nadine Capshaw since she was appointed to the funding committee last month, it's given me a new perspective on the issue. I think my main concerns now revolve around some of the changes the women are lobbying for. It seems at times that the TCC is heading toward becoming more of a country club than an organization that has always set the bar with its dedication to serving the needs of the community of Royal."

They both fell silent when the waitress brought them mugs of beer.

"I understand your and some of the other members' concerns," Gil said when Ginny moved away to serve another table. "And I know that some of the additions being made to the club's services for our members are viewed as unnecessary. But the way I see it, the more opportunities we offer, the better the chance our membership will stay strong and enable us to continue assisting the community."

"I guess you have a point," Josh conceded. He waited until Ginny had set their plates of food in front of them before he continued. "Speaking of our services, how do you like the new day care center? Is it living up to your expectations for your son?"

"It's exceeded them," Gil answered, cutting into his steak. "Cade looks forward to being with his friends each day and it's a load off my mind, knowing that while I conduct TCC business, he's being looked after right down the hall."

"The director seems to be pretty good with kids," Josh said, taking a bite of his steak.

Gil nodded. "Kiley Roberts is amazing. I can't believe some of the things Cade has learned since starting at the day care center last month." He smiled fondly as he talked about his son. "He can tie his own shoes now and is able to recognize a few basic words when he sees them."

"That's pretty good for a four-year-old, isn't it?" Josh asked. He really didn't know if it was or not. But then he didn't know much about what little kids learned at any age.

"Kiley has a real way with kids. She makes a game out of learning and they soak it up like sponges." Gil grinned. "Even getting Cade to go to bed is easier because she told them how important it is to get plenty of rest at night so they can play with their friends the next day."

Josh finished his dinner and took a drink of his beer. "She's asked for more money from the funding committee and I've been stopping by the center to see what the funds would be used for, and to determine whether I should recommend increasing the day care's yearly budget."

"Yeah, I heard Beau grousing about it the other day." Gil paused for a moment. "I know the decision to appropriate more money to the day care center's budget is entirely up to the funding committee. But for what it's worth, I think it would be money well spent." Something on one of the many televisions around the bar suddenly caught his attention. "Damn!"

Josh looked up to see a picture of Alex Santiago on one of the national evening news broadcasts. The anchorman reported that although Alex had been found, the investigation into his mysterious disappearance was ongoing. The reporter asked that anyone having seen Alex during the months he had been missing to please contact the state investigator, Britt Collins. He wrapped up the segment with a statement that all leads were being followed and that several members of the prestigious Texas Cattleman's Club had been questioned as persons of interest in the case.

Clearly angered by the report, Gil shook his head. "I don't like that the TCC is being disparaged by any of this. Our reputation has always been impeccable and every member of the club is carefully screened before they're granted membership. This Collins woman has already interrogated Chance McDaniel, Dave Firestone and myself. Who's she going to single out next?"

"It's my guess she'll investigate every one of us if she has to," Josh said, finishing his beer. "I've heard she's quite thorough."

"She'd do well to look elsewhere for possible suspects," Gil stated flatly.

Josh motioned for the waitress to bring their checks. "I wouldn't worry too much about the TCC's reputation. We've always been above reproach. We can weather this and anything else that casts a shadow of doubt over our integrity."

"You're right, but the club has been the subject of more than one negative news report lately," Gil reminded.

"Have there been any more leads in the vandalism of the day care center?" Josh asked, picking up the slip of paper the waitress placed facedown in front of him. "The last I heard the police think it might have been teenagers."

"That's what I heard, too." Gil reached for his check. "They're the only ones I can think of that might be stupid enough to mess with the TCC. The lead detective did tell me they found a partial fingerprint, but when they ran it through the national database there weren't any matches. He thinks it might be one of the members' kids."

Josh nodded as he removed his wallet from the inside pocket of his suit coat and tossed several dollars on the table to cover his dinner and a generous tip. "Kids are the only ones stupid enough to do something like this. Anyone else knows better than to come into our house and destroy any part of it. But you'd think a kid of one of our members wouldn't even think about it."

"Well, whoever it is, they've bit off more than they realize," Gil agreed. "I personally can't think of a single member, no matter what they think of the day care center, who doesn't want them held accountable for what they've done." Checking his watch, he rose to leave. "I guess I'd better get over to the Whelans' and pick up Cade. Thanks for sharing dinner with me, Josh."

Rising to his feet, Josh followed his friend out of the bar and walked to his car in favor of having the valet bring it to him. On the drive home, he thought a lot on what Gil had said about the day care center. It was true that the more the TCC had to offer, the better the chances of maintaining a full roster of members. And after seeing the way Kiley dealt with the kids, he knew firsthand that she was good at her job and the day care center was top-notch. Had he been looking at the club's need for a child care facility through jaded eyes?

Josh had to admit it was highly possible. He and his twin brother, Sam, had been raised by a man who made no secret that he thought a woman's place was in the home taking care of her own children and not outside of it working a job or playing tennis while someone else looked after her kids. For the most part, he had agreed with their father and it wasn't until he'd watched Kiley work with the kids that he was starting to question his steadfast opinion.

Maybe his thinking would have been different if his mother had lived long enough to really have an influence on his and Sam's lives. But other than what he saw from the pictures his dad had shown him,

Josh couldn't honestly say he recalled much about his mother.

Turning his car up the long drive leading to his ranch house, he decided to take Alex's advice and not make any rash decisions about his recommendation to the funding committee. He had the rest of the month to observe what went on at the day care center and he owed it to Kiley, as well as the members of the TCC, to give it a fair evaluation before he decided one way or the other.

On Saturday afternoon when Kiley parked in front of Josh's barn, her pulse sped up as she watched him walk toward her car. If she had thought he looked good yesterday when he stopped by the day care center, it couldn't compare to the way he looked today. In a suit and tie the man looked very handsome. In worn jeans, a blue chambray shirt, boots and a wide-brimmed black cowboy hat, he was downright devastating. Who knew he had been hiding such wide shoulders and narrow hips beneath the expensive fabric of those Armani suits?

"Right on time," he said, smiling as he opened her car door for her. "Good, you're wearing jeans."

Silently chastising herself for her wayward thoughts about the man, she took a deep breath and got out of the car. "You didn't think I'd wear heels and a dress to walk through a feedlot, did you?"

He laughed. "You wore a dress the other day."

"That's because I was going before your committee to ask for more money for the day care center," she said, turning to open the back door of the car. "You've seen me in slacks and a blouse every time since then."

The look in his blue gaze stole her breath. "And you've looked very nice in everything I've seen you in."

Surprised by the compliment, she didn't even think to protest when he gently moved her out of the way, opened the rear door, then unbuckled the safety straps and lifted her daughter from the car seat. "Are you ready to ride a horse, Emmie?" he asked.

Seated on his forearm, Emmie clapped her little hands together. "Me wide ponies."

"You didn't say anything about riding," Kiley accused, glaring at him. He knew she hadn't wanted to pay him a visit to begin with, let alone spend more time with him by going for a horseback ride.

"I didn't think of it until just a short while ago." He smiled at her happy daughter. "I thought this little lady might enjoy it."

"I'm sure she would," Kiley said without thinking. As soon as the words passed her lips, she knew she'd made a huge mistake and played right into his hands.

Josh gave her a triumphant grin as he placed his free hand to the small of her back. "Then it's settled."

"You're manipulating the situation, the same as you did yesterday afternoon," she said tightly as he guided her toward the corral where two saddled horses stood, their reins tied to the top rail of the fence.

"Not really." He opened the gate to the corral and led her over to a pinto mare. "I wasn't sure how experienced you are with horses, so I had my foreman saddle Daisy. She's the most gentle horse I own. You can ride, can't you?"

"Yes, but it's been a while since I've had the opportunity," Kiley admitted, patting the horse's neck.

"Do you need help mounting?" Josh asked from behind her.

She shook her head as she untied the reins and raised her leg to mount up. "I think I can manage."

Unfortunately, she was short and the horse was quite tall. When she put her foot in the stirrup, her knee was even with her chin and made it all but impossible to pull herself up into the saddle.

"Here, let me help," Josh said.

Before she realized what he intended, she felt his hand cup her backside and, as if she weighed nothing, he gave her the boost she needed to mount the mare. Her cheeks felt as if they were on fire when she settled herself in the saddle. Thankfully her daughter provided the distraction Kiley needed to regain her composure.

"Pony," Emmie said delightedly, touching the mare's mane.

When Kiley reached for her, Emmie stubbornly shook her head and put her arms around Josh's neck. "Wide a pony."

"You're going to ride a pony with me," Kiley explained.

Her daughter's blond pigtails swayed as she shook her head. "No!"

"Emmie," Kiley warned, keeping her tone firm but gentle.

Her little chin began to wobble and tears filled her big brown eyes. "No, pease."

"She can ride with me," Josh offered softly.

Emmie nodded her head. "Wide."

Kiley wasn't happy, but she finally nodded her consent. It wasn't that she didn't think Josh would keep her daughter safe. It was a matter of Emmie becoming too attached to him. She had watched her little girl's reaction when some of the children's fathers arrived at the end of the day to take them home and it was clear Emmie missed a paternal influence in her life.

As Kiley watched Josh untie the reins of the bay gelding and effortlessly swing up into the saddle while still holding Emmie, her heart ached. Her daughter deserved to have two parents, but it hadn't worked out that way and there was no sense lamenting the fact that she didn't.

"Me wide pony," Emmie said happily when Josh settled her on his lap and nudged his horse into a slow walk.

By the time they rode through the gate into the pasture beyond, Kiley had to admit that although she had been against the outing and still resented the way Josh had controlled everything, she wouldn't have missed the excitement on Emmie's face for anything. Her little girl was having the time of her life.

"She seems to be enjoying herself," Josh said, smiling when Emmie braced both hands on the saddle horn and grinned over her shoulder at him.

Kiley nodded. "She's always loved animals, but horses and ponies are her favorites. Even before she could sit up on her own, she had a stuffed pony that she wouldn't let out of her sight."

"Does her dad like horses?" he asked. "Maybe that's where she gets it from."

"No, he hasn't been in the picture since right after she was born," Kiley said, shrugging.

"I'm sorry," Josh said, sounding sincere.

"Don't be." She stared off into the distance. "Emmie and I are better off without him."

"He doesn't have any contact at all with you and Emmie?" He sounded disapproving.

Shaking her head, she smiled. "No. Mark signed over all legal rights to her so he wouldn't have to pay child support."

Josh stopped the bay gelding to turn and look at her. "And you're okay with that?"

"Actually, I'm just as glad I don't have to deal with him," she said honestly, reining in the mare. "But it breaks my heart for Emmie. When she gets a little older she'll start wondering why her dad didn't want anything to do with her."

"It's his loss," Josh stated flatly. "He's the one missing out and it sounds to me like the bast—" he stopped, looked down at Emmie, then, grinning, finished "—the jerk doesn't have the sense to know it."

She didn't know why she had opened up to Josh, but it was no secret in Royal that Mark Roberts cared little or nothing for anyone but himself. Of course, he wasn't a part of the same social set as Josh and his friends, so she doubted Josh had ever heard of Mark or his reputation for being his own number one fan.

"I know it's none of my business, but why did you marry him?" Josh asked, frowning.

"You're holding her." Kiley smiled fondly at her pride and joy. "I became pregnant and his grandfather insisted that he had to do the 'right thing' and marry me."

"You didn't have to go along with it," he pointed out.

"It appears that my sister isn't the only one in the

Miller family who makes poor choices when it comes to the men she gets involved with," Kiley said without thinking.

"Ouch."

"Oh, I'm sorry," she said, realizing that Josh thought she meant him. It was true that he had broken Lori's heart, but he was just one of a long list of men Lori had fallen for over the years. "I didn't mean you in particular," she hurried to add. "I just meant Lori seems to always fall for men who are all wrong for her."

He shrugged. "Lori's a great girl. But her attention span isn't all that long."

When he didn't say more, Kiley wondered what he meant by that comment. Lori wasn't known for seeing anyone for very long, but he made it sound as if she was the one who'd dumped him instead of the other way around. But Lori had said...

"That's why you said the day care center was your dream job," he said, drawing Kiley back to the present. "As long as you have to work to support yourself and Emmie, it's better to have her with you."

"By having her with me, I don't have to worry about missing any of her childhood milestones or wonder if someone else is taking good care of her," Kiley said, nodding.

He looked thoughtful, as if mulling over what she had told him before glancing down at Emmie. "Uh-oh. It looks like this little cowgirl is going to miss part of the ride."

When she looked over at her daughter leaning back against Josh, she smiled. Emmie was fast asleep.

"I think it was probably the rhythmic movement of the gelding's slow walk and the fact that she has been extremely excited about seeing the horses. When the adrenaline level starts to drop off, the little ones are usually asleep in no time." She stopped the mare. "Do you want me to take her?"

Smiling, he shook his head. "No, she's fine. Besides, I'd hate to wake her."

They fell silent as they rode along a creek on the far side of the pasture before turning back. Maybe Josh wasn't such a bad guy after all, Kiley decided.

As they rode across the wide pasture, Kiley found herself glancing at Josh holding her daughter securely to his wide chest and a warm feeling began to fill her. Was there ever a more endearing sight than a man tenderly holding a child?

When she remembered how surrounded she'd felt with his chest pressed to hers and the latent strength of his arms holding her close as he made love to her that night, a streak of longing coursed through her at the speed of light. Her heart skipped a beat and she had to remind herself to breathe. Where had that come from? And what on earth was wrong with her?

Josh Gordon was the very last man her heart should be fluttering over. If he and some of the other funding committee members had their way about it, the day care center would close and she would be out of a job—her dream job. She would be much better off focusing on that than to be thinking about how passionate he had been or how cherished she'd felt when he'd made love to her.

When he and Kiley rode the horses back into the corral, Josh was careful not to wake Emmie as he dismounted the bay. He had never before noticed how cute a little kid was when they were sleeping. Of course, he hadn't been around kids enough to know whether they all looked innocent and sweet or if it was just Emmie.

How in the name of hell could Roberts have walked away from her and Kiley? Why hadn't he at least wanted to be a big part of his kid's life?

Josh shook his head as he turned to help Kiley down from the mare. "Emmie's going to be disappointed that she slept through most of her first horseback ride."

Kiley nodded as she took Emmie from him and lifted her daughter to her shoulder. "Thank you, Josh. She really enjoyed it while she was awake and she'll be talking about petting the horses for days."

The sound of her soft voice saying his name and the sweet smile she gave him caused a warmth like nothing he had ever known to rush through him. He had to clear his throat before he could speak. "It was my pleasure, Kiley. We'll have to do it again soon. Maybe Emmie will be able to stay awake through the entire ride next time."

Emmie stirred against Kiley's shoulder and, raising her head, sleepily looked around. "Ponies." When she realized the ride was over, tears filled her eyes and she looked as if her heart had been broken. "Wide... a pony."

Josh felt like he'd taken a piece of candy or a favorite toy from her. "Do you mind if I hold her on the saddle while I lead the horses into the barn?" he asked Kiley. "You know, give her a little more riding time?"

"No, I don't mind," she said, wiping a big tear from Emmie's round little cheek. "Would you like for Josh to give you another ride on the pony?"

Emmie nodded and held both of her arms out for him to take her. "Wide a pony."

Without a moment's hesitation, he took her from her mother and set her on the gelding's saddle. "Hold on to the saddle horn," he instructed, showing her where to put her hands. Emmie gave him a smile that he wouldn't have missed for anything. "We'll come back for the mare," he said, turning to Kiley. "That way, she'll get to ride twice."

Putting his arm around Emmie to make sure she didn't slide off the saddle, Josh loosely held the reins as he urged the gelding into a slow walk. All of his horses had been well-trained and he was confident the animal wouldn't just take off. But he wasn't taking any chances, either.

Once the bay was tied to a grooming post inside the barn, Josh and Emmie returned to the corral to get the mare. From the look on Emmie's face, he had made some major points with her. The child was grinning from ear to ear by the time the mare was tied beside the gelding.

"Bobby Ray, would you start grooming the mare?" Josh called to his foreman at the far end of the barn. "I'll be back in a few minutes to take care of the bay." Lifting Emmie from the saddle, he walked back out to where Kiley stood by the corral gate, talking to Bobby Ray's wife. "I see you've met my housekeeper, Martha," he said, smiling at the two women.

"Oh, my word," Martha said, her face splitting into a wide grin when she spotted Emmie. "What a beautiful little angel!"

"Would you like for Martha to show you her new kittens?" Josh whispered to Emmie as if they were sharing a big secret. For reasons he didn't want to dwell on, he wanted to prolong her and Kiley's departure.

"Wanna see kitties," Emmie said happily.

"Is it all right to take her to see the two kittens we adopted from the animal shelter?" Martha asked Kiley.

"That would be fine," Kiley answered, smiling. "I'm sure she would like that."

When Josh set Emmie on her feet, she readily took Martha's hand and waved at him and her mother. "Bye."

"She's a great kid," Josh said, watching his housekeeper and Emmie walk back into the barn.

"Thanks."

"I feel like I should be the one thanking you," he said truthfully. "I've really enjoyed getting to see the wonder on her face."

Kiley nodded. "Every day is a big adventure for a two-year-old."

"I'm sure it can be an adventure for you, as well," he said, thinking about how difficult it had to be, raising a child with no help.

She laughed. "Well, there have been a couple of times when her adventures have turned into my disasters."

The delightful sound of Kiley's laughter did strange things to his insides and he didn't think twice about reaching out to pull her into his arms. "Thank you for letting me share in Emmie's latest adventure," he said, hugging her close.

Her body pressed to his felt wonderful even through the many layers of their clothing. When she leaned back to look up at him with her luminous brown eyes,

Josh couldn't have stopped himself from kissing her if his life depended on it.

Slowly lowering his head, he gave her the chance to call a halt to things. To his relief, her eyes fluttered shut as his mouth covered hers. Soft and sweet, her lips clung to his, reminding him of that night in her sister's apartment. A spark ignited in his belly and his lower body began to tighten predictably. He had suspected part of the reason that night had gone as far as it did was because of an undeniable chemistry between them. Now he knew for certain he was right. The reality of her response surpassed his memory of that night, and he knew absolutely that a force of nature was at work drawing them together.

Forcing himself to keep the kiss brief and non-threatening, he eased away from the caress instead of deepening it as he would have liked. "I've been wanting to do that for the past few days," he said, smiling down at her.

Kiley took a quick step back. "Th-that shouldn't… have happened."

"I'll be damned if I'm sorry it did."

"I… We should go," she said, looking a little flustered. Unless he missed his guess, she felt the magnetic pull as strongly as he did and it scared her senseless.

Before either of them could say anything more, Martha and Emmie returned from the barn.

"Me petted kitties," Emmie said excitedly.

"Tell Mr. Gordon thank you for inviting us to see the ponies and the kitties," Kiley said, her gaze not quite meeting his.

"Tank you," Emmie said politely.

Taking the little girl by the hand to lead her to the

car, he smiled. "You're very welcome, Emmie. We'll go for another ride the next time you come back to my ranch. Would you like that?"

The toddler nodded until her curly pigtails bounced. "Yes."

He opened the back door of Kiley's car and lifted Emmie into the car seat. Stepping back, he waited until Kiley buckled the safety straps and closed the car door before he reached up to brush a strand of blond hair from her smooth cheek.

"Drive safe."

She nodded as she hurriedly turned to get in behind the steering wheel. "I'll see you next week at the day care center."

"Yeah," he said, smiling confidently as he watched her turn the car around and start back up the drive to the main road. "You'll see me before then, too."

He had forgotten to tell Kiley about the partial fingerprint the detectives had found when they investigated the vandalism at the day care center and that after running it through their database, they had concluded the perpetrator didn't have a criminal record. It wasn't anything that couldn't wait until he saw her at the day care center, but as far as he was concerned it was reason enough to pay her a visit that evening. Besides, they still had yet to discuss their night together, and she might be more inclined to talk about what happened in the privacy of her own home.

Whistling a tune, he walked back to the barn to help his ranch foreman finish grooming the horses. Now that he had plans for the evening, he suddenly couldn't wait to get them started.

Four

Driving across town after picking up a pizza, Josh thought about what Kiley had told him earlier that afternoon while they were riding his horses. She had never received help from her ex-husband. As chairman of the funding committee, he knew exactly what her salary was. The TCC paid her the going rate for a day care center director, but it wasn't something she would ever get rich from. In fact, he wouldn't be the least bit surprised if she was struggling to make ends meet.

Suddenly several things became quite clear, causing a knot to form in his gut. Kiley had called working at the day care center her dream job. But aside from being able to be with Emmie, she needed to keep her position for two very important reasons. She needed to provide for herself and Emmie, and she probably couldn't afford the rising cost of child care if she worked any other job.

Now he felt guilty as hell for being so closed-minded about the day care center. To a certain degree he had been on the same page with Beau Hacket and Paul Windsor. His father had raised him and his twin with the misguided belief that a woman's place was in the home, taking care of her own kids. Period.

But what they had all failed to take into consideration was the fact that women not only had the right to enjoy recreational activities the same as men, but that some women didn't have a choice but to be out in the workforce. They had to hold a job to help their families make ends meet or, as was Kiley's case, be her family's only support.

Determined to be more open-minded in the future, he turned into the entrance of a subdivision and started watching street signs for Cottonwood Lane. It seemed to be a nice enough neighborhood, but he could tell that it was older and some of the houses were in desperate need of repairs, if not a complete renovation.

When he turned onto Kiley's street, he hadn't gone far when he spotted her older Ford sedan parked in the driveway of a small bungalow. He pulled his Mercedes in behind her car. The lights were on inside the house and he would bet that she and Emmie were probably getting ready for dinner.

"Right on time," he said, grabbing the pizza box and getting out of his car.

Walking up to the front door, he rang the bell and waited. When Kiley opened the door, his heart stalled and he couldn't believe how hard it was to take in his next breath. Dressed in a pink T-shirt that gave him a pretty fair idea of the size and shape of her breasts, and black leggings that hugged her slender legs like a second skin, she could easily tempt a saint to sin.

He forced himself to give her what he hoped was an innocent smile as he presented the pizza. "Dinner is served."

She looked confused. "Josh, what are you doing here?"

"I thought you'd be tired after today's outing and might not feel like cooking," he said suddenly, wondering if he'd lost his mind. It was clear Kiley was trying to keep him at arm's length. Why couldn't he accept that?

Emmie peeked out from behind her mother's legs. As soon as she recognized him, she started looking around the yard. "Ponies. Wanna wide ponies."

"I'm sorry, Emmie. The horses were tired and I left them at my ranch to rest," he said, hoping it was a good enough explanation for a two-year-old. He held out the box for her to see. "But I brought pizza for dinner."

The temptation of pizza worked its magic and, grinning, the little girl clapped her tiny hands. "Petza."

Kiley didn't look happy. "I normally make sure she has a more healthy dinner."

"I thought of that," he said, rocking back on his heels. "That's why I ordered the vegetable pizza with real cheese on a hand-tossed, whole-grain crust."

He was actually pretty proud of himself for thinking of the nutritional value for a change. Normally, when he had pizza it was loaded with meat, there wasn't the hint of a vegetable on it and the crust was as thick as a slice of Texas toast.

"Petza, Mommy," Emmie said, tugging on the tail of Kiley's T-shirt.

"Oh, all right," she finally said, stepping back.

When he entered the house, Josh looked around. It was exactly as he thought it would be—very warm and homey. The furniture was older and a bit worn, but everything was neat and clean, and looked very comfortable.

Noticing a couple of place mats on the coffee table, he raised an eyebrow. "Dinner in front of the TV?"

"Saturday is movie night for Emmie and me," Kiley explained. "I was just about to make tuna sandwiches." Walking into the kitchen, she returned to put another place mat down on the coffee table along with three small plates. "Would you like a glass of iced tea? I'm sorry I don't have anything stronger."

"I'll have whatever you're having," he said, placing the pizza box on the table with the plates. He waited until she returned with two glasses of iced tea and a small cup of milk with a straw built into the lid. "What are we watching this evening?"

"A classic cartoon about a mermaid princess who wants to be a real girl," Kiley said, dishing up slices of pizza. "It's one of Emmie's favorites."

Their fingers brushed when she handed him his plate, and it felt like a jolt of electric current traveled up his arm and exploded somewhere around his solar plexus. As quickly as she jerked her hand back, Josh knew beyond a shadow of doubt that she had felt it, too.

"Me pincess," Emmie said, nodding as Kiley fastened a bib around her neck to protect her pink footed pajamas with fairy-tale princesses on them. It was obvious the toddler was ready for bed and Josh would bet his last dollar that she fell asleep well before the movie was over.

While her mother cut the slice of pizza on her plate into little pieces, Emmie suddenly took off running down the hall.

"Where did she go?" he asked, confused.

Kiley smiled. "She's going to show you that she's a real princess."

When the little girl returned, she was wearing a gold-colored plastic crown with jewels painted on it. It was a little too large for her head and it kept sliding to one side, but she wore it as proudly as if it were the Crown Jewels.

"Me pincess," she said again as she picked up one of the bite-size pieces of pizza and put it into her mouth.

"Yes, you are," Josh said, unable to stop smiling. For some reason, he found everything the kid did to be cute as hell, and he was fascinated by her enthusiasm and delight in the simplest of things.

When he caught Kiley staring at him, he frowned. "What?"

"N-nothing," she said, picking up the remote control. Pushing a couple of buttons, she started the DVD and in no time Emmie became completely engrossed in the cartoon.

As they ate, he noticed Kiley glancing at him and then Emmie several times, but she remained strangely silent. Before he could ask her what was wrong, she paused the DVD player.

"If you'll excuse us, I need to finish getting her ready for bed," she said, taking Emmie by the hand.

While she took her daughter down the hall to the bathroom to wash her face and hands and brush her teeth, Josh took their plates and the empty pizza box into the kitchen. When he returned to the living room, he had barely settled himself on the couch when Emmie came running in to climb up on the cushion beside him.

Grinning up at him, she jabbered something that he assumed meant she wanted him to start the movie again. Fortunately Kiley was right behind her. Maybe she could translate toddler speak.

"Does she want me to start the movie again?" he asked, wondering why Kiley had stopped just inside the room. She looked as if she'd seen a ghost. "Is something wrong?"

His question seemed to snap her out of whatever she'd been thinking and, giving him a slight smile, she shook her head. "Please go ahead and take the player off Pause."

When Kiley started to sit in the armchair, Emmie shook her head and, getting down, took hold of her mother's hand. "Mommy," she said determinedly, tugging Kiley toward the couch.

"I think she wants you to sit with us," Josh said, deciding he owed the kid a debt of gratitude.

Kiley didn't look all that happy about it, but she did as her daughter wanted, and after Emmie climbed up beside him, she sat down on the other side of the little girl to finish watching the cartoon. Within ten minutes, Emmie surprised him yet again when she crawled over to sit on his lap and lean back against his chest.

Kiley started to move to the opposite end of the couch, but Josh put his arm around her shoulders to stop her. "The princess is about to go to sleep. If you move, it might disturb her," he whispered close to her ear.

He felt a tremor course through her before she gave him an exasperated look. "What are you doing, Josh?"

"Watching the movie with you and Emmie."

"You know what I mean," she said, shaking her head.

"Could we discuss this after she goes to sleep?" he asked, stalling.

The truth was, he didn't know why he felt the need to get close to Kiley. Normally women with little kids were the last females he wanted to get close to. But that wasn't the case with Kiley. Maybe it was that night three years ago that compelled him, or it could be the fact that the more he learned about her and her daughter, the more he wanted to know. He wasn't sure. But he had always followed his gut instinct and it was telling him not to be too hasty—to take his time and explore what was drawing him to them.

"She's asleep," Kiley said quietly as she reached for Emmie.

"If you'll lead the way, I'll carry her for you," Josh said, cradling the toddler to him as he rose to his feet. "She's as limp as cooked spaghetti."

Kiley's soft laughter caused a warm feeling to spread throughout his chest. "Children don't have the stress adults have. When they fall asleep they're completely relaxed."

Following her down the hall to Emmie's room, he placed the little girl on the smallest bed he had ever seen. He waited for Kiley out in the hall while she pulled the covers over Emmie and kissed her goodnight.

"I didn't know they made beds that little," he said when they walked back into the living room.

"It's a toddler bed." She turned off the DVD player

and removed the disk. "Emmie is too old for a crib and too little for a twin-size bed."

"That makes sense."

Staring at him for a moment, she finally asked, "Why did you come by tonight, Josh?"

"I forgot to mention this afternoon that the detective in charge of the vandalism case told Gil Addison that they analyzed a fingerprint found at the day care center," he stated.

"Were they able to find out who it belonged to?"

He shook his head. "It didn't match anyone in their database, so whoever was behind the destruction doesn't have a criminal record."

Kiley straightened the afghan on the back of the couch. "I was hoping by now the authorities would have someone in custody or at least have an idea of who the person was."

"From all indications, they think it might be a couple of the TCC members' kids," Josh said from behind her.

"And this couldn't have waited until Monday?" When Kiley turned to face him, her heart skipped a beat. He was way too close for comfort.

His slow grin sent goose bumps shimmering over her skin. "It probably could have, but I wanted to see you again."

"We spent the afternoon with you. Wasn't that enough?" she asked, wishing her voice didn't sound so darned breathless.

Slowly reaching out, he put his arms around her. She knew he was intentionally giving her a chance to back away, but for the life of her, she couldn't seem to get her feet to move.

"No, it wasn't enough," he said, smiling. "I wasn't able to give you a proper goodbye kiss this afternoon."

"Josh, it wasn't a good idea then and it's an even worse idea now." Why couldn't she make her tone sound more convincing?

"Why do you say that, Kiley?" he asked, brushing his mouth over hers.

"I… Well…it just…is," she said, sounding anything but sure. She needed time to think, but he was making it impossible.

As she stared up into his darkening blue eyes, he lowered his mouth to hers and any protest she was about to make went right out the window. She had tried for the past three years to forget how his lips felt moving over hers, how masterful his kiss was. It had been a subtle reminder when he'd kissed her earlier that afternoon at his ranch. But that paled in comparison to the way he was kissing her now.

Tasting and teasing, he traced her mouth with his tongue until she parted her lips on a soft sigh. When he slipped inside to gently explore her inner recesses, a delicious heat began to slowly glide its way through her and her knees suddenly felt as if they were made of rubber. When she raised her arms to his shoulders, he caught her to him, and the feel of his hard masculine body pressed against her softer form felt absolutely wonderful. It had been so very long since she'd been held by a man, felt the carefully controlled strength of his caress and the excitement of his lips claiming hers.

Lost in the delicious feelings, it took a moment for her to realize that Josh had brought his hand up to cup her breast. Even through her clothing the feel of his thumb chafing the tight tip caused a tingling sensa-

tion to travel straight to the most feminine part of her.
A longing like nothing she'd ever known threatened
to swamp her.

The ringing of her phone suddenly broke through
the sensual haze Josh had created and helped to re-
store some of her sanity. Pulling from his arms, her
hand trembled when she reached to pick up the cordless unit. She immediately recognized her sister's number on the caller ID.

"I-It's…Lori. I'll…call her back…in a few minutes," she said, struggling to catch her breath. "You
should probably…go, Josh."

Josh stared at her for several long seconds before
he finally nodded. "Tell Lori I said hello." He started
for the door, then, turning back, reached up to run his
index finger along her cheek. "I know that you're reluctant to acknowledge that it even exists, but whatever this is between us hasn't diminished. If anything,
it's stronger now than it was that night."

"Josh—"

Giving her a quick kiss, he opened the front door.
"I'll see you Monday afternoon."

Unable to form a coherent sentence, Kiley watched
him leave before she sank down on the couch. Her
head was still spinning from his kiss, but it was what
she had noticed when she watched him and Emmie together that made her feel as if the rug had been pulled
out from under her.

She had always thought that Emmie looked like
her. They both had the same hair and eye color. But
watching Josh and her daughter together, Kiley had
noticed several similarities that had her questioning
everything she thought she was sure of. Emmie had

the same smile as Josh, the same patrician nose, and although her eyes were brown instead of blue, they were the same shape as his.

Shaking her head to clear it, Kiley rose from the couch and wandered into the spare bedroom she used for an office. Sitting down at the desk, she booted up her laptop and brought up a website that she hoped would prove that she'd lost her mind.

A half hour later, Kiley stared off into space as the gravity of her findings sank in. She had calculated everything twice and there was no way to deny it. There was a very real possibility that, instead of her ex-husband, Josh Gordon was Emmie's father.

Kiley waited until the following morning to call her sister back. She was still trying to come to terms with the probability of Josh being Emmie's father. But the more she thought about it, the more it explained.

Emmie looked absolutely nothing like Mark. He had an olive complexion, black hair and a distinct Roman nose. Nothing like her daughter's facial features. And then there were the numbers that added up against Mark being her father.

Kiley had always thought she became pregnant a few weeks later, when she and Mark patched things up after that night in her sister's apartment. But the more she thought about it, the less likely that was the date she had conceived. If she calculated Emmie's birth by that, Emmie had been born three weeks early. But when she calculated it by the night she and Josh made love, Emmie had arrived right on time.

She knew that wasn't conclusive proof. Only a DNA test would be proof positive. But everything added up to suggest that Josh was more likely Emmie's father than Mark.

Deciding that she would end up completely overwhelmed by it all if she didn't distract herself, she dialed her sister's number. "Hi, Lori," Kiley said when her sister answered the phone. "I'm sorry I missed your call last night. I was…um, busy."

"No problem," Lori said cheerfully. "I figured you were probably having trouble getting my adorable niece tucked in for the night."

"Saturday nights are easy. Emmie always falls asleep during the movie and it's just a matter of carrying her to bed," Kiley said, wondering how she was going to bring up the subject of Lori's relationship with Josh. From what he had said about Lori being a great girl, it didn't sound like the breakup had been as disastrous as her sister had described at the time.

"I tried calling yesterday afternoon to see if you wanted to go help me start my Christmas shopping, but you weren't home." Lori laughed. "You know me. I always wait until the last minute to buy gifts for everyone and I need your opinion. Otherwise, I go into panic mode and buy something completely inappropriate for everyone." It was so typical of Lori. She had procrastination down to an art form.

"I put all of the gifts I'm giving into layaway this past fall." Kiley smiled. "It doesn't feel as expensive when I pay a little out of each paycheck and I'm able to put a little more thought into what I'm giving."

"You always were the smart one of the Miller girls," Lori said, laughing.

"There are only two of us," Kiley reminded.

"Just ask Mom and Dad, they'll tell you I'm not the

brightest bulb in the chandelier," Lori said. "Especially when it comes to men."

"Did you break up with your latest boyfriend?" Kiley asked, not at all surprised. Lori's relationships never seemed to last more than a few months.

"No, Sean and I are actually doing quite well," Lori said, sounding amazed. "We've even started talking about moving in together."

"Maybe he's Mr. Right," Kiley said, hoping her sister could find someone who loved her in spite of her flightiness.

"I'm actually thinking he might be," Lori said, sounding extremely hopeful.

"By the way, you'll never guess who I've been having to work with on funding for the day care center," Kiley said, hoping Lori would volunteer some information about her breakup with Josh.

"Who?" Lori asked, her interest obviously piqued.

"Josh Gordon," Kiley stated, awaiting her sister's reaction.

"Oh, Josh is very nice," Lori said, sounding sincere. She laughed suddenly. "In fact, he's one of Royal's most eligible bachelors. I think the two of you should get together. You'd make a really great couple and you need to start dating again."

"I'm not in the market to be part of a couple now or in the future," Kiley said, shaking her head. She knew her sister was teasing her, but she wasn't in the mood.

"That's a shame, because Josh really is a terrific guy," Lori stated.

Kiley frowned. "Now, hold it. Didn't you tell Mom and Dad that he broke your heart when he ended things with you?"

There was a long pause before her sister answered. "Well, it didn't exactly happen the way I told Mom and Dad. You know they're convinced that I make some pretty poor choices in my relationships."

"It must run in the family," Kiley muttered, unable to stop herself.

"Hey, Mark Roberts was the only guy you dated that they didn't approve of," Lori reminded her. "And we both know they were right about him."

Kiley took a deep breath. She didn't want to discuss her brief marriage. "Tell me the real story behind your breakup with Josh."

"We had been dating for a couple of months, but there were times when we'd go for a week or so without seeing each other." Lori paused, then went on. "You know me. I got bored. I sort of started going out with someone else and everything was going great. I saw Josh when we could get together and the other guy when we couldn't." She sighed audibly. "At least, everything was going great until Josh caught us."

"Lori!"

"I know, it was a dumb thing to do," her sister said, sounding contrite. "When Josh found out I was seeing this other guy, I begged him to let me tell Mom and Dad that he was the one who lost interest and ended things between us."

"Why?"

"Because I didn't want to listen to them tell me that I'd screwed up again." Lori sighed. "Josh and I both knew it wasn't a forever kind of relationship from the beginning. When I asked him to help me save face by going along with me telling everyone that he'd found someone else and dumped me, he was really nice and agreed."

Kiley couldn't believe what she'd just heard. "So all this time, we've been thinking that he's a snake in an Armani suit, when in fact he was innocent of doing anything wrong?"

"That just about sums it up," Lori admitted. "Please don't tell Mom and Dad. Things are going great with Sean and I and I'd rather not have strained relations with them when I take him to meet them at the end of this week."

"Don't worry. It's your place to tell them what really happened—not mine," Kiley assured her sister. "I've never been a tattletale and I'm not going to start now. But Josh doesn't deserve their condemnation and they deserve to know the truth. You really should set the record straight." She didn't like lying to anyone, but especially not to their parents.

"I know, and I promise I'll confess soon." She paused. "I'd better go. Sean is here to take me to brunch. Give Emmie hugs and kisses for me."

"I will," Kiley said absently as she ended the call.

How could everything that she'd been so certain about change so quickly?

She had never questioned that Mark was Emmie's father. Hadn't even given it a second thought. But now she knew there was every likelihood that he wasn't. She had also never doubted, until recently, that Josh was the unfeeling jerk who had broken her sister's heart. Finding out that he had been the innocent party in their breakup, yet he'd been generous enough to allow Lori to make him out to be the bad guy in order to save face with their parents, was almost more than Kiley could comprehend.

What else had she been wrong about? And why was she so darned relieved to hear that Josh wasn't a heartbreaking reptile after all?

Five

Josh cursed the weather as he made his way across the ice-covered mud at the job site for the new Duncan Brothers Western Wear store. Hot one week, cold the next, it had been nothing short of bizarre for the past several weeks. But today it had taken a particularly nasty turn. It had been raining since before daylight, but it had only been in the past hour that it started sleeting. With the temperature steadily dropping all day, it had finally reached the freezing point and conditions were deteriorating rapidly. Deciding it was just too dangerous for his men to walk the iron girders of the structure, he'd made the decision to shut the job down for the day and send the crew home. No building was worth risking a man's life.

Climbing into his SUV, he quickly dialed the Gordon Construction offices. "Sam, I've shut down the

Duncan job site and I'm heading home," he said without preamble.

"I figured that was going to happen," his twin brother agreed. "I'm getting ready to go by the clubhouse and pick up Lila, then head home. She had a yoga class at the gym for pregnant mothers and as bad as the roads are getting, I don't want her trying to drive."

Josh didn't blame his brother. Sam's wife, Lila, was only a few months away from having their twins and if Josh had a pregnant wife, he knew he'd be just as cautious.

A sudden thought occurred to him that sent apprehension knifing through him. Kiley and Emmie were at the day care center and wouldn't be able to leave until all of the other kids had been picked up. By that time the roads would be so slick he didn't want to think about what might happen.

"I may see you at the clubhouse," he said, starting his Navigator's powerful engine. It was his work truck and for the first time since he bought it, he was glad it had all-wheel drive. "The day care center's director and her little girl are going to need help getting home."

"Oh…really?" His brother drawled the words. "I didn't think you went for women with kids."

"Can it, bro," Josh said, irritated with his twin. "She lives over in the Herndon subdivision and you know how winding the highway is out that way."

"Yeah, I think the engineer who laid out that road must have been part sidewinder," Sam said, his tone disgusted. "It's bad enough driving that way when the weather's clear, but on days like this it's pure suicide."

"I know. That's why I'm taking them home with

extremely rare for us to get weather like this, I can't remember ever driving on it."

"I have and I can tell you that it's no picnic." When they reached the doors, he set Emmie on her feet. "Stay here. I'll go get my SUV and pull it under the canopy so you both stay dry."

"I need to get Emmie's car seat," she said, digging in her tote bag for her car keys.

"There's no sense in either of us breaking our necks trying to walk across a sheet of ice. After I get my truck, I'll drive over to your car and get the car seat." He took her keys from her. "When I come back for you and Emmie, I'll park under the canopy and you can show me how to install it in the backseat."

He had to go so slow that it took several minutes to get to his Navigator and drive over to the other side of the lot in order to retrieve the car seat, then get back to the clubhouse entrance. The SUV kept wanting to fishtail and Josh was more certain than ever that he'd made the right decision to come after Kiley and Emmie.

When he finally drove from under the canopy at the club's front entrance and headed for home, the car seat had been installed, and Kiley and Emmie were safely buckled into their seats. Gripping the steering wheel with both hands, Josh hoped the truck was heavy enough to get at least a little traction, but he wasn't counting on it. Just beyond the TCC's parking lot, a semi hauling a tanker had slid through the intersection and into a deep ravine on the opposite side of the road. If a rig that size had trouble with skidding, what chance did his much lighter SUV have?

Slowly steering the truck out onto the street, Josh didn't draw another breath until he had it straightened out and headed down the highway toward his ranch. The streets were completely deserted, and as they passed car after car off in the ditches lining the road, he decided that although he'd made the right decision about taking Kiley and Emmie to the ranch, it was going to be one hell of a long drive home.

As Josh slowly steered his SUV onto the lane leading up to his ranch house, Kiley finally relaxed enough to unclench her fists. The five-mile trip from the TCC clubhouse to his ranch had taken the better part of an hour and had been more than a little nerve-racking. She had lost count of the vehicles they'd passed that had slid off the road, and there were several times it felt as if the Navigator was going to join them. Fortunately, Josh was an excellent driver and managed to control the truck.

Although she was reluctant to admit it even to herself, she was glad he had insisted that she and Emmie go home with him. There was no way she'd have made it to her subdivision without having an accident. The highway had too many curves, and combined with her inexperience driving on ice, it would have made it impossible not to end up in a ditch. The thought that Emmie might have been hurt caused a chill to snake up her spine.

"Are you cold?" Josh asked, reaching for the heater. "We're almost at the house, but I can turn the heat up if you need me to."

She shook her head. "Thank you, but I'll be fine."

When Josh finally parked the SUV in the attached four-car garage and shut off the engine, he pushed a button on the remote clipped to the driver's sun visor to close the door behind them. "It may have taken a while to get here, but we made it safe and sound."

"Thank you," she said, meaning it. "I can't believe how bad the roads are."

He nodded. "I'm afraid we'll have to make our own dinner. I called Martha earlier this afternoon when the weather started to fall apart and told her and Bobby Ray to go on home. They have a ten-mile drive to their place and I wanted to make sure they got there before the roads got too bad."

Kiley stared at him for a moment. The fact that he was concerned for his housekeeper's and foreman's safety caused her opinion of him to go up several notches.

"I make dinner for Emmie and myself every evening," she said, smiling. "I think I can manage making dinner for the three of us."

He grinned. "Good. I'm afraid my culinary skills only extend as far as boiling water for ramen noodles or packaged macaroni and cheese."

"I thought most Texas men were born knowing how to grill," she teased as she reached for the door handle.

"Wait," he said, getting out of the truck to walk around to her side. Opening the door, he extended his hand to help her down from the seat. "I do know how to grill, but I'm not going to risk life and limb in this weather to walk out to the barbecue pit to burn a couple of steaks."

She laughed. "Where's your sense of adventure?"

"I used it up on that drive home," he said, his smile fading. He reached up to thread his fingers through her hair. "I'm glad you made the decision to come home with me." He leaned down to brush her lips with his.

"I couldn't stand the thought of you trying to navigate all those curves."

Her pulse sped up. "Josh—"

He placed his finger to her mouth to silence her. "I don't want you to worry. Contrary to what happened three years ago, I swear I can be trusted."

Before she could respond, he turned to open the Navigator's back door and reached in to unbuckle Emmie. "She's sound asleep," he whispered, gently lifting her daughter from the car seat.

Kiley's breath caught when Emmie roused, saw who held her, then put her arms around his neck and trustingly laid her head on his shoulder. Her daughter was friendly by nature, but she had never taken to anyone as quickly as she had Josh. Did Emmie somehow sense that he was supposed to be someone special in her life?

Following Josh as he led the way into the house, she couldn't help but wonder what she was going to do about her suspicions that Josh might be Emmie's real father. How was she supposed to even start that conversation? She couldn't very well say, "Oh, by the way, I suspect the child you're holding might be your daughter." That wasn't something just thrown out as a casual comment.

Deciding to keep her silence for the time being in hopes an opportunity presented itself, Kiley followed Josh through the mudroom into the spacious kitchen. When he turned on the lights, she caught her breath as she looked around. The black marble countertops and white custom-made cabinets were gorgeous, but it was the restaurant-size stainless-steel appliances that really caught her eye. They would make cooking an absolute joy.

"This kitchen is a dream come true for anyone who loves to cook," she stated as they continued down a hall to the front foyer. "Do you entertain a lot?"

"I always have our employee Fourth of July barbecue here because I have a bigger yard than my brother." He held Emmie while Kiley removed her sleeping daughter's jacket. "And Sam is in charge of hosting the company Christmas party." He waited until she removed her coat, then handed Emmie to her to take off his. "We sometimes take turns having a couple of dinner parties throughout the year for clients, but that's about it."

While he hung up their coats in a closet close to the front door, Kiley admired the cream-colored marble floor in the foyer and the sweeping staircase leading to the upper level. Everything about Josh's house indicated that he had spared no expense when he'd had it built.

"Hungee," Emmie murmured, waking up to look around.

"Hey there, princess," Josh said, smiling as he closed the closet door.

"Ponies," Emmie said with a shy smile.

Josh laughed and the rich sound did strange things to Kiley's insides. "The ponies are in the barn having their dinner now, but I promise when the weather gets better I'll take you to see them again. Will that be okay?"

Emmie nodded, then put her arms around Kiley's neck. "Hungee, Mommy."

"Then I suppose I'd better find something to make

for dinner," Kiley said, tickling her daughter's tummy. When Emmie dissolved into giggles, she turned to Josh. "Is there anything special you were planning to have Martha make, or should I just search to see what you have?"

"Martha always keeps the refrigerator and pantry fully stocked, so whatever you want to fix is fine with me," he answered. He led the way back to the kitchen. "If you'll tell me what to do, I can probably help a little." He grinned. "And if you need boiling water, I'm your man."

Kiley laughed as she set her tote bag on the kitchen island and reached inside for one of Emmie's ponies. "I'll be sure to remember that." Handing her daughter the toy, she asked, "Could you keep an eye on her while I get started?"

"Do you think she'd like to watch something on TV?" he asked. "I have satellite, as well as access to all kinds of movies and television shows on demand. I'm sure I can find something suitable."

She didn't normally allow Emmie to watch a lot of television, but these weren't normal circumstances. "There is a pony cartoon that I let her watch on occasion."

"I'll find it," Josh promised. Turning to Emmie, he asked, "Would you like to go into the family room with me to see if we can find the pony show on TV?"

"Yes, pease," Emmie said, nodding until her blond pigtails bobbed up and down.

When she watched her child put her little hand in Josh's and walk into the family room with him, Kiley bit her lower lip to keep it from trembling. Her little girl deserved to have a daddy. But how was she going to work up the nerve to share her suspicions with Josh? And if she did manage to find the courage, how receptive would he be? Mark had rejected Emmie, even though he thought she was his child. Would Josh do the same?

"Don't go there," she muttered, shaking her head.

There was one more thing she needed to do that might possibly help her with her decision about talking to Josh. As soon as the weather cleared and things got back to normal, she would call to ask Mark about his blood type. If that ruled out any possibility of him being Emmie's biological father, then she would somehow find the courage to talk to Josh. Until then it would be better to remain silent and turn her attention to a more pressing matter—finding something to make for dinner.

"You're a great cook," Josh said, sitting back from the dining room table. "That was fantastic."

Kiley gave him a smile that sent heat racing through his veins. "I'm glad you liked it, but a simple chicken casserole and some steamed vegetables isn't exactly gourmet fare."

"Would you like to know a little secret about most men?" he asked, grinning.

"Oh, this should be good," she said, laughing. "By all means, please tell me."

Standing, he picked up their plates to carry them to the kitchen, then leaned down to whisper close to her ear. "Most guys really don't care what we eat as long as it's good and there's plenty of it."

She smiled as she wiped off Emmie's face and

hands. "There should be an addendum to that statement."

He arched one eyebrow. "Oh, yeah? What's that?"

"Men really don't care as long as they don't have to cook it," she shot back.

He laughed. "That's a given, honey."

While he put their dishes in the dishwasher, Kiley got Emmie ready for bed. He wasn't sure how other women were with their kids, but Kiley was nothing short of amazing with hers. He couldn't believe how prepared she was. She not only carried toys to entertain Emmie in that tote bag, she also had a change of clothes for her daughter, toddler-size cutlery and an array of healthy snacks.

He decided right then and there that if he ever found himself in a survival situation, he wanted Kiley and her magic tote bag with him. She was prepared for every contingency and managed to get it all in a nice, neat little canvas bag about the size of a large box of cereal.

Walking into the family room to sit down on the couch, he wasn't at all surprised when the lights blinked a couple of times, then went off completely. The generator kicked on automatically and the lights immediately came back on, making him glad that he had thought to add the auxiliary power source when he built the house. The three of them might be stranded until the ice melted, but they would be warm and wouldn't go hungry.

Emmie suddenly came running into the family room as fast as her little legs would carry her. Dressed in the smallest pair of pink sweats he'd ever seen, the little girl's hair was a cloud of damp blond curls around her shoulders and her eyes were wide. She was clearly excited about something. Jumping into this lap, she waved her hands and her big brown eyes sparkled as she jabbered for all she was worth.

"What's she saying?" he asked when Kiley walked in and sat down in the armchair.

Kiley smiled. "She's trying to tell you about the lights going out while she was in the bathtub."

"I promise we won't have to worry about the lights going out again," Josh assured the little girl. He didn't know if she was frightened or just trying to tell him about the experience, but he figured a little reassurance wouldn't hurt.

"Is the house on auxiliary power now?" Kiley asked, putting the clothes Emmie'd had on earlier in the tote bag.

He nodded as he picked up the television's remote control. "I was just getting ready to see if the local news has a report on how widespread the outages are."

As they watched the news, they learned that Royal and the surrounding area had been virtually shut down by the ice storm. There were only a few pockets of people who still had electricity, but as the ice brought down more trees and power lines, the utility company expected those to be without power by morning.

When the news program ended, Kiley got up and walked over to him and Emmie. "She's asleep."

"Do you want me to carry her to bed for you?" he asked, careful to keep his voice low.

She shook her head. "It might frighten her if she wakes up by herself in a strange place." She lifted her daughter to her shoulder. "I'll just lay her down on the love seat until I go to bed."

After laying Emmie on the love seat, Kiley started to sit back down in the armchair, but he caught her hand in his. "Sit here."

"Josh, I'm not overly comfortable—"

"It will be easier to talk without disturbing Emmie," he reasoned, interrupting her.

She stared at him for several long seconds before she slowly lowered herself to the cushion. "I suppose you're right. She normally isn't a light sleeper, but that's at home in her own bed."

"I've been thinking about the sleeping arrangements," he said, nodding.

"And just what about them?" she demanded, looking suspicious.

He couldn't keep from chuckling. "Calm down. There are two master suites—the one down here that you used to give Emmie a bath, and one upstairs. There are also four more bedrooms upstairs. I thought you could take your pick of where you and Emmie are going to sleep. But common sense tells me that little kids and stairs aren't always a good mix."

"Oh." She paused for a moment. "Thank you. That's very considerate. But since your things are in the master suite down here, I assume it's your room?"

He nodded. "Martha has a bad knee and it's easier for her to clean and make the bed if she doesn't have to go up and down the stairs all the time."

Her slow smile sent heat straight to the pit of his belly. "You're one surprise after another, Josh Gordon."

He frowned. "Why do you say that?"

"Not everyone would be that considerate of their housekeeper," she answered.

"I've known Martha and Bobby Ray all my life," he said, shrugging. "When they had to sell off their herds because of the drought, they were in danger of losing their ranch. I offered them jobs because I knew they wouldn't accept help otherwise."

"I can understand that. It's a matter of pride." She seemed to visibly relax as they continued to talk. "Were they able to keep their land?"

He nodded. "They didn't have the money to start over, but since the ranch has been in Bobby Ray's family for over five generations, they wanted to keep it for their grandson. By working for me, they have enough money for their needs, as well as being able to keep the ranch."

"And you make adjustments in your life, so they're able to continue doing that," she said softly.

"Something like that," he answered, feeling a little uncomfortable. He hadn't thought about it as anything more than what it was—the right thing to do.

Deciding it was time to change the focus of their conversation, he grinned. "You know what we need to do tomorrow?"

"I can't imagine," she said, giving him the smile that never failed to send his hormones racing.

"We need to decorate this place for Christmas." He pointed to the corner beside the stone fireplace. "That's where I put the tree the first holiday after I moved in."

"You haven't decorated since then?" she asked, frowning.

"I haven't really had the time." He had, but he hadn't seen any reason to decorate since he was the only one around to appreciate it. "Do you think the tree should go there or somewhere else?"

"By the fireplace is fine," Kiley agreed, hiding a yawn behind her delicate hand. "Emmie and I put ours up on Sunday afternoon. She's going to love getting to decorate another one. But where are you going to get one in this weather?"

"I have a seven-foot artificial tree stored in the garage. But we can talk more about it tomorrow. You're tired," he said, rising to his feet. Holding out his hand to help her up from the couch, he pulled her into his arms. "I'm going to give you a good-night kiss, Kiley." When she started to protest, he put his index finger to her lips. "Just a kiss. Then I'm going to go upstairs—"

"We can sleep—"

He reached up to lightly run the pad of his thumb over her full lower lip, interrupting her protest. "It's all right. I'll take the suite upstairs."

He felt a slight tremor course through her at his touch and without hesitation brought his mouth down to replace his thumb. Careful to keep the kiss non-threatening, Josh barely brushed her lips with his as he waited for an indication from Kiley that she wanted him to take the caress to the next level. When she slowly raised her arms to his shoulders and leaned into him, he felt a moment of triumph. She wanted more, but teasing her with a featherlight touch, he continued to wait. He wanted an indication of her eagerness for his kiss, wanted to know she was impatient for him to give her the kiss she deserved.

Nibbling at her perfect mouth, Josh sensed her increased frustration when a tiny moan escaped her slightly parted lips and she pressed herself closer. "Do you want me to kiss you, Kiley?"

"I…shouldn't," she said, sounding delightfully breathless.

He leaned back to look down at her. "But you do."

"Yes."

It was all he needed to hear, and lowering his head, he covered her mouth with his to give them both what they wanted. Soft and yielding, Kiley had the sweetest lips. Coaxing her to open for him, he deepened the kiss, sending a shaft of heat straight to the region south of his belt buckle.

When she sagged against him, Josh caught her to him. He had no idea why, but even with several inches' difference in their heights, no other woman had ever felt as perfect in his arms as Kiley did. Thinking about how flawlessly they fit together reminded him of that night three years ago and caused his body to harden with need so fast it left him feeling light-headed.

Pulling her more fully against him, he knew the moment Kiley felt his arousal pressed firmly to her. Her breathing quickened and instead of pulling away as he thought she might, she tightened her arms around his shoulders and seemed to melt into him.

The knowledge that she wanted him as much as he wanted her sent his blood pressure sky-high and he sensed that it wouldn't take much for either of them to throw caution to the wind and give in to the explosive chemistry between them. But that wasn't what Josh wanted. When they made love that night in her sister's apartment, their coming together had been frenzied and desperate. And they had both thought they were making love with someone else.

When they made love again—and there wasn't a doubt in his mind that was exactly what was going to eventually happen—he wanted them to take their time. He wanted them to explore each other thoroughly and completely until there was no doubt in either of their minds whom they were making love with.

Slowly easing away from the kiss, Josh took a deep breath. Looking down into her pretty brown eyes still glazed with desire, it was all he could do to keep from resuming the kiss and letting the chips fall where they may.

"J-Josh, I—"

"Shh, honey," he interrupted, kissing the tip of her nose. He released her to walk over to the love seat and pick up her daughter. "Let's get you and Emmie settled in my bedroom. Then I'm going to go upstairs and take a shower cold enough to freeze the balls off a pool table."

Six

The following afternoon, Kiley sat on the couch watching as Josh let Emmie help him put a seven-foot artificial tree together in the corner by the fireplace. It was taking twice as long as it should to assemble the tree because of his "helper." But he didn't seem to mind and patiently waited for her daughter to bring him each branch from the piles he had sorted by length earlier that morning.

Yawning, Kiley laid her head back against the back of the couch. She was completely exhausted and it wasn't hard to figure out why. The kiss they'd shared last night had made her feel as if she would go into total meltdown, and if that hadn't been enough to keep her eyes wide open the entire night, Josh's insistence that she and Emmie sleep in his room was.

The entire suite had that clean, masculine scent

she'd come to associate with him, but when she'd crawled under the covers of his king-size bed, she'd had the sense of being surrounded by him. That had triggered memories of the night he had accidently made love to her, and an accompanying restlessness stronger than anything she could have ever imagined kept her tossing and turning the rest of the night.

"Mommy, see," Emmie said, climbing up on the couch beside her.

Opening her eyes, Kiley smiled at her beautiful little girl. "What do you want me to see, sweetie?"

Emmie beamed as she pointed to the corner by the fireplace. "Twee."

"It's beautiful," Kiley said as she watched Josh plug in the multicolored lights. "You did a really good job helping put it together."

When the tree's branches seemed to instantly come alive with hundreds of twinkling stars, Emmie's eyes widened and she clapped her little hands. "Pwetty."

"It does look pretty good, doesn't it?" Josh grinned. "Would you like to put the angel on the top, Emmie?"

Nodding, Emmie scrambled down from the couch to hurry over to him. As they searched the boxes of ornaments for the tree topper, Kiley couldn't help but notice once again the similarities between them. She had already noticed they had the same eyes and nose, but she now realized that Emmie's hair was closer to Josh's light brown shade than her own dark blonde.

As she watched, Josh lifted Emmie to place the angel on the top of the tree. When they turned to get her opinion, Kiley sucked in a sharp breath. Even their smiles were the same.

She still intended to go through the motion of calling Mark to ask about his blood type, but there was no longer any doubt who had fathered her precious little girl. Emmie looked just like Josh. Confirming the fact was just a matter of formality.

"How does it look?" Josh asked.

"Other than being a bit crooked, it looks fine," she answered automatically.

Setting Emmie on her feet, he walked over to stand in front of her. "Are you feeling all right?"

"Y-yes. Why do you ask?"

"You just looked so—" he paused as if searching for the right word "—preoccupied."

Shaking her head, she forced a smile. "I'm just a little tired. That's all."

He stared at her for several long seconds before nodding. "I didn't sleep all that well myself." He smiled. "I couldn't seem to stop thinking about that kiss and—"

"I didn't say I wasn't able to sleep last night," she interrupted, reluctant to admit to him that she had suffered the same problem.

"You didn't have to, honey," he said, reaching out to tenderly caress her cheek with his calloused palm. "The dark circles under your eyes told me that much."

She wasn't sure she liked Josh's knowing that he had been the reason for her exhaustion. Thinking quickly, she grasped the first excuse that came to mind. "Children tend to be restless sleepers."

Josh stared at her a moment longer. "If you say so," he finally said, turning back toward the boxes of ornaments. She could tell he didn't believe her for a minute, but at least he hadn't pressed the issue.

By the time they finished decorating the tree, Emmie had started rubbing her eyes sleepily and

Kiley knew it was time for her daughter to take a nap. "Emmie, would you like for me to read one of your books to you?"

"Ponies," Emmie said, reaching into Kiley's tote bag.

While she read her daughter's favorite book, Kiley noticed that Josh collected the empty ornament boxes, then, setting one aside, took the others back out to the storage area of the garage. When he came back in, he sat down in the armchair next to the couch. Every time she glanced up, he was staring at her, and she wondered what was running through his mind.

"She's asleep," he finally said, getting up to walk over and lift her daughter from Kiley's lap. Carrying her over to the love seat, she watched him cover Emmie with a colorful Native American blanket. "Would you like a cup of coffee? I made a fresh pot while you were reading to the pony princess," he said, chuckling.

"A cup of coffee sounds wonderful." Maybe the caffeine would help chase away some of her fatigue. "How do you take yours?" she asked, rising to her feet.

"I'll get it." He grinned. "You cooked dinner yesterday evening and, unless a tropical heat wave sweeps through the area to melt all this ice off the roads, you'll probably be cooking again this evening and maybe tomorrow evening. The least I can do is bring you a cup of coffee."

Telling him how she liked her coffee, Kiley sat back down on the couch. For the past few years she had thought of him as a man who couldn't be trusted—an unfeeling jerk who had broken her sister's heart. And in the past several months, she'd come to think of him as the uncaring chairman of the TCC funding committee who, along with some of his fellow committee members, wanted nothing more than to see the day care center fail and her be out of a job.

But the more she got to know him, the more she had to admit that Josh was different than she had perceived him to be. Even before her sister finally confessed that their breakup hadn't gone quite the way she'd told everyone, Kiley had started to realize that he wasn't such a bad guy after all.

If he was as heartless as she'd first thought, he wouldn't have given her a month's worth of the extra money she had asked for and the chance to prove to him that it was needed for the day care center. Nor would he have been concerned for her and Emmie's safety and insisted on driving them to his ranch, rather than her trying to get them home on a treacherous, ice-glazed road.

"Here you go." Laughing, Josh handed her a steaming mug. "Coffee-flavored milk with a little sweetener."

She smiled. "I suppose you're one of the coffee purists?"

He nodded as he sat down beside her. "I like it black, and the stronger the better."

"Aside from the taste, if I drank it like that, I'd never go to sleep." She set her cup on a coaster on the end table. "I didn't even start drinking coffee until after I had Emmie. It was the only way I could stay awake during the day after staying up all night with a colicky baby."

"So when you told me that your ex-husband left

right after Emmie was born, you meant immediately after?" he asked, frowning.

"Mark moved out four days after she was born." Kiley shrugged. "Looking back on it, I'm just as glad that he did. Taking care of a baby was enough to keep me busy. I didn't need a demanding, immature male to deal with at the same time."

"What about your mom or your sister?" Josh asked, sounding genuinely interested. "Surely they helped out."

She nodded. "They were there for me as much as they could be. But they both had to work. Besides, Emmie was my baby to take care of."

He seemed to think over what she had just told him before he finally nodded. "I can understand your sense of responsibility, but it couldn't have been easy. What about some time for yourself?"

"If by that you're asking if I've seen anyone since she was born, the answer is no." She smiled lovingly at her little girl sleeping so peacefully on the love seat. "It might have been extremely difficult at times, but there isn't a single second of it that I regret. I don't need a social life—I have my daughter. Nothing is more important to me than being her mother."

Setting his coffee on the end table, Josh moved closer to her. "You're a great mom and Emmie is a great kid," he said, pulling her into his arms.

"Josh, what are you doing?" she asked, wishing her tone had been a bit more demanding.

"I'm trying to remind you that besides being a great mom, you're a beautiful, desirable woman." He brushed her mouth with his. "You want to know what I think?"

"Probably not," she said, wondering why she couldn't be more assertive. All he had to do was take her into his arms and she seemed to lose every ounce of common sense she'd ever possessed.

He rested his forehead against hers. "I think you need to hear that on a regular basis." Kissing his way down her cheek, she could feel his smile against her skin. "I know you'd rather not think about it, but I know firsthand just how passionate and desirable you are."

A shiver of awareness streaked up her spine and for the first time in years, she was keenly aware of how long it had been since she'd felt anything even close to passion and desire. "You're right," she said, meaning it. "I'd rather not think about that night."

"But it's something neither of us will ever forget, honey." He kissed his way down the side of her neck. "I know every time I look at you, it's just about all I'm able to think about," he admitted as he nibbled at the rapidly beating pulse at the base of her throat. "We might have made love by mistake, but I can't say I'm sorry about it."

"I—I…thought you…were Mark," she said defensively.

"And I thought you were Lori." He cupped her cheeks with his hands and lifted her gaze to meet his. "But that doesn't negate the fact that something happened between us that night that was nothing short of amazing."

As she stared into his remarkable blue eyes, Kiley knew what he said was true. She had never felt anything even close to the connection, the intimacy she had experienced with Josh. It was as if their souls had touched.

"You felt it, too," he stated. It wasn't a question, and she knew by the look on his handsome face that it would be futile to deny it.

Instead of waiting for her response, he lowered his head. The moment their lips met, Kiley felt as if stars burst behind her closed eyes and it seemed that time came to a halt. The awareness she felt whenever she was around him became a magnetic pull that she found impossible to resist, and she couldn't have kept herself from melting against him if her life depended on it.

When he traced her lips with his tongue, she automatically parted them on a soft sigh, inviting him to deepen the caress. As he tenderly stroked her inner recesses, Kiley marveled at how exciting and arousing it was each time he kissed her. Josh Gordon was an expert, and there wasn't a doubt in her mind that he could seduce a marble statue with nothing more than his talented mouth.

Sliding his hand from her back along her side, when he cupped her breast and teased the puckered tip with the pad of his thumb, Kiley thought she would be swamped by the seemingly endless waves of heat sweeping over her. The sensations were so exquisite, she felt branded by his gentle touch.

"Kiley…honey, there's something…going on between us," he said, sounding as out of breath as she felt. "It started that night in your sister's apartment… and it's just as strong now, if not stronger, than it was then." He gave her a kiss so tender it brought tears to her eyes. "All I'm asking is that you acknowledge that."

She couldn't deny that there was something drawing them together much like a bee was drawn to a field of wildflowers. But she wasn't altogether sure she was ready to admit it either.

"We do seem to share an awareness of sorts," she said, choosing her words carefully. She tried to be honest without revealing the full impact of his effect on her.

To her surprise, instead of arguing with her to try to get her to admit that it was more than a mild attraction between them, Josh kissed her soundly, then, releasing her, stood up. "That's all I needed to hear." He took her hand in his and, pulling her to her feet, handed her the box he had set aside earlier. "Could you do me a favor and decorate the mantel, while I take care of hanging a few lights around the front door?"

Relieved and much more comfortable with his shift of focus, she nodded. "After I finish, I'll start dinner."

"Sounds like a plan," he said, giving her a lingering kiss that caused her toes to curl into the plush carpet.

As she watched him turn and stroll down the hall toward the front door, she sighed. How could life become so complicated in such a short span of time?

Opening the box he'd handed her, she placed holly and pinecones along the top of the mantel. It had been so much easier to think of Josh as the heartbreaking Ebenezer Scrooge of the TCC funding committee. She almost wished that she still could. It would be a lot less stressful than the reality of the kind, thoughtful man that he had turned out to be.

On Wednesday afternoon, Josh stood in his family room, staring at the Christmas tree he and Emmie had put up the day before. When had his house become so damned big and empty? He had lived in the place for over five years and in all that time, he couldn't think of a single time that he had felt as alone as he did at that moment.

After the morning news reported that the roads were clear and that power had been restored to the subdivision where Kiley lived, they'd gone to the TCC clubhouse to get Kiley's car, then he'd come home to work. But he hadn't expected to find himself listening for Kiley as she moved around in the kitchen cooking or the sound of Emmie's delightful giggles as she played with her toy ponies.

"You're losing it, Gordon," he muttered as he walked down the hall to his office.

He liked being a bachelor—liked living alone. He could do what he wanted, when he wanted, and there wasn't anyone but himself to worry about. Besides, he had work to do and didn't have time for anything else.

An hour later, he uttered a heartfelt curse and turned off his computer. He had been working on the same bid sheet since he'd sat down and gotten absolutely nowhere with it. All he had been able to do was sit there wondering what Kiley and Emmie were doing.

Had the house been warm enough when they arrived home? Did she need him to check out the plumbing to make sure the water pipes hadn't frozen from the low temperatures and caused a leak? What were they planning to have for dinner? Did they miss having him around?

Rising from his desk chair, he walked out of his office and straight through the house to the door leading to the garage. He grabbed a jacket on the way through the mudroom and within minutes, Josh was driving down the highway toward Royal.

By the time he knocked on Kiley's door, he was confident his plans for the evening were set. He would see if she needed anything, then he fully intended to pick up takeout at his favorite Chinese restaurant, go back home and work on the bid sheet he needed to turn in for the new addition to the women's crisis center over in Somerset.

"Josh, I didn't expect to see you again until Monday afternoon," Kiley said, looking confused when she let him in. "Is something wrong?"

"No, I just wanted to check in and make sure you and Emmie made it home all right." He realized how lame his excuse sounded. Picking up the phone and giving her a call would have accomplished the same thing.

"Hi," Emmie said, grinning as she ran up to him and held up her arms.

"Hi," he said, picking her up. "How's the pony princess?"

She surprised him when she put her little arms around his neck to give him a big hug, then started jabbering excitedly. He looked to Kiley for a translation.

"Emmie thinks you're here for dinner and a movie," Kiley said, smiling. "She wants you to stay."

"And what does her mom want?" he asked, lightly running his index finger along her smooth cheek.

As she stared up at him, he felt her turn ever so slightly into his touch. It was almost imperceptible, but there was no denying it had happened.

"I was going to pick up Chinese on the way home,"

he said, trailing his finger over her lower lip. "Why don't we have it delivered here?"

"Okay," she said, suddenly taking her daughter from him and backing away. "I'll give Emmie a bath and get her ready for bed. That way she can go to sleep while we watch the movie."

He had a good idea why she had retreated. Unless he missed his guess, she was frightened by the strength of the chemistry between them. Hell, it was pretty unsettling for him as well. But he knew beyond a shadow of doubt that if they didn't explore it further, he would end up regretting it for the rest of his life. He had a feeling she would, too.

Two hours later, Josh couldn't help but smile as he sat on Kiley's couch, waiting for her to finish getting Emmie tucked in for the night. They had stuffed themselves on lo mein and egg rolls, then watched the movie about the little mermaid princess again. And if anyone had told him a week ago that he would be happy staying in, watching a kids' cartoon for the second time in less than a week, he would have told them they were in serious need of psychiatric evaluation.

It wasn't that he was a player or ever had been. But his idea of a good time had always been taking a woman to dinner, maybe a little dancing afterward, and seeing where the evening led them.

He suddenly sat up straight as the realization set in that he hadn't even asked Kiley out on a date. They had spent a week and a half seeing each other as often as he could arrange, shared some extremely passionate kisses and, even though it had been three years ago and due to a case of mistaken identity, they had made love. But he hadn't taken her out for a night on the town.

Deciding to remedy that oversight, he waited for her to walk back into her living room. "Kiley, come over here and sit down. I have something I need to ask you."

"What would that be?" she asked, looking as if she dreaded what he might want to know.

When she sank down on the cushion beside him, he put his arms around her. "I know this is short notice, but would you be my date for the TCC's Christmas Ball on Saturday night?"

"That's all?" she asked, visibly relaxing.

Nodding, Josh frowned. "What did you think I wanted to ask you?"

She stared at him for a moment before she finally shook her head and smiled. "I…wasn't sure."

Pulling her closer, he lowered his mouth to hers to nibble and nip at her lower lip. "As much as I enjoy spending time with Emmie watching the mermaid cartoon, I'd like to take her mother out for dinner and an evening of dancing."

He felt a shiver course through her. "Josh, I don't usually…go out."

"How long has it been since you went dancing?" he asked, kissing his way to the slight hollow at the base of her throat.

"I…uh…before Emmie was born," she said, sounding distracted.

"You're joking." He leaned back to look at her. "You haven't gone out since your divorce?"

"No."

"Surely you've enjoyed an evening with some of your friends," he said, having a hard time believing that she hadn't at least had a girls' night out.

She shook her head. "All of my friends are married

and most of them have children. We're all too busy. Besides, going to clubs is expensive."

He pulled her back against his chest for a comforting hug. She had just confirmed his suspicion that she struggled to make ends meet, and he suddenly wanted to find her ex-husband and give him a lesson in facing up to his responsibilities that the man wouldn't soon forget.

"Having kids doesn't mean you can't get out and socialize." He kissed her forehead. "I'm not an expert by any means, but I think interaction with other adults would be a necessity after dealing with kids all the time."

"I didn't say I don't spend time with my friends," she said, defensively. "We sometimes get together on Saturday afternoons for shopping trips to the mall. And tomorrow I'm going to lunch with Piper Kindred."

"I think that's great, honey." He cupped her cheek with his palm and, staring into her warm brown eyes, he smiled. "But I want to take you out on a date. I want to hold you in my arms when we dance and remind you of what a beautiful, desirable woman you are."

"I'd have to find a dress and arrange for someone to watch Emmie," she said, her tone uncertain. "And I'm not sure that it isn't frowned on for employees of the Texas Cattleman's Club to attend special events like the Christmas Ball."

Frowning, Josh shook his head. "Let's clear up something right now. Members of the TCC might be affluent, but we aren't snobs. I can't think of anyone who would have a problem with you being my date for the evening."

"Not even Beau Hacket or Paul Windsor?" she

asked, arching one perfect eyebrow. "I'm sure one of them would have something to say."

"Beau Hacket will be too busy bragging about his son Hack's latest accomplishments to think of anything else. And the biggest issue with Paul Windsor would be him trying to put the moves on you." Grinning, he shook his head. "That's an opportunity I don't intend to give Windsor or anyone else."

"I don't know, Josh. It's been so long since—"

"Just say yes, Kiley."

"I probably wouldn't be able to get a sitter on such short notice," she hedged.

He pulled his cell phone from his shirt pocket and handed it to her. "Call your parents and see if they can keep Emmie for the night."

"Why?"

"It's going to be late by the time we leave the ball, then we would have to drive the fifty miles up to Midland and back to get her," he answered. "I just figured you might not want to disturb her sleep."

Kiley stared at him for several seconds before she nodded and handed his phone back to him. "I'll use the phone in my office."

While she went to make the call to ask her parents about keeping Emmie Saturday evening, Josh thought of something else he needed to do. Kiley had mentioned she would need to find a dress for the ball, and he could imagine just what a dent the price of an evening gown would make in her budget. If she'd let him, he would like nothing more than to make things easier for her by giving her one of his credit cards to use. But if there was one thing he had learned in the past week and a half, it was how fiercely independent she was. She would no doubt tell him where he could put his card, as well as tell him to find someone else to go to the ball with him.

Deciding that he could use a little assistance with his idea, he made a mental note to call Piper Kindred first thing tomorrow. He had heard that she and Kiley had become friends when Piper taught a CPR class at the TCC clubhouse, and he had known Piper for years. He knew he could count on her to help him out.

"What did they say?" he asked when Kiley walked back into the living room.

"They're thrilled that I'm going to the ball," she said, frowning as she sat back down on the couch beside him. "My mother even told me it's past time that I started dating again."

"Your mom sounds like a wise woman," he said, pulling Kiley to him. He was a bit surprised that her mother approved of Kiley going to the ball with him, considering the story Lori had planned on telling them after they broke up. Either Kiley's mother had forgotten who he was or, at some point in the past three years, Lori had come clean and told them the truth about how their brief relationship had ended.

Deciding it didn't matter, he gave Kiley a kiss that sent his blood pressure sky-high and caused his jeans to feel as if they were a few sizes too small. "I'm sure she just wants you to be happy."

"I know, but I'm so…out of practice at the whole dating thing," she said, shrugging one slender shoulder.

"The ball may be our first date, but it's not like we haven't spent a lot of time together in the past couple of weeks," he said, kissing her temple. "And let me assure you that I plan on spending a lot more with you in the future."

"Josh, I have Emmie…to think about." She melted against him. "I have to think of what's best for her."

He knew Kiley's reluctance stemmed from her concern that Emmie might become too attached to him and end up being hurt, not to mention the possibility of being rejected herself. The way that bastard of an ex-husband had walked out on her and Emmie, it was no wonder she was afraid of taking a chance on another relationship.

His heart came to a screeching halt and he had to take a deep breath. What the hell was he thinking? He wasn't looking for anything long-term, was he?

It was true that he had been relentless in getting close to Kiley because he wanted her to admit there was an overwhelming chemistry between them. And she had done that. But beyond that, he hadn't given it much thought. Did he want to try exploring something exclusive with her?

He wasn't sure. But he was certain of one thing. Just the thought of anyone, himself included, causing her or Emmie any kind of distress was more than he could tolerate. Nor could he stand the thought of Kiley in the arms of another man.

"Honey, I give you my word that I will gladly walk through hell and back before I hurt you or Emmie in any way," he assured her.

Needing to make sure she understood that he meant every word he said, Josh lowered his mouth to hers. For reasons he didn't care to analyze too closely, all he wanted to do was make Kiley happy, to show her

how special she was to him and to make things easier
for her and her delightful little girl.

When Kiley placed her hand over his heart, the
warmth of her palm and the feel of her caressing his
chest through the fabric of his chambray shirt set
off little electric charges throughout his being. Heat
rushed through his veins and his body hardened with
an urgency that left him feeling light-headed.

At that moment, nothing would have pleased him
more than to remove both of their clothes and make
love to her right there on her couch. But Kiley wasn't
ready and he didn't care how many cold showers he
had to endure, he wasn't going to rush her. When they
made love again, it would be because it was what they
both wanted, what they could no longer resist.

"I think I'd better leave," he said, breaking the kiss.

As he gazed down at her, he came close to losing his
resolve. The passion and desire in her luminous brown
eyes was breathtaking and he knew as surely as he
knew his own name, they would be making love soon.

"If you and Emmie need anything, don't hesitate to
let me know," he said, standing up. He took her hand
to help her to her feet, then led her over to the door.
Brushing her perfect lips with his, he smiled. "I'll see
you when I drop by the day care center on Friday afternoon, Kiley."

Seven

The following day, when Kiley parked her car outside the Royal Diner, she checked the time on her cell phone. She was running a little late and she hoped that Piper had already found them a booth.

"Over here, Kiley," Piper called to her.

Spotting her friend, Kiley smiled and made her way toward the back of the newly renovated diner. A paramedic working out of Royal Memorial Hospital, Piper had been the instructor for the first-aid and CPR classes Kiley had arranged for the TCC employees. She had wanted to make sure that in case of an emergency with the children at the day care center, everyone knew exactly what to do and how to administer aid if it was needed.

"Sorry I'm late," she said, sliding into the booth on the opposite side of the table from her friend. "I had to wait for one of my volunteers to arrive to help Carrie with the children's afternoon activities."

Piper shook her head. "Don't worry about it. I just got here myself."

"So what's up?" Kiley asked, picking up the plastic-covered menu. "When you called the other day you sounded a little panicked."

"I need your help," Piper said, looking a bit uncomfortable. "I know I've probably put it off way too long, but I need a dress for the Christmas Ball and we both know I'm a lot more comfortable in jeans and a flannel shirt than I am in an evening gown." She grinned. "I was hoping you'd go with me this afternoon to help pick it out."

"Of course I'll go with you," Kiley answered, relieved that nothing was seriously wrong. "In fact, I was going to look for a dress for the ball myself this afternoon. Josh Gordon asked me to be his date."

Piper grinned. "Keep your friends close and your enemies closer?"

Kiley grinned sheepishly. "Something like that."

"I knew there had to be something going on between the two of you," Piper said, nodding. "Your reaction to him a few weeks back was just a little too strong for there not to be."

"Well, at that time I thought he was about as trustworthy as a snake," she said, laughing. "But I've recently discovered that he isn't all that bad." Even her parents had revised their opinion of Josh and didn't seem to question her decision to start seeing him after her sister confessed her role in their breakup three years ago.

"Josh is a really nice guy," Piper agreed. "In fact,

most of the members of the TCC are basically good guys. Some of them might have a few rough edges, but they really do try to live by the TCC code."

As they continued to chat about who they thought would be attending the ball and the type of dresses they wanted to look for, Kiley noticed a woman with dark brown hair sitting at a table close by. She had finished her lunch, but seemed to be taking great interest in what they had to say. So much so that Kiley could tell she was delaying her departure. Only when the conversation turned to the shopping trip they were planning to find dresses for the event did the woman get up to go pay her bill and leave.

"Did you notice that woman eavesdropping?" Piper asked as they watched her walk up to the counter to pay for her meal.

Kiley nodded. "I wonder who she is."

"I don't know, but I intend to find out," Piper said, motioning for Amanda Battle, the manager of the diner, to come over to their booth.

"How can I help you two?" Amanda asked, smiling.

"Who was that woman sitting at the table next to us?" Piper asked, cutting right to the heart of the matter.

Amanda glanced toward the front of the diner where the woman was just leaving. "That was Britt Collins, the detective in charge of investigating Alex Santiago's kidnapping."

"That explains why she was so interested when we started talking about the TCC," Kiley commented.

Suddenly distracted by the tall, dark-haired man entering the diner, Kiley placed her napkin on the table. She had tried to phone her ex-husband the day before to inquire about his blood type, but he hadn't returned her call. She wasn't going to let him get away without answering her question now.

"If you two will excuse me, I see someone I need to talk to," she said. "I'll be right back."

Walking over to his table, Kiley wasn't surprised when he looked around as if trying to find a way to escape.

"What do you want?" he asked, clearly unhappy about seeing her again. "I figured when I didn't call you back yesterday that you'd get the idea that I don't want to have anything to do with you or the brat."

"You couldn't possibly want to avoid having to talk to me as much as I want to avoid talking to you," Kiley said, wondering what she'd ever seen in the man. "I only called yesterday because I need to know your blood type."

"What do you need that for?" he demanded as if she'd asked him to reveal some deep, dark secret.

"It's for Emmie's medical records," she said, thinking quickly.

"Is that it?" he asked, looking suspicious.

"That's it," she assured him. When he told her his blood type, she nodded. "Thank you."

Without another word, she turned to walk back to the booth where Piper still sat talking to Amanda. Kiley had known in her heart that her suspicions were well-founded, but to have them confirmed was almost more than she could come to terms with.

She had done enough research on blood types and establishing paternity by that method to know that for the past three years the man she had thought to be Emmie's father, wasn't. Now all she had to do was

find the right time and way to tell Josh Gordon that
the little girl he fondly called the "pony princess" was
his daughter.

Driving across Royal, Josh went through four traffic lights on yellow and, looking both ways, rolled
through two stop signs as he sped toward Kiley's.
When she'd called, she wouldn't tell him what was
wrong, only that it was urgent that she see him right
away.

When he finally pulled into her driveway, he barely
had the engine turned off before he was out of the car
and sprinting his way up to her door. Not bothering to
knock before he entered the house, he stopped short
when he spotted Kiley sitting in the armchair beside
the couch, glaring at him.

"Are you and Emmie all right?"

"We're just fine," she answered. "But you're not."

A strong sense of relief washed over him. She was
upset, but otherwise, she and Emmie were okay. "So
what's wrong?"

"You know what's wrong," she accused, her brown
eyes sparkling with anger. "How dare you?"

"How dare I what?" He feigned ignorance, but he
had a good idea why she was in a snit.

"You used my friendship with Piper to steer me to
the dress shop where you had made arrangements to
pay for my dress," she accused.

He glanced at the garment bag from one of Royal's
exclusive boutiques draped over the back of the couch.
He'd figured she wouldn't be overly happy with him,
but he hadn't counted on her being downright furi-

ous that he had arranged to buy the dress she would be wearing to the Christmas Ball.

Slowly closing the door, he looked around as he walked farther into the living room. "Have you already got Emmie in bed for the night?"

"Yes. Why?"

He nodded. "That's good. I'd hate for her to have to listen to us argue. It might upset her."

"There isn't going to be an argument," Kiley insisted. "You're going to take your dress and leave."

"Sorry, honey, you're going to have to keep it," he said, grinning. "It isn't my size." He knew immediately that a flippant remark was the wrong thing to say.

Her eyes narrowed and her cheeks turned crimson as her obvious anger rose. "You bought it. You can keep it, take it back or stick it where the sun never shines." She shook her head. "It really doesn't matter to me. Just take it and go."

"Now, honey—"

"Don't you 'now, honey' me, Josh Gordon." She stood up and came to stand in front of him. "Let's get something straight right now," she said, poking him in the chest with her index finger. "I'm not a charity case. I pay my own way."

After her reaction to his glib comment, he knew better than to grin. But damn she was cute when she was all fired up about something.

"I understand that you want to be independent and I respect that, Kiley," he said, reaching out to put his arms around her. When she tried to push herself free, he tightened his arms and pulled her more fully against him. "But I also know an evening gown wasn't something you planned to buy." He brought his hand up to lift her chin until their gazes met. "I asked you to go with me to the ball because I wanted you to have a good time, not to wreck your budget."

"I could have charged it," she insisted.

"I know that," he said, nodding. "But the point I'm trying to make is this—when I take a woman out for the evening, I want her to relax and enjoy herself. I don't want her having to worry about how she's going to pay for the dress she's wearing."

Before she could argue with him further, Josh lowered his mouth to hers. Unyielding at first, he moved his lips over hers until she melted against him. Then, using his tongue, he sought entry to lightly stroke and tease her inner recesses. No other woman had ever tasted sweeter and he knew without question that if he wasn't already, he could quickly become addicted to kissing her.

Bringing his hand up under the hem of her sweatshirt, he released the front clasp of her bra to cup her breast with his palm. Caressing the soft, full mound, he grazed the beaded tip with the pad of his thumb, causing a tiny moan to escape her parted lips. His body responded instantly and he didn't think twice about pressing himself to her. He wanted her to feel what she did to him, how she made him want her.

As he eased away from the kiss, he stared down into her passion-glazed brown eyes. "I'm still angry with you," she said stubbornly.

"I know, honey." Nodding, he removed his hand from her shirt. "But please believe me when I tell you it was never my intention to upset you. All I wanted to do was make it easier on you." He kissed her until they both gasped for breath. "Now, I'm going to go back home because if I don't, I'm going to take you into the bedroom and spend the rest of the night making love to you."

She worried her lower lip for a moment before she spoke. "Josh, we need to talk."

"Is it something that can wait?" he asked, knowing that if he didn't put distance between them, and damned quick, he wouldn't have the strength to leave.

"I suppose so," she said, nodding.

"Good." He pressed his lips to hers for a quick kiss, then, setting her away from him, walked to the door. "Because right now, I have to get back to my place. I have an ice-cold shower waiting on me and a sleepless night ahead." He laughed in an attempt to release some of the tension gripping him. "I think it's about time for me to get started on it."

As Kiley watched Josh close the door behind him, she caught her lower lip between her teeth. She had started to tell him that Emmie was his daughter. But when he stopped her, she had readily gone along with putting off the inevitable for just a bit longer. She couldn't decide if she was being a coward for not insisting that he listen to her, or just being cautious.

For one thing, she wasn't quite sure how to start the conversation, nor was she looking forward to his reaction to the news. There was no doubt he would be shocked. But there was also the possibility that he would think she was trying to use her daughter to sway his recommendation to the funding committee. He knew how important her job was to her and how much it meant to be able to be with Emmie while she still made a living to support them.

Unfortunately, time was not on her side. The more

he was around Emmie the greater the chance he would realize she not only looked like him, the timeline for her birth supported that he had fathered her.

Kiley took a deep breath as she reached for the garment bag with her new evening gown and walked down the hall to hang it in her closet. The funding committee would be meeting next week and unless something happened to further complicate the matter or the perfect opportunity presented itself, she might do well to wait until the day care center's fate had been decided.

Then she had every intention of making him listen to her whether he wanted to hear what she had to say or not.

On Saturday evening when Kiley opened the door, her breath caught. Josh looked utterly devastating in his tailored black tuxedo. But it was the look of appreciation in his blue eyes that caused her heart to skip several beats.

"You look so beautiful, Kiley." He stepped just inside the door to take her in his arms and give her a soft, lingering kiss. "I'll be the envy of every man at the ball."

"I was just thinking something very similar about you and the women attending the ball," she said, smiling.

They hadn't seen each other since their argument over the evening gown. He had been busy working up bids for construction jobs, as well as overseeing several Gordon Construction job sites. But that wasn't to say that they hadn't had contact. He'd had flowers delivered to her at the day care center the day before, and he'd called her last night to ask about her day and see that she and Emmie were doing all right.

"Is the pony princess okay with staying at your folks'?" he asked, as he helped her with her evening wrap.

Nodding, Kiley picked up her sequined clutch. "I don't know who was more excited about her spending the night with them, Emmie or my parents. She has them wrapped around her little finger."

Josh laughed as he placed his hand to her elbow and guided her out to his car. "She has that effect on just about everyone. She's an adorable little girl."

"Thank you," Kiley said, hoping she had made the right decision to wait until after the funding committee meeting to tell him that Emmie was his daughter.

Kiley jumped when Josh kissed her forehead. "I don't know what's running through that pretty head of yours," he said, helping her into the passenger seat of his Mercedes. "But frowning isn't allowed this evening. Only smiles."

As he drove them to the TCC clubhouse for the club's biggest event of the year, Kiley decided he was right. Even if she hadn't made the decision to wait to tell him about Emmie, tonight wasn't a good time. When they talked, they would need privacy and plenty of time to sort everything out.

When Josh stopped the car at the front entrance, he handed his keys to a valet, then came around the front of the car and opened the passenger door for her. "This is beautiful, Josh," she said, looking around as she got out of the car.

The TCC's maintenance crew had strung white twinkle lights into an arched tunnel over the entrance

for the ball's attendees to walk through. Comple-
mented by big red velvet bows, the effect was magical.

"Haven't you attended one of these in the past?"
he asked, tucking her hand into the crook of his arm
as they started to walk through the tunnel of lights.

"No, I didn't move to Royal until I graduated from
college and Mark wasn't a member of the club," she
answered as she looked at all the pretty decorations.

"Wait until you see how they've decorated inside,"
he said, smiling as the doorman opened the big ornate
oak entrance door for them. "The club spares no expense in making this *the* event of the year."

Inside the foyer gorgeous red and white poinsettias
had replaced the usual flower arrangements on the hall
tables, and big bows adorned the tops of every doorway. "This is absolutely beautiful," she said, taking it
all in. "How long will they leave it this way?"

"They'll take everything down the day after New
Year's," he said as they walked past several groups
of couples greeting each other just outside the Grand
Ballroom.

"I'm glad it will be like this the day of the children's
Christmas program," she commented. "It will make
everything so much more festive."

His smile sent a delicious warmth spreading
throughout her body. "What day is the program?"

"This coming Tuesday."

"I'll make sure I'm free," he promised, kissing her
temple.

"To check up on the use of the extra funds?" she
asked.

"No." He stopped to gaze down at her from his
much taller height. "I'll be there because Emmie is

in the program and her beautiful mother will be directing it."

His low, intimate tone caused her knees to wobble and a delightful little flutter to stir in the pit of her stomach. But it was the spark of desire she detected in his intense gaze that stole her breath and sent a shiver of need streaking up her spine.

To distract herself from the sudden tension gripping her, she pointed toward a couple standing by the doors to the Grand Ballroom. "There's Piper and her fiancé, Ryan Grant." Concentrating on the emerald-green gown her friend had chosen the day they went shopping, Kiley walked over to hug her. "You look beautiful, Piper. The gown complements your red hair perfectly."

"Thank you." Piper smiled. "I was thinking the same thing about you. I know I told you the other day, but that black dress is gorgeous and looks like it was made just for you."

While Josh and Ryan talked about the new Western wear store Gordon Construction was building, Kiley smiled at Piper. "Are you feeling a little more confident?"

Piper grinned. "If by that you mean, do I still feel like a fish out of water in a dress, the answer is yes." She laughed. "But the look on Ryan's face when he saw me in it for the first time was well worth it."

Kiley knew what her friend meant. The look of appreciation in Josh's eyes had been absolutely breathtaking and she knew for certain it was one she would never forget.

As the conversation wound down, they walked into the ballroom and Kiley continued to marvel at the elaborate decorations. Dark green holly ringed gold-and-silver tapers that served as centerpieces on the round banquet tables, which were covered with pristine white tablecloths. But it was the fifteen-foot Douglas fir Christmas tree in one corner at the front of the room that caused her to catch her breath. It was huge, perfectly shaped and decorated with thousands of blue twinkle lights. A huge silver loopy bow served as a tree topper, its wide ribbon streamers cascading elegantly down over the branches. The effect was stunning.

Kiley enjoyed listening to the conversation at their table throughout dinner. They were seated with Piper and Ryan, Alex Santiago and his fiancée, Cara Windsor, and Josh's twin, Sam, and his wife, Lila. The brothers entertained them all with stories of how they had traded places in a variety of situations and the many pranks they pulled on their friends. And Ryan shared some humorous anecdotes about his days on the rodeo circuit. Alex seemed rather quiet throughout the evening, but that was understandable. He still suffered from amnesia and had no memory of his childhood or past events, but he did seem to enjoy listening to his friends tell about their antics.

Sitting beside her, Piper leaned close. "Are you enjoying yourself?"

"Absolutely," Kiley answered. "I love my daughter more than life itself, but I hadn't realized how much I missed social situations and adult conversation." Smiling, she asked, "How about you? Still feeling like a fish out of water?"

Piper laughed. "I've never been a 'girlie' girl by any

stretch of the imagination, but dressing up and pretending to be one isn't as bad as I thought it would be."

When Ryan claimed Piper's attention, Alex Santiago smiled at her from across the table. "I hear you are doing amazing things at the day care center."

"I'm not sure how amazing it is, but I love what I do," Kiley answered, smiling back. "The children's Christmas program is next week. We'd love to have you join us if you're feeling up to it."

"I think I would like that," Alex said, looking thoughtful.

As Alex turned to greet a fellow TCC member, Josh's twin brother, Sam, spoke up. "In a couple of years we'll be needing the services of the day care center for our twins."

"Even if I decide I'm not going to go back to work, I'll probably need the respite." Lila laughed. "Especially if they're anything like Sam."

When the band started playing, Kiley and Josh sat in companionable silence for a time as they listened to the music. But when the singer introduced a slow song, Josh smiled as he rose to his feet and held out his hand. "Would you like to dance, honey?"

"I haven't danced in so long, I've probably forgotten how," she answered, laughing as she placed her hand in his.

"It's just like riding a bicycle," he said, leading her out onto the dance floor. "Once you learn, you never forget."

As he took her in his arms and placed his hand at her back, Kiley's heart skipped a beat and her knees threatened to give way. The feel of his warm palm caressing the skin exposed by the low-cut back of her gown was intoxicating and caused a longing within her stronger than anything she could have ever imagined.

"We'll have to do this again sometime." He pulled her close to whisper in her ear. "Although I have recently discovered there's a lot to be said for staying in on Saturday nights."

His breath feathering over her ear and the heat from his hand on her back reminded her of just how long it had been since she'd been held by a man as they danced, how much she missed the closeness. She briefly wondered if anyone watched them, but everything around them seemed to fade into nothingness as she stared into Josh's heated gaze.

"Y-You really like eating in front of the television and watching cartoon movies?" she asked, hoping to distract herself from the heat swirling throughout her body.

Shrugging, he smiled. "Watching the show with the pony princess is a lot of fun. But it really starts to get interesting after she's gone to bed and I get to hold and kiss her enticing mother."

The evidence of his rapidly hardening body pressed to her stomach made her feel as if her insides had been turned to warm pudding and she found herself clinging to him for support. "Josh—"

"I'm not going to lie to you, Kiley," he said, his expression turning serious. "I want you and nothing would please me more than to take you home, get you out of this slinky black dress and sink myself so deep inside of you that we both forget where you end and I begin. But that isn't going to happen unless it's what you want, too."

Staring up into his smoldering blue eyes, her heart

began to beat double time and her breathing became shallow. Before they took such an important step, she really needed to tell him about being Emmie's father. "Josh, I...want you, too. But—"

Pressed tightly against her, she felt his body surge at her admission. "There's no 'buts' about it. Do you want me, Kiley?"

"Yes, but we need to talk about something first," she said, wondering why she couldn't sound more insistent.

"Honey, we can talk as much as you want later on," he said, leading her off the dance floor. They stopped by their table for her clutch and evening wrap and came face-to-face with Sam as they turned toward the exit.

"Hey, where are you two going? The night's still young," he said, his eyes twinkling mischievously.

"Can it, bro," Josh said, glaring at his twin.

Seemingly unaffected by his brother's displeasure, Sam turned to her. "It was very nice to meet you, Kiley. If this boneheaded brother of mine gives you any problems, you just let me know."

Kiley smiled and nodded. "I enjoyed meeting you and Lila, as well."

"You and Lila have a nice evening and I'll see you at work on Monday, Sam," Josh said over his shoulder as he hurried her toward the exit. Fortunately the other couples were out on the dance floor and they didn't have to explain their early departure to anyone else.

As they stood beneath the twinkling white lights as they waited for the valet to bring Josh's Mercedes to the front entrance, she felt compelled to try again to tell him about Emmie before things between them went any further. "Josh, please. It's really important that I talk to you about—"

He cut her off with a deep, lingering kiss, then, lightly running his finger along her jaw, he smiled. "I give you my word that we'll discuss whatever is on your mind tomorrow. But tonight is all about us, Kiley. This thing—this need—between us has been building since you walked into the meeting room to address the funding committee, and it's past time we explored it."

Her pulse raced as he helped her into the car, then drove away from the TCC clubhouse. There was no question that the chemistry between them was explosive, but was she ready to take what seemed like the next natural step with Josh? She still hadn't managed to tell him that he was Emmie's real father.

"We aren't going back to my house?" she asked when he steered the Mercedes toward his ranch.

The look he gave her sent heat sweeping throughout her entire body and she forgot anything else she was about to say. "You've slept in my bed without me," he said, his voice low and intimate. "But not tonight." Reaching across the car's console, he took her hand in his and raised it to his mouth to kiss. "Tonight I'm going to hold you and make love to you the way you were meant to be loved. And I'm not about to let anything interrupt that."

The promise in his words and the look on his handsome face caused her to shiver with anticipation, and by the time they reached his ranch, she knew she really didn't have any choice in the matter. Heaven help her, she wanted to once again experience the power of his lovemaking, needed to feel as cherished as when he'd made love to her that night three years ago.

Eight

When they reached his place, Josh led her directly into his bedroom, closed the door and turned on the bedside lamp. Taking her wrap and sequined clutch from her, he placed them on the dresser, then, turning back, he took her in his arms. Any second thoughts she might have had evaporated like the morning mist on a warm summer's day when he lowered his head to capture her lips with his.

His firm mouth moved over hers with an expertise that left her breathless, and she realized that no other man's kiss had ever caused her to react quite the way Josh's did. With sudden clarity, she knew no other man's kiss ever would.

Running his hands along her sides, he nibbled his way down the side of her neck to the base of her throat. "Honey, would you like to know what I've been thinking ever since you opened your door this evening and I saw you in this slinky black dress?"

"I—I'm not sure," she admitted. She shivered with anticipation when he brought his hand up and trailed his index finger along the V neckline of her gown.

"All I've been able to do is think of ways to take it off you," he whispered, kissing her collarbone and the valley between her breasts. "And when we were dancing I wasn't sure I wouldn't lose my mind."

"Wh-why?" She had to concentrate hard to keep from melting into a puddle at his feet.

"When I put my hand to your bare back I couldn't help but imagine how it would feel to caress every inch of your soft skin." There was such passion in his deep baritone, a wave of heat streaked from the top of her head to the soles of her feet.

Her knees threatened to give way and Kiley placed her hands on his chest to steady herself. "I'd like to touch you, too."

The look in his eyes stole her breath a moment before he stepped away from her to remove his tuxedo jacket and tug his shirt from the waistband of his trousers. He held her gaze with his, and neither of them said a word as he unfastened the stud closures, then shrugged out of the shirt and tossed it aside.

Her hand trembled as she reached out to run her fingers over his padded pectoral muscles and the taut ridges of his abdomen and stomach. The light sprinkling of hair covering his hard flesh tickled her palm and reminded her of the marvelous contrasts between a man and a woman.

When he shuddered from her light touch, she smiled. "Your body is perfect, Josh."

He brought his hands up to brush the stretchy fabric from her shoulders, then kissed the newly exposed skin. "Having you explore my chest feels wonderful, honey. But I want to touch you, too." As he pushed the evening gown down her arms, then over her hips into a shimmery black pool at her feet, Kiley's pulse raced at the look of appreciation in his smoldering blue eyes. When he discovered that she wasn't wearing a bra, his sharp intake of breath caused an interesting little flutter deep in the pit of her stomach. "You're beautiful, Kiley."

Cupping her breasts with his hands, he alternated kissing and teasing her beaded nipples, sending waves of heat sweeping over her. But when he took one of the tight buds into his mouth to explore her with his tongue, the sensations coursing through her were so intense, she felt as if she might faint.

"J-Josh… Oh, my."

"Does that feel good, Kiley?"

Unable to form a coherent thought, all she could do was nod.

"Do you want me to take off the rest of our clothes?" he asked, continuing to taunt the overly sensitive tip.

"Y-yes."

Dressed in nothing but her panties and high heels, she stepped out of the dress at her feet and braced her hands on his shoulders for him to remove her black velvet shoes. When he straightened, she watched him quickly kick off his own shoes, then unzip his tuxedo trousers to shove them and his boxer briefs down his legs. He tossed them and his socks onto the rapidly growing pile of their clothing. When he turned to face her, Kiley's breath lodged in her throat.

She'd been right. Josh's body was—in a word—perfect. His shoulders were impossibly wide, his muscles well-defined and his torso lean. But as her gaze traveled lower, her eyes widened. Josh wasn't just perfect, he was magnificent.

Fully aroused and looking at her as if she were the most desirable creature on earth, he stepped forward to hook his thumbs in the waistband of her lace panties. "I want to feel all of you against me," he said, his intimate tone sending another flash of heat flowing through her.

Once the scrap of silk and lace had been added to the pile of clothes, he took her back into his arms, and the feel of skin against skin caused her knees to give way. He caught her to him and Kiley thought she might go into complete meltdown. His firm, hair-roughened flesh pressed to her smooth feminine skin, the hard length of his erection nestled against her soft belly, set off tiny little sparks skipping over every nerve in her body.

"Honey, I think it would probably be a good idea if we get into bed while we both still have the strength to get there," he said, his warm breath feathering the hair at her temple.

He led her over to the bed and while she pulled back the navy satin duvet and got into bed, he reached into the drawer of the bedside table. Tucking a small foil packet under his pillow, he stretched out beside her and pulled her to him.

"I'm going to try to go slow, honey," he said, giving her a kiss so tender it brought tears to her eyes. "But I've wanted you again for so damned long, I'm not sure that's going to be possible."

"A couple of weeks isn't…all that long," she said, trying to catch her breath.

"I'm not referring to seeing you at the meeting of the funding committee," he said, skimming his hand down her side to her hip. Caressing her thigh, his movements were slow and steady. "I'm talking about how long it's been since we made love the first time. I haven't been able to forget that night three years ago. If I had known your name, I would have tried to find you. But I didn't think asking your sister was the right thing to do, especially since I started distancing myself from her after that night."

His impassioned words created a longing inside of her stronger than anything she had ever experienced before, and she knew that whether she had realized it or not, she had wanted him since that night, as well. But before she could tell him, he parted her to gently touch the tiny nub nestled within and she suddenly felt as if she would go up in flames. His light teasing strokes and the feel of him testing her readiness for him caused a coil of need to tighten deep in the most feminine part of her, and she couldn't stop herself from moving restlessly against him.

Wanting to touch him as he touched her, Kiley slowly slid her hand over his chest, then down his rippled abdomen and beyond. When she found him, her heart skipped several beats at the sheer strength of his need. His body went completely still and a groan rumbled up from deep in his chest as she measured his length and girth with her palm, then explored the softness below.

"Kiley…nothing would make me happier…than to have you touch me like this…for the rest of the night," he said haltingly. When he caught her hands in his, he sounded as if he couldn't take in enough air. "But I want you so damned much…I'm not going to last… if you keep that up."

The look in his eyes sent her temperature soaring, and her need for him grew with each passing second. If they didn't make love soon, she knew for certain she would be reduced to a cinder.

"P-please make love to me, Josh."

He reached under his pillow, quickly arranged their protection, then kissed her with a passion that caused her head to swim. Before she could fully recover, he held her gaze with his as he nudged her knees apart and rose over her.

"Show me where you want me, Kiley," he said, taking her hand in his to place it on his hardened body.

Her heart pounded as she guided him to her and she felt his blunt tip slowly begin to enter her. His gaze never wavered from hers as he eased himself forward and she knew she'd never felt more complete than she did at that moment.

"It feels so good to be inside of you," Josh whispered as he gathered her to him.

Before she could respond, he set a slow pace and Kiley felt as if she were being swept away by the exquisite sensations filling her entire being. Wrapping her arms around his wide shoulders, she held him to her as the coil of need deep within her tightened to the empty ache of unfulfilled desire. But all too soon, she found herself climbing toward the pinnacle, and apparently sensing that she was poised on the edge of finding the satisfaction they both sought, Josh quickened the pace of his lovemaking.

Heat and light flashed behind her tightly closed eyes as she was suddenly set free from the tension holding her captive. Waves of pleasure flowed over her and Kiley had to cling to Josh to keep from being consumed by the exquisite intensity of it all. He thrust into her one final time, then, groaning her name, he joined her in the all-encompassing pleasure of mutual release. As they slowly drifted back to reality it felt as if their souls had been united to become one, and she knew beyond a shadow of doubt that if she hadn't already done so, she was close to losing her heart to the man holding her so securely in his arms.

"You're amazing, honey," he said, kissing her until they both gasped for air.

"That was…breathtaking," she murmured, still trying to come to terms with her newfound realization.

Levering himself to her side, he pulled her close. "Are you all right?"

Deciding there would be plenty of time to analyze her feelings for him later, she kissed his chin. "'All right' doesn't begin to describe how incredible I feel right now, Josh."

She felt his body stir against her leg a moment before a wicked grin appeared on his handsome face. "That's good, because I'm going to spend the rest of the night reminding you of just how incredible we are together."

And to her utter delight, he did just that.

The following Monday afternoon, Kiley gathered some festive paper and a memory stick. "Carrie, will you and Lea be able to watch the children until I get back? I need to walk down to the administrative office to get the programs printed for the Christmas show tomorrow."

"Sure thing." Carrie nodded toward the children sleeping on colorful mats on the floor. "They should nap for another thirty minutes or so. Lea and I can just start story hour a little early if you aren't back when they wake up," she added, referring to the volunteer Kiley hoped to add as a paid staff member after the first of the year.

Nodding, Kiley headed for the door. "I shouldn't be too long."

As she walked down the hall, she couldn't stop thinking about her night with Josh. Never in all of her twenty-eight years had she experienced that level of passion or felt more cherished than she had in his arms. But as wonderful as her night with him had been, once he had taken her back to her place the following morning, reality had intruded as she remembered the unresolved issues between them.

She sighed. He had made it easy to forget that the funding committee would be meeting at the end of the week and she still had no indication if he would recommend additional funds for the day care or side with Beau Hacket and Paul Windsor in hopes of seeing the center close. And then there was the matter of finding the right words to tell him that he was Emmie's father.

If she told him now, how would he react? As fond as he seemed to be of Emmie, Kiley was almost positive he would accept and love her. But her main concern was that he might think she was trying to use her daughter to influence his recommendation to the funding committee. For that matter, it could cross his mind that she had made love with him for that same purpose.

She really didn't think he would consider her making love with him a ploy to keep her job. As if by unspoken agreement, neither of them mentioned the day care center's future when they were away from the TCC clubhouse. But she wasn't so sure he would take the news about Emmie being his child as well. That's why she had made the decision not to tell him until after the funding committee met. If she withheld the information, then there would be no question about her motives. And besides, it wasn't like a couple of days would make a difference. Josh was Emmie's biological father and there wasn't anything that would ever change that fact.

Lost in thought, she paid little attention to the group of teenage boys gathered in one of the alcoves she passed as she walked down the main hallway. At least, she didn't until she heard one of them mention her name.

"I'm telling you it's just a matter of time before that damned Roberts woman and her day care center full of rug rats are history," she heard one of the boys say.

Stopping just out of sight of the sitting area, she shamelessly listened to what the group had to say.

"What makes you think the day care center is going to close, Hack?" another boy asked. "From what I hear it's doing pretty good."

"Well, when it got torn up, my old man said whoever did it had done the club a big favor," Hack said, sounding smug. "He said he had enough influence on the funding committee to see that what the insurance didn't cover would be taken out of the center's budget and that it would run out of money by spring. He even told me he'd thank the vandal if he knew who he was." The boy laughed. "I told him he could just buy me a new truck and we'd call it even."

"You're full of it, Hack," one of the boys scoffed. "There's no way you're the vandal the police are looking for. And your dad wouldn't let you get away with doing something like that here at the TCC."

"Yeah, man, why would you say something like that?" another one asked.

"I know how to work the old fart. He thought I was joking with him." Laughing, the teenager added, "I wanted him in a good mood when I asked for my new ride."

"In other words, he got what he wanted, now you figure he owes you," the scoffer said slowly.

Kiley had heard enough. If what he boasted about was true, Beau Hacket's son had been responsible for the damage done to the day care center. But whether it turned out he was the vandal or not, his claim needed to be investigated.

The Christmas programs forgotten, Kiley walked straight to one of the house phones to have the switchboard operator page Josh. He had stopped by the day care center earlier on his way to lunch with Gil Addison and she hoped they were still in the restaurant or possibly in the bar.

"Josh Gordon here," he said, coming on the line a couple of minutes later.

"I know who vandalized the day care center," Kiley said, careful to keep her voice quiet.

"Kiley?"

"Yes. I just overheard someone bragging about it," she said, deciding not to say the culprit's name aloud for fear of alerting the boys that she had overheard their conversation.

"Where are you?" he asked.

"On the house phone in the main hallway," she answered, keeping an eye on the sitting area. The boys were still there. "Hurry, Josh. He's in a group of teenagers in the alcove across from the Grand Ballroom."

"Gil and I will be right there."

In no time, Josh and Gil came jogging down the hall toward her. "It's Beau Hacket's son," she whispered when they stopped beside her.

"Are you sure?" Josh asked.

She nodded. "The other boys called him Hack and he mentioned his father being on the funding committee."

"It really doesn't surprise me," Gil said, shaking his head. "Hack is a real smart-ass and there isn't a lot I would put past him."

Josh nodded. "And Beau has a blind spot when it comes to that kid. He never makes him face the consequences of his actions."

"Beau isn't going to have a choice this time," Gil said, pointing toward the two plainclothes detectives who had just entered the clubhouse.

"We phoned the police right after you called," Josh explained.

When the detectives joined them, Kiley relayed what she had heard. "They didn't realize I was eavesdropping," she finished.

"Do you know the boys' parents?" the older policeman asked. "They'll need to be called."

"From what he said, I think the Hacket boy acted alone," Kiley said, hoping the other boys weren't deemed guilty by association. They had sounded as appalled at the Hacket boy's claims as she had been.

"We need all of their parents present before we question them," the younger detective advised.

"Since the club has a policy of not allowing anyone underage on the premises without being accompanied by a parent, I'm pretty sure their dads are all here," Gil said, glancing into the alcove. He walked over to the house phone. "I'll have them paged."

While Gil called the switchboard, the police officers walked into the alcove and advised the boys that as soon as their parents arrived, they had some questions they wanted to ask them.

Putting his arm around her shoulders, Josh held Kiley to his side as they walked the short distance to the sitting area. "Are you doing okay, honey?"

"I'm fine," she said, nodding. "I'm just glad we found out who was behind the vandalism and why, even if it was a little disconcerting to hear him admit everything."

"I can't believe he did all that just to make points with his dad in hopes of getting the truck he wanted," Josh said, shaking his head. He grunted. "That kid needs a reality check."

"How do you think Beau will react when he finds out his son was behind all of the destruction?" she asked, checking her watch.

"Knowing Beau, he won't take the news well." Josh shrugged. "But it looks like we aren't going to have to wait to find out."

Looking up, Kiley watched Beau Hacket coming down the hall toward them like a charging bull. "What the hell's going on?" he demanded. If the scowl on his face was any indication, Josh was right about him not taking the news well.

"We know who was behind vandalizing the day care center," Josh answered.

"Who was it?" Beau asked, glancing into the sitting area. The blood drained from his face when he spotted his son among the four boys seated in the alcove. "This had better be some kind of joke."

As the detectives questioned the boys and sorted through the facts, they dismissed all of them but Hack. The teenager didn't look nearly as confident now as he had when the interrogation started.

"Who are you going to believe, Dad? Me or them?" Hack demanded, looking up at his father defiantly.

"Don't lie to me, son," Beau said firmly. "You know I'd never condone you breaking the law."

"I'm telling you, I didn't do it," the boy lied.

"We collected a partial fingerprint when we first investigated the vandalism," the younger policeman advised. "It's enough that once we take you down to the station and fingerprint you, we should be able to establish either your innocence or your guilt."

"I'm going to jail?" Hack asked, looking alarmed for the first time since the detectives arrived. "You're gonna get me out of this, aren't you, Dad? I did it for you," the boy said, unaware that he had just confessed.

"I don't know if I can, son." Beau looked from one detective to the other. "Is there any way to make this right without my boy having a criminal record?"

"It's up to the Texas Cattleman's Club if they want to press charges," the older detective advised. "But we're going to read him his rights and take him down to the station for further questioning. I would suggest you get in touch with your lawyer, Mr. Hacket. Your kid is facing charges of vandalism, criminal mischief and anything else we can think to charge him with." He gave Beau a pointed look. "Although this is the most serious, I don't have to tell you, this isn't the first time he's been in trouble."

Beau looked miserable when he turned to Josh and Gil. "What do you guys think? If I make full restitution for the damages do you think we can let this thing go?" he asked hopefully. "I give you my word I'll do whatever it takes to make this right."

"That's not up to us," Gil said, shaking his head. "This will have to be voted on by the executive board."

"While you all sort this out, we'll take Junior here down to the station." The younger police officer stepped behind Hack to put handcuffs around the teenager's wrists. "You have the right to remain silent...." The detectives led Hack toward the main exit as they continued to read him his rights.

"Can you call an emergency meeting of the board, Gil?" Beau asked, reaching for the cell phone clipped to his belt. Making a quick call to his lawyer, Beau turned back to Josh and Gil. "I can't tell you how much it would mean to me for Hack not to end up with a police record over this."

"Before this goes any further, I have a question for you, Beau," Josh said, folding his arms across his wide chest. "What are you going to do about your son? His complete lack of respect for people and property, as well as his self-discipline, are all but nonexistent. There's going to come a day when you can't pay his way out of the trouble he gets into."

Gil nodded. "I agree with Josh, Beau. I'll call an

emergency meeting for this evening, but if I recommend that the board let you do what you're proposing, we need an assurance from you that something like this won't happen again to us or anyone else in the community."

Surprisingly, instead of getting angry at Josh and Gil for pointing out that something needed to be done with his son, Beau nodded. "I give you my word that he won't be getting into any more trouble. I've threatened to send him to a military school in the past."

"You go on down to the police station with your son and we'll let you know what the board decides," Gil advised.

"There's one more thing that I want done," Josh said as Beau turned to leave.

"What's that?" the man asked, sounding as if he would agree to just about anything.

"When he vandalized the day care center, your son spray-painted a very derogatory word on the wall in reference to Ms. Roberts," Josh stated flatly. "I think an apology is in order. And it had better be sincere."

Beau nodded. "I can't tell you how sorry I am that this happened, Ms. Roberts. Believe me when I say I never intended for my objections to the day care center to cause my son to do something like this. I give you my word, I'll find a way to make this right."

"Apology accepted," Kiley said, suddenly uncomfortable at being the center of attention.

Beau nodded, then turned to Gil and Josh. "I'll be down at the police station. Could you let me know as soon as the board makes a decision?"

Gil nodded. "I'll call you one way or the other."

As they watched Beau hurry toward the exit, Josh

turned to Gil. "While you phone the executive board members, I'm going to walk Kiley back to the day care center," Josh said, putting his arm around her.

"Will you be there tonight for the meeting?" Gil asked as they walked out into the hallway.

Josh wasn't a member of the executive board, but unless it was a closed session, any member in good standing could attend. And since he had witnessed the police's questioning, Kiley wasn't sure he wouldn't be asked to give an account of what had taken place.

"I figure I'll throw my support behind Beau sending Hack off to military school," Josh said, nodding. "I think he could benefit from the discipline and structure of a military academy. It would probably be the best thing that ever happened to that kid."

"At this point, it sure won't hurt," Gil agreed. "And since his dad is one of our own, I'm pretty sure we can get the justice we want without leaving Hack with a criminal record." He smiled at Kiley. "I'll see you a little later this afternoon when I come to get Cade."

"Do you think the board will go along with what you and Gil have in mind?" Kiley asked when Gil left to go back to his office.

Josh nodded as they walked down the hall. "Every member of the TCC is sworn to live by its code— 'Leadership, Justice and Peace.' And we've got a long history of policing our own, as well as righting a lot of injustices for those outside of the club. This is something we can take care of ourselves."

"Hack will be taught a lesson without a criminal record and the club won't suffer further scandal," she guessed.

"That's it. He's seventeen and would have probably

been charged as an adult. This way he'll get the chance to clean up his act without the stigma of having been in trouble with the law." When they stopped at the day care center's door, he took her into his arms. "Thank you for catching him for us."

"I really didn't do anything but eavesdrop." She smiled. "But now that the mystery is solved, I'm glad I won't have to worry about coming in to work one morning and finding the place destroyed again."

He gave her a long, deep kiss. "Now that I have that meeting, I won't be able to see you until sometime tomorrow."

"Are you planning on attending the children's Christmas program tomorrow afternoon?" she asked, feeling the familiar flutter of desire begin deep in the pit of her belly.

"Of course." His deep chuckle caused the fluttering inside of her to go berserk. "I wouldn't think of missing the pony princess's singing debut."

Kiley's chest swelled with emotion. "She's going to be thrilled to see you there."

"I think Gil said the program is in the main ballroom?" he asked.

"Yes."

He nodded and gave her a quick kiss. "I'll call you this evening and let you know the outcome of the board's vote."

As she watched Josh walk away, Kiley caught her lower lip between her teeth to keep it from trembling. Any doubts she had about him accepting Emmie as his daughter had just been erased. Very few men would make sure they attended a toddler's Christmas program if they didn't care a great deal for the child. And once he learned he was Emmie's father, Kiley believed he would be the loving daddy that her daughter had always deserved.

But where did she fit into the equation?

Kiley knew that he liked kissing her and there was no doubt he desired her. But could he ever love her?

Her heart stalled and it suddenly became difficult to draw her next breath. She had known the night they made love that she was in danger of doing it, but had she actually fallen for him?

Knowing in her heart that was exactly what had happened, she slowly opened the door to the day care center. She wasn't comfortable with it and it certainly added another wrinkle to an already complicated situation. But there was no denying it, either.

Whether she liked it or not, she had fallen head over heels in love with Josh Gordon.

Nine

The next afternoon, Josh stopped his SUV at the TCC
clubhouse entrance, got out and tossed the keys to one
of the valets. He had just enough time to find himself
a seat in the Grand Ballroom before the day care center's Christmas program started.

If anyone had told him a few weeks ago that he
would be rushing to attend something put on by a
bunch of little kids, he would have questioned their
sanity. But now? He'd walk through hell if he had to
in order to keep from disappointing one cute little girl
and her beautiful mother.

He frowned as a woman standing by the door to
the ballroom handed him a program with a brightly
colored holiday design. When had Kiley and Emmie
become so important to him? And how had it happened so quickly?

His mouth went as dry as a wad of cotton as he entered the ballroom and found himself a seat. Surely
he hadn't fallen in love with Kiley. He knew he liked
her a lot and the chemistry between them was nothing short of amazing. But love?

Giving himself a mental shake, he almost laughed
out loud at his own foolishness. He had to be losing it.
There wasn't any question that he was in lust with the
woman. But that didn't mean he was in love with her.

And he could even understand his feelings for
Emmie. She was a cute, friendly little girl and it would
take a heartless bastard not to find her completely
adorable.

He sat down next to an older couple close to the
front of the portable stage that had been set up next
to the Christmas tree. Seeing the decorated tree, he
couldn't help but think about dancing with Kiley the
night of the ball. That one dance had been all it took
for them to decide to leave the gala and go back to his
place for the most incredible night he'd spent in the
past three years.

"We're here to see our grandson," the woman said,
smiling. "And you?"

Before he could tell the beaming grandmother he
was a friend of the day care center's director and her
little girl, Christmas music filled the room and the
kids began to take their places on the stage. When he
spotted Emmie in her red velvet dress, pigtails bob-
bing as she skipped along, he couldn't stop grinning.
She had to be the cutest kid ever.

As the program began, there were several times
Josh found himself laughing out loud. Kiley and her
helpers had to lead wandering kids back to their places,

hand giant plastic candy canes back to the little ones who dropped theirs and take a giant bell away from one of the preschool boys when he used it to bop one of the little girls on the head. Josh enjoyed the program immensely and he was certain the rest of the crowd had, too.

When the kids sang the last song, Kiley thanked everyone for attending, told the parents that the day care was dismissed for the rest of the afternoon and then motioned for Josh to come up to the stage. "Would you mind watching Emmie for a moment while I get everything cleared up here?" she asked.

"No problem," he said, picking up the toddler. "We'll be over by the tree."

As he carried her over to look at the decorative ornaments on the tree, he marveled at the fact that he was actually watching after a kid and didn't mind it at all. "Did you see this ornament, Emmie?" he asked, pointing to Santa's sleigh with eight tiny reindeer hanging from one of the branches.

"Ponies," Emmie said, her little face beaming as she pointed at it.

Tickling her tummy, he laughed. "You've got a one-track mind, princess."

"Your daughter is very cute," the woman who had sat next to him throughout the program said as she and her husband walked over with their grandson in tow. "She looks just like you." Josh smiled and started to correct her, but the woman didn't give him the chance. "Do you have a cell phone?" she asked.

"Yes, do you need to use it?" He unclipped his phone from his belt and handed it to her.

"I'll use the camera on your phone to take your

picture with her here by the tree, if you'll return the favor and take one of us with our grandson," she said, pulling a digital camera from her purse.

"Sure," Josh agreed. He wouldn't mind having a picture of himself and Emmie, and if the woman wanted to think they looked alike, what would it hurt?

After the pictures had been taken and the couple moved on, he checked the gallery on his phone to see how the photo had turned out. He smiled at the image. Perched in the crook of his arm, Emmie had her hand resting on his cheek and the sweetest grin he had ever seen on her cute little face.

But his smile suddenly faded as he looked at his image and then Emmie's. He normally didn't pay any attention to who resembled who. He had a mirror image of himself in his twin brother, Sam, and didn't figure he looked like anyone else. Staring at the picture suddenly had him changing his mind.

He had never before seen himself and Emmie together—not in a mirror or a picture. And since he hadn't been looking for any similarities between the two of them, he hadn't given it so much as a fleeting thought. But there was no denying that Emmie looked a lot like him. He could see glimpses of Kiley in Emmie's big brown eyes and the delicate shape of her face, but the child had his nose and smile. And their hair color was almost exactly the same shade.

"Did you enjoy the program?" Kiley asked, walking up to them.

Looking up, he clipped the phone back on his belt as he nodded. "Are you finished for the day?"

"Yes. The children have all been turned over to their parents and the props have been stored in my office," she said as she took Emmie from him to set her on her feet. Helping the little girl into her coat, she zipped it up. "Would you like to come over and help us bake and decorate sugar cookies for the rest of the afternoon?"

Suddenly needing to put space between them, Josh shook his head. "I'll have to take a rain check on that. I need to get back to one of the job sites," he lied. What he needed was time to think.

"We'll save some for you," she said, oblivious to the turmoil beginning to roil through him.

He nodded. "I'll see you tomorrow."

"At the meeting of the funding committee?" she asked.

"Yeah." He kissed Kiley's cheek and the top of Emmie's head, then started toward the exit to the ballroom.

As he walked out of the clubhouse and got into his SUV, he sat there for several long minutes staring blindly at the steering wheel. He knew Kiley had expected him to at least drop by that evening after he finished with his duties at Gordon Construction. But he needed time to think, time to do some calculating and then decide what he was going to do.

Beyond learning how to protect himself and his partner when they made love, he hadn't paid much attention in sex education class. Hell, he couldn't think of a teenage boy who did. They all had more hormones than good sense and were too busy hoping to get lucky with one of the cheerleaders to give things like the gestation of a woman's pregnancy a lot of thought. But it didn't take a Rhodes scholar to figure out that there was more than just a possibility, there was a very real probability, that the cute little girl he called the pony princess was his daughter.

Standing in the hall outside of the meeting room, Kiley dried her sweaty palms on her khaki slacks as she tried to think of what she could say this time to convince the members to approve the increase in the day care center's budget that she hadn't gone over the last time they'd met. Of course, when Josh gave her the money to cover one month of the extra funds she'd asked for, he had promised that if he saw a need for the TCC day care center, he would personally recommend that the committee approve her request. But he hadn't mentioned making a decision and she hadn't asked.

"Ms. Roberts, the committee is ready to see you now." When she looked up, one of the members was holding the door for her to enter the meeting room.

As she walked up to the conference table, Josh was busy entering notes into his electronic tablet and barely raised his head to acknowledge her presence. A sinking feeling began to settle in the pit of her stomach.

"Ms. Roberts, have your needs for the day care center changed since our last meeting with you?" he asked, finally looking at her.

Confused by his all-business tone and cool demeanor, she shook her head. "No, I still need the extra money to supplement what the committee has already appropriated for the center."

Why was he acting so indifferent to the situation? He had stopped by the center enough times to know what the funds would be used for and that if she didn't get them the TCC day care center would have to close by spring.

He gave her a short nod. "I'm going to excuse my-self from the discussion and vote because of our re-lationship, but I'll come down to the day care center after the meeting is over to let you know the outcome."

Effectively dismissed, there was nothing left for her to do but go back to the center and wait for Josh to explain himself. But as she walked back to the center she felt her cheeks heat as her anger rose.

She could understand that he had no choice but to excuse himself from the issue because of a conflict of interest. But surely he could have given his report on what he had observed of the day-to-day running of the center. And why was he acting so aloof? Was it his way of telling her that she had little or no chance for additional funding? If that was the case, the day care center would be closing down shortly after the first of the year.

"Merry Christmas, Kiley," she muttered sarcasti-cally.

As soon as the holidays were over, she would have to start looking for another job. She had no doubt she could find something at another day care center, but she would have to accept whatever position they had open and she could only hope that it paid well enough for her to make ends meet for herself and Emmie.

By the time Josh opened the door and entered the day care center an hour later, Kiley wasn't certain she wanted to hear the official outcome of the vote. At least not until after the holidays were over.

"Let's go into your office," he suggested.

Nodding, she led the way to the former storage room that served as her office. When he closed the door behind them, she shook her head. "You don't have to tell me the outcome of the funding committee's vote," she said, sitting in the hard wooden desk chair. "I knew when I was summarily dismissed what the outcome would be." She took a deep breath in an effort to calm herself. "What I'd like to know is what these past few weeks have been about, since you clearly never intended to recommend additional funding for the day care center."

"The issue was tabled until a later date. But before we get into that, I have a couple of questions for you." His eyes narrowed. "Are you aware that I'm Emmie's father?"

Thrown off guard by his unexpected question, she slowly nodded. "Y-yes."

"Is that why your ex-husband refused to have anything to do with her? Did he know or suspect that she wasn't his child?" he demanded.

"No. As far as Mark is concerned, he still thinks he fathered her." Anticipating his next question, she met his angry gaze head-on. "And before you ask, I didn't realize it was even a possibility until you came by my house that first night with the pizza. That's when I noticed that Emmie looks a lot like you."

He rose to his feet to pace the small area in front of her desk. "Why didn't you tell me as soon as you suspected it was a possibility?"

"I wanted to confirm my suspicions before I talked to you about it," she defended herself.

His eyes narrowed. "And you've done that?"

She stood up to face him. "Yes."

"When?"

"The day I went to lunch with Piper, I saw my ex-husband in the Royal Diner and asked him about his blood type." She shook her head. "I had done enough research on the internet to know immediately that there was no way Mark could be her biological father."

Josh stopped pacing to glare at her. "That was a week ago, Kiley. What were you waiting on? Didn't you think I had the right to know I have a daughter?"

"Oh, no, you don't, buster," she fumed, walking up to stand toe to toe with him. "You're not going to make me feel guilty about not telling you right away that Emmie is your child. Not when I was doing everything I knew how to do to keep from making you think I was trying to use her to influence your recommendation to the funding committee." She poked him in the chest with her finger. "But I shouldn't have bothered because you never intended to give the day care center a fair chance anyway, did you?" She turned away, then whirled back to add, "And just for the record, I intended to tell you as soon as the funding committee made a final decision and settled the day care center's fate once and for all. That way I couldn't be accused of something I wasn't guilty of."

"Let's leave the day care center out of this for the moment," he hissed. "I want to finish talking about my daughter."

"Our daughter," Kiley corrected. "And there's really nothing to discuss. I won't try to stop you from being part of Emmie's life, if that's what you want. But I have two conditions before I'll agree to anything."

His expression was dark and guarded. "What kind of conditions?"

"I don't want your money to help support her. I'm perfectly capable of providing for my child."

"Our child," he reminded. "And let me make one

thing perfectly clear right now. It will be a cold day in hell before you tell me what I will or won't do to see that she's taken care of."

Kiley counted to ten as she tried to keep tears from welling in her eyes. How could she love him so much when she was so darned angry with him? So disillusioned?

"We can cover that another time," she finally managed to get out around the lump clogging her throat. "The most important stipulation I have is that you love her. Emmie deserves that and if you can't be the daddy she needs, I'd rather you not try to have a relationship with her at all."

A muscle worked furiously along his jaw. "I can't believe you think I would do otherwise." Staring hard at her for what seemed like an eternity, he finally turned and opened the door to her office. "We'll talk about this later when we're both thinking more clearly."

Through the office window looking out into the day care center, Kiley watched Josh march across the room and leave before she walked back around her desk on shaky legs. Sinking into her chair, she buried her face in her hands. Even before her sister had admitted that Josh wasn't the snake she'd led their family to believe, Kiley's instincts had told her that he wasn't a bad guy. Had she been wrong about him? Was she destined to be like her sister and see traits in a man that simply weren't there? Why hadn't he been able to see that she had handled the situation the best way she knew how?

A sudden thought had her sitting up straight in the chair. Could Josh have gotten the issue of the day care center tabled as a way of retaliation? Was he getting

even with her for not telling him when she first suspected that he was Emmie's father?

She wasn't sure. But a day care center full of children wasn't the place to have an emotional meltdown.
There would be plenty of time for that when she got
home and let go of the tight grip she held on her emotions.

Feeling as if her heart had been shattered into a mil-
lion pieces, Kiley did her best to pull herself together.
Fate may have set her and Josh on a path three years
ago with the conception of Emmie that would entwine
their lives forever, but that didn't mean she was going
to let it break her. She was a survivor. She had made it
through the inevitable end of her disastrous marriage
and the emotional pain of seeing her child rejected
by the man she'd thought until recently was Emmie's
father. She could certainly weather having her heart
broken by Josh Gordon's deceit and betrayal.

She straightened her shoulders, stood up and with
a smile firmly in place, walked out into the day care.
She might be suffering from a broken heart that she
was certain could never be mended, as well as facing the probability of losing her dream job in a few
months, but until then, she had parents and children
who were counting on her. And she wasn't going to
let them down.

Sitting in his darkened family room, Josh took a
swig from the half-empty beer bottle in his hand as he
stared at the Christmas tree he and his daughter had
put up during the ice storm. His daughter. He tightly
closed his eyes as a wave of emotion surged through
him. Dear God, he had a child.

The mere thought had him running his hand over his face in an attempt to wipe away the tangled feelings that had threatened to swamp him since discovering Emmie was his daughter. He had been crazy about the kid before. But now that he knew she belonged to him—that she was his own flesh and blood—it caused a tightness in his chest that was almost debilitating. He had never felt such love in his entire life and it had been almost instantaneous.

And then there were his feelings for her mother. What he had thought to be nothing more than a strong case of lust had turned out to be far more than he could have ever imagined.

His heart slammed into his rib cage with the force of a physical blow and he had to take several deep breaths as he gave in and acknowledged the emotion that he had avoided putting a name to. He'd fallen hopelessly in love with Kiley and he hadn't even seen it coming.

He'd known that he wanted to spend all of his time with her and that he desired her more than he had any woman in his entire life. But not once had it occurred to him that he was falling in love with her.

As the certainty of the emotion settled in, he knew he wanted to be the man to hold her while she slept at night, wanted to wake up with her each morning and spend the rest of his life spoiling her the way her jerk of an ex-husband never had. He wanted to help her raise Emmie and wanted to give her more babies for them to love and enjoy.

Unfortunately, he was almost positive he had destroyed any possibility of her ever allowing him to do that when he'd refused to talk to her about it further.

And he really couldn't say he blamed her. They had things they needed to work out and spending the past few days holed up in his house brooding about it all wasn't accomplishing anything.

"You blew it, Gordon," he muttered miserably as he opened his eyes to stare at the bottle in his hand.

Drinking the last of the beer, he set the empty bottle down on the end table next to the other three he had polished off earlier. He had overreacted to the entire situation when he'd confronted her at the day care center and driven the only woman he had ever loved—would ever love—from his life. Most likely for good.

Josh sighed heavily. Now that he'd had a few days to cool down and started looking at things rationally, he could understand Kiley's wanting to be positive about who had fathered Emmie before she approached him about it. It just made good sense to handle it that way.

He could even appreciate her reasoning for not wanting to tell him until after the funding committee decided on the additional funds for the day care center, too. She hadn't wanted there to be any question about her motives. He respected and admired that kind of integrity.

And although her fears were unfounded, he even got why she was afraid he wouldn't step up to the plate and be the father Emmie needed. She was trying to protect her child—their child—and there was no way in hell he would ever fault her for that. He would be disappointed in her if she didn't.

As he sat there staring at the twinkling lights on the tree, he thought back over the past few weeks. Spending time with her and Emmie had given him a glimpse of what his life with them could be like, and he wanted that more than he wanted his next breath.

He smiled through the mist of emotion gathering in his eyes. He'd enjoyed the nights they spent together eating in front of the television while they watched a movie, even if it had been the same cartoon both times. Then, after the pony princess was tucked into bed for the night, he loved sitting on the couch with Kiley, holding her close, talking to her and kissing her until they both gasped for breath.

He had even loved taking on the responsibility of being their protector. Initially, Kiley hadn't appreciated his insistence that he drive her and Emmie to his place to ride out the ice storm. But just the thought of her having an accident on the icy roads or either one of them being cold and uncomfortable in a house without heat and electricity had been more than he could bear.

Sighing heavily, he uttered a curse word that he only used around the guys or when he did something stupid like smash his thumb with a hammer. He loved them both unconditionally and that was something that would never change. But he was afraid he had come to that realization too late.

Unable to sit still, he stood up, gathered the beer bottles and went outside to the shed to toss them in the recycle bin. Standing in his backyard, he stared up at the star-studded night sky. He wanted it all—Kiley, Emmie and to be the best husband and father he could possibly be. But what could he do to get them back to where they had been, to make things right between him and Kiley?

He wasn't sure there was anything he could do to repair the damage he had caused to their relationship.

But the one thing he did know for certain was that he had to try. If he didn't, he knew as surely as the sun rose in the east each morning, he would regret it every second of every day for the rest of his life.

Ten

Two days before Christmas, Kiley sat in her living room watching Emmie play with the pony castle her grandparents had given her the night Kiley and Josh went to the Christmas Ball. She had spent a miserable few days wondering how she could have handled the situation with Josh any differently. After going over everything time and again, she had come to the conclusion that she couldn't.

Telling him about her suspicions before she had concrete evidence would have definitely made it appear as if she had some sort of agenda to use Emmie to keep the day care center open, as well as made her look utterly foolish if it had turned out he wasn't. Or he might have even thought she was somehow trying to extort money from him to support a child who wasn't his.

Sighing, she rose from the chair and walked into the kitchen to put her coffee cup in the dishwasher. To a point, she could understand Josh's angry reaction. Learning that he had a two-year-old child had to have been a huge shock. But that was no reason not to give her explanation serious consideration.

And then there was his promise to give the day care center a fair evaluation. Why hadn't he reported his observations and then excused himself from the vote for the additional funds for the facility? He knew that was the only chance the day care center had to survive. The only reasons she could think of to explain his actions were either he hadn't been impressed with the services she was providing to the children of the TCC members or he was retaliating against her for not telling him about Emmie. And that hurt almost as much as his unwillingness to listen to her.

Lost in thought, she jumped when the phone rang. It was probably her parents, asking her what time she thought she and Emmie would be arriving Christmas day to exchange gifts. But when she checked, the Texas Cattleman's Club number was displayed on the caller ID.

"Kiley, I'm sorry to bother you, but we need you here at the clubhouse," Gil Addison said when she answered.

"Is something wrong?" she asked. Now that Beau Hacket's son had been dealt with over the vandalism and was scheduled to attend a military school in central Texas immediately after the first of the year, she hoped nothing else had happened to the day care center.

"No," he assured her. "We just need to talk to you about your future employment here at the club."

Great, on top of everything else, they were going to fire her two days before Christmas. "I'll be there—" she glanced at the clock "—in about an hour."

"That will be great," he said, sounding cheerful. "We'll see you then."

When he hung up, she stared at the phone. She had thought Gil was quite happy with the job she was doing. Now it appeared he was happy to be rid of her.

Getting herself and Emmie ready to face the inevitable, she wondered why the TCC had decided to terminate her contract early, instead of waiting until it closed the day care center in the spring. "Your daddy probably had something to do with that," she said without thinking.

"Daddy?" Emmie asked, clearly confused. She looked around the room as if searching for something.

"No, sweetie," Kiley said, mentally chiding herself as they left the house and she strapped Emmie into her car seat. Two-year-olds tended to parrot everything they heard and since he hadn't come around them in the past few days, she had no idea if Josh intended to be a real father to Emmie or not. "Mommy made a mistake."

Twenty minutes later when she drove into the clubhouse parking lot, she recognized several cars and couldn't help but wonder why Piper and Ryan were at the club. She thought they were busy making final wedding arrangements. In fact, she thought everyone would be busy with last-minute shopping or traveling to spend the holidays with family.

"We might as well get this over with, Emmie," she said, lifting her daughter from the car seat to walk up to the front door.

The door opened before she could reach for the handle. "I'm glad you were able to make it on short notice," Piper said, grinning.

Kiley frowned. "What are you doing here?"

"They've called an emergency meeting of the funding committee," Piper said, hurrying her down the hall to the ballroom. "I'm here to give you moral support."

Before they entered the room, Kiley set Emmie on her feet to remove their coats. "Ryan isn't on the committee," she commented as she straightened. "What's really going on, Piper?"

"Ryan's here to support you, too." Her friend smiled mysteriously. "So are the majority of the parents who have kids in the day care center."

"Piper, I appreciate their support, but I doubt it will make a difference," she said tiredly. She hadn't slept well since arguing with Josh and didn't anticipate her insomnia getting better any time soon.

"Come on." Piper urged her toward the closed ballroom doors. "This won't take long. I promise."

Taking Emmie by the hand, Kiley opened the door to the big room, walked inside and looked around. Tables had been set up on the stage the day care had used and the funding committee members were seated behind them, looking at her expectantly.

Most of the parents and their children from the day care center sat in rows of chairs in front of the stage, and she was grateful for their support even though it probably wouldn't influence the committee's vote.

"Ms. Roberts, would you please approach the committee?" Josh asked, drawing her attention to him.

She had purposely avoided looking at him when she entered the room. But as she turned her attention his way, her breath caught. Instead of a suit and tie like the other male members on the panel were wearing, he was dressed in boots, jeans and a chambray shirt. She didn't think he had ever looked as handsome as he did at that moment. But why was he dressed so casually?

Walking up to the front of the room, she was surprised when Josh grinned and stood up. "It would be a conflict of interest for me to preside over this meeting, as well as vote on the future of the day care center. For that reason, I'm excusing myself," he said, handing the gavel to Beau Hacket. "I do, however, retain my right to report my observations on the center's operation and give my recommendation of action on the issue." He walked to the end of the stage, descended the steps and came to stand beside her.

"What's going on?" she demanded under her breath.

"Just wait," he whispered close to her ear.

"Can we at least sit down?" she asked. Why did they have to humiliate her by firing her in front of everyone?

"No. Just listen," he said, smiling at her. Her heart skipped a beat at the warmth she detected in his brilliant blue eyes.

"Up," Emmie said, patting Josh's leg.

Without a moment's hesitation, he picked up their daughter and held her close. "How's my little princess?" he asked, causing Kiley's chest to swell with emotion. Even if he couldn't care for her, there was no doubt how he felt about their daughter. It was easy to see Josh loved their daughter with all his heart.

"It's been brought to our attention that the funding committee needs to review our calculations for the day care center's budget," Beau stated, drawing everyone's attention back to the panel of men. "We've also been asked by Gil Addison to review Ms. Roberts's contract for the position of day care center operator."

Here it comes, Kiley thought. This was where they were going to terminate her contract. But why did they have to ruin Christmas for her and Emmie? Why couldn't they have waited until after the first of the year?

"I make a motion to start the discussion," Paul Windsor said when Beau gave him a nod.

When one of the other members seconded the motion, Beau looked directly at Josh. "I think you have something to report?"

Josh nodded and, with Emmie perched on his forearm, stepped forward. "After Ms. Roberts addressed the committee at the first of the month requesting additional funds for the day care center, I made periodic visits to see how she was running the operation and to determine if the money was actually needed."

"And what were your findings?" Beau asked, surprising Kiley with his even tone and pleasant expression. Apparently, his way of "making things right" for what his son had done was to at least appear interested and congenial.

"I've observed Ms. Roberts in several different situations at the day care center and I can honestly say I was extremely impressed by her dedication and how well she was able to relate to the kids," he said, making eye contact with every one of the panel members. "She gives each child individual attention and makes them all feel like everything they show or tell her is of the utmost importance. I've also observed her methods of discipline and I was amazed by the kindness and respect she showed." He chuckled. "The little boy in question happily accepted his 'time out' without protest or her having to raise her voice above normal." He turned to look at her and the expression on his handsome face was breathtaking. "And I doubt anyone could have done a better job of putting on an entertaining and enjoyable children's Christmas program."

The crowd of parents broke their silence with applause and several even called out words of encouragement and support.

When the parents quieted down, he continued, "In conclusion, I would like to add that the TCC has a top-notch day care center." His gaze never wavered from hers. "And we have the dedication and expertise of Kiley Roberts to thank for it. I recommend that you vote to keep the day care center open and appropriate the funds needed to keep it running."

"I would like to add that I think the TCC should renegotiate her contract to include a raise and a five-year extension," Gil Addison said, walking up to stand beside Josh.

The group of parents once again erupted in a round of applause and loud cheers.

Tears filled her eyes and Kiley couldn't have found her voice to save her soul. Josh's heartfelt endorsement was more than she could have possibly hoped for and proved that no matter what their differences were, he wasn't going to hold them against the club's day care center.

"Thank you," she mouthed, looking at the only man she would ever love. She just wished their problems could be resolved as easily as the fate of the day care center. Unfortunately, she wasn't sure that was going to be the case.

Beau banged the gavel to bring order back to the meeting. "Are there any other comments?"

"My son, Cade, has learned more at the TCC day care center in the past couple of months than he ever did at the child care facility he used to attend," Gil stated.

"All of the children love Miss Kiley," Winnie Bartlett added. "My daughters are disappointed on the weekends when they can't go to school."

"I move to adopt Josh Gordon's recommendations," the only female on the panel said, grinning.

"I second the motion," one of the men chimed in.

"Then I guess all there is left to do would be to bring it to a vote," Beau said, smiling. "All those in favor of the recommendations set forth by Josh Gordon and Gil Addison, please raise your hands."

When every member of the funding committee, including Beau and his cohort Paul Windsor, raised their hands high in the air, Beau nodded. "It's unanimous. The motion carries," he said, bringing down the gavel to seal the fate of the day care center.

Kiley couldn't believe what had just taken place. She had been summoned to the TCC clubhouse, expecting to be fired. Now she had job security for the next five years, as well as a raise.

Amid the thunderous cheers and standing ovation, Beau Hacket pounded the gavel on the table several times. "Order, please." He looked at Josh. "I think there's something else Josh wants to say."

She frowned. What on earth could he possibly have to add?

Still holding Emmie, Josh took Kiley by the hand and led her up onto the stage. Kiley's heart pounded so hard, she wasn't sure it wouldn't create a hole in her chest. What was he up to now?

"The reason I felt it would be a conflict of interest for me to preside over the meeting today was because, as many of you know, I've been seeing Kiley for the past few weeks," he stated, glancing down at her. His smile and the light she detected in his eyes caused her to feel warm all over. "I didn't feel I could vote without bias on an issue that involves the woman I love."

As the crowd clapped their approval, Kiley looked at Piper, standing with her fiancé, Ryan Grant. Smiling, tears filled her friend's eyes. "It's going to work out, Kiley," she mouthed. "I'm so happy for you."

Feeling as if she were in a bizarre dream, Kiley looked up at Josh. They still had problems. But for the first time in days, she felt there might be a glimmer of hope that things could work out between them, at least where Emmie was concerned.

"There's one more thing before we adjourn," Josh said, quieting the well-wishers. "I'd like to thank you all for coming to the club on such short notice to support Kiley and the day care center."

He grinned and whispered close to her ear, "Now let's get out of here. I have something at the ranch I want to show Emmie and we have some things we need to talk over."

They were silent as they made their way through the crowd to the clubhouse parking lot, and by the time they reached his SUV, Kiley felt as if she had regained some of her equilibrium. Josh had taken her by surprise when he made the recommendations for the day care center and his public announcement that he loved her had caused her head to spin. But now that she was able to think more clearly, her cautious nature took over. Just because he said he loved her didn't mean things would automatically work out for them.

Parking the truck by the corral gate, Josh looked over at the woman in the passenger seat beside him. Kiley was the only woman he had ever loved—would ever love. And he had to make things right between them.

"Thank you for allowing me to bring the two of you out here to the ranch," he said, reaching over to take her hand in his. "I wanted to give Emmie her Christmas present."

Kiley nodded, looking cautious. "I'm sure she'll love whatever you have for her."

He had hurt her emotionally and she was being careful. He could understand that and he didn't blame her one bit. He had been a complete jackass and he wasn't fool enough to think that telling her he loved her in front of a crowd was going to make everything okay. It was going to take some serious groveling on his part to make it up to her. He was prepared to do that and whatever else it took to get her to give him another chance.

"Wanna see ponies," Emmie chimed in from the backseat. Apparently she had recognized the barn when he stopped the truck.

"I think that can be arranged, princess," he said, smiling in the rearview mirror at the most precious little girl in the entire world. She and her mother were his whole world, and if Kiley would give him the chance, he would spend every minute of every day proving it to them.

Getting out of the Navigator, he came around the front to open Kiley's door and help her down from the seat. Then, getting Emmie from her car seat, he set her on her feet. "Are you ready to see the ponies?"

Emmie clapped her hands. "Pet a pony."

"You can do more than pet a pony," Josh said, smiling. "You can ride one."

Her little face lit up with glee as she nodded. "Wanna wide."

"We're not dressed for horseback riding," Kiley said, frowning. "Was that the reason you were dressed so casually for the meeting? You intended to go for a ride afterward?"

He shrugged. "I'm not going riding, but since a suit and tie aren't appropriate attire for a barnyard, I figured jeans were my best bet."

"I don't understand," Kiley said, looking confused.

"Emmie's Christmas present is in the barn," he said, grinning.

Kiley shook her head. "You didn't."

He nodded. "I sure did. My daughter likes ponies, she gets a pony."

"You're going to spoil her, Josh Gordon."

"That's my intention." He wanted to tell Kiley he intended to spoil her, too, but that would have to wait until a little later.

When Bobby Ray led the fat Shetland pony from the barn, already saddled and ready to ride, the look on Emmie's face was one Josh knew he would never forget. "Pony! Pony!" his daughter chanted excitedly.

"This is Rosy," he said, lifting Emmie to set her on the saddle. "She's your pony."

"Me pony?" The child's delight was priceless and he wouldn't have traded seeing it for the entire world.

Strapping a blue toddler-size riding helmet on her head, Josh walked beside the pony as he led her around the corral several times until he noticed Martha waiting at the corral fence. He had made arrangements in advance for his housekeeper to watch Emmie while he tried to straighten out things with Kiley.

Lifting his daughter down, he handed the lead rope back to Bobby Ray. "You can ride again a little later, princess. Do you think you could go with Martha now and have some lunch while I talk to your mommy?"

Grinning, Emmie waved as she and Martha walked toward the house. "Bye-bye."

"She's amazing, Kiley," he said, staring after their little girl. "You've done a wonderful job with her."

"She's my world," Kiley said, smiling for the first time since they left the TCC clubhouse.

"Do you have room in that world of yours for me?" he asked, gently touching her smooth cheek.

"Josh, please…" she said, starting to turn away from him. "I don't want to hear it if you don't mean it."

Reaching out, he pulled her into his arms. She tried to push away from him, but he locked his arms around her. He was determined to settle things between them. It was the only possible chance they had of building a future together.

"Kiley, don't just quit on us." Placing his finger beneath her chin, he tilted her head until their gazes met. "I know I hurt you, but hear me out before you make the decision to walk away from what we have together."

She stared at him for several long seconds before she spoke. "Besides Emmie, just what do you think we have, Josh?"

"Love," he answered. "I love you and you love me. And it's something I have every intention of fighting for. I meant it when I announced it at the meeting. I love you, Kiley."

"You didn't feel that way the other day." She shook her head. "You walked out in the middle of quite possibly the most important conversation we'll ever have— the one about our daughter."

The emotional pain and disappointment he saw in the depths of her pretty brown eyes made him feel as if he'd been punched in the gut. But it was no less than he deserved.

"I know I acted like a complete bastard, and I regret that more than you'll ever know," he said honestly. "I left because I needed time to come to grips with everything. I know it's no excuse for my behavior or the accusations I hurled at you, but it's the truth. I was never more shocked in my entire life than I was when I figured out Emmie is mine. But what angered me the most was that you knew and didn't tell me as soon as you suspected I could be her father."

"I didn't want to be an alarmist in case I was wrong," she said defensively. "Nor did I want you to think I was using Emmie to try to keep the day care open."

He nodded. "I understand that now that I've had time to think straight. And I admire you for handling

it the way you did. But at the time, all I could think
was that you'd deceived me."

"And I felt you had betrayed me when you put off
the day care issue at the funding meeting," she shot
back. "You had assured me you were going to give the
day care center a fair evaluation. But that afternoon
you acted like it was an inconvenience for me to even
request the additional funds."

"To tell you the truth, the day care center was the
last thing on my mind at that point," he said, meaning it. "I asked that the issue of additional funding be
tabled because I figured with my state of mind, it was
the only fair thing I could do."

"Why did you call an emergency meeting of the
funding committee today to decide the day care's
fate?" she asked, frowning. "Couldn't it have waited
until after the first of the year?"

"I wanted to make sure that issue was dealt with
and out of the way so I could concentrate on fixing the
mess I had made with you." He brushed her lips with
his. When she didn't protest, he took that as a positive sign and went on. "I love you, Kiley. And I take
full responsibility for our argument." He kissed her
forehead. "If you'll let me, I want to spend the rest of
my life making it up to you for acting the way I did."

As she stared up at him, tears filled her eyes, and
knowing he had caused her to cry made him feel as
if someone tried to rip out his heart. "Josh, you don't
have to say that." She shook her head. "I'm not going
to try to stop you from being with Emmie."

"Honey, I know that." Giving her a kiss that had her
clinging to him for support and him feeling as if his
jeans had become too small in the stride, he smiled.

"What I'm trying to tell you is that I don't just want Emmie. I want you, too. I love you more than life itself. I want to marry you and raise a whole house full of kids just like our beautiful little girl."

"Josh, I don't know—"

"Do you love me, Kiley?"

Tears streamed down her cheeks as she nodded.

"Will you marry me?"

"I—I'm not sure—"

Kissing her again, he felt like he'd run a marathon by the time he raised his head. "Are you sure now?"

"I—I… You're not making it easy to think," she said, looking delightfully confused.

"Just say yes, Kiley," he commanded.

As she continued to look at him, he could tell the moment she gave in to what he knew they both wanted. "Y-yes."

"Thank God!" Releasing her, he reached into the front pocket of his jeans and pulled out the red velvet box he had carried with him since stopping by the jewelry store on the way to the TCC clubhouse earlier that morning. "Kiley, will you marry me?"

Laughing, she covered her mouth with both hands. "You already asked me that and I said yes."

"Say it again." He laughed as he opened the box, removed the one-carat solitaire diamond ring inside and slipped it on her finger. "And keep saying it until we celebrate our seventy-fifth wedding anniversary."

"Yes, I'll marry you, Josh Gordon," she said, throwing her arms around his neck.

"Good." He gave her a quick kiss, then, taking her by the hand, led her toward the house.

"Are we going to tell Emmie?" she asked.

"No. We can tell her later, after we've talked to your folks. I know they're going to have a lot of tough questions about my being Emmie's father and how that all came about." He kissed the top of her head. "But we'll do that together."

"Will you go with me to their place on Christmas Day?" she asked.

He nodded. "We can go to Midland to see your parents and on the way back home, we can stop by and tell my brother that we're going to be a family. But right now, I have something else in mind." He chuckled as he closed the corral gate behind them. "And standing in the middle of a barnyard isn't exactly the place I want to do it."

"You're incorrigible, Josh Gordon," she said, laughing with him.

"No, honey. I'm a man in love with the most desirable woman on the planet," he said, pulling her back into his arms for another kiss.

"I love you, Josh," she said softly.

"And I love you, Kiley." Grinning, he took her hand in his. "Now let's go inside the house and get started planning our life together."

* * * * *

"You are obnoxious and uptight at times. Other times…"

She circled a hand in the air, trying to pluck out one or two of his less irritating traits. "Other times you surprise me, Mr Ambassador. Like tonight, for instance, when you got behind the bar. You went above and beyond the call of duty there."

"I'm a man of many talents," he said smugly. "And that reminds me. I was promised payment for services rendered."

"So you were. Have you given any thought to what form that payment should take?"

"Oh, sweetheart, I haven't thought of anything else all evening."

Red flags went up instantly. Gina knew she was playing with fire. Knew the last thing she should do was slide her feet off his lap and curl them under her, rising to her knees in the process.

All she had to do was look at him…

* * *

The Diplomat's Pregnant Bride
is part of the Duchess Diaries duet:

Two royal granddaughters on their way to
happily ever after!

THE DIPLOMAT'S
PREGNANT BRIDE

BY
MERLINE LOVELACE

MILLS
BOON

Published in Great Britain 2013
by Mills & Boon, an imprint of Harlequin (UK) Limited,
Eton House, 18-24 Paradise Road, Richmond, Surrey TW9 1SR

© Merline Lovelace 2013

ISBN: 978 0 263 90493 2

51-1213

Harlequin (UK) policy is to use papers that are natural, renewable and recyclable products and made from wood grown in sustainable forests. The logging and manufacturing processes conform to the legal environmental regulations of the country of origin.

Printed and bound in Spain
by Blackprint CPI, Barcelona

To my gorgeous niece Cori and Jane and the
rest of the crew at Clayton on the Park, in Scottsdale.
Thanks for the inside look at the ups and downs
of an event coordinator's life!

Prologue

I could not have asked for two more beautiful or loving granddaughters. From the first day they came to live with me—one so young and frightened, the other still in diapers—they filled the empty spaces in my heart with light and joy. Now Sarah, my quiet, elegant Sarah, is about to marry her handsome Dev. The wedding takes place in a few hours, and I ache with happiness for her.

And with such worry for her sister. My darling Eugenia has waltzed through life, brightening even the sourest dispositions with her sparkling smile and carefree, careless joie de vivre. Now, quite suddenly that carelessness has caught up with her. She's come face-to-face with reality, and I can only pray the strength and spirit I know she possesses will help her through the difficult days ahead.

Enough of this. I must dress for the wedding. Then it's off to the Plaza, which has been the scene of so many significant events in my life. But none to match the delight of this one!

From the diary of Charlotte,
Grand Duchess of Karlenburgh

One

Gina St. Sebastian forced a smile to hide her gritted teeth. "Good Lord, you're stubborn, Jack."

"*I'm* stubborn?"

The irate male standing before her snapped his sun-bleached brows together. Ambassador John Harris Mason III was tanned, tawny-haired and a trim, athletic six-one. He was also used to being in charge. The fact that he couldn't control Gina or the situation they now found themselves in irritated him no end.

"You're pregnant with my child, dammit. Yet you refuse to even discuss marriage."

"Oh, for…! Trumpet the news to the whole world, why don't you?"

Scowling, Gina craned her neck to peer around the bank of gardenias shielding her and Jack from the other guests in the Terrace Room of New York City's venerable Plaza Hotel. With its exquisitely restored Italian Renaissance ceiling and crystal chandeliers modeled after those in the Palace of Versailles, it made a fabulous venue for a wedding.

A wedding put together on extremely short notice! They'd had less than two weeks to pull it off. The groom's billions had eased the time crunch considerably, as had the miracle worker Dev Hunter employed as his executive assistant. Gina had done all the planning, though, and she would not allow the man she'd spent one wild weekend with to disrupt her sister's wedding day.

Luckily no one seemed to have heard his caustic comment. The band was currently pulsing out the last bars of a lively merengue. Sarah and Dev were on the dance floor, along with the St. Sebastians' longtime housekeeper, Maria, and most of the guests invited to the elegant affair.

Gina's glance shot from the dancers to the lace-clad woman sitting ramrod-straight in her chair, hands crossed on the ebony head of her cane. The duchess was out of earshot, too, thank God! Hearing her younger granddaughter's pregnancy broadcast to the world at large wouldn't have fit with her notions of proper behavior.

Relieved, Gina swung back to Jack. "I won't have you spoil my sister's wedding with another argument. Please lower your voice."

He took the hint and cranked down the decibels, if not his temper. "We haven't had ten minutes alone to talk about this since you got back from Switzerland."

As if she needed the reminder! She'd flown to Switzerland exactly one day after she'd peed on a purple stick and felt her world come crashing down around her. She'd had to get away from L.A., had to breathe in the sharp, clean air of the snow-capped Alps surrounding Lake Lucerne while trying to decide what to do. After a day and a night of painful soul-searching, she'd walked into one of Lucerne's ultramodern clinics. Ten minutes later, she'd turned around and walked out again. But not before making two near-hysterical calls. The first was to Sarah—her sister, her protector, her dearest friend. The second, unfortunately, was to the handsome, charismatic and thoroughly annoying diplomat now confronting her.

By the time Sarah had made the frantic dash from Paris in response to her sister's call, Gina's jagged nerves had smoothed a little. Her hard-won poise shattered once again, however, when Jack Mason showed up on the scene. She hadn't expected him to jump a plane, much less express such fierce satisfaction over her decision to have their child.

Actually, the decision had surprised Gina as much as it had Jack. She was the flighty, irresponsible sister. The good-time girl, always up for a weekend skiing in Biarritz or a sail through the blue-green waters of the Caribbean. Raised by their grandmother, she and Sarah had been given the education and sophisticated lifestyle the duchess insisted was their birthright. Only recently had the sisters learned how deeply Grandmama had gone into debt to provide that lifestyle. Since then, Gina had made a determined effort to support herself. A good number of efforts, actually. Sadly, none of the careers she'd dabbled in had held her mercurial interest for very long.

Modeling had turned out to be a drag. All those hot lights and temperamental photographers snapping orders like constipated drill sergeants. Escorting small, select tour groups to the dazzling capitals of Europe was even more of a bore. How in the world could she have imagined she'd want to make a career of chasing down lost luggage or shuffling room assignments to placate a whiny guest who didn't like the view in hers?

Gina had even tried to translate her brief sojourn at Italy's famed cooking school, the Academia Barilla, into a career as a catering chef. That misguided attempt had barely lasted a week. But when her exasperated boss booted her out of the kitchen and into the front office, she'd discovered her apparently one real talent. She was far better at planning parties than cooking for them. Especially when clients walked in waving a checkbook and orders to pull out all the stops for their big event.

She was so good, in fact, that she intended to support herself and her child by coordinating soirees for the rich and famous. But first she had to convince her baby's father that she neither needed nor wanted the loveless marriage he was offering.

"I appreciate your concern, Jack, but…"

"Concern?"

The handsome, charismatic ambassador kept his voice down as she'd requested, but looked as though he wanted let loose with both barrels. His shoulders were taut under his hand-tailored tux. Below his neatly trimmed caramel-colored hair, his brown eyes drilled into her.

Gina couldn't help but remember how those eyes had snared hers across a crowded conference room six weeks ago and signaled instant, electric attraction. How his oh-so-skilled mouth had plundered her throat and her breasts and her belly. How…

Oh, for pity's sake! Why remember the heat that had sizzled so hot and fast between them? That spontaneous combustion wouldn't happen again. Not now. Not with everything else that was going on in their lives.

"But," she continued with a forced smile, "you have to agree a wedding reception is hardly the time or place for a discussion like this."

"Name the time," he challenged. "And the place."

"All right! Tomorrow. Twelve noon." Cornered, she named the first place she could think of. "The Boathouse in Central Park."

"I'll be there."

"Fine. We'll get a table in a quiet corner and discuss this like the mature adults we are."

"Like the mature adult at least one of us is."

Gina hid a wince. The biting sarcasm stung, but she had to admit it wasn't far off the mark. The truth was she'd pretty much flitted through life, laughing at its absurdities, always counting on Sarah or Grandmama to bail her out of trouble every time she tumbled into it. All that changed about ten minutes after she peed on that damned stick. Her flitting days were over. It was time to take responsibility for herself and her baby.

Which she would.

She would!

"I'll see you tomorrow."

Chin high, she swept around the bank of gardenias.

Jack let her go. She was right. This wasn't the time or the place to hammer some sense into her. Not that he held much hope his calm, rational arguments would penetrate that thick mane of silvery blond curls or spark a glimmer of understanding in those baby-doll blue eyes.

He'd now spent a total of five days—one long, wild weekend and two frustrating days in Switzerland—in Gina St. Sebastian's company. More than enough time to confirm the woman constituted a walking, talking bundle of contradictions. She was jaw-droppingly gorgeous and so sensual she made grown men go weak at the knees, but also friendly and playful as a kitten. Well-educated, yet in many ways naive beyond belief. And almost completely oblivious to the world around her unless it directly impacted her, her sister or her dragon lady of a grandmother.

Pretty much his exact opposite, Jack thought grimly as he tracked her progress across the crowded room. He came from a long line of coolheaded, clear-thinking Virginians who believed their vast wealth brought with it equally great responsibility. Jack's father and grandfather had served as advisors to presidents in times of national crisis. He himself had served in several diplomatic posts before being appointed the State Department's ambassador-at-large for counterterrorism at the ripe old age of thirty-two. As such, he'd traveled to some of the most volatile, violent trouble spots in the world. Recently he'd returned to State Department headquarters in Washington, D.C., to translate his hard-won field knowledge into policies and procedures that would improve the security of U.S. diplomatic personnel around the world.

His job demanded long days and long nights. Stress rode on his shoulders like hundred-pound weights. Yet he couldn't remember any issue, any recalcitrant bureaucrat or political pundit, who frustrated him as much as Gina St. Sebastian. She was pregnant with his child, dammit! The child he was determined would carry his name.

The child he and Catherine had tried so hard to have.

The familiar pain knifed into him. The feeling wasn't as vicious as it had once been, but was still ferocious enough to carve up his insides. The lively conversation around him faded. The flower-bedecked room blurred. He could almost see her, almost hear her Boston Brahman accent. Catherine—brilliant, politically savvy Catherine—would have grasped the irony in his present situation at once. She would have...

"You look like you could use a drink, Mason."

With an immense effort of will, Jack blanked the memory of his dead wife and turned to the new groom. Dev Hunter held a crystal tumbler in one hand and offered one to Jack with the other.

"Scotch, straight up," he said dryly. "I saw you talking to Gina and figured you could use it."

"You figured right."

Jack took the tumbler and tipped it toward the man who might soon become his brother-in-law. Not might, he amended grimly as they clinked glasses, would.

"To the St. Sebastian sisters," Hunter said, his gaze shifting to the two women standing with their heads together across the room. "It took some convincing, but I got mine to the altar. Good luck getting yours there."

The Scotch went down with a well-mannered bite. Jack savored its smoky tang and eyed the sisters. They were a study in contrasts. Dark-haired Sarah was impossibly elegant in a clinging ivory gown with feathered clasps at each shoulder and glowed with the incandescent beauty of a bride. Blonde, bubbly Gina was barely six weeks pregnant and showed no signs of a baby bump. She was still slender but more generously endowed than her sister. Her flame-colored, body-hugging, strapless and backless sheath outlined her seductive curves to perfection.

Jack's fingers tightened on the tumbler. Six weeks after the fact and he could still remember how he'd positioned those seductive hips under his. How he'd buried his hands in her silky hair and lost himself in that lush body and those laughing blue eyes.

They'd used protection that weekend. Went through a whole damned box of it, as he recalled. So much for playing the odds.

"I'll get her to the altar," he vowed. "One way or another."

Hunter raised a brow but refrained from comment as his bride smiled and crooked a finger. "I'm being summoned. I'll talk to you again when Sarah and I get back from our honeymoon."

He handed his empty tumbler to a passing waiter and started for his wife, then turned back. "Just for the record, Mason, my money's on Gina. She's got more of the duchess in her than she realizes. And speaking of the duchess…"

Jack followed his glance and saw the silver-haired St. Sebastian matriarch thumping her way toward them. A long-sleeve, high-necked dress of ecru lace draped her slight frame. A trio of rings decorated her arthritic fingers. Leaning heavily on her cane with her left hand, Charlotte dismissed her new grandson-in-law with an imperious wave of the right.

"Gina says it's time for you and Sarah to change out of your wedding finery. You only have an hour to get to the airport."

"It's my plane, Charlotte. I don't think it'll leave without us."

"I should hope not." Her ringed fingers flapped again. "Do go away, Devon. I want to talk to Ambassador Mason."

Jack didn't consciously go into a brace but he could feel

his shoulders squaring as he faced Gina's diminutive, indomitable grandmother.

He knew all about her. He should. He'd dug up the file the State Department had compiled on Charlotte St. Sebastian, once Grand Duchess of the tiny principality of Karlenburgh, when she fled her Communist-overrun country more than five decades ago. After being forced to witness her husband's brutal execution, she'd escaped with the clothes on her back, her infant daughter in her arms and a fortune in jewels hidden inside the baby's teddy bear.

She'd eventually settled in New York City and become an icon of the social and literary scenes. Few of the duchess's wealthy, erudite friends were aware this stiff-spined aristocrat had pawned her jewels over the years to support herself and the two young granddaughters who'd come to live with her after the tragic death of their parents. Jack knew only because Dev Hunter had hinted that he should tread carefully where Charlotte and her granddaughters' financial situation were concerned.

Very carefully. Jack's one previous encounter with the duchess made it clear her reduced circumstances had not diminished either her haughty air or the fierce protectiveness she exhibited toward her granddaughters. That protectiveness blazed in her face now.

"I just spoke with Gina. She says you're still trying to convince her to marry you."

"Yes, I am."

"Why?"

Jack was tempted to fall back on Gina's excuse and suggest that a wedding reception was hardly the proper place for this discussion. The steely look in the duchess's faded blue eyes killed that craven impulse.

"I think the reason would be obvious, ma'am. Your granddaughter's carrying my child. I want to give her and the baby the protection of my name."

The reply came coated with ice. "The St. Sebastian name

provides more than enough cachet for my granddaughter and her child."

Well, hell! And he called himself a diplomat! Jack was delivering a mental swift kick when the duchess raised her cane and jabbed the tip into his starched shirt front.

"Tell me one thing, Mr. Ambassador. Do you honestly believe the baby is yours?"

He didn't hesitate. "Yes, ma'am, I do."

The cane took another sharp jab at his sternum.

"Why?"

For two reasons, one of which Jack wasn't about to share. He was still pissed that his father had reacted to the news that he would be a grandfather by hiring a private investigator. With ruthless efficiency the P.I. had dug into every nook and cranny of Gina St. Sebastian's life for the past three months. The report he submitted painted a portrait of a woman who bounced from job to job and man to man with seeming insouciance. Yet despite his best efforts, the detective hadn't been able to turn up a single lover in Gina's recent past except John Harris Mason III.

Furious, Jack had informed his father that he didn't need any damned report. He'd known the baby was his from the moment Gina called from Switzerland, sobbing and nearly incoherent. He now tried to convey that same conviction to the ferocious woman about to skewer him with her cane.

"As I've discovered in our brief time together, Duchess, your granddaughter has her share of faults. So do I. Neither of us have tried to deceive the other about those faults, however."

"What you mean," she countered with withering scorn, "is that neither of you made any protestations of eternal love or devotion before you jumped into bed together."

Jack refused to look away, but damned if he didn't feel heat crawling up the back of his neck. Wisely, he sidestepped the jumping-into-bed issue. "I'll admit I have a lot to learn yet about your granddaughter but my sense is she doesn't lie. At least not about something this important," he added with more frankness than tact.

To his relief, the duchess lowered the cane and leaned on it with both hands. "You're correct in that assessment. Gina doesn't lie."

She hesitated, and a look that combined both pride and exasperation crossed her aristocratic features. "If anything, the girl is too honest. She tends to let her feelings just pour out, along with whatever she happens to be thinking at the time."

"So I noticed," Jack said, straight-faced.

Actually, Gina's exuberance and utter lack of pretense had delighted him almost as much as her luscious body during their weekend together. Looking back, Jack could admit he'd shucked a half-dozen layers of his sober, responsible self during that brief interlude. They hadn't stayed shucked, of course. Once he'd returned to Washington, he'd been engulfed in one crisis after another. Right up until that call from Switzerland.

The duchess reclaimed his attention with a regal toss of her head. "I will say this once, young man, and I suggest you take heed. My granddaughter's happiness is my first—my *only*—concern. Whatever Eugenia decides regarding you and the baby, she has my complete support."

"I wouldn't expect anything less, ma'am."

"Hrrrmph." She studied him with pursed lips for a moment before delivering an abrupt non sequitur. "I knew your grandfather."

"You did?"

"He was a member of President Kennedy's cabinet at the time. Rather stiff and pompous, as I recall."

Jack had to grin. "That sounds like him."

"I invited him and your grandmother to a reception I hosted for the Sultan of Oman right here, in these very rooms. The Kennedys attended. So did the Rockefellers."

A distant look came into her eyes. A smile hovered at the corners of her mouth.

"I wore my pearls," she murmured, as much to herself as to her listener. "They roped around my neck three times before draping almost to my waist. Jackie was quite envious."

He bet she was. Watching the duchess's face, listening to her cultured speech with its faint trace of an accent, Jack nursed the hope that marriage to her younger granddaughter might not be such a disaster, after all.

With time and a little guidance on his part, Gina could learn to curb some of her impulsiveness. Maybe even learn to think before she blurted out whatever came into her mind. Not that he wanted to dim her sparkling personality. Just rein it in a bit so she'd feel comfortable in the restrained diplomatic circles she'd be marrying into.

Then, of course, there was the sex.

Jack kept his expression politely attentive. His diplomatic training and years of field experience wouldn't allow him to do otherwise. Yet every muscle in his body went taut as all-too-vivid images from his weekend with Gina once again grabbed him.

He hadn't been a saint since his wife died, but neither had he tomcatted around. Five women in six years didn't exactly constitute a world record. Yet the hours he'd spent in that Beverly Hills penthouse suite with Gina St. Sebastian made him come alive in ways he hadn't felt since…

Since Catherine.

Shaking off the twinge of guilt that thought brought, Jack addressed the woman just coming out of her reverie of presidents and pearls.

"Please believe me, Duchess. I want very much to do right by both your granddaughter and our child."

Those shrewd, pale eyes measured him for long, uncomfortable moments. Jack had faced cold-blooded dictators whose stares didn't slice anywhere as close to the bone as this white-haired, seemingly frail woman's did.

"You may as well call me Charlotte," she said finally. "I

suspect we may be seeing a good deal of each other in the weeks ahead."

"I suspect we may."

"Now, if you'll excuse me, I must help Sarah prepare to depart for her honeymoon."

Two

After Sarah changed and left for the airport with Dev, Gina escorted her grandmother and Maria down to the limo she'd ordered for them.

"I'll be a while," she warned as the elevator opened onto the Plaza's elegant lobby. "I want to make sure Dev's family is set for their trip home tomorrow."

"I should think that clever, clever man Dev employs as his executive assistant has the family's travel arrangements well in hand."

"He does. He's also going to take care of shipping the wedding gifts back to L.A., thank goodness. But I need to verify the final head count and see he has a complete list of the bills to expect."

The duchess stiffened, and Gina gave herself a swift mental kick. Dang it! She shouldn't have mentioned those bills. As she and Sarah knew all too well, covering the cost of the wedding had come dangerously close to a major point of contention between Dev and the duchess. Charlotte had insisted on taking care of the expenses traditionally paid by the bride's family. It was a real tribute to Dev's negotiating skills that he and Grandmama had reached an agreement that didn't totally destroy her pride.

And now Gina had to bring up the sensitive subject again! It was Jack's fault, she thought in disgust. Their confrontation had thrown her off stride. Was still throwing her off. Why the heck had she agreed to meet him for lunch tomorrow?

She was still trying to figure that one out when the limo pulled up to the Plaza's stately front entrance. The driver got out to open the door but before his two passengers slid into the backseat, the duchess issued a stern warning.

"Don't overtax yourself, Eugenia. Pregnancy saps a woman's strength, especially during the first few months. You'll find you're more fatigued than usual."

"Fatigue hasn't been a problem yet. Or morning sickness, knock on…"

She glanced around for some wood to rap. She settled for wiggling a branch of one of the massive topiary trees guarding the front entrance.

"My breasts are swollen up like water balloons, though. And my nipples ache like you wouldn't believe." Grimacing, she rolled her shoulders to ease the constriction of her tight bodice. "They want *out* of this gown."

"For pity's sake, Eugenia!" The duchess shot a glance at the stony-faced limo driver. "Let's continue this discussion tomorrow, shall we?"

Nodding, Gina bent to kiss her grandmother's cheek and breathed in the faint, oh-so-familiar scent of lavender and lace. "Make sure you take your medicine before you go to bed."

"I'm not senile, young lady. I think I can manage to remember to take two little pills."

"Yes, ma'am."

Trying to look properly chastised, she helped the duchess into the limo and turned to the Honduran native who'd become a second mother to her and Sarah. "You'll stay with her, Maria? I shouldn't be more than another hour or two. I'll have a car take you home."

"Take as long as you need. *La duquesa* and I, we'll put our feet up and talk about what a fine job you did organizing such a beautiful wedding."

"It did come off well, didn't it?"

Maria beamed a wide smile. "*Sí, chica,* it did."

Buoyed by the compliment, Gina returned to the reception room. Most of the guests had departed. Including, she saw after a quick sweep, a certain obnoxious ambassador who'd shown up unexpectedly. She should have had him escorted out when he first walked in. Being summarily ejected from the wedding would have put a dent in the man's ego. Or maybe not. For a career diplomat, he seemed as impervious to Gina's snubs as to her adamant refusal to marry him.

He didn't understand why she wouldn't even consider it for their baby's sake. Neither did the duchess. Although Grandmama and Sarah both supported Gina's decision to go it alone, she knew they wondered at her vehemence. On the surface, John Harris Mason III certainly made excellent husband material. He was rich, handsome and charming as the devil when he wanted to be.

It was what lurked below the surface that held Gina back. Every story, every bio printed about the charismatic diplomat, hinted that Jack had buried his heart with the young wife he'd first dated in high school and married the day they both graduated from Harvard. From all reports, Catherine Mason had been every bit as smart, athletic and politically involved as her husband.

Gina knew in her heart she couldn't compete with the ghost of his lost love. Not because she lacked her own set of credentials. The Duchy of Karlenburgh might now be little more than an obscure footnote in history books, but Grandmama could still hold her own with presidents and kings. What's more, she'd insisted her granddaughters be educated in accordance with their heritage. Gina had actually graduated from Barnard with a semi-decent grade point average.

She'd pretty much majored in partying, though, and to this day had zero interest in politics.

She might have cultivated an interest for Jack. Had actually toyed with the idea during that crazy weekend. For all her seemingly casual approach to life and love, she'd never met anyone as fascinating and entertaining and just plain hot as Jack Mason.

Any thoughts of fitting into the mold of a diplomat's wife went poof when Gina discovered she was pregnant. There was no way she could dive into politics *and* marriage *and* motherhood at the same time. She already felt as though she were on an emotional roller coaster. All she could think about right now, all she would *allow* herself to think about, was proving she could take care of herself and her baby.

"You put on a helluva party, lady."

Smiling, she turned to Dev's gravel-voiced buddy from his air force days. Patrick Donovan now served as Dev's executive assistant and pretty much ruled his vast empire with an iron fist.

"Thanks, Pat."

Tall and lanky and looking completely at home in his Armani tux, Donovan winked at her. "You decide you want to come back to L.A., you let me know. We could use someone with your organizational skills in our protocol office. Seems like we're hosting some bigwig industrialists from China or Germany or Australia every other week."

"I appreciate the offer but I'm going to try to break into the event-planning business here in New York. Plus, I'm thinking about moving in with Grandmama for the next eight months or so."

If the duchess would have her. They'd all been so busy these past few weeks with Sarah's wedding, Gina hadn't found the right time to broach the subject. Her sister heartily endorsed the plan, though. Both she and Gina hated the thought of the duchess living alone now that Sarah was moving out.

Okay! All right! So Gina needed a place to stay until she landed a job and became self-supporting. Despite her determination to prove herself, she had to have a base to build on. Grandmama wouldn't object to letting her move in. Probably.

"I've got some pretty good contacts in New York," Patrick was saying. "You want me to make a few calls? Grease the skids a little?"

"I need to do this on my own, Pat. But thanks for the offer."

"It stays on the table," he said with a shrug as he wrapped an arm around her shoulders and gave her a squeeze. "Call me if you change your mind. Or better yet, let your new brother-in-law know. Dev is complete mush right now. He'd set you up with your own agency if you so much as hint that's what you want. And let me know if you want me to close up your apartment in L.A. and have your things shipped here."

"I will. Thanks again."

Gina climbed out of a cab some two hours later. The Dakota's red sandstone turrets poked against the darkening night sky, welcoming her to the castlelike apartment complex that was one of New York City's most prestigious addresses. The duchess had bought an apartment here shortly after arriving in New York City. The purchase had put a serious dent in her cache of jewels, but careful investments during those first years, along with the discreet sale of a diamond bracelet here, a ruby necklace there, had allowed Charlotte to maintain the apartment and an elegant lifestyle over the decades.

Keeping up the facade had become much tougher in recent years. The jewels were gone. So were most of the haute couture gowns and designer suits that once filled her grandmother's closet. With her love of the classic retro look, Sarah had salvaged a number of the outfits and saved money by not splurging on new clothes for herself, but she'd had to struggle to cover the bills from her own salary.

Dev, bless him, wanted to make things easier for his wife's grandmother. But like the wedding expenses, taking over the duchess's financial affairs involved delicate negotiations that had yet to reach a satisfactory conclusion. Which put the burden on Gina's shoulders. She couldn't just move in and expect her grandmother to support her. She had to pay her own way.

On that determined note, she thanked Maria for staying so late and told her to sleep in the next morning. "I'll make breakfast for Grandmama."

The Honduran looked dubious. "Are you sure, *chica? La duquesa,* she likes her egg poached just so."

"I know. It has to sit for exactly four minutes after the heat's turned off."

"And her tea. It must be…"

"The Twinings English Black. I've got it covered. The car's waiting for you. Go home and get some rest."

Maria obviously had her doubts but gathered her suitcase-sized purse. "I'll see you tomorrow."

Gina was up and waiting when her grandmother walked into the kitchen just after eight-thirty the next morning. The duchess was impeccably dressed as always in a calf-length black skirt and lavender silk overblouse. Her hair formed its usual, neat snowy crown atop her head, but Gina saw with a quick dart of concern that she was leaning more heavily than she normally did on her cane.

"Good morning," she said, masking her worry behind a cheerful smile. "I got a text from Sarah a while ago. She says it's balmy and beautiful in Majorca."

"I expect it is. Are you doing breakfast?"

"I am. Sit, and I'll bring your tea."

Surprised and just a little wary, the duchess seated herself in the sunny breakfast room off the kitchen. Its ivy-sprigged wallpaper, green seat cushions and windows overlooking

Central Park seemed to bring the bright May spring right into the room.

Gina poured hot water over the leaves she'd measured into her grandmother's favorite Wedgwood teapot and placed the pot on the table. While the Twinings Black steeped, she popped some wheat bread in the toaster and brought a saucepan of water back to a boil before easing two raw eggs out of their shells. The sight of the yolks gave her a moment's qualm, but it passed. Still no twinge of morning nausea, thank God! With any luck, she'd escape that scourge altogether.

"Here we are."

She hadn't kept the yolks from breaking and going all runny, but the duchess thanked her with a smile and buttered her toast. Sensing there was something behind this special effort, she munched delicately on a corner of toast and waited patiently.

Gina pulled in a deep breath and took the plunge. "I was wondering, Grandmama…"

Dang! Admitting she was a screwup and needed to come live with her grandmother until she got her life in order was harder than she'd anticipated.

"I thought perhaps I might stay with you until I get a job. If you don't mind, that is."

"Oh, Eugenia!" Charlotte's reaction came swift and straight from the heart. "Of course I don't mind, my darling girl. This is your home. You must stay for as long as you wish. You and the baby."

Gina wasn't crying. She really wasn't. The tears just sort of leaked through her smile. "Thanks, Grandmama."

Her own lips a little wobbly, the duchess reached for her granddaughter's hand. "I admit I wasn't looking forward to rattling around this place by myself now that Sarah's moving out. I'm delighted you want to stay here. Will you need to fly back to L.A. to pack up your things?"

"Dev's assistant, Patrick, said he would take care of that if I decided to stay in New York."

"Good!" Charlotte gave her hand a quick squeeze and picked up her fork. "Now, what's this Sarah told me about you wanting to go into the catering business?"

"Not catering. Event planning. I did a little of it in L.A. Just enough to know I'm better at organizing and throwing parties than..." She managed a watery chuckle. "Than everything else I've tried."

"Well, you certainly did an excellent job with the wedding."

The praise sent Gina's spirits winging. "I did, didn't I?" She preened for a moment, her tears forgotten. "And the photographer from Sarah's magazine shot some amazing video and stills. He gave me a disk with enough material to put together a portfolio. I just emailed it to the woman I'm interviewing with this afternoon."

Her grandmother paused with her fork halfway to her lips. "You have an interview this afternoon?"

"I do. With Nicole Tremayne, head of the Tremayne Group. TTG operates a dozen different event venues, three right here in the city."

"Hmm. I knew a Nicholas Tremayne some years ago. Quite well, actually." Her thoughts seemed to go inward for a moment. Shaking them off, she lowered her fork. "This Nicole must be his daughter. If so, I'll call him and..."

"No, Grandmama, please don't."

The urgent plea brought a look of surprise. "Why ever not?"

"I want to do this on my own."

"That sentiment does you justice, Eugenia, but..."

"You don't have to say it. I know my track record doesn't suggest I'll make a very reliable employee. When you add the fact that I'm pregnant, it'll be a miracle if I land any job. I want to try, though, Grandmama. I really do."

"Very well. I'll refrain from interfering."

"Thank you. Dev and Patrick made the same promise. And I'll get Jack to do the same when I meet him for lunch today."

The duchess tilted her head. Sudden interest gleamed in her faded blue eyes. "You're having lunch with Jack? Why? I thought you'd said all you have to say to him."

"I did. Several times! The man won't take no for an answer."

"So again I ask, why are you having lunch with him?"

"He badgered me into it," Gina admitted in disgust. "You can see why I don't want to marry him."

The duchess took her time replying. When she did, she chose her words carefully.

"Are you sure, Eugenia? I treasure every moment I had with your mother and with you and Sarah, but I speak from experience when I say raising a child on your own can be quite terrifying at times."

"Oh, Grandmama!"

Her eyes misted again. Blinking furiously, Gina bared her soul. "I'm scared out my gourd. I admit it! The only thing that makes me even think I can do this is you, and the love you lavished on Sarah and me. You filled our lives with such joy, such grand adventures. You still do. I can give that to my child. I know I can."

A smile started in her grandmother's eyes and spread to Gina's heart.

"I know you can, too."

Gina had intended to spend the rest of the morning prepping for her interview with Nicole Tremayne. To her annoyance, her thoughts kept slipping away from party planning and instead landed on Jack Mason.

Her irritation increased even more when she found herself scowling at the few outfits she'd brought to New York with her. They were all flashy, all playful. Thigh-skimming skirts in bold prints. Tights in eye-popping colors. Spangled, midriff-baring T-shirts. Reflective of her personality, maybe, but not the image she wanted to project to Ms. Tremayne. Or to a certain ambassador-at-large.

Abandoning the meager offering, she went next door to Sarah's room and rummaged through the designer classics her sister had salvaged from their grandmother's closet. After much debate and a pile of discards strewn across the bed, Gina decided on wide-legged black slacks. She topped them with a summer silk Valentino jacket in pearl gray that boasted a flower in the same fabric on one lapel. The jacket strained a bit at the bust but gave her the mature, responsible air she was aiming for. A wad of cotton stuffed into the toes of a pair of sensible black pumps added to the look. As a final touch, she went light on the makeup and wrestled her waterfall of platinum-blond curls into a French twist. When she studied the final result in the mirror, she gulped.

"Oh, God. I look like Grandmama."

If the duchess recognized herself, she mercifully refrained from saying so. But Gina caught the slightly stunned look she exchanged with Maria as her new, subdued granddaughter departed for her lunch meeting.

If Gina had needed further evidence of her transformation, she got it mere moments after walking into the Boathouse. A favorite gathering place of tourists and locals alike, the restaurant's floor-to-ceiling windows gave unimpeded views of the rowboats and gondolas gliding across Central Park's Reservoir Lake. Both the lake and the trees surrounding it were showcased against the dramatic backdrop of the Manhattan skyline.

The Boathouse's casual bar and restaurant buzzed with a crowd dressed in everything from business to smart casual to just plain comfortable. Despite the logjam, Gina spotted Jack immediately. As promised, he'd secured a table tucked in a quiet corner that still gave an unobstructed view of the lake. She stood for a moment at the top of the short flight of steps leading down to the dining area and put a hand on the railing to steady herself.

Oh, Lord! Her hormones must be cartwheeling again. Why else would her knees get all wobbly at the way the sunlight streaked his tawny hair? Or her lungs wheeze like an old accordion at the sight of his strong, tanned hands holding up a menu? In the tux he'd worn to the wedding yesterday, Jack had wreaked havoc on her emotions. In a crisply starched pale blue shirt with the cuffs rolled up on muscled forearms lightly sprinkled with gold fuzz, he almost opened the floodgates.

She was still clinging to the wooden rail when he glanced up. His gaze swept the entrance area from left to right. Passed over her. Jerked back. He was too polished a diplomat to reveal more than a flash of surprise, but that brief glimpse gave Gina the shot in the arm she needed. Channeling the duchess at her most regal, she smiled at the head waiter, who hurried over to assist her.

"May I show you to a table?"

"Thank you, but I see the party I'm meeting."

She tipped her chin toward Jack, now rising from his chair. The waiter followed her gaze and offered a hand.

"Yes, of course. Please, watch your step."

Jack had recovered from his momentary surprise. Gina wasn't sure she liked the amusement that replaced it.

"I almost didn't recognize you," he admitted. "Are you going for a new look?"

"As a matter of fact, I am."

She took the seat next to him and considered how much to share of her plans. After a swift internal debate, she decided it might be good to let him know that she did, in fact, have plans.

"I'm also going for a new career. I have a job interview this afternoon with the head of the Tremayne Group. TTG is one of the biggest event-coordinating companies in the business, with venues in New York, Washington and Chicago."

The change in Jack was so subtle she almost missed it. Just a slight stiffening of his shoulders. She bristled, thinking he was going to object to her making a foray into the professional party world while carrying his child. Instead, he responded quietly, calmly.

"TTG also has a venue in Boston. My wife used them to coordinate our wedding."

Three

"Oh, Jack!"

Gina's soft heart turned instantly to mush. She didn't want to marry this man but neither did she want to hurt him. Ignoring the obvious inconsistency in that thought, she dug in her purse for her cell phone.

"I'm sorry. I didn't know you had that connection to TTG. I'll call and cancel my interview."

"Wait." Frowning, he put a hand on her arm. "I'll admit I would prefer not to see you pursue a career here in New York. Or anywhere else, for that matter. But…"

"But?"

Still frowning, he searched her face. "Are you really dead set against marriage, Gina?"

Her gaze dropped to his hand, so strong and tan against the paler skin of her forearm. The stress and confusion of the past weeks made a jumble of her reply.

"Sort of."

"What does that mean?"

She looked up and met his serious brown eyes. "I like you, Jack. When you're not coming on all huffy and autocratic, that is. And God knows we were fantastic together in bed."

So fantastic she had to slam the door on the images that thought conjured up.

"But I think…I know we both want more in a marriage."

He was silent, and Gina gathered her courage.

"Tell me about your wife. What was she like?"

He sat back, withdrawing his hand in the process. Withdrawing himself, as well. His glance shifted to the rowboats circling the lake. The ripples from their oars distorted the reflected images of the high-rises peeking above Central Park's leafy green tree line. The buildings seemed to sway on the lake's blue-green surface.

"Catherine was funny and smart and had a killer serve," he said finally, turning back to Gina. "She cleaned my clock every time we got on a tennis court. She might have turned pro if she hadn't lived, breathed and slept politics."

The waiter appeared at that moment. Gina ordered decaffeinated mango tea, Jack a refill of his coffee. They listened to the specials and let the menus sit on the table after the waiter withdrew. She was afraid the interruption had broken the thread of a conversation she knew had to be painful, but Jack picked it up again.

"Catherine and another campaign worker were going door-to-door to canvas unregistered voters for the presidential campaign. She suffered a brain aneurysm and collapsed. The docs say she was dead before she hit the sidewalk."

"I'm so sorry."

"We didn't learn until after the autopsy that she had Ehlers-Danlos syndrome. It's a rare, inherited condition that can cause the walls of your blood vessels to rupture. Which," he said as he eased a leather portfolio out from under his menu, "is why I prepared this."

"This" turned out to be a set of stapled papers. For a wild moment Gina thought they might be a prenup. Or a copy of a will, naming the baby as his heir if he should die as unexpectedly as Catherine had. Or…

"Your obstetrician will want a complete medical history

of both parents," he said calmly. "As far as I know, I haven't inherited any rare diseases but my father and grandfather both suffer from chronic high blood pressure and my mother is a breast cancer survivor. Who's your doctor, by the way?"

"I don't have one yet."

The frown came back. "Why the delay? You should've had your first prenatal checkup by now."

"It's on my list, right after getting resettled in New York and finding a job."

"Move the obstetrician to the top of the list," he ordered, switching into his usual take-charge mode. "I'll cover your medical expenses until you land a job."

"No, Mr. Ambassador, you won't."

"Oh, for…!"

He dropped the papers, closed his eyes for a moment and adopted a calm, soothing tone that made Gina want to hiss.

"Let's just talk this through. You're currently unemployed. I assume you have no health insurance. Few obstetricians will take you on as a patient unless there's some guarantee you can pay for their services."

"I. Will. Find. A. Job."

"Okay, okay." He held up a placating hand. "Even if you do land a job in the next few days or weeks, health benefits probably won't kick in for at least six months. And then they may not cover preexisting conditions."

Well, crap! Gina hadn't considered that. Her throat closed as her carefully constructed house of cards seemed to teeter and topple right before her eyes.

No! No, dammit! Hormones or no hormones, she would not break down and bawl in front of Jack.

He must have sensed her fierce struggle for control. His expression softened, and he dropped the grating, let's-be-reasonable tone. "This is my baby, too, Gina. Let me help however I can."

She could handle autocratic and obnoxious. Nice was

harder to manager. Shoving back her chair, she pushed away from the table.

"I have to go to the bathroom."

After some serious soul-searching, she returned from the ladies' room to find the waiter had delivered their drinks. Gina dumped artificial sweetener in her tea and took a fortifying sip before acknowledging the unpalatable truth.

"I guess I didn't think this whole insurance thing through. If it turns out I can't get medical benefits in time to cover my appointments with an obstetrician, I would appreciate your help."

"You've got it." He hesitated a moment before extending another offer. "Finding a good doctor isn't easy, especially with everything else you have going on right now. Why don't I call my chief of staff and have him email you a list of the top OB docs in the city? He can also verify that they're accepting new patients."

And coordinate the payment process, Gina guessed. Swallowing her pride, she nodded. "I'd appreciate that."

"Just call me when you decide on a doctor. Or call Dale Vickers, my chief of staff. He'll make sure your appointments get on my schedule."

"Your schedule?"

"I'll fly up from D.C. to go with you, of course. Assuming I'm in the country."

"Oh. Of course."

The sense that she could do this on her own was rapidly slipping away. Trying desperately to hang on to her composure, Gina picked up her menu.

"We'd better order. My appointment at the Tremayne Group is at two-thirty."

Jack's hand hovered over his menu. "This might sound a little crass but between Catherine's family and mine, we spent an obscene amount of money on our wedding. I could make a call and…"

"No!"

Gina gritted her teeth. Was she the only person in the whole friggin' universe who didn't have an inside connection at TTG? And the only fool who refused to exploit that connection? Sheer stubbornness had her shaking her head.

"No calls. No pulling strings. No playing the big ambassadorial cheese. I have to do this myself."

He lifted a tawny brow but didn't press the point. After signaling the waiter over to take their orders, he steered the conversation into more neutral channels.

The awkwardness of the situation eased, and Gina's spirits took an upward swing. Jack soon had her laughing at some of his more humorous exploits in the field and realizing once again how charming he could be when he wanted to.

And sexy. So damned sexy. She savored the lump crab cake she'd ordered for lunch and couldn't help admiring the way the tanned skin at the corners of his eyes crinkled when he smiled. And how the light reflecting off the lake added glints to the sun-streaked gold of his hair. When he leaned forward, Gina caught the ripple of muscle under his starched shirt. She found herself remembering how she'd run her palms over all that hard muscle. That tight butt. Those iron thighs. The bunched biceps and…

"Gina?"

She almost choked on a lump of crab. "Sorry. What were you saying?"

"I was asking if you'd consider coming down to D.C. for a short visit. I'd like to show you my home and introduce you to my parents."

The request was reasonable. Naturally Jack's parents would want to meet the mother of their grandchild. From the little he'd let drop about his staunchly conservative father, though, Gina suspected John Harris Mason II probably wouldn't greet her with open arms.

"Let's talk about that later," she hedged. "After I get settled and find a job."

They finished lunch and lingered a few minutes over tea and coffee refills. Gina's nerves had started to get jittery by the time they exited the Boathouse. Jack walked with her through the park now filled with bicyclers and in-line skaters and sun worshippers sprawled on benches with eyes closed and faces tilted to the sky.

A group of Japanese tourists had congregated at Bethesda Fountain and were busy snapping photos of each other with the bronze statue of the *Angel of the Waters* towering over them. At the shy request of one of the younger members of the group, Jack obligingly stopped to take a picture of the whole party. Everyone wanted a copy on their own camera so Gina ended up acting as a runner, passing him ten or twelve cameras before they were done. By the time they reached Fifth Avenue and Jack hailed a cab to take her to her interview, she was feeling the pressure of time.

"Keep your fingers crossed," she said without thinking as the cab pulled over to the curb.

Only as he reached to open the door for her did she remember that he would prefer she didn't land this—or any job—in New York. He made no secret of the fact that he wanted to put a ring on her finger and take care of her and their child. To his credit, he buried those feelings behind an easy smile.

"I'll do better than that. Here's a kiss for luck."

He kept it light. Just a brush of his lips over hers. On the first pass, at least.

Afterward Gina could never say for sure who initiated the second pass. All she knew was that Jack hooked a hand behind her nape, she went up on tiptoe and what had started as a friendly good-luck token got real deep and real hungry.

When he finally raised his head, she saw herself reflected in his eyes. "I...I have to go!"

He stepped back and gave her room to make an escape. She slid into the cab and spent the short drive to the Tremayne Group's headquarters trying desperately to remember all the reasons why she wanted—no, needed!—this job.

* * *

At three-ten, she was reiterating that same grim list. She'd been sitting in Nicole Tremayne's ultramodern outer office for more than half an hour while a harried receptionist fielded phone calls and a succession of subordinates rushed in and out of the boss's office. Any other time Gina would have walked out after the first fifteen or twenty minutes. She didn't have that luxury now.

Instead, she'd used the time to reread the information she'd found on Google about the Tremayne Group. She also studied every page in the slick, glossy brochure given out to prospective clients. Even then she had to unlock her jaw and force a smile when the receptionist finally ushered her into the inner sanctum.

Stunned, Gina stopped dead. This dark cavern was the command center of a company that hosted more than two thousand events a year at a dozen different venues? And this tiny whirlwind erupting from behind her marble slab of a desk was the famed Nicole Tremayne?

She couldn't have been more than five-one, and she owed at least four of those inches to her needle-heeled ankle boots. Gina was still trying to marry the bloodred ankle boots to her salt-and-pepper corkscrew curls when Nicole thrust out a hand.

"Sorry to keep you waiting. You're Eugenia, right? Eugenia St. Sebastian?"

"Yes, I…"

"My father had a thing for your grandmother. I was just a kid at the time, but I remember he talked about leaving my mother for her."

"Oh. Well, uh…"

"He should have. My mother was a world-class ball-breaker." Swooping a thick book of fabric swatches off one of the chairs in front of her desk, Tremayne dumped it on the floor. "Sit, sit."

Still slightly stunned, Gina sat. Nicole cleared the chair

next to hers and perched on its edge with the nervous energy of a hummingbird.

"I looked at the digital portfolio of your sister's wedding. Classy job. You did all the arrangements?"

"With some help."

"Who from?"

"Andrew, at the Plaza. And Patrick Donovan. He's…"

"Dev Hunter's right-hand man. I know. We coordinated a major charity event for Hunter's corporation last year. Three thousand attendees at two thousand a pop. So when can you start?"

"Excuse me?"

"One of the assistant event planners at our midtown venue just got busted for possession. She's out on bail, but I can't have a user working for TTG." Her bird-bright eyes narrowed on Gina. "You don't do dope, do you?"

"No."

"I'd better not find out otherwise."

"You won't."

Tremayne nodded. "Here's the thing. You have a lousy work record but a terrific pedigree. If you inherited half your grandmother's class and a quarter of her smarts, you should be able to handle this job."

Gina wasn't sure whether she'd just been complimented or insulted. She was still trying to decide when her prospective boss continued briskly.

"You also grew up here in the city. You know your way around and you know how to interact with the kind of customers we attract. Plus, the classy digital portfolio you sent me shows you've got a flair for design and know computers. Whether you can handle vendors and show yourself as a team player remains to be seen, but I'm willing to give you a shot. When can you start?"

Tomorrow!

The joyous reply was almost out before Gina caught it. Gulping, she throttled back her exhilaration.

"I can start anytime but there's something I need to tell you before we go any further."

"What's that?"

"I'm pregnant."

"And I'm Episcopalian. So?"

Could it really be this easy? Gina didn't think so. Suspicion wormed through her elation.

"Did my grandmother call you?" she asked. "Or Pat Donovan?"

"No."

Her jaw locked. Dammit! It had to have been Jack.

"Then I assume you talked to the ambassador," she said stiffly.

"What ambassador?"

"Jack Mason."

"Jack Mason." Tremayne tapped her chin with a nail shellacked the same red as her ankle boots. "Why do I know that name?"

Gina didn't mention that TTG had coordinated Jack's wedding. For reasons she would have to sort out later, that cut too close to the bone.

"Who is he," Tremayne asked, "and why would he call me?"

"He's a friend." That was the best she could come up with. "I told him about our interview and…and thought he might have called to weigh in."

"Well, it certainly never hurts to have an ambassador in your corner, but no, he didn't call me. So what's the deal here? Do you want the job or not?"

There were probably a dozen different questions she should ask before jumping into the fray. Like how much the job paid, for one. And what her hours would be. And whether the position came with benefits. At the moment, though, Gina was too jazzed to voice any of the questions buzzing around in her head.

"Yes, ma'am, I do."

"Good. Have my assistant direct you to the woman who handles our personnel matters. You can fill out all the necessary forms there. And call me Nikki," she added as her new employee sprang out of her chair to shake on the deal.

Gina left the Tremayne Group's personnel office thirty or forty forms later. The salary was less than she'd hoped for but the description of her duties made her grin. As assistant events coordinator she would be involved in all phases of operation for TTG's midtown venue. Scheduling parties and banquets and trade shows. Devising themes to fit the clients' desires. Creating menus. Contracting with vendors to supply food and decorations and bar stock. Arranging for limos, for security, for parking.

Even better, the personnel officer had stressed that there was plenty of room for advancement within TTG. The tantalizing prospect of a promotion danced before Gina's eyes as she exited the high-rise housing the company's headquarters. When she hit the still glorious May sunshine, she had to tell someone her news. Her first, almost instinctive, impulse was to call Jack. She actually had her iPhone in hand before she stopped to wonder why.

Simple answer. She wanted to crow a little.

Not so simple answer. She wanted to prove she wasn't all fun and fluff.

With a wry grimace, she acknowledged that she should probably wait until she'd actually performed in her new position for a few weeks or months before she made that claim. She decided to text Sarah instead. The message was short and sweet.

I'm now a working mom-to-be. Call when you and Dev come up for air.

She took a cab back to the Upper West Side and popped out at a deli a few blocks from the Dakota. Osterman's had occupied the same choice corner location since the Great Depression. Gina and Sarah had developed their passion for corned beef at the deli's tiny, six-table eating area. The sisters still indulged whenever they were in the city, but Gina's target tonight was the case displaying Osterman's world famous cheesecakes. With unerring accuracy, she went for a selection that included her own, her grandmother's and Maria's favorites.

"One slice each of the white chocolate raspberry truffle, the key lime and the Dutch apple caramel, please. And one pineapple upside down," she added on an afterthought.

The boxed cheesecake wedges in hand, she plucked a bottle of chilled champagne from the cooler in the wine corner. She had to search for a nonalcoholic counterpart but finally found it in with the fruit juices. Driven by the urge to celebrate, she added a wedge of aged brie and a loaf of crusty bread to her basket. On her way to check out she passed a shelf containing the deli's selection of caviars.

The sticker price of a four-ounce jar of Caspian Sea Osetra made her gasp. Drawing in a steadying breath, she reminded herself it was Grandmama's caviar of choice. The duchess considered Beluga too salty and Sevruga too fishy. Gina made a quick calculation and decided her credit card would cover the cost of one jar. Maybe.

"Oh, what the hell."

To her relief, she got out of Osterman's without having the credit card confiscated. A block and a half later she approached the Dakota with all her purchases.

"Let me help you with those!"

The doorman who'd held his post for as long as she could remember leaped forward. Although she would never say so to his face, Gina suspected Jerome assumed his present duties about the same time Osterman's opened its doors.

"You should have called a cab, Lady Eugenia."

Sarah and Gina had spent most of their adult years trying to get Jerome to drop their empty titles. They'd finally agreed it was a wasted effort.

"I'm okay," Gina protested as he tried to relieve her of her burdens. "Except for this."

She sorted through her purchases and fished out a wedge-shaped box. Jerome peeked inside and broke into a grin.

"Pineapple upside down! Trust you to remember my favorite."

Gina's emotions jumped on the roller coaster again as she thought about his devoted loyalty to her and Grandmama over the years.

"How could I forget?" she said with a suspicious catch to her voice. "You slipped me an extra few dollars every time I said I was going to Osterman's."

For a moment she thought the embarrassed doorman would pat her on the head as he'd done so many times when she was a child. He controlled the impulse and commented instead on the bottles poking out of her bag.

"Still celebrating Lady Sarah's wedding?"

"Nope. This celebration is in my honor."

Riding her emotional roller coaster to its gravity-defying apex, she poured out her news.

"I'm moving back to New York, Jerome."

"Lady Eugenia! That's wonderful news. I admit I was a bit worried about the duchess."

"There's more. I've got a job."

"Good for you."

"Oh," she added over her shoulder as she made for the lobby. "I'm also pregnant."

Four

Gina walked into the Tremayne Group's midtown venue at 9:30 a.m. the next morning. She didn't drag out again until well past midnight.

Her first impression was *wow!* What had once been a crumbling brick warehouse overlooking the East River was now a glass-fronted, ultra-high-rent complex of offices, restaurants and entertainment venues. TTG occupied a slightly recessed four-story suite smack in the center of the complex. The primo location allowed into a private ground-floor courtyard with bubbling fountains and a top-floor terrace that had to offer magnificent views of the river.

A young woman with wings of blue in her otherwise lipstick-red hair sat at a curved glass reception desk and fielded phone calls. Gina waited until she finished with one caller and put two others on hold to introduce herself.

"I'm Gina St. Sebastian. I'm the new…"

"Assistant coordinator. Thank God you're here! I'm Kallie. Samuel's in the banquet hall. He said to send you right up. Third floor. The elevators are to your right."

Gina used the ride to do a quick check in mirrored panels. She'd left her hair down today but confined the silky curls behind a wide fuchsia headband studded with crystals. A

belt in the same hot pink circled the waist of her apple-green
J. Crew tunic. Since this was her first day on the job she'd
gone with sedate black tights instead of the colorful prints
she preferred. She made a quick swipe with her lip gloss and
drew in a deep, steadying breath. Then the elevator door
glided open and she stepped out into a vortex of sound and
fury.

What looked like a small army of workers in blue overalls
was yanking folded chairs from metal-sided carrier racks,
popping them open and thumping them around a room full
of circluar tables. Another crew, this one in black pants and
white shirts, scurried after the first. They draped each chair
in shimmering green, the tables in cloth of gold. Right behind
them came yet another crew rattling down place settings of
china and crystal. The *rat-tat-tat* of staple guns fired by intent set designers erecting a fantastic Emerald City added
to the barrage of noise, while the heady scent of magnolias
wafted from dozens of tall topiaries stacked on carts waiting to be rolled to the tables.

Soaking up the energy like a sponge, Gina wove her way
through the tables to a wild-haired broomstick with a clipboard in one hand, a walkie-talkie in the other and a Blue-
tooth headset hooked over one ear. "Not *The Wizard of Oz,*"
he was shouting into the headset. "Christ, who does Judy
Garland anymore? This is the new movie. *Oz the... Oz the...*"

Scowling, he snapped his fingers at Gina.

"Oz the Great and Powerful," she dutifully asserted.

"Right. *Oz the Great and Powerful*. It's a Disney flick
starring Rachel Weisz and..."

More finger snaps.

"Mila Kunis."

"Right. Mila Kunis. That's the music the clients requested." The scowl deepened. "Hell, no, I don't! Hold on."

He whipped his head around and barked at Gina. "You
the new AC?"

"Yes."

"I'm Samuel DeGrange."

"Nice to…"

He brushed aside the pleasantries with an impatient hand. "Go upstairs and tell the DJ to pull his head out of his ass. The clients don't want Dorothy and Toto, for God's sake! Then make sure the bar supervisor knows how to mix the fizzy green juice concoction that's supposed to make the kids think they're dancing down a new, improved Yellow Brick Road."

Eight and a half hours later Gina was zipped into the Glinda the Good Witch costume that had been rented for her predecessor and making frantic last-minute changes to seating charts. Kallie the receptionist—now garbed as a munchkin—wielded a calligraphy pen to scribble out place cards for the twenty additional guests the honoree's mother had somehow forgotten she'd invited until she was in the limo and on her way from Temple with the newly bat mitz-vahed Rachel.

Another six hours later, Gina collapsed into a green-draped chair and gazed at the rubble. Iridescent streamers in green and gold littered the dance floor. Scattered among them was a forgotten emerald tiara here, an empty party-favors box there. The booths where the seventy-five kids invited to celebrate Rachel's coming of age had fired green lasers and demolished video villains were being dismantled. Only a few crumbs remained of the fourteen-layer cake with its glittering towers and turrets. The kids invited to the party had devoured it with almost as much gusto as the more than two hundred parents, grandparents, aunts, uncles, cousins and family friends had drained the open bar upstairs.

Gina stretched out her feet in their glittery silver slippers and aimed a grin at the toothpick-thin Tin Man who flopped into the chair beside her.

"This party business is fun."

"You think?" Samuel shoved back his tin hat and gave her a jaundiced smile. "Talk to me again after you've had an inebriated best man puke all over you. Or spent two hours sifting through piles of garbage to find a guest's diamond-and-sapphire earrings. Which, incidentally, she calls to tell you she found in her purse."

"At least she let you know she found it," Gina replied, laughing.

"She's one of the few. Seems like our insurance rates take another jump after every event." He slanted her a sideways glance. "You did good tonight, St. Sebastian. Better than I expected when I read your resumé."

"Thanks. I think."

"You need to keep a closer finger on the pulse of the party, though. The natives got a little restless before the cake was brought out."

Gina bit her lip. No need to remind her new boss that he'd sent her out to the terrace to shepherd some underage smokers back inside right when the cake was supposed to have been presented.

"I'll watch the timing," she promised.

"So go home now. I'll do the final bar count and leave this mess to the cleaning crew."

She wasn't about to argue. "I'll see you tomorrow."

"Nine sharp," he warned. "We've got a preliminary wedding consult. I'll talk, you listen and learn."

She popped a salute. "Yes, sir."

"Christ! You got enough energy left for that?" He didn't wait for an answer, just shooed her away. "Get out of here."

The *Oz the Great and Powerful* bat mitzvah set the stage for the dozens of events that followed during the busy, busy month of May. Almost before she knew it Gina was caught up in a whirl of wedding and engagement and anniversary and graduation and coming-of-age parties. She gained both experience and confidence with each event.

So much so that Samuel soon delegated full responsibility for computing and placing orders with the subs for everything from decorations to bar stock. He also tapped her for fresh ideas for themes and settings. In rapid succession she helped plan a white-on-white wedding, a red-and-black "Puttin' on the Ritz" debutante ball and a barefoot-on-the-beach engagement party at a private Hamptons estate. And then there was her grand coup—snaring Justin Bieber for a brief appearance at the national Girl Scout banquet to be held in the fall. He was in town for another event and Gina played shamelessly on his agent's heartstrings until every teen's favorite heartthrob agreed.

Not all events went smoothly. Frantically working her cell phone and walkie-talkie, Gina learned to cope with minor crises like a forgotten kosher meal for the rabbi, a groom caught frolicking in the fourth-floor bridal suite shower with the maid of honor and a drunken guest held hostage by an irate limo driver demanding payment for damage done to the vehicle's leather seats.

In the midst of all the craziness she unpacked the boxes Dev's assistant had shipped back from L.A. and welcomed her sister and her new brother-in-law home from their honeymoon. Gina and Sarah and the duchess were all teary-eyed when the newlyweds departed again, this time to look at homes for sale close to Dev's corporate headquarters in California.

Miracle of miracles, Gina also managed to snag an appointment with the top OB doc on the short list of three Jack had emailed. She suspected he'd used his influence or family clout to make sure she got in to see one of them. She didn't object to outside help in this instance. The health of her baby took precedence over pride.

As promised, she called Jack's office to let him know about the appointment. A secretary routed her to his chief of staff.

"This is Dale Vickers, Ms. St. Sebastian. The ambassador is in conference. May I help you?"

"Jack asked me to let him know the date and time of my prenatal appointment. It's Thursday of next week, at three-fifteen, with Dr. Sondra Martinson."

"I'm looking at his calendar now. The ambassador is unavailable next Thursday. Please reschedule the appointment and call me back."

The reply was as curt as it was officious. Gina held out the phone and looked at it in surprise for a moment before putting it to her ear again.

"Tell you what," she said, oozing sweetness and light, "just tell Jack to call me. We'll take it from there."

The man must have realized his mistake. Softening his tone, he tried to regain lost ground.

"I'm sorry if I sounded abrupt, Ms. St. Sebastian. It's just that the ambassador is participating all next week in a conference with senior State Department officials. They're assessing U.S. embassy security in light of recent terrorist attacks. I can't overstate the importance of this conference to the safety and security of our consular personnel abroad."

Properly put in her place, Gina was about to concede the point when he made a suggestion.

"Why don't I call Dr. Martinson's office and arrange an appointment that fits with the ambassador's schedule?"

"That won't work. We need to work around my schedule, too."

"I'm sure you can squeeze something in between parties for twelve-year-olds."

The barely disguised put-down dropped Gina's jaw. What was with this character? Sheer obstinacy had her oozing even more saccharine.

"I'm sure I can. After all, the tab for our last twelve-year-old's party only ran to sixty-five thousand dollars and change. Just have Jack call me. We'll work something out."

"Really, Ms. St. Sebastian, we don't have to trouble the ambassador with such a trivial matter."

Heat shot to every one of Gina's extremities. Given her normally sunny and fun-loving disposition, she'd never believed that old cliché about seeing red. She did now.

"Listen, asshole, you may consider the ambassador's baby a trivial matter. I'm pretty sure he won't agree. The appointment is for three-fifteen next Thursday. End of discussion."

As instructed, she arrived at Dr. Martinson's office a half hour prior to her scheduled appointment. The time was required for a final review and signature on the forms she'd downloaded from the office website. She hadn't heard from Jack or from his stick-up-the-butt chief of staff. So when she walked into the reception area and didn't spot a familiar face, she wasn't surprised.

What did surprise her was how deep the disappointment went. She'd been so busy she hadn't had time to dwell on the confused feelings Jack Mason stirred in her. Except at night, when she dropped into bed exhausted and exhilarated and wishing she had someone to share the moments of her day with. Or when her body reminded her that she wasn't its sole inhabitant anymore. Or when she happened to spot a tall, tanned male across the room or on the street or in the subway.

"Don't be stupid," she muttered as she signed form after form. "He's making the world safer for our embassy people. That has to take precedence."

She was concentrating so fiercely on the clipboard in her hand that she didn't hear the door to the reception area open.

"Good, I'm not late."

The relieved exclamation brought her head up with a jerk.

"Jack! I thought… Vickers said…"

Of all the idiotic times to get teary-eyed! How could she handle every crisis at work with a cheerful smile and turn into such a weepy wimp around this man? She had to jump off this emotional roller coaster.

"Vickers told me what he said." Grinning, he dropped into the chair beside hers. "He also told me what you said."

"Yes, well, you shouldn't piss off a preggo. The results aren't pretty."

"I'll remember that."

Guilt wormed through the simple, hedonistic pleasure of looking at his handsome face. She let the clipboard drop to her lap and made a wry face.

"You shouldn't have come. Vickers said you had a top-level conference going on all week."

"We wrapped up the last of the key issues this morning. All that's left is to approve the report once it gets drafted. I can do that by secure email. Which means," he said as he took the clipboard and flipped through the forms, "I don't have to fly back to D.C. right away. Here, you forgot to sign this one."

She scribbled her signature and tried not to read too much into his casual comment about extending his trip up from D.C. Didn't work. When he tacked on an equally casual in-vitation, her heart gave a little bump.

"If you don't have plans, I thought I might take you and the duchess to dinner tonight."

"Oh, I can't. I'm working a fiftieth anniversary party. I had to sneak out for this appointment."

"How about tomorrow?"

The bump was bigger this time. "Are you staying over that long?"

"Actually, I told Dale to clear the entire weekend."

"Ha! Bet he loved that."

"He's not so bad, Gina. You two just got off on the wrong foot."

"Wrong foot, wrong knee, wrong hip and elbow. How long has he worked for you, anyway?"

"Five years."

"And no one's ever told you he's officious or condescend-ing?"

"No."

"It has to be me, then." Grimacing, she rolled out the reason she suspected might be behind his aide's less-than-enthusiastic response to her call. "Or the fact that the paparazzi will have a field day when they hear you knocked me up."

"They probably will," he replied, not quite suppressing a wince. "But when they do, you might want to use a different phrase to describe the circumstances."

"Really? What phrase do you suggest I use, Mr. Ambassador?"

He must have seen the chasm yawning at his feet. "Sorry. I didn't mean to come across as such a pompous jerk."

The apology soothed Gina's ruffled feathers enough for her to acknowledge his point. "I'm sorry, too. I know the pregnancy will cause you some embarrassment. I'll try not to add to it."

"The only embarrassing aspect to this whole situation is that I can't convince the beautiful and very stubborn mother of my child to marry me."

She wanted to believe him, but she wasn't that naive. She chewed on her lower lip for a moment before voicing the worry that had nagged her since Switzerland.

"Tell me the truth, Jack. Is this going to impact your career?"

"No."

"Maybe not at the State Department, but what about afterward? I read somewhere that certain powerful PACs think you have a good shot at the presidency in the not-too-distant future."

"Gina, listen to me." He curled a knuckle under her chin and tipped her face to make sure he had her complete attention. "We met, we were attracted to each other, we spent some time together. Since neither of us were then, or are now, otherwise committed, the only ones impacted by the result of that meeting are you, me and our baby."

"Wow," she breathed. "That was some speech, Mr. Ambassador. Those PACs may be right. You should make a bid for the Oval Office. You'd get my vote."

He feathered the side of her jaw with his thumb. "I'd rather get your signature on a marriage license."

Maybe…maybe she was being blind and pigheaded and all wrong about this marriage thing. So he didn't love her? He wanted her, and God knew she wanted him. Couldn't their child be the bridge to something more?

The thought made her cringe inside. What kind of mother would pile her hopes and dreams on a baby's tiny shoulders?

"We've had this discussion." Shrugging, she pulled away from his touch. "Let's not get into it again."

Surprise darkened his brown eyes, followed by a touch of what could have been either disappointment or irritation. Before Gina could decide which, a nurse in pink-and-blue scrubs decorated with storks delivering bundles of joy popped into the waiting room.

"Ms. St. Sebastian?"

"Right here."

"If you'll come with me, I'll get your height and weight and show you to an exam room."

Gina pushed out her chair. Jack rose with her. The nurse stopped him with a friendly smile. "Please wait here, Mr. St. Sebastian. I'll come get you in a few minutes."

The look on his face was more than enough to disperse Gina's glum thoughts. Choking back a laugh, she floated after the nurse. When Jack joined her in the exam room five minutes later, she was wearing a blue paper gown tied loosely in the front and a fat grin.

"I set her straight on the names."

"Uh-huh."

"Come on," she teased. "You have to admit it was funny."

The only thing in Jack's mind at the moment was not something he could admit. How could he have forgotten how full and lush and ripe her breasts were? Or had her pregnancy enhanced the creamy slopes he glimpsed through the front opening of her gown?

Whatever! That one glimpse was more than enough to put him in a sweat. Thoroughly disgusted, he was calling himself all kinds of a pig when the doctor walked in.

"Hello, Ms. St. Sebastian. I'm Dr. Martinson."

Petite and gray-haired, she shook hands with her patient before turning to Jack. "And you're Ambassador Mason, the baby's father?"

"That's right."

"I read through your medical and family histories. I'm so pleased neither of you smoke, use drugs, or drink to excess. That makes my job so much easier."

She included Jack in her approving smile before addressing Gina.

"I'm going to order lab tests to confirm your blood type and Rh status. We'll also check for anemia, syphilis, hepatitis B and the HIV virus, as well as your immunity to rubella and chicken pox. I want you to give a urine sample, as well."

Her down-to-earth manner put her patient instantly at ease…right up until the moment she extracted a pair of rubber gloves from a dispenser mounted on the wall.

"Let's get the pelvic exam out of the way, then we'll talk about what to expect in the next few weeks and months."

She must have caught the consternation that flooded into Gina's china blue eyes. Without missing a beat, the doc snapped on the gloves and issued a casual order.

"Why don't you wait outside, Ambassador Mason? This will only take a few moments."

Five

When Jack accompanied Gina out of the medical plaza complex and into the early throes of the Thursday evening rush hour, he was feeling a little shell-shocked.

The news that he would be a father had surprised the hell out of him initially. Once he'd recovered, he'd progressed in quick order from consternation to excitement to focusing his formidable energy on hustling the mother of his child to the altar. Now, with a copy of *A Father's Guide to Pregnancy* tucked in the pocket of his suit coat and the first prenatal behind him, he was beginning to appreciate both the reality and the enormity of the road ahead.

Gina, amazingly, seemed to be taking her pregnancy in stride. Like a gloriously painted butterfly, she'd gone through an almost complete metamorphosis. Not that she'd had much choice. With motherhood staring her in the face, she appeared to have shed her fun-loving, party-girl persona. The hysterical female who'd called Jack from Switzerland had also disappeared. Or maybe those personas had combined to produce this new Gina. Still bubbling with life, still gorgeous beyond words, but surprisingly responsible.

She'd listened attentively to everything the doctor said, asked obviously well-thought-out questions and made careful notes of the answers. She also worked the calendar on her iPhone with flying fingers to fit a visit to the lab for the required blood tests and future appointments with Dr. Martinson into her schedule.

In between, she fielded a series of what had sounded like frantic calls from work with assurances that yes, she'd confirmed delivery of the ice sculpture; no, their clients hadn't requested special permission from the New York City Department of Corrections for their grandson currently serving time at Rikers to attend their fiftieth wedding anniversary celebration; and yes, she'd just left the doctor's office and was about to jump in a cab.

Jack waited on the sidewalk beside her while she finished that last call. The sky was gray and overcast but the lack of sunshine didn't dim the luster of her hair. The tumble of shining curls and the buttercup-yellow tunic she wore over patterned yellow-and-turquoise tights made her a beacon of bright cheer in the dismal day.

Jack stood beside her, feeling a kick to the gut as he remembered exploring the lush curves under that bright tunic. Remembering, too, the kiss they'd shared the last time he put her in a cab. He'd spent more time trying to analyze his reaction to that kiss than he wanted to admit. It was hot and heavy on his mind when Gina finished her call.

"I have to run," she told him. "If you still want to take Grandmama and me to dinner, I could do tomorrow evening."

"That works."

"I'll check with her to make sure tomorrow's okay and give you a call."

He stepped to the curb and flagged a cab. She started to duck inside and hesitated.

Was she remembering the last time he'd put her in a cab, too? Jack's stomach went tight with the anticipation of taking her in his arms again. He'd actually taken a step forward when she issued a tentative invitation.

"Would you like to see where I work?"

The intensity of his disappointment surprised him, but he disguised it behind an easy smile. "Yeah, I would."

"It'll have to be a brief tour," she warned when they got in the cab. "We're in the final throes of an anniversary celebration with two hundred invited guests."

"Not including the grandson at Rikers."

She made a face. "Keep your fingers crossed he doesn't break out! I have visions of NYPD crashing through the doors just when we parade the cake."

"You parade cakes?"

"Sometimes. And in this instance, we'll do it very carefully! We're talking fifteen layers replicating the Cape Hatteras lighthouse that stands on the spot where our honorees got engaged."

She thumbed her iPhone and showed Jack an image of the iconic black-and-white striped lighthouse still guarding the shores of North Carolina's Outer Banks.

"We're doing an actual working model. The caterer and I had several sticky sessions before we figured out how to bury the battery pack in the cake base and power up the strobe light at the top without melting all his pretty sugar frosting into a black-and-white blob."

"I'm impressed."

And not just with the ingenuity and creativity she obviously brought to her new job. Enthusiasm sparkled in her blue eyes, and the vibrancy that had first snared his interest bubbled to the surface again.

"Hopefully, our clients will be impressed, too. We're decorating the entire venue in an Outer Banks theme. All sand, seashells and old boats, with enough fishnet and colorful buoys to supply the Atlantic fleet."

Unbidden and unwanted, a comparison surfaced between the woman beside him and the woman he'd loved with every atom of his being. The vivid images of Catherine were starting to fade, though, despite Jack's every effort to hang on to them. He had to dig deep to remember the sound of her laughter. Strain to hear an echo of her chuckle. She'd been so socially and politically involved. So serious about the issues that mattered to her. She had fun, certainly, but she hadn't regarded life as a frothy adventure the way Gina seemed to. Nor would she have rebounded so quickly from the emotional wringer of Switzerland.

As his companion continued her lighthearted description of tonight's event, Jack's memories of his wife retreated to the shadows once again. Even the shadows got blasted away when he and Gina exited the elevators onto the third floor of the Tremayne Group's midtown venue.

They could be on the Outer Banks, right at the edge of the Atlantic. Bemused, Jack took in the rolling sand dunes, the upended rowboat, the electronic waves splashing across a wall studded with LED lights.

"Wow. Is this all your doing?" he asked Gina.

"Not hardly. Mostly my boss, Samuel, and...uh-oh! There's Samuel now. He's with our big boss. 'Scuse me a minute. I'd better find out what's up."

Jack recognized the diminutive woman with the salt-and-pepper corkscrew curls at first look. Nicole Tremayne hadn't changed much in the past eight years. One of the underlings in her Boston operation had handled most of the planning for Jack's wedding to Catherine, but Nicole had approved the final plans herself and flown up from New York to personally oversee the lavish affair.

He saw the moment she recognized him, too. The casual glance she threw his way suddenly sharpened into a narrow-eyed stare. Frowning, she exchanged a few words with Gina, then crossed the floor.

"John Harris Mason." She thrust out a hand. "I should have made the connection when Gina demanded to know if Jack Mason had contacted me."

"I hope you told her no. She almost bit off my head when I offered to call and put in a word for her."

"She did? Interesting."

Chin cocked, Tremayne studied him through bird-bright eyes. She wasn't so crass as to come out and ask if he were the father of Gina's baby but Jack could see the speculation rife in her face.

"I was sorry to hear about your wife," she said after a moment.

"Thank you."

God, what a useless response. But Jack had uttered it so many times now that the words didn't taste quite as bitter in his mouth.

"Are you still in Boston?" she asked.

"No, I'm with the State Department now. Right now I'm assigned to D.C."

"Hmm." She tapped a bloodred nail against her chin. "Good to know."

With that enigmatic comment she excused herself and returned to her underlings. Gina rushed over a few moments later.

"I'm so sorry, Jack. We'll have to postpone the tour. I've got to take care of an ice-sculpture crisis."

"No problem. Just let me know if tomorrow evening's a go for the duchess."

"I will."

The following evening was not only a go, but the duchess's acceptance also came with an invitation for drinks at the Dakota prior to dinner.

Jack spent all that day at the NYPD Counterterrorism Bureau established after 9/11. While coordination between federal, state and local agencies had increased exponentially since that horrific day, there was always room for improvement. The NYPD agents were particularly interested in Jack's recent up-close-and-personal encounter with a rabidly anti-U.S. terrorist cell in Mali. They soaked up every detail of the terrorists' weaponry and tactics and poured over the backgrounds of two Americans recently ID'd as part of the group. Since the parents of one of the expatriates lived in Brooklyn, NYPD was justifiably worried that the son might try to slip back into the country.

Jack in turn received in-depth briefings on the Counterterrorism Bureau's Lower Manhattan Security Initiative. Designed to protect the nation's financial capital, the LMSI combined increased police presence and the latest surveillance technology with a public-private partnership. Individuals from both government and the business world manned LMSI's operations center to detect and neutralize potential threats. Jack left grimly hopeful that this unique public-private cooperative effort would prove a model for other high-risk targets.

He rushed back to his hotel and had his driver wait while he hurried upstairs to change his shirt and eliminate his five-o'clock shadow. A half hour later he identified himself to a uniformed doorman at the castlelike Dakota. The security at the famed apartment complex had stepped up considerably after one of its most famous tenants, John Lennon, was gunned down just steps away from the entrance years ago. Jack had no problem providing identification, being closely scrutinized and waiting patiently while the doorman called upstairs.

"The duchess is expecting you, sir. You know the apartment number?"

"I do."

"Very good." He keyed a remote to unlock the inner door. "The elevators are to your left."

A dark-haired, generously endowed woman Jack remembered from the wedding reception answered the doorbell. She wore a polite expression but he sensed disapproval lurking just below the surface.

"*Hola.* I am Maria, housekeeper to *la duquesa* and auntie to Sarah and Gina."

Auntie, huh? That explained the disapproval. She obviously considered him solely responsible for the failure of the box of condoms he and Gina had gone through during their sexual extravaganza.

"Good evening, Maria. I saw you at Sarah's wedding but didn't get a chance to introduce myself. I'm Jack Mason."

"*Sí,* I know. Please come with me. *La duquesa* waits for you in the salon."

He followed her down a hall tiled in pale pink Carrara marble. The delicate scent of orange blossoms wafted from a Waterford crystal bowl set on a rococo side table. The elegant accessories gave no hint of how close the duchess had come to financial disaster. Jack picked up faint traces of it, however, when Maria showed him into the high-ceilinged salon.

The room's inlaid parquet floor was a work of art but cried for a hand-knotted Turkish carpet to soften its hard surface. Likewise, the watered silk wallpaper showed several barely discernible lighter rectangles where paintings must have once hung. The furniture was a skillful blend of fine antiques and modern comfort, though, and the floor-to-ceiling windows curtained in pale blue velvet gave glorious views of Central Park. Those swift impressions faded into insignificance when Jack spotted the woman sitting ramrod-straight in a leather-backed armchair, her cane within easy reach. Thin and frail though she was, Charlotte St. Sebastian nevertheless dominated the salon with her regal air.

"Good evening, Jack."

She held out a veined hand. He shook it gently and remembered her suggestion at the wedding that he use her name instead of her title.

"Good evening, Charlotte."

"Gina called a few moments ago. She's been detained at work but should be here shortly."

She waved him to the chair beside hers and smiled a request at Maria. "Would you bring in the appetizer tray before you leave?"

When the housekeeper bustled out, the duchess gestured

to a side table holding a dew-streaked bucket and an impressive array of crystal decanters.

"May I offer you an aperitif?"

"You may."

"I'm afraid I must ask you to serve yourself. The wine is a particularly fine French white, although some people find the Aligoté grape a bit too light for their tastes. Or…"

She lifted the tiny liqueur glass sitting on the table next to her and swirled its amber liquid.

"You may want to try *žuta osa*. It's produced in the mountains that at one time were part of the Duchy of Karlenburgh."

The bland comment didn't fool Jack for a second. He'd responded to too many toasts by foreign dignitaries and downed too many potent local brews to trust this one. He poured a glass of wine instead.

Maria returned with a silver tray containing a selection of cheeses, olives and prosciutto ham slices wrapped around pale green melon slices. She placed the tray on a massive marble-topped coffee table within easy reach of the duchess and her guest.

"Thank you." Charlotte gave her a smile composed of equal parts gratitude and affection. "You'd better leave now. You don't want to miss your bus."

"I'll take a later one."

Her quick glance in Jack's direction said she wasn't about to leave her friend and employer in his clutches. The duchess didn't miss the suspicion in her dark eyes.

"We're fine," she assured the woman. "Go ahead and catch your bus."

Maria looked as though she wanted to dig in her heels but yielded to her employer's wishes. The kitchen door swished shut behind her. Several moments later, her heavy footsteps sounded in the hall.

"Actually," Jack said when he resumed his seat beside the duchess, "I'm glad we have some time alone."

"Indeed?"

"As you know, Gina and I didn't spend all that much time together before our lives became so inextricably linked."

"I am aware of that fact."

Deciding he'd be wise to ignore the pained expression on Charlotte's face, Jack pressed ahead. "I'm just beginning to appreciate the woman behind your granddaughter's dazzlingly beautiful exterior. I'm hoping you'll help me add to that portrait by telling me a little more about her."

One aristocratic brow lifted. "Surely you don't expect me to provide ammunition for your campaign to convince Gina to marry you?"

"As a matter of fact, that's exactly what I'm hoping you'll provide."

"Well!" The brow shot up another notch. "For a career diplomat, you're very frank."

"I've found being frank works better than tiptoeing around tough issues."

"And that's how you categorize my granddaughter?" the duchess said haughtily. "A tough issue?"

"Ha!" Jack didn't bother to disguise his feelings. "Tough doesn't even begin to describe her. To put it bluntly, your granddaughter is the toughest, stubbornest, most irritating issue I've ever dealt with."

Oh, hell. The frozen look on his hostess's face said clearer than words that he'd overshot his mark. He was just about to apologize profusely when the facade cracked and the duchess broke into somewhat less than regal snorts of laughter.

"You do know," she responded some moments later, "that Gina says exactly the same thing about you?"

"Yes, ma'am, I do."

Still chuckling, she lifted her glass and tossed back the remainder of the amber liquid.

"Shall I pour you another?" Jack asked.

"Thank you, no. My doctor insists I limit myself to one a day. He's a fussy old woman, but he's kept me alive this long so I suppose I can't complain. Now, what do you want to know about Gina?"

Feeling as though he'd managed to negotiate a particularly dangerous minefield, Jack relaxed. "Whatever you feel comfortable sharing. Maybe you could start when she was a child. What kind of mischief did she get into?"

"Good heavens! What kind didn't she get into?" A fond smile lit the duchess's clouded blue eyes. "I remember one incident in particular. She couldn't have been more than seven or eight at the time. Maria had taken her and Sarah to the park. Gina wandered off and threw us all into a state of complete panic. The police were searching for her when she showed up several hours later with a lice-infested baglady in tow. She'd found the woman asleep under a bush and simply couldn't leave her on the cold, hard ground. I believe the woman stayed with us for almost a week before Gina was satisfied with the arrangements we worked out for her."

Charlotte's wry tale added another piece to the mosaic that was Gina St. Sebastian. Jack was trying to assemble the varied and very different sections into a coherent whole when the front door slammed.

"It's me, Grandmama. Is Jack here yet?"

The question was accompanied by the thud of something heavy hitting the table in the hall. Wincing, the duchess called out an answer.

"He is. We're in the salon."

With a kick in his pulse, Jack rose to greet her. His welcoming smile faltered and came close to falling off his face when she waltzed into the salon.

"Sorry I'm late."

"Eugenia!" the duchess gasped. "Your hair!"

"Pretty, isn't it?" Gina patted her ruler-straight, bright purple locks and shot her grandmother a mischievous grin. "We're doing a manga-themed birthday party tomorrow afternoon. I'm Yuu Nomiya."

"I don't have the faintest idea who manga or Yuu are, but I sincerely hope that color isn't permanent."

"It'll come out after a few washings." With that blithe assurance, she gave Jack an apologetic smile. "I'm sorry I kept you waiting. We haven't missed our dinner reservation, have we?"

"We've plenty of time." He struggled to keep his eyes on her face and off the neon purple framing it. "Would you like something to drink? I'm doing the honors."

"God, yes!"

She dropped onto the sofa in an untidy sprawl and caught the suddenly disapproving expressions on the two faces turned in her direction.

"What? Oh! I don't want anything alcoholic. Just tonic, with lots of ice."

Jack delivered the tonic and listened while Gina tried to explain the concept of Japanese manga comics to her grandmother. In the process, she devoured most of the contents of the appetizer tray.

To her credit, the duchess appeared genuinely curious about the phenomenon now taking the world by storm. Or perhaps she just displayed an interest for her granddaughter's sake. Whatever the reason, she asked a series of very intelligent questions. Gina answered them with enthusiasm…at first. Gradually, her answers grew shorter and more muddled. At the same time she slipped lower against the sofa cushions. When her lids drooped and she lost her train of thought in midsentence, the duchess sighed.

"Eugenia, my darling. You're exhausted. Go to bed."

The order fell on deaf ears. Her granddaughter was out like a light.

"I warned her," Charlotte said with affectionate exasperation. "The first few months especially sap a woman's strength."

"Dr. Martinson said the same thing."

"We'll have to forego dinner, Jack. She needs to rest."

"Of course."

When the duchess grasped her cane and aimed the tip at her sleeping granddaughter, he pushed out of his chair.

"Don't wake her."

Bending, he eased her into his arms. She muttered something unintelligible and snuggled against his chest. The scent and the feel of her tantalized Jack's senses. His throat tightening, he growled out a request for directions.

"Which way is her bedroom?"

Six

Gina was having the best dream. She was cradled in strong arms, held against a warm, hard chest. She felt so safe, so secure. So treasured. Like something precious and fragile, which even in her dream she knew she wasn't. Savoring the sensation of being sheltered and protected, she ignored a pesky pressure low in her belly and nuzzled her nose into something soft and squeezy.

The soft and squeezy, her hazy mind determined a moment later, was her pillow. And that irritating pressure was her bladder demanding relief. She pried up an eyelid and made out the dim outlines of her bedroom. The faint glow of the night-light always left on showed she was tucked under the satin throw she normally kept folded at the foot of the bed. She was also fully dressed.

Grunting, she got an elbow under her and sat up. Her slept-in clothes felt scratchy and twisted and tight. Long strands of purple hair fell across her eyes. She brushed them back and tossed aside the throw. Still groggy, she made her way to the bathroom. Once back in the bedroom she shed her clothes and slid into bed, between the sheets this time.

Sleep tugged at her. She drifted toward it on the vague

remnants of her dream. Those strong arms… That steady pulse of a heartbeat under her cheek…

"Jack?"

She sat up again, suddenly and fully awake, and flipped onto her other hip. The covers on the other side of the bed lay smooth and flat. Intense and totally absurd disappointment made her scrunch her face in disgust.

"Idiot! Like the man's going to crawl into bed with you? Right here, in the apartment? And Grandmama only a snore away?"

She flopped back down and yanked the sheet up to her chin. In almost the next breath, her disappointment took a sharp right turn into thigh-clenching need. The hunger shot straight from her breasts to her belly. From there it surged to every extremity, until even her fingernails itched with it.

She stared at the ceiling, her breath coming hot and fast. Images fast-forwarded in her mind. Jack leaning over her, his muscles slick and taunt. Jack laughing as she rolled him onto his back and straddled him. Jack's hands splayed on her naked hips and his jaw tight while he rose up to meet her downward thrust.

Oh, man! She should have expected this. One of the pamphlets Dr. Martinson had provided specifically addressed the issue of heightened sex drive during pregnancy. The rampaging hormones, the supersensitive breasts, the increased blood supply to the vulva— Taken together they could brew up a perfect storm of insatiable physical hunger.

Gina was there. Smack in the eye of the storm. She ached for Jack. She wanted him on her and in her and…

"Oh, for Pete's sake!"

Throwing off the sheet, she stalked to the antique dressing table with its tri-fold mirror, marble top and dozens of tiny drawers. She couldn't begin to count the number of hours she'd spent at this table. First as a youngster playing dress-up in Grandmama's pearls and Sarah's lacy peignoir. Then as a preteen, giggling with her girlfriends while they pirouetted in panties and training bras to show off their budding figures. After that came the high school years of mascara and eye shadow and love notes and trinkets from a steady stream of boys drooling over her nicely filled-out curves.

The notes and trinkets were long gone but her trusty vibrator was tucked in its usual drawer. She didn't have to resort to it often, but this…this gnawing hunger constituted a medical emergency.

So much of an emergency that the relief was almost instantaneous. And too damned short-lived! Gina tried to go from limp and languid into sleep. Jack kept getting in the way. Had he been bummed about dinner? Did he and Grandmama go without her? Would he try to see her again before he flew back to Washington?

She was forced to wait for the answers to those questions. With the manga birthday party set to kick off at 11:00 a.m., she had to leave for work before the duchess emerged from her bedroom. Maria came in at midmorning on Saturdays so Gina got no help from that quarter, either.

She toyed with the idea of calling Jack during the short subway ride to midtown, but all-too-vivid memories of last night's searing hunger kept her cell phone in her purse. The memories raised heat in her cheeks. She suspected that hearing his voice, all deep and rich, would produce even more graphic effects. She wasn't showing up for work with her nipples threatening to poke through bra and blouse.

That didn't stop said nipples from sitting up and taking notice, however, when Jack contacted her just after nine-thirty.

"How are you doing, sleepyhead?"

"Better this morning than last night." Jamming the phone between her chin and shoulder, she initialed the final seating plan and handed it to Kallie to add table numbers to name tags. "Sorry I zonked out on you."

"No problem. The duchess didn't want to leave you, so we ordered in."

"Corned beef on rye from Osterman's, right?"

"How did you know?"

"That's what we usually order in."

"We had a nice, long talk while we ate, by the way."

"Uh-oh! Did she leave any stones from my misspent youth unturned?"

"One or two. She said you'll have to turn over the rest yourself. She also said she was meeting with her opera club this evening. So that leaves just us. We can do a make-up dinner. Unless you have to work…"

He'd left her an easy out. It said much for Gina's state of mind that she didn't even consider taking it.

"I'm doing the party kickoff but Samuel's taking cleanup. I should be done here by three."

"I'll pick you up then."

"Kind of early for dinner," she commented.

"We'll find something to do."

His breezy confidence took a hit when she slid into the cab he drove up in. Groaning, she let her purpled head drop onto the seat back.

"Next time I tell you I'm helping with a birthday party for a slew of eight- and nine-year-olds, be kind. Just shoot me right between the eyes."

"That bad, huh?"

"Worse."

"Guess that means you're not up for a stroll down Fifth Avenue."

"Do I look like I'm up for a stroll?"

"Well…"

She angled her head and studied him through a thick screen of purple-tipped lashes. "You, bastard that you are, appear relaxed and refreshed and disgustingly up for anything."

Jack laughed and decided not to bore her with the details of his day, which had kicked off at 4:32 a.m. with a call from the State Department's twenty-four-hour crisis monitoring desk. They reported that an angry crowd had gathered at the U.S. Embassy in Islamabad, and a debate was raging within the department over whether to reinforce the marine guard by flying in a fleet antiterrorist security team. Thankfully, the crowd dispersed with no shots fired and no FAST team required, but Jack had spent the rest of the morning and early afternoon reading the message traffic and analyzing the flash points that had precipitated the seemingly spontaneous mob.

Although the crisis had been averted, Jack knew he should have jumped a shuttle and flown back to D.C. His decision to remain in New York another night had surprised him almost as it had his chief of staff, Dale Vickers.

Jack had first met Dale at Harvard, when they both were enrolled in the Kennedy School of Government. Like Jack, Dale had also gone into the Foreign Service and had spent almost a decade in the field as a Foreign Service Officer until increasingly severe bouts of asthma chained him to a desk at State Department headquarters. *Chained* being the operative word. Unmarried and fiercely dedicated, Vickers spent fourteen to sixteen hours a day, every day, at his desk.

Jack appreciated his second-in-command's devotion. He didn't appreciate the disdain that crept into Vickers's voice after learning his boss intended to stay another night in New York.

"We've kept your relationship with Ms. St. Sebastian out of the press so far, Ambassador. I'm not sure how much longer we can continue to do so."

"Don't worry about it. I don't."

"Easy for you to say," Dale sniffed, displaying the prissy side he didn't even suspect he possessed. "Media relations is my job."

"I repeat, don't worry about it. If and when the story breaks, Ms. St. Sebastian and I will handle it."

That was met with a short, charged silence. Jack had worked with Vickers long enough now to know there was more to come. It came slowly, with seeming reluctance.

"You might want to discuss the slant we should give Ms. Sebastian's pregnancy with your father, Ambassador. He expressed some rather strong views on the matter when he called here and I told him you were in New York."

"First," Jack said coldly, "I don't want you discussing my personal affairs with anyone, including my father. Second, there is no slant. Gina St. Sebastian is pregnant with my child. What happens next is our business. Not the media's. Not the State Department's. Not my father's. Not yours. Got that?"

"Yes, sir."

"Good. I'll let you know when I book the return shuttle to D.C."

Fragments of that conversation played in Jack's mind now as he studied the purple-tipped lashes framing Gina's eyes. When his gaze drifted from those purple tips to her hair, he found himself repressing an inner qualm at the prospect of bumping into some member of the paparazzi. Jack could only imagine his father's reaction to seeing Gina splashed across the tabloids in her manga persona.

John Harris II still mourned Catherine's death but in recent years he'd turned his energy to finding a suitable replacement. Preferably someone with his daughter-in-law's family wealth and political connections. He would accept an outsider if pushed to the edge. But Gina…?

"What are you thinking?" she asked, yanking Jack back to the present.

Everything fell away except the woman next to him. He relaxed into a lazy sprawl, his thighs and hips matched with hers. "I'm thinking I skipped lunch. How about you? Did you scarf down whatever you ordered up for that slew of eight-and nine-year-olds?"

"Puh-leez." Her shoulders quivered in an exaggerated shudder. "My system can only take so much sugar."

Her system, and her baby.

Only now did Gina appreciate the 180-degree turn her diet had taken. She'd cut out all forms of alcohol the moment she'd suspected she was pregnant. After her initial appointment with Dr. Martinson, she'd also cut out caffeine and started tossing down neonatal vitamins brimming with iron and folic acid. She hadn't experienced any middle-of-the-night cravings yet but suddenly, inexplicably, she had to have a foot-long smothered in sauerkraut.

"How does a picnic sound?" she asked. "One of my favorite street vendors works a corner close to Bryant Park. We could grab a couple of fat, juicy hot dogs and do some serious people watching."

"I'm game."

Bryant Park encapsulated everything Gina loved about New York. Located between 5th and 6th Avenues and bounded on the eastern side by the New York Public Library, it formed an island of leafy green amid an ocean of skyscrapers. On weekdays office workers crowded the park's benches or stretched out on the lawn during their lunch hours. If they had the time and the ambition, they could also sign up for a Ping-Pong game or backgammon or a chess match. Out-of-towners, too, were drawn to the park's gaily painted carousel, the free concerts, the movies under the stars and, glory of glory, the superclean public restrooms. Chattering in a dozen different languages, tourists wandered the glassed-in kiosks or collapsed at tables in the outdoor restaurant to take a breather from determined sightseeing.

This late in the afternoon Gina and Jack could have snagged a table at the Bryant Park Grill or the more informal café. She was a woman on a mission, however. Leaning forward, she instructed the cab driver to cruise a little way

past the park and kept her eyes peeled for an aluminum-sided
cart topped by a bright yellow umbrella.

"There he is. Pull over."

Mere moments later she and Jack carried their soft drinks
and foil-wrapped treasures into the park. Gina had ordered
hers doused with a double helping of sauerkraut. Jack had
gone the more conservative mustard-and-relish route. The
scent had her salivating until they snagged an empty bench.

"Oh, God," Gina moaned after the first bite. "This is almost better than sex."

Jack cocked a brow and paused with his dog halfway to
his mouth.

"I said 'almost.'"

If she'd had a grain of common sense, she would have
left it there. But, no. Like an idiot, she had to let her mouth
run away with her.

"Not that I've had anything to compare it to in the past
couple of months," she mumbled around another bite.

"We can fix that."

Jack tossed the words out so easily, so casually, that it
took a second or two for his meaning to register. When it
did, Gina choked on the bite she'd just taken.

"I've been doing my assigned reading," he said as he gave
her a helpful thump on the back. "*A Father's Guide to Pregnancy* says it's not uncommon for a woman's libido to shoot
into the stratosphere, particularly during the first trimester.
It also warned me not to feel inadequate if I don't satisfy
what could turn into an insatiable appetite."

He didn't look all that concerned about the possibility.
Just the opposite. The wicked glint in his brown eyes posi-
tively challenged Gina to give him a shot.

She wanted to. God, she wanted to! Just looking at his
beautiful mouth with a tiny smear of mustard at the corner made her ache to lean in and lick it off. She had to gulp
down a long slug of Sprite Zero to keep from giving in to
the impulse.

"I appreciate the offer," she said with what she hoped was a cheeky smile. "I'll keep it in mind if I run out of batteries."

"Ouch."

He put on a good show of being wounded, but when the laughter faded from his eyes she saw the utter seriousness in their depths.

"I know you want a relationship based on more than just sex, Gina. I'm hoping we can build that partnership."

"I know you are."

"We're not there yet," he admitted with brutal honesty, "but we're getting closer."

Ha! He could speak for himself. She was standing right on the edge, and every moment she spent with this man cut more ground from under her feet. All it would take was one gentle push. She'd fall for him so fast he wouldn't know what hit him.

Unfortunately, everything else would fall with her. Her fledgling career. Her self-respect. Her pride. She was just starting to feel good about herself. Just beginning to believe she could be the responsible parent she wanted so desperately to become.

Oh, hell! Who was she kidding? She would dump it all in a heartbeat if Jack loved her.

But he didn't. Yet.

So she wouldn't. Yet.

Consoled by the possibilities embedded in that little three-letter word, she tried to keep it light. "Too bad this isn't horseshoes. We would score points for close. Let's just…let's just press on the way we have been and hope for a ringer."

Stupid metaphor but the best she could come up with at the moment. Jack looked as if he wanted to say more but let it go. They sat knee-to-knee in the sunshine and devoured their hot dogs. Or more correctly, Gina devoured hers. Jack had set his on the unwrapped foil to pop the top of his soft drink. He took a long swig and rested the can on his knee while he watched two twentysomethings duking it out at the Ping-Pong table. The crack of their paddles smacking the ball formed a sharp counterpoint to the carousel's merry tune and the traffic humming along 6th Avenue.

"This is nice," Jack commented. "I don't get to just sit and bask in the sun much anymore."

"Uh-huh."

He stretched an arm along the back of the bench. "Did you come here often when you were growing up?"

"Yep."

Her abbreviated responses brought his gaze swinging back to her just in time to catch the covetous looks she was giving his not-yet-consumed weenie. She didn't bother to plead innocence.

"Are you going to eat that?"

"It's all yours. Or shall I go get you another one doused with sauerkraut?"

She gave the question serious consideration before shaking her head. "This will do me."

The remains disappeared in two bites. Semi-satisfied, Gina leaned against the bench and stretched out her legs. His arm formed a comfortable backrest as she replied to his earlier query.

"I couldn't even hazard a guess how many times I've been to Bryant Park. Maria used to bring Sarah and me to ride the merry-go-round or ice-skate on Citi Pond. Grandmama would come, too, after shopping on Fifth Avenue or to wait while we girls hit the library."

"Your grandmother's a remarkable woman."

"Yes, she is."

"Are she and Sarah the only family you have left?"

"There are some distant cousins in Slovenia. Or maybe it's Hungary. Or Austria. To tell the truth, I'm not real sure which countries got which parts of Karlenburgh after the duchy was broken up."

"Has Charlotte ever gone back?"

"No, never. She doesn't say so, but I know it would be too painful for her."

"What about you?" He toyed with the ends of her hair, still straight, still purple. "Have you ever visited your ancestral lands?"

"Not yet. I'd like to, though. One of these days…"

She could sit here for hours, she thought lazily. Listening to the crack of the Ping-Pong paddles, watching the tourists nose through the kiosks, nestling her head on the solid heat of Jack's arm. She didn't realize her eyelids had fluttered shut until his amused voice drifted down to her.

"You going to sleep on me again?"

"Maybe."

"Before you zone out completely, let's set a date for you to make a visit to D.C. My folks are anxious to meet you."

That woke her up. The little she knew about Jack's family suggested they probably wouldn't welcome her with open arms. Not his father, anyway. But she'd promised. Digging into her purse, she checked the calendar on her iPhone.

"I can't do next weekend. Does the second weekend in June work for you?"

"I'll make it work. Go back to sleep now."

Seven

Gina ended up making the jaunt down to Washington a week earlier than expected. Her change of plans kicked off the following Thursday morning with a summons to Samuel's office, where her boss relayed a request from the head office.

"Nicole just called. She needs you to fly down to D.C. You've got a reservation on the two-twenty shuttle."

"Today?"

"Yes, today. TTG's coordinating a black-tie reception and private, prerelease movie showing for two hundred tomorrow evening."

"And Elaine needs help?"

Elaine Patterson managed the TTG's Washington venue. Gina had met the trim, elegant brunette once when she'd flown to New York for a meeting with Samuel.

"Elaine's father had a heart attack. She's in Oregon and her assistant just checked into the ICU with a bad case of pancreatitis, whatever the hell that is. The rest of the staff is too junior to handle a function this large. Nicole wants you to take charge."

Samuel shoved a folder across his desk. "Here are faxed copies of the timetable, menu, floor plans, proposed setup, list of suppliers and contact phone numbers. I had them also email copies so you'll be able pull 'em on your iPad in case you need to make changes on the fly. You can stay in the venue's bridal suite. It's fully equipped and stocked."

"But…"

"I'll cover the consult you have scheduled for this afternoon."

"What about the Hanrahan retirement party on Saturday? I'm lead on that."

"I scanned the file. From the looks of the checklist, you've got everything in good shape. I'll take care of the last few prep tasks and get Kallie to pull floor duty with me."

Gina thought fast. She'd have to call Maria to see whether she could come in Sunday and check on Grandmama. If she could, Gina might extend her stay in D.C. for another day, possibly two.

The prospect of spending those days with Jack made her heart do its own version of a happy dance. She could feel it skittering and skipping as she let drop a casual comment.

"My calendar's pretty light on Monday. I don't have anything scheduled that can't be moved. I may take some comp time and stay over in Washington."

"Fine by me." He flapped a hand. "Just get your butt in gear."

She got her butt in gear!

A call made while the cab whisked her uptown confirmed Maria would be happy to check on *la duquesa* Sunday afternoon. When Gina dashed in and explained the arrangement, Grandmama issued an indignant protest.

"I'm neither crippled nor incapacitated, Eugenia. There's no need for Maria to come all the way in to check on me."

"She's not doing it for you, she's doing it for me."

"Really," the duchess huffed. "It's not necessary."

"I know. Just humor me, okay? The thing is, I may stay

over in D.C. a day or two. Jack wants me to meet his parents.
If they're available, I'll try to cram in a visit."

"Indeed?"

That bit of news stifled any further objections from her
grandmother. Her faded blue eyes lingered thoughtfully on
Gina's face for a moment before she commented dryly, "How
fortunate the purple washed out of your hair."

Extremely fortunate, Gina thought as she rushed into the
bedroom. She hurried out again after stuffing toiletries, a
sequined tuxedo jacket she appropriated from Sarah's closet,
black satin palazzo pants and some casual clothes into a
weekender.

"I'll call you," she promised, dropping a kiss on her
grandmother's cheek.

She hit the lobby and had Jerome flag her a cab to La-
Guardia. Collapsing in the backseat, she fished out her phone
and called Jack. His cell phone went to voice mail, so she
left a quick message. For added insurance, she called his
office and got shuffled to his chief of staff. Her nose wrin-
kling, she asked Vickers to advise his boss that she was flying down to Washington.

"Certainly, Ms. St. Sebastian."

He sounded a little more polite but about a mile and half
from friendly. Gina wanted to ask him what his problem was
but she suspected she already knew the answer.

She made her flight with all of five minutes to spare.
When the adrenaline rush subsided and the plane lifted off,
she rested her head against the seat back. The next thing she
knew, the flight attendant was announcing their imminent
arrival at Ronald Reagan National Airport. Gina blinked
the sleep out of her eyes and enjoyed her view through the
window of the capital's marble monuments.

The short nap left her energized and eager to plunge into
the task ahead. She wheeled her weekender through the airport with a spring in her step and exited into a beautiful June

day only slightly tainted by the exhaust pluming out of the cars and taxis and shuttles lined up outside the terminal.

Gina didn't have to dig deep to know why she was so jazzed. The idea that Nicole trusted her enough to step in at the last minute and take charge of a major event had given her self-confidence a shot in the arm.

Then there was the chance she might cram in some time with Jack. That possibility prodded her to whip out her cell phone and take it off airplane mode. The flashing icon indicating a text from Jack put a smile on her lips.

Just heard you're en route to D.C. Call when you arrive.

She crossed the street to the parking garage and aimed for the rental car area while she tried his private number. He answered on the second ring.

"You're here?"

The sound of his voice moved the smile from her lips to her heart. "I'm here. Just got in."

"This is a surprise. What brought you to D.C.?"

For once she managed to catch herself before blurting out the truth. He didn't need to know the possibility of spending some time with him was one of the reasons—the main reason—she'd jumped at this job.

"I'm a last-minute stand-in to coordinate an event tomorrow night."

"Which event?"

"A fancy-schmancy cocktail party and prerelease showing of the new action flick starring Dirk West."

Gina wasn't a real fan of the shoot-'em-up, blow-'em-up type movies West had been making for several decades but she knew every new release pulled in millions.

"The event's being hosted by Global Protective Services," she told Jack. "According to their company propaganda, they're—"

"One of the largest private security contractors in the

world," he interrupted. "They have more boots on the ground in Afghanistan right now than the U.S. military. Rumor is they put up most of the money for the movie. Probably because the script makes a very unsubtle case for decreasing the size of our standing armies and increasing the use of private mercenaries."

Holding the phone to her ear, Gina skimmed the Hertz reservation board to find the parking slot for the car Kallie said would be waiting for her.

"Sounds like this shindig would be right up your alley," she commented as she started down the long row of parked vehicles, "but I didn't see your name on the attendee list."

"That's because I declined the invitation. I might have to rethink that, though, if you're going to be working the event."

"Oh, sure," she said with a laugh. "Screw up the head count, why don't you?"

"I won't eat much," he promised solemnly.

"Well…" She found her car and tossed her briefcase onto the passenger seat. "I guess I can add you to the list."

"That takes care of tomorrow, then. What's on your agenda tonight?"

"I've got what's left of the TTG crew standing by." She slid into the driver's seat but waited to key the ignition. "We're going to go over the final task list and walk through the venue."

"How long will that take?"

"I have no idea."

She hesitated a moment before laying the possibility of an extended stay on him. Would she really be up to meeting his parents after working this event? Yes, dammit, she would.

"I told Samuel I might take a couple extra days in D.C. If it fits with your schedule and theirs, maybe we could work in a visit with your folks."

"We'll make it fit. I'll give them a call and arrange a time. Where are you staying?"

"At TTG's L'Enfant Plaza venue. We have a full bridal suite on the top floor."

"A bridal suite, huh?" His voice dropped to a slow, warm caress. "Want some company?"

God, yes! She gripped the phone, almost groaning at the idea of rolling around with Jack on the Tremayne Group's signature chocolate-brown sheets. Instant, erotic images of their bodies all sweaty and naked buzzed in her head like a swarm of pesky flies.

"Thanks for the offer," she said, making a valiant attempt to bat away the flies, "but I'd better pass."

Somewhat to her disappointment Jack didn't press the issue.

"You sure you can't sneak away for an hour or two and have dinner with me?" he asked instead.

Desire waged a fierce, no-holds-barred, free-for-all with duty. The old, fun-loving Gina would have yielded without a second thought. The new, still fun-loving but not quite as irresponsible Gina sighed.

"Sorry, Jack. I really need to spend this afternoon and evening prepping for the event."

He conceded with his usual easy charm. "I understand. I'll see you tomorrow."

Jack disconnected, swung his desk chair around and settled his gaze on the slice of Washington visible from his third-floor office. Since he held ambassadorial rank, he rated a full suite at the State Department's main headquarters on C Street.

The thirties-era building was originally designed to house the War Department, but the war planners outgrew it before it was completed. When they moved into the Pentagon in 1941, State inherited this massive structure constructed of buff-colored sandstone. It and its more modern annexes were located in the area of D.C. known as Foggy Bottom, so named because this section of the city was once a dismal, gray-misted swamp. Many of the talking heads who filled today's airwaves with their dubious wisdom liked to suggest the decisions coming out State were still pretty foggy and swampy.

The windows in Jack's office gave a narrow view down 21st Street to the National Mall, with the Lincoln Memorial at one end and the Washington Monument at the other. On good days he could almost catch the glitter of sunlight bouncing off the reflecting pool. The view didn't hold a particle of interest at the moment.

All his thoughts centered on Gina. The news that she was coming to Washington had proved the only bright spark in an otherwise grim morning spent reviewing casualty reports and incident analyses from twenty years of attacks on U.S. diplomatic outposts. Just the sound of her voice and merry laugh lightened his mood.

Thoughtfully, Jack tipped back his chair. Simply knowing that Gina was here, on his home turf, sparked a need that dug into him with sharp, fierce claws. Her image was etched in his mind. Those bright blue eyes. That luscious mouth. The tumble of white-blond curls.

The image shifted, and he pictured her manga'ed mane. God, what if she was still sporting that look? He could only imagine his father's reaction. The thought produced a wry grin as he swung his chair around and dialed his parents' number.

Jack brought his tux in to the office with him the next morning and changed before leaving work that evening. Anxious to see Gina, he arrived at L'Enfant Plaza early.

The plaza was named for Pierre Charles L'Enfant, the French-born architect recruited by General LaFayette to serve as an engineer with George Washington's Continental army. A long rectangle, the plaza was bordered on three sides by an amalgamation of office buildings, government agencies, retail shops and hotels. One of I. M. Pei's iconic glass pyramids dominated the center. A sister to the pyramid in front of the Louvre, it rose from a lower level with gleaming majesty.

The spot was a good choice for evening events. Foot and vehicle traffic died out when the surrounding offices emptied, leaving plenty of underground parking for guests. Or they could hop off the Metro and let the escalators whisk them up to the plaza. Jack had opted for plan B and emerged from the Metro's subterranean levels into a balmy June evening. Tiny white lights illuminated the trees lining two sides of the plaza. Centered between those sparkling rows, the lighted pyramid formed a dramatic backdrop for lavishly filled buffet tables and strategically placed carving stations.

Two dozen or so other early arrivals grazed the tables or clumped together in small groups with drinks in hand. Jack took advantage of the sparse crowd and lack of lines to hit one of the S-shaped bars set up close to the pyramid. He kept an eye out for Gina as he crossed the plaza but didn't spot either her blond curls or a waterfall of purple. Nor did he find a bartender behind the ebony-and-glass counter. He angled around to check the other bars and saw an attendant at only one. Flipping and tipping bottles, the harried attendant splashed booze and mixers into an array of glasses and shoved them at the tuxedoed waitstaff standing in line at his station.

The fact that three of the four bars weren't ready for action surprised Jack until he spotted Gina, a male in a white shirt and black vest and a plump female with a radio clipped to her waist hurrying out onto the plaza. The man peeled off in the direction of one unattended bar, the woman aimed for another. Gina herself edged behind the ebony S where Jack stood.

"Shorthanded?" he asked as she whipped bottles of champagne out of a refrigerated case and lined them up on the bar.

She rolled her eyes. "Just a tad."

When she started to attack the foil caps, he moved behind the bar to help. She flashed him a grateful look and set him to popping corks while she extracted champagne flutes from a rack beneath the counter.

"I should be in the media center making a last check of the seating," she told him, "but I've been on the phone with the bar subcontractor for twenty friggin' minutes. He's supposed to be sending replacements for their no-shows. You can bet this is the last time the jerk will do business with TTG."

The fire in her eyes told Jack that was a safe bet.

"Keep your fingers crossed the replacements get here before the real hordes descend," she muttered as she began pouring champagne into the tall crystal flutes.

He nodded toward the crowd emerging from the bank of elevators. "I think they're descending."

"Crap." She slapped the filled flutes onto a tray and hooked a finger at one of the waitstaff. "You're over twenty-one, right?"

"Right."

"Take this and start circulating."

"I'm a food server," he protested.

"Not for the next half hour, you're not. Take it! I've cleared it with your boss."

Champagne sloshing, she thrust the tray at him and reached under the counter for more flutes.

"Good thing the subcontractors aren't union," she said fervently. "My ass would be grass if I got TTG crosswise of the culinary workers and bartenders local."

Jack eyed the racks of glasses, bottles and nozzles behind the counter. Everything appeared to be clearly labeled.

"I've fixed a few martinis and Manhattans in my time. I'll pull bar duty until your replacements arrive. You go do your thing in the media center."

"No way! I can't let you sling booze. You're a guest."

"I won't tell if you don't. Go. I've got this."

Jack had no trouble interpreting the emotions that flashed across her expressive face. He could tell the instant the idea of John Harris Mason III dishing up drinks at Global Protective Service's big bash struck her as too irresistible to pass up.

"All right," she conceded, laughter sparkling in her eyes. "But let's hope Nicole doesn't hear about this. My ass won't just be grass. It'll be mowed and mulched."

"And it's such a nice ass." He couldn't help it. He had to reach behind her and caress the body part under discussion. "Trust me, sweetheart, I won't let anyone mow or mulch it."

She backed away and tried to look stern, but the light still danced in her eyes. "I can't believe you just did that."

Jack couldn't believe it, either. He'd do it again, though, in a heartbeat. Or better yet, drag her upstairs to that bridal suite she'd mentioned and caress a whole lot more than her ass. Sanity intruded in the form of the gray-haired senior senator from Virginia.

Thomas Dillon broke away from the group he was with and strolled over to the bar. "Jack?"

The senator looked from him to Gina and back again. Clearly he didn't understand what an ambassador-at-large was doing behind the drinks counter, but he contained his confusion behind a broad smile.

"I thought I recognized you, son. How's your father?"

"He's still kicking butt and taking names, Senator. What can I get you to drink?"

"Pardon me?"

"I'm pulling special duty tonight. What would you like?"

Despite the near-disastrous start, the remainder of the event went off without a hitch. Most of the invitees were jaded Washingtonians who had attended too many black-tie functions to do more than guzzle down the free booze and food, but Jack heard more than one guest comment on the quality of both.

His replacement arrived before he'd had to mix up more than a dozen drinks. He surrendered his post with some reluctance and mingled with the other guests. Jaded they might be, but the arrival of the movie's star started a low buzz. Gina had returned to the plaza and stood next to Jack while Dirk West graciously made the rounds.

"Wow," she murmured, eyeing his shaved head and six-feet-plus of tuxedo-covered muscle. "He looks tougher in real life than he does on the screen."

Tough, and extremely savvy. West worked the crowd like a pro and seemed to sense instinctively the real power brokers and potential backers. He might have been aided in that by the CEO of Global Protective Services, who stuck to the star's side like a barnacle and made a point of steering him over to Jack.

"This is Ambassador John Harris Mason," he said by way of introduction. "He's the man who faced down a cell of armed insurgents in Mali a few years ago."

"I read about that." West crunched Jack's hand in his. "Sounded like a pretty hairy situation. I might have to send a script writer to ferret out the details that didn't get into print."

Jack could have told him not to bother since most of the details were still classified but West had already turned his attention to Gina.

"And who's this?"

The bronze-edged name tag pinned to her lapel should have given him a clue. He ignored it, concentrating all his star power on her face.

"Gina St. Sebastian." She held out her hand and had it enfolded. "I'm with the Tremayne Group. We're coordinating this event."

West's appreciative gaze made a quick trip south, edged back up. "You ever considered taking a shot at acting, Ms. St. Sebastian?"

"I've toyed with the idea once or twice."

"If you decide to do more than toy, you give me a call."

Global's CEO was more interested in Jack's connections

at the State Department than the acting aspirations of the hired hands.

"I hear you've got a meeting with the Senate Intelligence Committee next week regarding embassy security, Ambassador. I've got some ideas in that regard."

"I'm sure you do."

"I'd like to discuss them with you. I'll have my people call and set up an appointment."

His mission accomplished, he steered West to the next group. Jack waited until they were out of earshot to fill Gina in on his conversation with his parents.

"I got ahold of my folks. They're anxious to meet you, but mother's chairing a charity auction tomorrow evening so I told them we'd drive down for Sunday brunch."

"Sunday brunch works for me."

"Good. That leaves tomorrow for just you and me."

She started to comment, but spotted the plump brunette with the radio clipped to her waist signaling from across the plaza.

"Gotta go. It's almost showtime."

She turned, spun back and flashed one of her megawatt smiles.

"Thanks for helping out earlier. Remind me to pay you for services rendered."

"I will," he murmured to her retreating back. "I most certainly will."

Jack carried fantasies of the various forms that payment might take with him into the plush media hall. They teased his thoughts all through Dirk West's explosive attempts to single-handedly save the world from evil. But not even his wildest imaginings could compete with reality when a tired but triumphant Gina invited him up to the bridal suite several hours later.

<u>Eight</u>

Gina had tried to convince Jack he didn't need to hang around while she signed off on the final tally sheets and supervised the breakdown. She'd honestly tried. Yet she couldn't suppress a little thrill of pleasure when he insisted on waiting for her to finish up.

So she'd extended the invitation to join her upstairs. When they entered the lushly appointed suite, though, all she wanted to do was plop down on the sofa, kick off her shoes and plunk her feet on the coffee table. Which was exactly what she did. And all she would have done if Jack hadn't plopped down beside her!

"That's some view," he commented lazily, his eyes on the dramatic vista of the floodlit capital dome framed by the suite's windows.

"Mmm."

She only half heard him. Her mind was still decompressing after the pressure-packed night. He responded by tugging loose his bow tie and popping the top button of his dress shirt before patting his lap.

"Here."

She blinked, suddenly very much in the present. She didn't trust either his simple gesture or her body's instant response to it. He read the sudden wariness in her face and patted his thighs again.

"I've been told I give a pretty good foot massage. Swing your feet up and see if you agree."

Oooooh, yeah! Gina most definitely agreed. Ten seconds after he went to work on her toes and arch, she was approaching nirvana. Groaning with pleasure, she wedged deeper into the corner of the sofa.

"If you ever decide to give up ambassadoring, you could make a bundle plying the foot trade."

"I'll keep that in mind."

Curious, she eyed him through the screen of her lashes. "What *are* you going to do when you give up ambassadoring?"

"Good question."

His clever, clever fingers worked magic on the balls of her right foot before moving to the left.

"What about those PACs I read about?" she asked. "The ones that think you've got the makings of a future president?"

"*Future* being the operative word. There are a few steps I'd have to take in between."

"Such as?"

"Running for public office, to start with. I've been just a career bureaucrat up to this point."

"Su-u-ure you have. I wonder how many career bureaucrats go toe-to-toe with armed terrorists."

"Too many, unfortunately. Still, elected office is almost a required stepping stone to anything higher. Except for the war heroes like Washington and Eisenhower, almost all of our presidents served as either governors or members of Congress."

"So run for governor. Or Congress. You'd make a great senator or representative. More to the point, someone's got to get in there and straighten out that mess."

"Am I hearing right?" Ginning, he pulled on her toes.

"This enthusiastic endorsement can't be coming from the same woman who's called me obnoxious and uptight and a few other adjectives I won't repeat."

"You are obnoxious and uptight at times. Other times…" She circled a hand in the air, trying to pluck out one or two of his less irritating traits. "Other times you surprise me, Mr. Ambassador. Like tonight, for instance, when you got behind the bar. You went above and beyond the call of duty there."

"I'm a man of many talents," he said smugly. "And that reminds me. I was promised payment for services rendered."

"So you were. Have you given any thought to what form that payment should take?"

"Oh, sweetheart, I haven't thought of anything else all evening."

Red flags went up instantly. Gina knew she was playing with fire. Knew the last thing she should do was slide her feet off his lap and curl them under her, rising to her knees in the process.

All she had to do was look at him. The tanned skin, the white squint lines at the corners of his eyes, the square chin and the strong, sure column of his throat. Like a vampire hit with a ravenous hunger, her weariness disappeared in a red flash. She had to taste him. Had to lean forward and press her mouth to the warm skin in the V of his shirt. Had to nip the tendons in his neck, the prickly underside of his chin, the corner of his mouth.

And of course, he had to turn his head and capture her lips with his. There was nothing gentle about the kiss. Nothing tentative. It went from zero to white-hot in less than a heartbeat. Mouths, teeth, tongues all engaged. Hips shifted. Hands fumbled. Muscles went tight.

Jack moved then, tipping her back onto the cushions. He came down with her, one leg between hers, one hand brushing her hair off her face. Careful not to put all his weight on her middle but taut and coiled and hungry.

She could feel him get hard against her hip. The sensation shot a hot, fierce rush through her veins. Shoving his jacket lapels aside, she tugged his starched shirt free of the satin cummerbund and tore at the buttons. When she got to the shoulder muscle underneath, she ran her palm over the smooth curve, then felt it bunch under her fingers as Jack's hand went to her waist. The two buttons on her borrowed sequin jacket proved a flimsy barrier. Jack peeled back the lapels and came to a dead stop. Every muscle and tendon in his body seemed to freeze.

"God."

It was half prayer, half groan. His brown eyes hot with desire, he brushed a finger along the lace trimming her demi-bra.

"Good thing I didn't know this was all you had on under those sequins. It was hard enough making it through the movie."

Gina tucked her chin and surveyed her chest with something less than enthusiasm. The underwired half cup of black silk and lace mounded her breasts almost obscenely.

"I've gone up another whole size," she muttered in disgust. "I had to buy all new bras."

Jack picked up on her tone and wisely didn't comment. Good thing, because she probably wouldn't have heard him. All it took was one brush of his thumb over her sensitized nipple and she was arching her back. And when he tugged down the lace and caught the aching tip between his teeth, every part of her screamed with instant, erotic delight.

She arched again, and he took what she offered. His hands and mouth and tongue drove her higher and higher. The knee he wedged between her thighs and pressed against her center almost sent her over the edge.

"Wait!" Gasping, she wiggled away from the tormenting knee. "Wait, Jack!"

He raised his head, a shudder rippling across his face. Disgust followed a moment later.

"Sorry. That was a little more than you probably expected to pay for my bartending services."

When he started to sit up, Gina grabbed his lapels and kept him in place. "Hold on, Ambassador. That little tussle doesn't even constitute minimum wage. I just…I just thought we should shed a few more layers."

Jack stared down at her, eyes narrowed. He knew as well as she did they wouldn't stop at a few layers. He was damned if he'd give her a chance to change her mind, though. Getting the stubborn Gina St. Sebastian into bed ranked almost as high up there as getting her to the altar.

"Shedding is good," he said with a crooked grin that masked his sudden iron determination. "I'll start."

His tux jacket hit the floor. The cummerbund and shirt followed a moment later. He held out a hand and helped her to her feet, taking intense satisfaction from the play of her greedy hands over his bare chest.

Once he'd disposed of the sequined jacket, he helped her shimmy out of her black satin pants. His self-control took a severe hit when he got a look at the hipsters that matched her black lace bra. They dipped to a low V on her still-flat belly and barely covered her bottom cheeks.

He cupped his hand over those sweet, tantalizing curves and brought her against him. He saw her eyes flare when she felt him against her hip, rock-hard and rampant. Her head tipped. Red singed her cheeks.

"Okay," she exhaled in a low, choked voice. "I really, really need to make payment in full. But the two of us going to bed together doesn't change anything."

The hell it didn't.

Jack kept that thought to himself as he scooped her into his arms and strode toward the bedroom.

The Tremayne Group had done their guest suite up right. A king-size bed sat on a raised dais, its chocolate-brown comforter draping almost to the floor. Mounds of brown, aqua and silver-trimmed pillows piled high against the padded headboard. Floor lamps gave the corners of the room a subdued glow, while a crystal dish filled with creamy wax pebbles emitted a faint scent of vanilla.

Jack absorbed the details with the situational awareness that was as much instinct as training. That alertness had kept him alive in Mali and served him well in so many other tense situations. But it shut down completely when he stretched Gina out on the soft, fluffy ocean of brown. Her hair spilled across the comforter in a river of pale gold. Her eyes were hot blue and heavy. Her long, lush body drove every thought from his mind but one.

Aching for her, he yanked down the zipper of his pleated black slacks. He discarded them along with his socks and jockey shorts, joined her on the bed and ran his hand over the flat planes of her belly.

"You are so incredibly gorgeous."

Her stomach hollowed under his palm even as she gave a breathless, delighted chuckle.

"Flattery will get you everywhere, Ambassador."

He slid his hand under the lace panties and found the wet heat at her center. Her head went back. Her lips parted. As Jack leaned down to cover her mouth with his, he realized he didn't want to be anywhere but here, with this woman, tasting her, touching her, loving her.

He was rougher than he'd intended when he stripped off her underwear. More urgent than he ever remembered being when he pried her knees apart and positioned himself between her thighs. And when she hooked her calves around his and canted her hips to fit his, he lost it.

Driven by a need that would shock the hell out of him when he analyzed it later, he thrust into her. It was a primal urge. An atavistic instinct to claim his mate. To brand her as his. Leave his scent on her. Plant his seed in her belly.

Except he'd already done that.

The thought fought its way through the red haze of Jack's

mind. He went stiff, his member buried in the hot satin that was Gina. Hell! What kind of an animal was he? He levered up on his elbows, blinking away the sexual mists that clouded his vision. When they cleared, he saw Gina glaring up at him.

"What?" she demanded.

"I didn't mean to be so rough. The baby…"

"Is fine! I, however, am not."

To emphasize her point, she hooked her calves higher on his and clenched her vaginal muscles. Jack got the message. Hard not to, since it damned near blew off the top of his head. He slammed his hips into hers again. And again. And again.

They could only spend so many hours in bed. Theoretically, anyway. Jack would have kept Gina there all day Saturday but even he had to come up for air. Since they wouldn't drive down to his parents' house in Richmond until the following day, he offered to show her his favorite spots in D.C. She approved the proposed agenda, with two quick amendments.

"I'd like to see where you live. And where you work."

Jack had no problem with either. Gina had packed clothes for the weekend but he had to get rid of his tux before he could appear in public again. That naturally lent itself to a first stop at his town house.

It was classic Georgetown. Three narrow stories, all brick. Black shutters. Solid brass door knocker in the shape of a horse's head. Gina's nose wrinkled when Jack mentioned that the detached garage at the back had once been slave quarters, but she was gracious enough to acknowledge he'd taken occupancy of the ivy-covered premises long after those tragic days.

The framed photo of Catherine still occupying a place of honor on the entryway table gave her pause, though. Almost as much as it gave Jack. He stood next to Gina as she gazed at the black-and-white photo.

It was one of his favorite shots. He'd taken it after losing yet another tennis match to his hypercompetitive wife. She laughed at the camera, her racquet resting on her shoulder. Her dark hair was caught back in a ponytail. A sweatband circled her forehead. All her energy, all her pulsing life, shone in her eyes.

"I bet she kept you jumping," Gina murmured.

"She did."

Almost too much.

The thought darted into Jack's mind before he could block it. That energy, that formidable legal mind, the all-consuming passion for politics. He'd had to march double time to keep up with her. More than once he'd wished she'd just relax and drift for a while.

The thought generated a sharp jab of guilt. Jack had to work to shrug it off as he left Gina to explore the town house's main floor and went upstairs to change. He came back down a half hour later, showered and shaved and feeling comfortable in jeans and his favorite University of Virginia crewneck.

"You sure you want to swing by my office? There's not a whole lot to see but we can make a quick visit if you want."

Gina forced a smile. The pictures of his wife scattered around the town house had gotten to her more than she would admit. She'd spotted several shots of Catherine alone. Several more of Catherine with Jack. The perfect marriage of smarts and ambition.

And here Gina was, trying desperately to anchor herself after years of flitting from job to job, man to man. Her life to this point seemed so frivolous, so self-centered. How could Jack have any respect for her?

She buried her crushing doubts behind a bright smile. "I've never been to the State Department. I'd like to see it."

"Okay, but don't say I didn't warn you."

Gina took Jack's disclaimer with a grain of salt. It should have been a teaspoon, she decided when he escorted her through State's echoing marble halls and into his impressive suite of offices.

The first thing she noticed was the view from the windows of the outer office. It cut straight down 21st Street to the Lincoln Memorial Reflecting Pool and presented a narrow, if spectacular, slice of Washington.

The second item that caught her attention was the individual in jeans, a button-down yellow shirt and round eyeglasses hunched over a computer. She shouldn't have been surprised that Jack's people were dedicated enough to come in on weekends. And when he introduced her to his chief of staff, she tried hard to bury her antipathy behind a friendly smile.

"I'm glad to finally meet you, Dale."

That was true enough. She'd been curious about this man. More than curious. She wasn't usually into stereotypes, but her first glimpse of Dale Vickers pegged him immediately as a very short, very insecure male suffering from a rampaging Napoleon complex. He kept his desk between him and his boss. Also between him and Gina. She had to reach across it to shake his hand. He acknowledged her greeting with a condescending nod and turned to his boss.

"I didn't know you were coming in this morning."

What a prick! Gina couldn't see why Jack put up with him until she spotted the framed 4x6 snapshot on the man's workstation. Catherine *and* Jack *and* Dale Vickers with their arms looped over each other's shoulders. All smiling. All wearing crimson sweatshirts emblazoned with the Harvard logo.

Images of Catherine Mason hovered at the back of Gina's mind for the rest of the day. She managed to suppress them while Jack gave her a private tour of the State Department's hallowed halls. Ditto when they took advantage of the glorious June afternoon to stroll the banks of the Potomac and cheer the scullers pushing against the vicious current.

After browsing the upscale shops in Georgetown Mall,

Jack took Gina to his favorite Thai restaurant later that evening. The owner greeted him with a delighted hand pump.

"Mr. Ambassador! Long time since we see you."

"Too long, Mr. Preecha."

The slender Asian whipped around, checked his tables and beamed. "You want by the window, yes? You and...?"

He made a heroic effort to conceal his curiosity when Jack introduced Gina. She felt it, though, and as soon as they were seated and their drink order taken, the question tumbled out.

"Did you and Catherine come here often?"

"Not often. We'd only lived in D.C. four or five months before she died. Do you like shumai? They serve them here with steamed rice and a peanut ginger sauce that'll make you swear you were in Bangkok."

The change of subject was too deliberate to ignore. Gina followed the lead.

"Since I have no idea what shumai are and have never been to Bangkok, I'll take your word on both."

Shumai turned out to be an assortment of steamed dumplings filled with diced pork, chicken or shrimp. She followed Jack's lead and dipped each morsel in ginger or soy sauce before gobbling it down. Between the dumplings, steamed rice, golden fried tofu triangles, some kind of root vegetable Gina couldn't begin to pronounce and endless cups of tea, she rolled out of the restaurant feeling like a python just fed its monthly meal. Too stuffed for any more wandering through Georgetown. Almost too stuffed for sex. When she tried to convince Jack of that sad state of affairs, though, he just laughed and promised to do all the work.

He followed through on his promise. The chocolate-brown sheets were a tangled mess and Gina was boneless with pleasure when he finally collapsed beside her.

For the second night in a row she fell asleep in his arms. And for the second morning in a row, she greeted the day cradled in the same warm cocoon.

She came awake slowly, breathing in Jack's scent, twitching her nose when his springy chest hair tickled her nose. It felt right to cuddle against his side. Safe and warm and right.

Slowly, without Gina willing them, the images she'd glimpsed of Jack's wife yesterday took form and shape in her mind. For an uneasy moment, she almost sensed Catherine's presence. Not hostile, not heartbroken at seeing her husband in bed with another woman, but not real happy, either.

"We'd better get up and get moving."

Jack's voice rumbled up from the chest wall her ear was pressed against. "Sunday brunch is a long-standing family tradition," he warned, stroking her hair with a lazy touch. "Hopefully, it'll just be us and my parents today but you should be prepared for the worst."

"Great! Now he tells me."

She could do this, Gina told herself as she showered and blow-dried her hair and did her makeup. She could run the gauntlet of Jack's family, all of whom had known and no doubt adored his wife. She wasn't looking forward to it, though.

And damned if she couldn't almost hear Catherine snickering in the steamy air of the bathroom.

Nine

Light Sunday–morning traffic was one of the few joys of driving in Washington. Jack's Range Rover whizzed through near deserted streets and crossed the 14th Street Bridge. The Jefferson Memorial rose in graceful symmetry on the D.C. side of the bridge. The gray granite bulk of the Pentagon dominated the Virginia side. From there they shot south on 395.

Once south of the Beltway, though, Jack exited the interstate and opted instead to drive a stretch of the old U.S. Highway 1. Gina understood why when he pulled into the parking lot of the Gas Pump Café just outside Woodbridge.

"We won't sit down for brunch until one or two. And this place," he said with a sweeping gesture toward the tin-roofed cafe, "serves the best biscuits and gravy this side of the Mason-Dixon line."

Gina hid her doubts as she eyed the ramshackle structure. It boasted a rusting, thirties-era gas pump out front. Equally rusty signs covered every square inch of the front of the building. The colorful barrage advertised everything from Nehi grape soda to Red Coon chewing tobacco to Gargoyle motor oil. The scents of sizzling bacon and smoked sausage that emanated from the café, though, banished any doubts the place would live up to Jack's hype.

It didn't occur to Gina that he'd made the stop for her sake until they were seated at one of the wooden picnic tables. He obviously didn't consider the slice of toast and half glass of orange juice she'd downed while getting dressed adequate sustenance for mother and child. She agreed but limited her intake to one biscuit smothered in gravy, two eggs, a slab of sugar-cured ham and another glass of juice. Since it was just a little past nine when they rolled out of the café, Gina felt confident she would be able to do justice to brunch at one or two o'clock.

She also felt a lot more confident about meeting Jack's family. Strapped into the Range Rover's bucket seat, she patted her tummy. "Hope you enjoyed that, baby. I sure did."

Jack followed the gesture and smiled. "Have you started thinking about names?"

She didn't hesitate. "Charlotte, if it's a girl."

"What if it's a boy?"

She slanted him a sideways glance. He'd left his window cracked to allow in the warm June morning. The breeze lifted the ends of his dark gold hair and rippled the collar of his pale blue Oxford shirt. He'd rolled the cuffs up on his forearms and they, too, glinted with a sprinkling of gold.

She guessed what was behind his too-casual question. If Jack won his on-going marriage campaign, he no doubt envisioned hanging a numeral after his son's name. John Harris Mason IV. Not for the first time, Gina wondered if she was being a total bitch for putting her needs before Jack's. Why did she have to prove that she could stand on her own two feet, anyway? This handsome, sophisticated, wealthy man wanted to take care of her and the baby. Why not let him?

She sighed, acknowledging the answers almost before she'd formulated the questions. She would hate herself for giving up now. That had been her modus operandi her entire adult life. Whenever she got bored or developed a taste for something new, she would indulge the whim.

But she couldn't quit being a mother. Nor did she want to give up a job she'd discovered she was good at. Really good. Then again, who said she had to quit? The Tremayne Group's Washington venue had plenty of business.

All of which was just a smoke screen. The sticking point—the real, honest-to-goodness sticking point—was that Jack didn't love her. He'd been completely honest about that. Although…the past two nights had made Gina begin to wonder if what they did feel for each other might be enough. Uneasy with that thought, she dodged the issue of boys' names.

"I haven't gotten that far," she said lightly. "Tell me about your parents. Where they met, how long they've been married, what they like to do."

Jack filled the rest of the trip with a light-handed sketch of a family steeped in tradition and dedicated to serving others. His mother had been as active in volunteerism over the years as his father had in his work for a series of presidents.

Gina might have been just the tiniest bit intimidated if she hadn't grown up on stories of the literary and social giants Grandmama had hobnobbed with in her heyday. Then, of course, there was her title. Lady Eugenia Amalia Thérése St. Sebastian, granddaughter to the last Duchess of Karlenburgh. That and five bucks might get her a cup of coffee at Starbucks but it still seemed to impress some people. Hopefully, she wouldn't have to resort to such obvious measures to impress Jack's folks.

She didn't. Fifteen minutes after meeting John II, Gina knew no title would dent the man's rigid sense of propriety. He did not approve of her refusal to marry his only son and give his grandson the Mason name.

"Now, John," his wife admonished gently. She was a soft-spoken Southern belle with a core of tempered steel beneath her Donna Karan slacks and jewel-toned Versace tunic. "That's a matter for Gina and Jack to decide."

"I disagree."

"So noted," Ellen Mason said dryly. "Would you care for more iced tea, Gina?"

There were only the four of them, thank goodness. They were sitting in a glass-enclosed solarium with fans turning overhead. A glorious sweep of green lawn shaded by the monster oaks that gave the place its name filled the windows. The Masons' white-pillared, three-story home had once been the heart of a thriving tobacco plantation. The outlying acres had been sold off over the decades, but the current owner of Five Oaks had his lord-of-the-manner air down pat.

"I'd better not," Gina replied in response to Ellen's question. "I'm trying to cut out caffeine. Water with lemon would be great."

Jack's mother tipped ice water from a frosted carafe and used silver tongs to spear a lemon wedge. "We didn't worry about caffeine all those years ago when I was pregnant. That might explain some of my son's inexhaustible energy."

Her guest kept a straight face, but it took some doing. Ellen's son was inexhaustible, all right. Gina had the whisker burns on her thighs to prove it.

"I know you must have questions about this side of your baby's family tree," the older woman was saying with a smile in her warm brown eyes. "We have a portrait gallery in the upper hall. Shall I give you a tour while Jack and his father catch up on the latest political gossip?"

"I'd love that."

The duchess had taken Gina and Sarah to all the great museums, both at home and abroad. The Louvre. The Uffizi. The Hermitage. The National Gallery of Art in Washington. As a result Sarah had developed both an interest in and an appreciation for all forms of art. Gina's knowledge wasn't anywhere near as refined but she recognized the touch of a master when she saw it. None of the portraits hanging in the oak-paneled upstairs hall had that feel. Still, the collection offered a truly fascinating glimpse of costumes and hairstyles from the 17th century right down to the present.

Gina paused before the oil of Jack's grandfather. He wore the full dress uniform of an army colonel, complete with gold shoulder epaulets and saber. "My grandmother knew him," she told Ellen. "She said he and your mother-in-law attended a reception she once gave for some sultan or another."

"I've read about your grandmother," her hostess commented as they moved to the next portrait, this one of Ellen and her husband in elegant formal dress. "She sounds like an extraordinary woman."

"She is." Lips pursed, Gina surveyed the empty space at the end of the row. "No portrait of Jack and Catherine?"

"No, unfortunately. We could never get them to sit still long enough for a formal portrait. And..." She stopped, drew in a breath. "And of course, we all thought there was plenty of time."

She turned and held out both hands. Gina placed hers in the soft, firm fold.

"That's why I wanted this moment alone with you, dear. Life is so short, and so full of uncertainties. I admire you for doing what your heart tells you is right. Don't let Jack or his father or anyone else bully you into doing otherwise."

The brief interlude with Ellen made her husband a little easier to bear. John II didn't alter his attitude of stiff disapproval toward Gina but there was no disguising his deep affection for his son. He not only loved Jack. He was also inordinately proud of his son's accomplishments to date.

"Did he tell you he's the youngest man ever appointed as an ambassador-at-large?" he asked during a leisurely brunch that included twice-baked cheese grits, green beans almondine and the most delicious crab cakes Gina had ever sampled.

"No, he didn't," she replied, silently wishing she could

sop up the béchamel sauce from the crab cakes with the crust of her flaky croissant.

"Then he probably also didn't tell you some very powerful PACs have been suggesting he run for the U.S. Senate as a first step toward the White House."

"Dad…"

"Actually," Gina interrupted, "I read about that. I know those PACs love Jack. And he and I talked about his running for office the other night."

John II paused with his knife and fork poised above his food. "You did?"

"Yep. I told him he should go for it."

"Dad…"

Once again the father ignored the son's low warning. His lip curled, and a heavy sarcasm colored his voice. "I'm sure our conservative base will turn out by the thousands to support a candidate with an illegitimate child."

"That's enough!"

Jack shoved away from the table and tossed down his napkin. Anger radiated from him in waves. "We agreed not to discuss this, Dad. If you can't stick to the agreement, Gina and I will leave now."

"I'm sorry." The apology was stiff but it was an apology. "Sit down, son. Please, sit down."

Ellen interceded, as Gina suspected she had countless times in the past. "Jack, why don't you take our guest for a stroll in the rose garden while I clear the table and bring in dessert?"

Gina jumped up, eager for something to do. "Please, let me help."

"Thank you, dear."

A decadent praline cheesecake smoothed things over. Everyone got back to being polite and civilized, and Ellen deftly steered the conversation in less sensitive channels.

Gina thought they might make it through the rest of the

visit with no further fireworks. She nursed that futile hope right up until moments before she and Jack left to drive back to Washington. At his mother's request, he accompanied her into her study to pick up a flyer about an organization offering aid to abused children overseas she wanted him to look at.

That left Gina and John II standing side by side in the foyer for a few moments. An uncomfortable silence stretched between them, broken when he made an abrupt announcement.

"I had you investigated."

"What?"

"I hired a private investigator."

Gina's brows snapped together, and her chin tipped in a way that anyone familiar with the duchess would have recognized immediately as a warning signal.

"Did you?"

"I wanted him to chase down rumors about the other men you might have been involved with."

Her hand fluttered to her stomach in a protective gesture as old as time. "The other men I might have screwed, you mean."

He blinked at the blunt reply, but made no apology. "Yes."

The thought of a private investigator talking to her friends, asking questions, dropping insinuations, fired twin bolts of anger and mortification. Gina's chin came up another inch. Her eyes flashed dangerously.

"Why go to the expense of a private investigator? A simple DNA test would have been much cheaper."

"You were in that clinic in Switzerland. Jack flew over right after you called him. I told him to insist on a paternity test, but…" He broke off, grimacing. "Well, no need to go into all that now. What I want to say is I accept that you're carrying my grandchild."

"How very magnanimous of you."

The icy response took him aback. He looked as though

he wanted to say more, but the sound of footsteps stilled him. Both Jack and his mother sensed the tension instantly. Ellen sighed and shook her head. Her son demanded an explanation.

"What's wrong?"

"Nothing," Gina said before his father could respond. "Nothing at all. Thank you for a lovely lunch, Ellen."

She kissed the older woman's cheek before offering a cool glance and a lukewarm handshake to Jack's father.

"Perhaps I'll see you again."

He stiffened, correctly interpreting the threat buried in that polite "perhaps."

"I certainly hope so."

"All right," Jack said as the Range Rover cut through the tunnel of oaks shading the drive. "What was that all about?"

Gina wanted to be cool about it, wanted to take the high road and shrug off the investigation as inconsequential, but her roiling emotions got the better of her. She slewed around as much as the seat belt would allow. Anger, hurt and suspicion put a razor's edge in her words.

"Did you know your father hired a P.I. to investigate me?"

"Yes, I…"

"With or without your approval?"

"Christ, Gina." His glance sliced into her. "What do you think?"

She was still angry, still hurt, but somewhat mollified by his indignation. Slumping against the seat back, she crossed her arms. "Your father's a piece of work, Ambassador."

Which was true, but probably not the smartest comment to make. Jack could criticize his father. He wouldn't appreciate an outsider doing so, however, any more than Gina would tolerate someone making a snide comment about the duchess. The tight line to Jack's jaw underscored that point.

"I'm sorry," she muttered. "I shouldn't have said that."

He accepted the apology with a curt nod and offered one

of his own. "I'm sorry, too. I should have told you about the investigation. The truth is I didn't know about it until after we got back from Switzerland and then it just didn't matter."

Her anger dissipated, leaving only an urgent question. "Why not, Jack? Didn't you…? Don't you have any doubts?"

"No. Not one." The rigid set to his shoulders eased. His reply was quiet and carried the ring of absolute truth. "We may disagree on a number of important issues, marriage included, but we've always been honest with each other."

Her eyes start to burn. She refused to cry, she flatly refused, but she suddenly felt miserable and weary beyond words. "Look," she said tiredly, "this has been a busy few days. I may have overdone it a bit. I think…I think I'd better fly back to New York this evening."

He knifed her a quick look. "Is it the baby?"

"No! The baby's fine."

"Then it's my father." Another sharp glance. "Or is it us?"

"Mostly us." She forced a smile. "You have to admit we didn't get much sleep the past two nights. I need to go home and rack out."

"Is that what you really want?"

"It's what I really want."

The drive back to D.C. took considerably less time than the drive down to Richmond. No cutting off to ramble along Route 1. No stops at picturesque cafés. Jack stuck to the interstate, and Gina used the time to check airline schedules. She confirmed a seat on a 7:20 p.m. flight to New York. It was a tight fit, but she could make it if she threw her things in her weekender and went straight to the airport.

"You don't have to wait," she told Jack as he pulled into the parking garage at L'Enfant Plaza. "I can grab a cab."

"I'll drive you."

She was in and out of TTG's guest suite in less than twenty minutes. A quick call ensured the cleaning crew would come in the following day. The key cards she sealed in an envelope and slid under the door to the main office. Elaine Patterson, manager of the Washington venue, was due back tomorrow. Gina would coordinate the after-event report with her and tie up any other loose ends by email.

Her emotions were flip-flopping all over the place again when Jack pulled up at the airport terminal. Part of her insisted she was doing the right thing. That she needed to pull back, assess the damage to her heart done by the nights she'd spent in his arms. The rest of her ached for another night. Or two. Or three.

If Jack were experiencing the same disquiet, it didn't show. He left the Range Rover in idle and came around to lift out her weekender. His expression was calm, his hand steady as he buried it in her hair and tilted her face to his.

"Call me when you get home."

"I will."

"And get some rest."

"Yes, sir."

"I'll see you at our next doctor's appointment, if not before."

Before would be good, she thought as she closed her eyes for his kiss. Before would be very good.

When she climbed out of a cab outside the Dakota almost seven hours later, her ass was well and truly dragging. Her flight had been delayed due to mechanical problems before being canceled completely. The passengers had sat for well over an hour on the plane before being shuffled off and onto another. She'd called Jack once she was aboard the alternate aircraft so he wouldn't worry, and again when she landed at LaGuardia.

Since they'd touched down at almost midnight, she didn't call her grandmother. The duchess would have gone to bed hours ago and Gina didn't want to wake her. Feeling dopey with exhaustion, she took a cab into the city. Jerome wasn't on duty and she didn't know the new night doorman except to nod and say hello. Wheeling her suitcase to the elevator, she slumped against the mirrored wall as it whisked her upward.

The delicate scent of orange blossoms telegraphed a welcome to her weary mind. She dropped her purse and key next to the Waterford crystal bowl filled with potpourri. Her weekender's hard rubber wheels made barely a squeak as she rolled it over the marble tiles.

She'd crossed the sitting room and was almost to the hall leading to the bedrooms when she caught the sound of a muffled clink in the kitchen. She left the suitcase in the hall and retraced her steps. Light feathered around edges of the swinging door between the dining room and kitchen. Another clink sounded just beyond it.

"Grandmama?"

Gina put out a hand to push on the door and snatched it back as the oak panel swung toward her. The next second she was staring at broad expanse of black T-shirt. Her shocked glance flew up and registered a chin shadowed with bristles, a mouth set in a straight line and dark, dangerous eyes topped by slashing black brows.

Ten

Everything Gina had ever learned or heard or read about self-defense coalesced into a single, instinctive act. Whipping her purse off her shoulder, she swung it with everything she had in her.

"Hé!" The intruder flung up his arm and blocked the savage blow. *"Várj!"*

"Várj yourself, you bastard!"

Gina swung again. This time his arm whipped out and caught the purse strap. One swift tug yanked it out of her hands.

"If you've hurt my grandmother…"

She lunged past him into the kitchen. Her fingers wrapped around the hilt of the largest knife in the upright butcher-block stand.

"Jézus, Mária és József!" The stranger chopped his hand down on her wrist, pinning it to the counter. "Stop, Eugenia. Stop."

The terse command pierced her red haze of fear but her heart still slammed against her chest as the questions tumbled out. "How do you know my name? What are you doing here? Where's my grandmother?"

"The duchess is in her bedroom, asleep, I presume. I am

here because she invited my sister and me to stay. And I know your name because we're cousins, you and I."

"Cousins?"

"Of a sort."

When she tugged her wrist, he released his brutal grip. A smile softened the stark angles of his face. "I'm Dominic. Dominic St. Sebastian. I live in Budapest, but my parents came from Prádzec. Your grandmother's home," he added when she looked at him blankly.

It took her a moment to recognize the name of the town on the border between Austria and Hungary, in the heart of what was once the Duchy of Karlenburgh.

"I don't understand. When did you get here?"

"This afternoon." He gestured behind him to the coffee-maker just starting to bubble and brew on the counter. "It's midnight in New York, but morning in Hungary. My body has yet to adjust to the time change and craves its usual dose of caffeine. Will you join me for coffee and I'll explain how Anastazia and I come to be here, in your home."

"No coffee," Gina murmured, her hand fluttering to her stomach as she tried to absorb the presence of this dangerous-looking man in her grandmother's kitchen.

He was as sleek and as dark as a panther. Black hair, black shirt, black jeans slung low on his hips. The T-shirt stretched taut across a whipcord-lean torso. The hair was thick and razored to a ragged edge, as though he didn't have time or couldn't be bothered with having it styled.

"Tea, then?" he asked.

"Tea would be good." Slowly getting her wind back, Gina nodded to the cabinet behind his head. "The tea caddy is in there."

"Yes, I know." His smile reached his eyes. "The duchess told me to make myself to home. I took her at her word and explored the cupboards."

Whoa! This man's face cast in hard angles and tight lines was one thing. The same face relaxing into a lazy grin was something else again. Gina had a feeling Dominic St. Sebastian could have his pick of any woman in Budapest. Or pretty much anywhere else in the world.

The fact that he knew his way around a tea caddy only added to the enigma. While the fresh-made coffee dripped into the carafe, he brewed a pot of soothing chamomile. Moments later he and Gina were sitting across from each other with steaming mugs in hand.

"So," he said, slanting her a curious look. "The duchess never spoke to you of me or my family?"

His speech held only a trace of an accent. A slight emphasis on different syllables that made it sound intriguing and sexy as all hell. Wondering where he'd learned to speak such excellent English, Gina shrugged.

"Grandmama told my sister and me that we had some cousins, four or five times removed."

"At least that many times. So we could marry if we wished to, yes?"

The tea sloshed in her mug. "Excuse me?"

"We're well outside the degree of kinship forbidden by either the church or the law. So we could marry, you and I."

A sudden suspicion darted into Gina's consciousness. Despite the duchess's seeming acceptance of her granddaughter's single-and-pregnant status, was she resorting to some Machiavellian scheming?

"Just when did my grandmother invite you and your sister to New York?"

"She didn't. I had to come on business and since Anastazia had never been to the States, she decided to accompany me. When we phoned the duchess to arrange a visit, she invited us for tea. She was so charmed by my sister that she insisted we stay here."

Charmed by his sister? Gina didn't think so.

"How long will you be in New York?"

"That depends on how swiftly I conclude my business. But not, I hope, before I get a chance to know you and the duchess. I've heard many tales of her desperate flight after the duke's execution."

"She doesn't speak of those days. I think the memories still haunt her."

"Is that why she's never returned to Austria, or traveled to any part of what is now Hungary?"

"I think so."

"That's certainly understandable, but perhaps some day she will visit and allow Anastazia and me to return her gracious hospitality. She would find everything much changed."

"I'm sure she would."

"You must come, too. I would enjoy showing you my country, Eugenia."

"Gina, please. Grandmama's the only one who calls me Eugenia, and then it's generally because I've screwed up."

"And does that happen often?"

She made a face. "Far more often than either of us would like."

The tea and the European rhythm of Dominic's speech had combined to bring Gina the rest of the way down from the adrenaline spike of her scare. When she reached bottom, weariness hit like a baseball bat.

Her jaw cracked on a monster yawn. She barely got a hand up in time to cover it and gave Dominic a laughing apology.

"Sorry 'bout that. It's been a long day."

"For me, also." His mesmerizing onyx eyes held hers. "Shall we go to bed?"

Okay, she had to stop attaching sexual innuendo to every word that came out of the man's mouth.

They took their mugs to the sink. Dominic rinsed them while Gina emptied the coffeemaker. He flicked off the kitchen light as they passed through the swinging door, plunging them both into temporary blindness.

Gina had grown up in this apartment and was intimately familiar with every piece of furniture a mischievous girl could crawl under or hide behind. She also knew which sharp edges to avoid, blind or not. Instinctively, she angled to the left to skirt the corner of a marble-topped table.

The move brought her into contact with Dominic's thigh, and his hand shot out to save her from what he must have assumed was a near fall.

"Careful."

For the second time that night he'd captured her arm. Gina wasn't quite as quick to shake off his hold this time.

"Thanks. I assume Grandmama put Anastazia in my sister's room and you in the study?"

"Is the study the baronial hall with the oak paneling and crown molding?" he asked dryly.

"It is." They stopped outside the double sliding doors. "Here you go. I guess I'll see you in the morning. Correction. Make that later in the morning."

His fingers slid from her forearm to her elbow to her wrist. Raising her hand, he bowed and dropped a kiss on it with old-world charm right out of the movies.

"*Aludj jól,* Gina."

"And that means?"

"Sleep well."

"*Aludj jól,* Dominic."

She left him standing by the sliding doors and reclaimed her suitcase. No light shone from under the door to her grandmother's room, so Gina slipped quietly into her own. She was asleep almost before her head hit the pillow.

She woke mere hours later. Grunting at what felt like a bowling ball resting atop her bladder, she rolled out of bed and headed for the bathroom.

When she snuggled between the sheets again, sleep didn't descend as swiftly. And when it did, it brought confusing dreams of a shadowy figure whose hair morphed from black to gold to black again.

Since Samuel wasn't expecting her back from Washington for another day, possibly two, Gina didn't feel compelled to go in to the office the next morning. Good thing, because she didn't wake up a second time until almost nine.

She took her time in the shower, wondering if she'd dreamed that kitchen encounter last night. It was so surreal, and so unlike her grandmother to invite complete strangers to stay in their home. Maybe she was more tied to the land of her birth than she let on.

Gina followed the scent of coffee and cinnamon toast to the kitchen, where Maria was turning fresh toast onto a plate.

"There you are. Dominic told us, *la duquesa* and me, that you came in late last night."

"I just about jumped out of my skin when I came in last night and bumped into him." Dying for a cup of coffee, Gina poured a glass of apple juice instead. "I'm surprised Grandmama invited him and his sister to stay here."

"Me, as well. But they are very nice and have made your grandmother smile. You will see," Maria said, flipping the last of the toast onto the platter.

"Here, I'll take that."

The scene in the sunny, green-and-white breakfast room certainly seemed to give credence to Maria's comment. The duchess was holding court, her snowy hair in a crown of braids, her chin feathered by the high lace collar of her favorite lavender silk blouse. Her smile was far from regal, though. Wide and lively, it transformed her face as she carried on an animated conversation with her guests in their native language.

But it was those guests who stopped Gina in her tracks. In the bright light of day, Dominic appeared every bit as dangerous as he had last night. Must be that European, unshaved whisker thing. Or his preference for black shirts. This one was starched cotton and open-collared, showing just a hint of a silver chain at his throat.

The woman seated across from him was almost as riveting. Her hair fell well past her shoulders, as lustrous and raven-black as her brother's. Her cheekbones were high and sharp, her mouth a glistening red. Thick lashes framed dark eyes with just the hint of a slant. If the rest of her was as striking as that sculpted face, the woman could walk into any modeling agency in New York and sign a high six-figure contract within minutes.

All of a sudden Gina felt fat and dumpy and just a tad jealous of the way these two outsiders seemed to have glommed on to her grandmother. That lasted only until the duchess spotted her. Her lined face lit up with love.

"You're awake at last. Come and join us, dearest."

Dominic pushed back his chair and took the platter of toast so Gina could bend to give her grandmother a kiss. The look he gave her banished any lingering nasty thoughts. Fat and dumpy wouldn't have put such an admiring gleam in his eyes.

"Good morning, cousin. Did you sleep well?"

"Very."

"You must let me introduce my sister. Anastazia, this is…"

"Eugenia Amalia Therése," the brunette said in an accent noticeably heavier than her brother's.

She, too, pushed back her chair and came around the table. Holding out both hands, she kissed Gina's cheeks. "I have been so eager to meet you, cousin. I, too, was named for the Archduchess Maria Amalia of Parma." She wrinkled her perfect nose. "I am Anastazia Amalia Julianna. Such long names we have, yes?"

Despite her cover-model looks, she was open and friendly and engaging. Gina couldn't help but smile back.

"We do indeed."

"You must call me Zia. And I will call you Gina."

That thorny matter settled, they joined the others at the table. Gina helped herself to two slices of cinnamon toast while her grandmother gave them all a rare glimpse into the family archives.

"Poor Archduchess Maria Amalia," she said with a wry

smile. "Married against her will to a mere duke while two of her sisters became queens. Marie Antoinette of France and Marie Caroline of Naples and Sicily."

Charlotte took a sip of her tea and shared another historical tidbit.

"The three sisters were reportedly very close. They often exchanged letters and portraits and gifts. One of the last letters Marie Antoinette smuggled out of her prison was to Amalia."

"I'm told there's a miniature of their mother, the Empress Marie Therese of Austria, in your Metropolitan Museum of Art," Zia said eagerly. "It is one of the places I hope to visit while I am here."

"You must get Eugenia to take you. She spent many hours at the Met as a child."

"Oh, but I must not impose." The brunette turned her brilliant smile on Gina. "From what your grandmother has told us, you're very busy with your work."

"Actually, I'm off today. We can go this afternoon, if you like."

"I would! And you, Dom. You must come, too, to see this long-dead ancestor of ours."

His gaze met and held Gina's. His mouth curled in a slow smile. "I'll have to see if I can reschedule my afternoon appointment."

Gina didn't get a chance to corner her grandmother until midmorning. Zia had gone out onto the terrace to check her phone for voice messages and emails. Dominic retreated to the study to make some calls. As soon as he was out of the room, Gina pounced.

"Okay, Grandmama, 'fess up. What's behind this sudden spurt of hospitality to distant relatives you've never met."

"Really, Eugenia! I should hope I'm not so lacking in generosity as to let two young and very charming relations stay in a hotel when we have plenty of room here."

"But you don't know anything about them."

"That's what Dominic said when I extended the invitation. He tried to refuse, but I insisted."

"Did either of them tell you what they do for a living?"

"Dominic does some kind of security work. Anastazia just got her MD degree from Semmelweis University in Budapest."

Gorgeous and smart and a doc. Another nasty little worm of jealousy poked its head up. Gina might have started feeling dumpy and fat again if Dominic hadn't come back into the room.

"I'm yours for the afternoon, if you're sure you wish to…"

He broke off and pivoted on the balls of his feet in the direction of the hall. Startled, Gina strained to hear in the sudden silence and picked up a faint buzz.

"Oh, that's my phone. I left it in my purse on the hall table last night. Excuse me."

The call had already gone to voice mail when she fished the phone out of her jam-packed bag. She saw the name on caller ID and stabbed the talk button just in time.

"Hello, Jack."

"Hi, Gina. I just wanted to check and see how you're feeling after your long odyssey last night."

The sound of his voice stirred the usual welter of confused emotions. Despite her abrupt departure yesterday, she couldn't believe how much she missed him. How much she ached for him.

"I'm good," she said, "although I decided not to go in to work since I had the day off, anyway."

"So you're going to put your feet up and rest, right?"

"Pretty much. Although I did agree to take my cousins to the Met this afternoon."

"Cousins?"

"Two of them. Dominic and his sister, Anastazia. Their parents came from Prádzec, which was once part of the Duchy of Karlenburgh."

"And is now in Hungary."

Trust an ambassador-at-large to know that. The phone to her ear, Gina wandered toward the end of the hall. Dom sat next to her grandmother's chair and appeared to be amusing her with some anecdote.

"Did the duchess know they were coming?" Jack asked.

"They surprised her. Me, too! I thought Dom was a burglar when I came chest-to-chest with him last night."

"They were there, in the apartment when you got home?"

"They're staying here."

That was met with a short silence.

"What did you say their names were again?"

"Dominic and Anastazia St. Sebastian. She's just finished med school and he does something in security. Grandmama didn't get the specifics."

She caught a flash of sunlight as the terrace doors opened and Zia rejoined the group.

"Oh, there's Anastazia. I'd better go, Jack."

"Gina…"

"Yes?"

"About this weekend—"

"It was just me," she interrupted quickly. She hadn't had time to sort through everything that had happened during their days together. And the nights! Dear God, the nights.

"Chalk it up to hormones run amok. I'll talk to you soon, okay?"

"Okay."

She blew out a breath and hit the end button, but some of the emotions Jack had stirred must have shown in her face when she walked into the sitting room. She couldn't hide them from the duchess. Her faded blue eyes locked onto to Gina's.

"Who was that, dearest?"

"Jack."

"Hmm."

The odd inflection in that murmur snared the interest of

both guests. They were too polite to ask, however, and the duchess left it to Gina to elaborate.

"Jack Mason. He's an ambassador-at-large with the U.S. State Department in Washington."

Dominic's expression of casual interest didn't change but just for a second she thought she saw something flicker in his dark eyes. Like the duchess, he must have sensed there was more to the call than she wanted to reveal.

Oh, hell. Might as well let it all hang out.

"He's the father of my baby."

After Gina disconnected, Jack spent several long moments staring at the slice of the Mall viewable through his office windows. Their brief conversation ricocheted around in his mind.

Two of them. From Hungary. They surprised her. Chest-to-chest.

He wanted to believe it was his recent showdown with the Russian Mafia thugs who'd spilled across the borders of Eastern and Central Europe that prompted him to reach for the phone. Yet he couldn't get that chest business out of his head.

His chief of staff answered the intercom. "What's up, boss?"

"I need you to run a check on a pair from Hungary. They say they're siblings and are going by the names Dominic and Anastazia St. Sebastian."

Eleven

The next few days flew by. Gina got caught up at work. During her spare hours she showed Zia and Dominic the best of New York. She also delighted in the slow unfurling of her grandmother's memories. Prompted by her guests' presence and their gentle probing, the duchess shared some of her past.

She'd kept it locked inside her for so long that each anecdote was a revelation. Even now she would only share those memories that gave glimpses of a girl born into a wealthy, aristocratic family, one who'd grown up with all Europe as her playground. A fascinated Gina learned for the first time that her grandmother might have qualified as an Olympic equestrian at the age of fifteen had her family allowed her to compete. She'd retaliated for their adamant refusal by insisting she be allowed to study Greek and Roman history at Charles University in Prague.

"Prague is such a romantic city," the duchess mused to her audience of three over a dinner of Hungarian dishes prepared by Zia and Dominic as a small thank-you to their hostess.

Candles flickered in tall silver holders. The remains of the meal had been cleared away but no one was in a hurry to leave the table. A Bohemian crystal decanter of *pálinka* sat within easy reach. Double-distilled and explosively potent, the apricot-flavored brandy had been a gift from Zia and Dom. The duchess and her guests sipped sparingly from balloon-shaped snifters. Gina was more than content with a goblet of diet cranberry juice and the dreamy expression on her grandmother's face.

"That's where I first met the duke," the duchess related with smile. "In Prague. There'd been talk off and on about a possible liaison between our families but nothing had come of it at that point."

"So what was he doing in Prague?" Gina asked.

"He'd evidently decided it was time to take a wife, and came to find out if I was scandalously modern as the rumors said."

She took a sip of brandy and a faraway look came into her eyes.

"When he walked into the café where my friends and I were having dinner, I didn't know who he was at first. All I saw was this tall, impossibly handsome man with jet-black hair and the swarthy skin of his Magyar ancestors. Even then, he had such a presence. Every head in the café turned when he walked over to my table," she murmured. "Then he bowed, introduced himself, and I was lost."

The duchess paused, drifting on her memories, and Gina's gaze drifted to Dominic. His olive-toned skin and dark eyes indicted Magyar blood ran in his veins, too.

A nomadic, cattle-herding tribe that swept into Europe from the Steppes, the Magyars were often depicted in art and literature as the early Hungarian equivalent of America's Wild West cowboys. Gina was back in the 8th or 9th century, picturing Dominic riding fast and low in the saddle, when the intercom sounded.

She returned to the present with a start. The buzz brought the duchess out of her reverie, as well. A small frown of annoyance creased her forehead.

"I'll get it," Gina said.

She crossed to the intercom's wall unit and saw the flashing light signaling a call from the lobby. "Yes?"

"It's Jerome, Lady Eugenia. There's a gentleman to see you. Mr. John Mason."

Jack! Surprise and pure, undiluted delight flooded her veins.

"Send him up! Excuse me," she said to the three interested parties at the table. "I need to get the door."

She rushed to the entryway and out into the hall, wishing she'd spiffed up a little more for this evening at home. Oh, well, at least she still fit into her skinny jeans. And her crab-apple-green stretchy T-shirt did accent her almost-nursing-mother boobs.

When Jack stepped out of the elevator, Gina forgot all about her appearance and devoured his. Ohmanohman-ohman! Hungarian cowboys had nothing on tall, tanned Virginians.

The sight of him erased last weekend's awkward moments. Her hurt and indignation over learning that his father had hired a P.I. evaporated. Ditto the poisonous little barbs planted by his obnoxious chief of staff. Double ditto the ache in her heart when she'd spotted the pictures of Catherine at his home. Like the duchess had so many years ago, all Gina needed to do was look at this man and know she was lost.

"What are you doing here?"

"Two reasons. One, I didn't like the way our weekend ended. I'm still kicking myself for letting you leave with little more than a peck on the cheek."

"Oh. Well. I suppose we can correct that."

"You suppose right."

When he hooked her waist, she went into his arms eagerly, joyfully. He buried a hand in her hair and more than made up for any deficiencies in their parting.

Gina could have stayed there forever. The feel and the taste and the scent of him wrapped around her like warm silk. She felt his heart beating under her spread palms, breathed in the heady mix of aftershave and male.

When he raised his head, her heart was in her smile. "You said there were two reasons. What's the second?"

The pause was brief, hardly more than half a breath, but still noticeable.

"I missed you."

"Was it that hard to say?" she teased.

"You try it."

"I missed you." It came so easily she added a little embellishment. "Bunches."

The murmur of voices inside the apartment snagged Jack's attention. "Did I catch you at a bad time?"

"No, we finished dinner a while ago and are just sitting around the table talking. Come meet my cousins."

She led him to the dining room and had time to note widely varied reactions before she made the introductions. Zia's first glimpse of the newcomer brought her elbows off the table and a look of instant interest to her face. As her eyes raked Jack over, a slow, feline smile curved her lips.

Gina couldn't help herself. She was bristling like a barnyard cat when she noticed Dominic's expression. It was as shuttered as his sister's was open. The duchess's, on the other hand, was warm and welcoming.

"Good evening, Ambassador. It's good to see you again."

The title sent Zia's brows soaring. Her gaze whipped from Jack to Gina and back again, while Dominic slowly pushed his chair back from the table and stood.

"It's good to see you, too, Duchess." Jack crossed the dining room to take her hand. "I'm sorry to barge in like this."

"No need to apologize. Allow me to introduce my guests. They're visiting from Hungary."

"So Gina told me."

"Anastazia, may I present Ambassador Jack Mason."

He was at his most urbane with the sultry brunette. A smile, a lift of her hand, a light kiss on the fingers.

"You must call me Zia," she purred. "And I will call you Jack, yes?"

"Igen."

"How wonderful! You speak our language."

"Only enough to order a drink in a bar."

"In Hungary," she laughed, "that is more than enough. This is my brother, Dominic."

Jack rounded the table and extended his hand. It was a simple courtesy, a universal gesture recognized the world over. Yet there was something about the look accompanying it that made Gina pause. The message was subtle. Almost *too* subtle. She caught a hint of it, though, or thought she did.

So did Dominic. His smile took on a sardonic edge, his eyes a sudden glint as he shook Jack's hand.

"We've met before, Ambassador, although I doubt you'll remember."

"I remember. I also remember you were using another name at the time."

The two men ignored the surprise that produced among the women. Their gazes locked, they seemed to be engaged in a private and very personal duel.

"I was, indeed," Dominic drawled. "And you, as I recall, had not yet acquired your so very impressive diplomatic credentials."

The duchess's notions of propriety didn't include what was fast assuming the air of an Old West showdown in her dining room. With a touch of irritation, she thumped her hand on the table to get the combatant's attention.

"Do sit down, both of you. Jack, would you care to try this very excellent cognac? Or there's coffee if you prefer."

"Cognac, please."

"Gina, if you'll get another snifter perhaps Jack or Dominic will condescend to tell us where or when they met before."

The acidic comment found its mark. While Gina retrieved a cut crystal snifter from the graceful Louis XV china cabinet that took up almost an entire wall, the tension between the two men eased by imperceptible degrees. She brought the snifter to the table and splashed in the aromatic brandy as Dom yielded the floor to Jack with upturned palms.

"It's more your story than mine, Ambassador."

Jack accepted the snifter with a murmured thanks and addressed himself to the duchess. "Dominic and I met a number of years ago in Malta. I was on a UN fact-finding mission investigating the transshipment of young women kidnapped from Eastern Europe and sold to wealthy purchasers in the Arab world."

"Dear Lord!" The duchess shot her guest a sharp, questioning look, but he merely gestured for Jack to continue.

"While the UN team was in Malta, we heard rumors of a shipment coming in from Albania. We worked with Interpol and the Maltese authorities to intercept the trawler transporting the merchandise. There were six girls aboard, all between the ages of fifteen and twenty, all drugged to the gills."

Jack lifted the balloon goblet and swirled its contents. His gaze shifted from the duchess to the man sitting across of him.

"The captain of the trawler was killed in the cross fire. That's the word that was put out, anyway."

"What do you mean?" Gina demanded. "Was the captain killed or wasn't he?"

She didn't like where this was going. Had she and her grandmother been too trusting? Had they accepted too readily that Dom and Zia were who they said they were? With a sinking sensation, she remembered how dangerous Dom had seemed that first night, when she'd come home and surprised him in the kitchen.

"The captain went down," Jack confirmed, "but not in a cross fire. Evidently he spotted the intercept boats on his radar and started dragging the girls to the rail. He was going to throw them overboard and get rid of the incriminating evidence before we closed in. That's when he took a shot point-blank to the forehead."

Dom lifted a shoulder. "The bastard had one of those kids shoved against the rail. There was no time to negotiate."

"I don't understand." Gina frowned at her cousin. "Were you on one of the intercept boats?"

"I was on the trawler."

"What?"

He leaned forward, acknowledging her shock. "I was undercover, Gina. I'd been working to take down the head of that particular white slavery ring for months, but I couldn't allow the captain to murder those girls."

"Or blow your cover," Jack murmured in the stunned silence that followed.

Dom's glance slewed back to him. "Or blow my cover."

"Funny thing about that." Jack swirled his cognac again, his eyes never leaving Dom's face. "Interpol put out the word that the second crewman on the trawler escaped after being taken into custody. Yet there was never any record made of the arrest. And the officer who supposedly took the man into custody disappeared two days later."

Dom's smile didn't quite make it to his eyes. "The Albanians play rough."

Gina couldn't believe they were sitting in this elegant dining room, sipping brandy and cranberry juice from Baccarat crystal while calmly discussing kidnapped fifteen-year-olds and death on the high seas. She glanced at her grandmother and found the same incredulity on the duchess's face. Even Zia looked stunned. Evidently her brother's undercover persona was news to her, too.

"I'm curious," Jack said. "Where did you go from Malta, St. Sebastian?"

"I had several assignments. As did you, Mason."

"You're no longer with Interpol."

It was a statement, not a question, but Dominic responded

with a quick, slashing grin. "Not anymore. I'm now what you might term an independent entrepreneur."

And just like that, the ominous spell was broken. He was Gina's cousin again. Handsome, charming, exotic and more intriguing than she'd ever imagined.

She made the fatal mistake of saying so when she walked Jack to the door an hour later.

"I had no idea my cousin was an undercover agent."

"Isn't that the whole point of 'undercover'?"

The acerbic comment raised Gina's brows.

"I suppose," she replied. "But still, you have to admit it's all pretty James Bondish."

"If you say so. Are you tired?"

The abrupt change of subject made her blink. It also made her realize she wasn't the least tired. Probably because the hour was still relatively early. Either that, or the extraordinary conversation at the dinner table had stimulated her. Or just standing here, so close to Jack, set every one of her nerves to dancing.

"Not really. Why?"

"I'm staying at the Excelsior. It's only a few blocks from here. Do you feel like getting out for a little while? We still need to talk about last weekend."

Cold, hard logic dictated a negative. She still hadn't completely sorted through the confused feelings left over from their weekend together. Luckily, Gina had never been particularly concerned with logic. At that moment, looking up into Jack's brown eyes, all she knew was that she craved an hour or two or six alone with him.

She'd never been the kind to play games, much less hide her feelings. Coyness didn't factor anywhere into her makeup. A smile of eager anticipation slid into her eyes as she tipped her head toward the dining room.

"Hang loose. I'll tell Grandmama and the others not to wait up for me."

* * *

They opted to walk to the Excelsior. The June night was too balmy and the city lights too enticing to take a cab for a few short blocks. When they reached the lobby of the Dakota, she steered him away from the main entrance on West 72nd toward the inner courtyard.

"This way. It's shorter."

They exited on 73rd and cut back to Central Park West. Somehow Gina's hand found her way into Jack's as they strolled past the imposing bulk of the Museum of Natural History. And somehow, when they were in the elevator shooting up to his suite, his lips found hers.

She couldn't blame the heat that raced through her on hormones. It was Jack. All Jack. Only Jack. He stoked her senses. Fired her blood. She made herself wait until he keyed the door to his room before she pounced. Then there were no holds barred.

"I hope this is what you had in mind when you asked if I wanted to get out for a while," she muttered as she tore feverishly at his shirt buttons.

"Pretty much."

His voice was low and rough. So were his hands. Dragging up the hem of Gina's T-shirt, he cupped her aching breasts. All it took was one flick of his thumbs over her supersensitive nipples to have her moaning. On fire for him, she locked her mouth and her body with his. They were both half-naked when she threw a glance around the luxurious sitting room.

"There's a bed here somewhere, right?"

"Oh, yeah."

The bedroom was as palatial as the rest of the suite. All crown molding and watered silk wallpaper. Not that either of them noticed. The bed was the center of their focus. Four ornately carved posts. Champagne-colored gauze dripping from each corner. A silk duvet in the same color just begging to be yanked back.

Jack did the honors before tumbling Gina onto the cool sateen sheets. Standing beside the bed, he stripped off the rest of his clothes. Her greedy eyes feasted on his muscled chest. His washboard ribs and flat stomach. His rampant sex.

Gina had to cup him. Had to taste him. Rolling onto her knees, she scooted to the edge of the mattress and wrapped her hand around him. He was hot to her touch. Hot and ridged and already oozing. The milky bead at the tip of his erection stirred a deep, feminine thrill. The idea that she could bring her man to this point with just a kiss, just a stroke, set a torch to her own wild desire. Dipping her head, Gina took him in her mouth.

Jack stood it as long as he could. Then the atavistic need that had been building in him since the moment he'd walked into the duchess's apartment swept everything else aside. He wanted to claim this woman. Mark her as his.

Driven by that primal instinct, he pushed her onto the pillows and followed her down. She spread her legs for him willingly, eagerly, and Jack sank into her. Her hips rose, rammed into his. Once. Twice. Again. Then she opened her eyes and the red mist that had obscured Jack's mind cleared.

This was Gina of the bright, contagious smile.

Gina, who enticed and excited him.

Gina, who'd erased everything and everyone else from his mind.

Jack came out of a deep sleep with his customary, instant awareness. The hotel room was still dark, the silence deep, although a faint gray light was just beginning to show at the edge of the drapes blanketing the window.

Gina lay sprawled at his side. Soft puffs of air escaped her lips with each breath. Not quite snores but close enough to make him smile. With slow, careful moves he nudged down the knee digging into his hip and eased out of bed.

His slacks and shorts lay where he'd dropped them. He

pulled them on but left his belt unbuckled and shirt lying where it was as he crossed to the window. Lifting the drape a crack, he saw the city hadn't yet roared to life. Like Jack, it was enjoying the final quiet moments before the rush of the day.

He stared at the shadowy bulk of the Museum of Natural History across the street and tried to remember the last time he'd felt so relaxed. More important, the last time his world had felt so right. Not since Catherine, certainly.

Or even before.

The traitorous thought slipped in before he could block it. Only here, in the dim stillness, with Gina just a few feet away, could he admit the painful truth.

Catherine had been all brilliant energy. Athletic, competitive, totally committed to the causes she believed in. Loving and living with her had demanded the same high level output from Jack.

Would he have burned out? Would they?

Or would they have found what he'd somehow found so swiftly and so unexpectedly with Gina? Jack struggled to find the right word for it. It wasn't peace. Or contentment. Or certainty. God knew, there was nothing certain or predictable about Eugenia Amalia Therése St. Sebastian!

Nor was what he felt for her wrapped up in the baby. The fact she was carrying his child played, of course. No way it couldn't. But what had Jack by the throat right now was Gina. Just Gina.

Christ! Why didn't he just admit it? He was in love with her. Everything about her. Okay, she pissed him off royally at times. And yes, she was one of the most stubbornly hardheaded females he'd ever encountered. Yet everything inside him warmed at the thought of waking up next to her for the next…the next…

His jaw locked. Whirling, he strode back to the bed and sat on the edge.

"Gina. Wake up."

She grunted and tried to burrow into her pillow.

"Wake up."

"Wha…?" She raised a face half-obscured by a tangle of hair and blinked owlishly. "What?"

"Sit up a moment."

Grumbling, she rolled onto a hip and wiggled up against the headboard. The sheet came with her in a waterfall of Egyptian cotton.

"This better be good," she muttered.

She shoved her hair out of her face and tucked the sheet around her breasts, scowling at him through still sleepy eyes. He figured that was as good as he would get.

"Okay, here's the deal. I love you. I want to wake up beside you every morning for as long as we have together. The problem is, neither of us knows how long that might be."

He gripped her upper arms. His fingers dug into soft flesh as he pressed his point.

"I learned the hard way there are no guarantees. You… we have to grab whatever chance at happiness we have now, today. I understand you're still trying to sort through all the changes going on in your life right, but…"

"Wait! Just hold on!"

She pulled away from him, and Jack smothered a curse. He'd overplayed it. Pushed her too hard. He was falling back to regroup when she scrambled off the bed, sheet and all, and pointed a finger at him.

"You stay right where you are. I have to pee. And wash my face. And brush my teeth. Afterward, I'm going to come back to bed and you're going to repeat part of your speech."

"Which part?"

She looked over her shoulder on her way to the bathroom. The smile she sent him lit up the entire room.

"The I-love-you part."

Jack sat there, grinning like an idiot.

* * *

He was still grinning when he heard a faint click coming from the sitting room. A second later, the outer door thudded back against the wall and three men rushed in.

Jack reacted instantly. His one thought, his only thought, was to direct them away from Gina. Springing to the far side of the bed, he grabbed the only available weapon. He had his arm back to hurl the nightstand lamp when the bald giant leading the pack leveled a silenced semiautomatic. The beam of his laser sight painted a red eye dead-center in Jack's naked chest.

"Don't be foolish, Ambassador."

He recognized the voice even before Dominic St. Sebastian stepped from behind baldy's hulking frame.

Twelve

"Now," Gina said gleefully as she yanked open the bathroom door, "let's pick up where we…"

She stopped dead. Clutching the towel she'd wrapped around her like a sarong, she gaped in stunned disbelief at the frozen tableau that greeted her. Jack, gripping a table lamp like a baseball bat. A monster with a shaved head aiming a gun at his chest. Another stranger eying her half-naked body with a leer. And Dom, his dark eyes flashing an urgent message she couldn't even begin to interpret.

"Wh…?" She backed up an involuntary step, two, hit the bathroom door frame. "What…?"

"Very nice, Ambassador." The leering stranger's accent was so thick Gina's shocked mind could barely understand him. "Your woman would bring a good price, yes?"

"Jack! Dom!" Her frantic gaze whipped from one to the other. "What's going on?"

Dom stepped toward her, still telegraphing a signal that refused to penetrate her frantic brain.

"Listen to me, Gina. These men and I have some unfinished business to take care of, business that involves Jack. When you wake, you will understand."

"When I…when I wake?"

A small, apologetic smile altered his grim expression for a moment. Just long enough to distract Gina from the blow that clipped her chin and snapped her head back. She felt Dom catch her as she crumpled. Heard Jack snarl out a curse. Sensed some sort of violent movement on the other side of the room, followed by a low pop.

Then everything faded to black.

She came to slowly, dazed and disoriented. As the gray mist cleared, she discovered she was stretched on the unmade bed. Alone. With the towel draped over her naked body.

She also discovered that her jaw hurt like nobody's business. The ache cut through her lingering haze. A montage of images leaped into her head, sharp and cold and terrifying. The men. Dom. The gun with its ugly silencer.

"Jack!"

Terror engulfing her, Gina shoved off the bed. The violent lunge brought a dark, dizzying wave. She had to reach out a hand to steady herself for a moment, as the towel puddled around her ankles. As soon as the wave receded enough to reclaim her scant body covering, she rushed into the sitting room.

Nothing. No one. Not a table out of place. No overturned chairs. No Jack, or any strangers.

Or Dom.

She hadn't fully processed those moments right before her cousin clipped her, hadn't really understood the vivid images that had popped into her head. She strung them together now, and the pattern they formed made her want to retch.

Dom! Dear God, Dom! What was he involved in? Why had he led those men to Jack? What did they want?

Five exhausting hours later, Gina still didn't have an answer to any of those questions. Neither did the small army of city, state and federal officials who'd descended on the Excelsior in response to her 911 call.

Two uniformed NYPD officers arrived hard on the heels of hotel security. They were followed in a bewildering succession by two plainclothes detectives; a CSI team to scour the suite for fingerprints and other evidence; a grim-faced individual who identified himself as being with the city's counterterrorism unit; two agents from the regional FBI office; a liaison from the governor's office in Albany; a Department of Homeland Security rep and a tall, angular woman from the State Department's New York Office of Foreign Missions, who'd been sent at the urgent request of her boss to find out what the hell happened to Ambassador-At-Large Mason.

Senior FBI Agent Pamela Driskell assumed charge of the hastily assembled task force. It was done with tact and a smooth finesse that told Gina the agent had considerable prior experience dealing with prickly jurisdictional issues.

"Section 1114 of Title 18 U.S. Code assigns the FBI the responsibility for protecting officers and employees of the United States," she explained in a peaches-and-cream Southern drawl at odds with her short, no-nonsense hair and stocky frame. "Now tell me everything you know about this cousin of yours."

Gina started with the surprise visit by Dom and his sister and ended with last night's startling revelations.

"I didn't get all the details. Just that he and Jack—Ambassador Mason—crossed paths some years ago during a UN mission investigating white slavery."

Driskell shot a look at the State Department rep. "You know anything about that?"

"No, but I'll check it out."

Whipping out her BlackBerry, the woman turned away. Driskell swung back to Gina.

"What else?"

"Dom—my cousin—was an undercover agent at the time. Working for Interpol."

"That right? Well, we'll check that out, too. Now I think it's time we talk to your cousin's sister."

She flapped a hand to get the attention of everyone else in the suite.

"Y'all have any further questions for Ms. St. Sebastian? No? Okay, I'm taking her home. Kowalski and I will interview Anastazia St. Sebastian."

When Gina and her escort arrived, Jerome was at his station. Concern etched deep grooves in his seamed face, and his shocked gaze went to the bruise that had blossomed on her chin.

"It's not as bad as it looks," she assured the doorman.

Actually, it was worse but Jerome didn't need to know that.

"Two police officers arrived earlier," he reported.

Gina nodded. Driskell had requested NYPD dispatch the officers. Just in case Dom made an appearance.

"One officer's waiting in the lobby," Jerome said with a worried frown. "The other went up to the duchess's apartment. Can you tell me what's going on, Lady Eugenia?"

Special Agent Driskell started to intervene but Gina held up a palm. "It's okay. I've known this man all my life. I feel safer with him on the door than any five FBI agents."

Driskell hiked a brow but didn't argue the point. "We're investigating the suspected kidnapping of Ambassador Jack Mason," she said instead. "We have reason to believe Dominic St. Sebastian may be involved."

"No!" Jerome reeled back a step. "I don't believe it!"

"Why not?"

He had to stop and think about his instinctive denial. "I've seen Mr. St. Sebastian and his sister with the duchess," he said after a moment. "They're so good with her. So caring and solicitous."

Driskell's curled lip said what she thought of caring and solicitous. "What time did you come on duty this morning?"

"Nine o'clock."

Too late for the events that happened at the Excelsior hours earlier, but Driskell tried, anyway.

"Have you seen two men loitering anywhere in the vicinity? One big and bald? The other smaller, with a heavy accent?"

Jerome drew himself up, all wounded dignity under his summer uniform. "If I'd seen anyone loitering in the vicinity of the Dakota, you may rest assured I would have seen they were attended to."

"I'll take that as a no," Driskell said in her deceptively soft, magnolia-petal drawl.

The uniformed cop in the lobby reported no sighting of Dominic St. Sebastian, his suspected accomplices, or Ambassador Mason. The cop who'd been assigned to wait in the duchess's apartment gave the same report.

Gina only half heard him. Her attention went straight to her grandmother. The duchess sat as straight-spined as ever in her high-backed chair. Maria huddled with shoulders hunched in the chair beside hers. Both women showed worried, strained faces. And both jerked their heads up when Gina walked in.

"Eugenia!"

Relief flooded the duchess's face. Then she seemed to fold into herself, like someone who'd been granted a reprieve from her worst fears.

Gina rushed across the room and dropped to her knees beside the woman who'd always been her anchor. The terror she'd been holding at bay rose up again but she choked it back. She wasn't about to aggravate her grandmother's heart condition by indulging in a fit of hysterics like she really, really wanted to.

"I'm okay, Grandmama."

"What happened to your face?"

She hesitated but couldn't find any way around the truth. "Dom knocked me unconscious."

"No!"

The single syllable arced through the air like summer lightning. Sudden. Tense. Electrifying. Gina jerked her head around and saw Zia leap off the sofa. Her face was ablaze, her eyes feral.

"My brother would not strike a woman!"

"Guess again," Gina snapped.

"I don't believe you!"

The savage denial pulled her up short. Jerome and Anastazia. That made two people in less than five minutes who refused to accept Dom's role in the morning's events.

Her grandmother made a third.

"I can't believe it, either," the duchess said in a more shaky voice than Gina had ever heard coming from her. "Please, Eugenia. Introduce me to these people. Then for heaven's sake sit down and tell us what happened. Zia and Maria and I have been imagining every sort of horrible disaster."

The introductions didn't take much time. The telling took only a little longer. What could Gina add to the stark facts? She'd emerged from the bathroom. Found Dom and two strange men in Jack's suite. Dom stepped forward, knocked her out. She woke alone.

"I cannot understand any of this," Zia said fiercely. "But whatever happened, Dom had some reason for his actions."

Agent Driskell chose to exert her authority at that point. "We'd like to talk to you about your brother, Ms. St. Sebastian."

"It's Dr. St. Sebastian," Zia interrupted acidly.

"Right." The agent turned to the duchess. "Is there some place my partner and I can speak privately with Dr. St. Sebastian?"

"Yes, of course. Maria, will you show them to the breakfast room?"

The kitchen door swished behind them, leaving Gina and her grandmother alone for a few precious moments.

"Eugenia, for God's sake, be honest with me." The duchess held out a trembling hand. "Did you fall? Hurt yourself or the baby?"

"No." She took her grandmother's hand and sank into the chair Maria had just vacated. "Dom caught me before I hit the floor."

"He knocked you unconscious but didn't let you fall? This...none of this makes any sense."

"I know."

She was no closer to understanding when Agent Driskell and her partner departed some time later. Before leaving, Driskell gave Gina a business card imprinted with her office and cell phone numbers.

"There's a chance your cousin or whoever's he's working with may try to reach you. If they do, call me at once."

"I will," Gina promised, slipping the card into the pocket of her jeans. "And you'll call me immediately if they contact someone in Jack's office?"

Driskell nodded. "In the meantime, we'll pull the police officer here in the apartment but keep one in the lobby just in case."

With the agents' departure, an uneasy silence gripped the four women. Maria broke it by pushing heavily to her feet.

"You must eat, *Duquesa*. All of us must. I will make a frittata."

She swished through the swinging door to the kitchen, leaving Gina and the duchess to face a clearly worried Zia.

"I knew my brother had worked with Interpol," the Hungarian said with a deep crease between her brows, "but I was not aware he was...he was..." She waved a hand, as though trying to pull down the right word.

"An undercover agent?" Gina supplied.

"*Igen!* An undercover agent." Her accent reflected her agitation. The Eastern European rhythm grew more marked with each word. "Dominic never spoke of such things to me. Nor to our parents."

Gina wanted to believe her. Her aching chin dictated otherwise.

"He said last night he's no longer with Interpol," she reminded Zia coolly. "As I recall, he mentioned that he's now an independent entrepreneur. What, exactly, does that mean?"

Her cousin's eyes flashed. "I don't know. He has business all over. Many parts of the world. Something to do with security. But…I don't know."

She raked a hand through her silky black hair. She was dressed casually today in navy leggings and a belted, cream-colored tunic with a scoop neckline that dipped off one shoulder. Tall and slender and impossibly elegant, she stirred Gina's frumpy, dumpy feelings again.

Of course, it didn't help that she'd been in such a hurry to jump back into bed with Jack this morning that all she'd done in the bathroom was pee, splash her face with cold water and brush her teeth. Nor was her appearance uppermost in her mind when she'd come to. After her panicked 911 call, she'd scrambled into the same jeans and crab-apple stretchy T-shirt she'd worn last night. If she'd dragged a comb through her hair, she couldn't remember it. Makeup had never entered her mind. Aside from the ice pack Agent Driskell's partner had thrown together with a towel and minicubes from the wet bar to keep her jaw from swelling, Gina had given zero thought to how she looked.

She was feeling that omission now. She wanted a shower, a hairbrush, a change of clothes and another ice pack in the worst way. She hated to take the time for even a quick scrub, though. What if Agent Driskell called? Or Dom? Or Jack?

She was still debating the issue when Zia addressed the duchess. "This is very awkward for you," she said stiffly. "And for me. I think perhaps I should pack my things and… and Dom's…and go to a hotel."

The duchess frowned but before she could reply the cordless phone on the table beside her chair rang. Gina dived for it, praying fervently. Jack! Please, God, let it please be Jack!

"Hello?" Stabbing the talk button, she fumbled the receiver to her ear. "Hello?"

"Gina! Thank God!"

She had to strain to hear her sister's voice over the roar of some kind of engine.

"Grandmama called us early hours and hours ago," Sarah shouted above the noise. "She said you'd been in some kind of an incident. Are you okay?"

"I'm fine."

"The baby?"

Gina laid a hand over her still-flat stomach. Dom had caught her just as her knees crumpled. She hadn't hit the floor. Hadn't bruised anything but her chin. Which, she realized belatedly, must have been his intent.

"Also fine," she assured Sarah. "What's that noise? Where are you?"

"Just about to touch down at the 34th Street Heliport."

"You're here? In New York?"

"Dev ordered his private jet two minutes after Grandmama called. We'll be at the Dakota shortly. Gina, you're not hurt? You swear you're not hurt?"

"I swear."

"Okay, see you in a bit."

Gina cut the connection, battling the almost overwhelming urge to burst into tears. Dammit! These kamikaze hormones were killing her! But just knowing that the sister who always was and always would be her closest friend had rushed to New York on the basis of a single phone call made her want to bawl.

She fought back the tears and sent the duchess a tremulous smile. "That was Sarah."

"So I gathered. They're in New York?"

"They're about to touch down at the 34th Street Heliport."

Her grandmother's paper-thin eyelids fluttered down, as though in prayer. "Thank heavens."

When her lids lifted again, relief was stamped all across her face. "If anyone can get to the bottom of all this, Dev can."

Gina wasn't sure what her brother-in-law could do that two dozen assorted city, state and federal law officials couldn't. She'd put her money on Dev, though. He didn't have to play by the same rules those officials did.

"Now I must leave," Zia said, returning to the topic she'd introduced before the phone call. "Your other granddaughter comes, yes? You will need the bedroom for her."

"Why don't we wait until Sarah and Dev arrive before we decide that?" the duchess suggested.

Zia wasn't fooled. Neither was Gina. They both knew the duchess intended to keep their only connection to Dom on a short leash until Dev had a chance to talk to her.

Her cousin acknowledged as much with a curt nod. "Very well."

Then the stiffness went out of her spine. Like an elegant doll that suddenly lost its stuffing, Zia collapsed onto the sofa and put her head in her hands.

"Dominic is the best of all brothers," she said on a small moan. "I don't understand this. I don't understand any of this."

Her distress was so genuine, so obviously unfeigned. If Zia loved her brother even half as much as Gina loved Sarah, this crazy situation had to be tearing her apart.

The realization gave Gina more of a sense of kinship with her cousin than she'd felt at any point before. It brought her out of her chair and halfway across the sitting room before the buzz of the intercom sent her spinning toward the wall unit. The flashing number on the panel signaled a call from the lobby.

"It's Gina, Jerome."

"There's a gentleman to see you, Lady Eugenia. Mr. John Mason says..."

"Send him up!"

Thank God, thank God, thank God! Jack had returned from wherever he'd disappeared to.

She raced to the front door and flung it open. She was dancing from foot to foot in wild impatience when the elevator doors pinged open. Like a stork hit by lightning, she froze with one foot lifted in the air.

Jack's father stalked out of the elevator, his face red with suppressed fury. "What the hell have you involved my son in?"

Thirteen

She fell back a step, stunned by the vicious accusation. Before she could respond, before she could even think of a response, Zia came running down the hall.

"Come quickly! Special Agent Driskell's on the phone. She thinks they have a link to the kidnappers."

Gina spun on one heel and raced for the sitting room. Footsteps pounded behind her but she had no thought for Jack's father at the moment. Her heart pounding, she snatched up the phone the duchess held out and jammed it to her ear.

"This is Gina St. Sebastian. What's happening?"

"We just got a tip from Interpol," Pam Driskell said with barely suppressed excitement. "Antonio Cordi disappeared from their radar three days ago and may have entered the U.S. under a fake passport."

Like that told Gina anything!

"Who's Antonio Cordi?"

"He's the suspected capo of a vicious crime family operating out of southern Italy. Unfortunately, no one's been able to penetrate the family or get close enough to pin anything on him."

"You're kidding!" She gripped the phone with a white-knuckled fist. "What connection does Jack—Ambassador Mason—have to a Mafia don?"

A grim, white-faced John Harris Mason II surged into her field of view. "I can answer that."

Gina had the phone plastered against her ear, trying to assimilate John II's startling announcement, when she heard a commotion in the foyer. Her heart jumped into her throat.

Jack! Dom! Please God, let it be one of them!

She was hit with alternating waves of crushing disappointment and heartfelt joy when Sarah and Dev appeared. Waving a frantic hello, she relayed the latest development to Special Agent Driskell.

"Ambassador Mason's father is here at our apartment. He says he's got information about this Antonio Cordi."

"Keep him there! My partner and I are only a few blocks away. We'll return immediately."

Her thoughts whirling, Gina inserted the phone into its base. "Agent Driskell wants you to hang loose. She's on her way back here."

The thump of a cane against the parquet floor commanded her attention. "I believe introductions are in order, Eugenia."

"Oh. Right. Grandmama, Sarah, Dev, Zia...this is Jack's father, John Mason. John, this is my grandmother, sister, brother-in-law and...and cousin."

She hadn't intended the stumble over that last part. In her heart of hearts, Gina refused to believe Dom had gone over to the dark side. She still hadn't been able to come up with an explanation for his role in this morning's extraordinary events, though. Neither had his sister. Their unanswered questions hung over the room like a black cloud.

Zia acknowledged as much with a terse nod in the general direction of the newcomers. Which left Gina to pray the duchess hadn't heard the accusation flung at her by Jack's father in the hall a few moments ago. If Charlotte had, blood might yet be spilled.

Mason skated on that one, thank God. The duchess rose

from her chair with the aid of her ebony cane and held out a blue-veined hand.

"I'm sorry we have to meet under such unhappy circumstances, John. I may call you John, mightn't I?"

He gave a curt nod, his thoughts obviously spinning more on his son than on social niceties.

"Good, and you may call me Charlotte. Now, please, sit down and tell us what connection your son has to a Mafia don."

Mason a dismissive gesture with one hand. "I'll wait for the FBI."

Gina chalked the rudeness up to the worry that had to be gnawing at him but cringed at the expression his brush-off put on her grandmother's face.

"Gina says this FBI agent is on the way to take my statement. I'll wait and…"

"No, sir, you will not."

The duchess's cane whipped up and took aim at his chest.

"Look at that bruise on my granddaughter's chin," she commanded with icy hauteur. "If you have an explanation for why her cousin felt compelled to strike her and disappear into thin air with your son, I want to hear it. Now."

Gina guessed John II rarely, if ever, tucked his tail between his legs and backed off. He didn't exactly do either at that point, but he offered a stiff reply.

"I can't tell you why this…this cousin of Gina's struck her or how *he's* involved in this situation. I have my suspicions," he said, his jaw tight, "but nothing solid to base them on. All I can tell you is that I once headed a delegation chartered to examine international banking practices that shielded money laundering, both in the U.S. and abroad. We spent months in South America, more months in Europe digging into accounts reputedly owned by an Italian crime organization called the 'Ndrangheta."

"Go on," the duchess instructed as she resumed her seat. "And for heaven's sake, do sit down."

The demand for at least a semblance of normality drained the last of John II's hostility. He sank into a chair, looking suddenly haggard and far older than his years.

Gina and Sarah and Zia huddled together on the sofa. Dev took the straight-backed chair at the duchess's gilt-edged escritoire. Every pair of eyes was locked on Jack's father as he reduced what had to be a dramatic tale of international crime and intrigue to a few, stark sentences.

"We were in Rome. With the help of the Italian authorities, we'd actually begun to decipher the labyrinthine flow of third- and fourth-tier transactions. One of those tiers led to a member of the 'Ndrangheta named Francesco Cordi."

"I thought his name was Antonio," Gina said, frowning.

"Francesco is—was—Antonio's brother.

"Was?"

"Francesco's dead."

John scrubbed a hand over his face. It was evident to everyone in the room he still carried vivid memories of those days in Rome.

"He didn't like us nosing around in his business and decided to let us know about it. Two of my associates were incinerated when their vehicle was firebombed. We found out later I was next on the hit list. Fortunately—or unfortunately as it now turns out—Jack flew over to Rome at the first sign of trouble. He was with me when Francesco made his move." A fleeting smile creased the retired diplomat's face. "There wasn't a whole lot left of him to send home to his brother Antonio."

"Who's now here, in the States," Gina explained for Sarah and Dev. "The FBI says they got a tip that…"

The buzz of the intercom had her springing her off the sofa.

"That must be Agent Driskell and her partner now."

It wasn't. Her stomach sank like a stone when Jerome announced another visitor.

"I'm sorry to bother you, Lady Eugenia, but there's a Mr. Dale Vickers in the lobby."

Jack's obnoxious chief of staff. That's all she needed! Squeezing her eyes shut, Gina pressed her forehead against the wall.

"He wishes to speak with you. Shall I send him up?"

Hell, no! She knew darn well the officious little turd possessed no vital information relating to his boss's kidnapping. If he had, he would have taken it straight to the FBI. She would also bet he'd already used the weight of his office to extract every detail he could from them. Now he wanted to hear it straight from the horse's mouth.

She guessed she couldn't blame him. Vickers and Jack went back a long way. He had to be as shaken as everyone in the room. Sighing, Gina raised her head.

"Send him up."

Mere moments after the short, tightly wired Vickers said hello to Jack's father and was introduced to others, he confirmed Gina's cynical guess. The man had spoken to just about every local, state and federal official involved into the case.

"They can't tell me a damned thing beyond the basics. All they could confirm was that you and the ambassador were screwing around when he got snatched and…"

"Stop right there, young man!"

Incensed, the duchess tilted her chin to a dangerous angle.

"You will address Lady Eugenia with courtesy and respect or you will leave this apartment immediately."

"I…"

"Do we understand each other?"

"I just…"

"A simple 'yes, ma'am' will do."

"Yes, ma'am."

Despite the tension engulfing the room, Gina and Sarah exchanged a small smile. The sisters had seen their grandmother reduce bigger and stronger men than Dale Vickers to quivering blobs of sorry.

Vickers's next comment erased any inclination to smile, however. Too wired to accept the duchess's icily polite invitation to have a seat, he paced the sitting room.

"I know it was clutching at straws, but I even thought this might have something to do with the face-to-face between the ambassador and the CEO of Global Protective Services at that little soiree TTG put on last weekend."

Little soiree? Gina swallowed an indignant huff. She had to work hard to refrain from suggesting Vickers take a short leap off a tall building.

Unaware he'd ignited her fuse, the staffer proceeded to send her straight into orbit. "If Global's power structure thought the ambassador was going to undercut them on the fat embassy security contract they're trying to land, they might want him out of the picture. When I called Nikki, though, she assured me…"

"Whoa! Back up a minute. Did you just say you called Nikki?" Gina asked incredulously. "Nicole Tremayne? My boss?"

"Of course I called her. She appreciates the business we've sent TTG's way since you and the ambassador…uh…" He caught the duchess's warning glance. "Since you and the ambassador started seeing each other. But I knew she didn't understand the awkward position you put him in by enticing him to attend an event sponsored by Global."

Gina barely heard the last, insulting remark. She was still dealing with the shock of learning that Jack and his staff had funneled business to TTG.

Her pride crumbled. Like an old, rotted rowboat, it just fell apart right before her eyes. What a fool she was! All these weeks she'd thought, she'd actually believed, she was making her own mark at TTG.

She struggled to her feet. She refused to burst into tears in front of Vickers, but her throat was thick when she reminded the assembled group that Special Agent Driskell and her partner were expected at any moment.

"Sarah, would you show them in when they get here? I need to… I need to…"

She didn't trust herself to finish. With a vague gesture toward the arched hallway leading to the rear of the apartment, she turned on her heel. Her eyes were burning by the time she made it the bath linking her bedroom with Sarah's old room. She dropped the lid to the stool and sank down sideways, crossing both arms on the counter beside it.

Strangely, the tears didn't gush. Gina stared at the wall, her pride in shreds, and waited for the usual flood to burst through the dam. It took a moment for her to understand why the tsunami didn't happen.

None of it mattered. Not her job or TTG or Vickers's snide comments. The *only* thing that mattered right now was Jack's safety. She would eat crow or humble pie or black, slimy worms if that would bring him back to her.

She was still staring blankly at the wall when Sarah tapped on the bathroom door.

"Gina? Are you okay?"

"Mostly."

"May I come in?"

She mumbled an assent and almost lost it when her sister eased down onto her knees beside the stool. Gina had counted on Sarah to bail her out of so many of life's little catastrophes. Turned to her, too, to soothe the ruffled feathers of the men she'd fallen for, then dropped with such careless abandon.

"It'll be okay," Sarah murmured, stroking her hair. "It'll be okay. Judging by everything I've heard in the past few minutes, Jack's been in tight spots before. He'll find a way out of this one, too."

Halfway across town Jack was was hungry, hurting and totally pissed.

He'd been sitting on his ass for hours now in a wobbly

chair with one leg shorter than the other. His arms were twisted behind his back. Plastic restraints cut into his wrists. The wound from the bullet that had grazed his upper arm had scabbed over, but the trail of dried blood it left itched like the devil under the shirt and suit coat he'd been told to pull on before they'd departed his hotel suite.

Jack had complied with the order. Hell, with Dominic St. Sebastian cradling an unconscious Gina in his arms, Jack would have jumped out the eighth-story window if so ordered to prevent the bastard from hurting her any worse.

He'd had time these past hours to think about that, though. How fast St. Sebastian had put himself between Gina and his two pals with guns. How quickly he'd clipped her, then caught her before she hit the floor. As though he wanted to neutralize her and get her out of the picture immediately, before the other goons turned their weapons in her direction.

If so, he hadn't bothered to communicate his strategy to Jack. Or anything else, for that matter. St. Sebastian and the shorter of his two pals had disappeared right after they'd dumped Jack in this abandoned warehouse.

They'd left the shaved-head Goliath to stand guard. The giant had heaved his bulk up twice in the past six hours, both times to take a leak. He'd sprayed the grimy brick wall like a fire hose, adding his contribution to the stench of vomit, urine and rat feces littering what was obviously a hangout for homeless druggies. He'd also grunted into a cell phone a few times in a heavy dialect Jack couldn't understand but otherwise refused to say a word.

Shifting in his chair to ease the ache in his shoulder joints, Jack decided to take another shot at him. "Hey! Num nuts! I know you won't respond to English."

He tried Spanish again, then French, then his limited Russian. All he got was a sneer and a shake of the thug's massive head.

Okay. All right. Jack couldn't wait any longer. If the nine or ten layers of local, state and federal officials he knew had to be looking for him hadn't closed in on the warehouse by now, odds were pretty damned good they wouldn't. If Jack were going to get out of this mess, he had to do it on his own.

For the fifth or sixth time he did a visual sweep of the warehouse. Rat droppings weren't the only objects littering its dim, cavernous interior. A stained mattress, some moldy fast-food sacks and a scatter of rusted tin cans gave ample evidence of prior occupation. So did the syringes dropped on the concrete floor.

His glance lingered on the syringes. He'd considered those earlier but the damned things were plastic, not glass. Even if he could toe one within reach, somehow get it into his hands and break the barrel before the gorilla noticed, the plastic shard wouldn't cut through the restraints.

He'd have to go with a rusted can. The closest was about four feet away. Its lid was jagged and bent back, as though someone had used an old-fashioned can opener to get at the contents, then tossed it aside.

He couldn't wiggle the rickety chair that far without getting Goliath all excited. He had to take a dive. Probably more than one. He just hoped to hell he didn't knock himself unconscious when he hit the cement floor.

"Hey! You!"

Goliath slewed a disinterested glance Jack's way.

"I need to take a leak, too."

Hard to pantomime without the use of your arms. He tipped his chin toward his fly. When that didn't produce results, he nodded toward the urine-splashed wall, arced his arms behind him to clear the chair and started to push to his feet.

His guard grunted a warning. Jack ignored it. He was almost upright when the giant lunged out of his own chair and swung the beefy fist gripping his silenced semiautomatic.

The blow knocked Jack sideways. He crashed to the cement. The rickety chair went with him. Goliath said something that was obviously a warning and hooked a paw under

Jack's arm. Of course, he had to grab the one grazed by the bullet.

When Jack grimaced in pain, amusement lit Goliath's broad, flat face. He muttered a few words that no doubt translated to "serves you right, asshole" and righted the overturned chair. He shoved Jack into it and headed back to his own.

"I have to piss."

His jaw set, Jack started to rise again. And again, Goliath let fly with a backhanded blow. And this time, he couldn't be bothered to right the chair or haul his hostage up into it.

Jack's lips curled in a snarl. His eyes never left the gorilla's. Muttering profanities that only seemed to increase the big man's amusement, he got a grip on the rusted can he'd landed almost on top of. He maneuvered it with his fingertips until he turned the jagged lid inward. As he surreptitiously sawed at the plastic restraints, he wondered fleetingly how long it had been since his last tetanus shot. No matter. Lockjaw was the least of his worries right now. His gut told him Dominic St. Sebastian's pals played for keeps.

He got confirmation of that just moments after the giant's cell phone buzzed. Goliath picked up the instrument, glanced at the number displayed on the screen and hit Talk. Two grunts later, he set the phone down. A few moments after that, a door at the far end of the warehouse opened.

Still lying on his side, Jack curved his body so his front faced the door and his wrists were hidden behind his back. The damned can lid was slippery with blood from slicing into his skin, but the grim realization that it was now or never kept him razoring at the restraints.

He also kept his eyes on the three men who came through the door. One he recognized from the hotel. The second was a stranger. The third was Dominic St. Sebastian. His features seemed to freeze when he spotted the body sprawled on the concrete. Then his eyes caught Jack's. He flashed a swift, silent message, but before Jack could interpret that damned thing, the stranger took a wide-legged stance a few yards away. He was dressed in a sleek gray suit and white wing tips. A distant corner of Jack's mind was wondering who the hell wore wing tips anymore when a vicious smile cut across the man's swarthy face.

"I have waited a long time for this, Ambassador."

"That right?"

"I thought to take you in Washington, but security there is too tight. How convenient that you have a woman here in New York."

The jagged lid took another slice out of Jack's thumb. He couldn't work the lid too hard with the stranger's eyes on him, but he didn't give up.

"Convenient for you, maybe," he drawled. "Not so much for me. Who the hell are you, anyway?"

"I am Antonio Cordi, the brother of Francesco Cordi. Perhaps you remember him?"

"Yeah, I remember him. Hard to forget the man who tried to gun down my father."

"And failed, unfortunately. We don't often miss our targets."

"'We' being you and the other scumbags who comprise 'Ndrangheta."

Jack was all too familiar with the confederation of Italian families that rose to power after the Cosa Nostra's decline in the 1990s. By forming alliances with Central and South American drug cartels, 'Ndrangheta had gone global and was now one of the world's most powerful criminal organizations. Its members were up to their hairy armpits in drug trafficking, prostitution, extortion, weapons smuggling and kidnappings for ransom. One U.S. State Department white paper estimated that their illegal activities accounted for more than $43 billion in 2007 alone—or approximately three percent of Italy's total gross domestic product.

Jack had gotten up close and personal with only one member of the clan, when his dad had been tapped to lead a delegation exploring the extent to which the 'Ndrangheta's money laundering had infiltrated the international banking system. The delegation followed one of the links to Francesco Cordi. When they dug a little too deep, Cordi retaliated by going after the high-ranking members of the delegation. Two died when their car was firebombed. Jack flew to Rome as soon as he heard about it and was with his father when Cordi came after him.

He had no regrets about taking Cordi down. Not then, not now. Even though he'd been advised by several concerned Italian officials that every member of the 'Ndrangheta swore a blood oath to always, *always* avenge the death of one of their own.

So he wasn't surprised when Cordi's brother slid a hand inside the jacket of his pearl-gray suit. Or that the hand emerged holding a blue steel Beretta.

Fourteen

Gina had never been inside a military command post but she suspected they couldn't be any more crowded or more tense than the apartment once Special Agent Driskell and her partner arrived.

With the duchess's permission, the FBI agents commandeered the study to interview Jack's father in private. That left Gina, her grandmother, Sarah, Dev, Zia and the obnoxious Dale Vickers to pick at the buffet lunch Maria had miraculously managed to augment with the arrival of each new wave of visitors.

Gina re-ee-eally wanted to tell Vickers to find somewhere else to squat, but the man was so worried about his friend and boss she didn't have the heart to kick him out of their unofficial command center. Besides, he and Dev seemed to have formed an unlikely partnership.

She tried to set aside her animosity for Vickers and study the two men objectively as they sat across from her, with the remains of the buffet lunch still littering the table. Jack's chief of staff was in an expensive-looking suit with his tie loosened and the top button of his shirt popped. Dev wore jeans and a faded, light blue denim shirt with the sleeves rolled up. With his broad shoulders, close-cropped black hair and tanned skin, he looked as if he spent more time on his parents' New Mexico ranch than in boardrooms all around the globe. Yet anyone looking at the two men could easily pick out the power broker. Dev Hunter exuded the utter confidence that came with having built a multinational aerospace corporation from the ground up.

"Are you sure Jack had his cell phone on him when he left Washington?" he asked Vickers.

"I'm sure."

Frowning, Dev worked the buttons of his handheld device. "It's not emitting a signal."

"I could have told you that," Gina said. "Someone…"

She scrunched her forehead and ran through a mental litany of officials who'd responded to her 911 call. The NYPD detectives? The guy from the counterterrorism office? Pam Driskell? Aside from the short, stocky FBI agent, they were all pretty much a nameless, faceless blur now.

"I can't remember who, but someone ran a trace on Jack's cell phone within moments of showing up at the Excelsior. Maybe several someones. They said any recently manufactured cell phone has a built-in tracking device that allows eavesdroppers to pinpoint its location to within just a few feet."

"Unless the battery is removed," Dev muttered, playing with his gizmo. "Which must be the case here, or the ultra high frequency cargo container signal receptor we're developing for MilSatCom would pick it up."

"The what for the who?"

"I can't speak to the 'what,'" Sarah said as Dev continued to scowl at the instrument in his hand, "but the 'who' is the Military Satellite Communications System."

When both the duchess and Gina turned to stare at her, she smiled at their look of astonishment. "Don't be so surprised. I've been receiving a crash course on all things military since we got back from our honeymoon."

"You're serious?"

"As serious as the self-contained, bolt-on/bolt-off special operations surveillance system mounted in the belly of a C-130," she said solemnly.

Gina tried, she really tried, to picture her oh-so-elegant sister in one of the retro designer classic outfits she loved clambering around the belly of a C-130. Not that Gina knew what a C-130 was, exactly.

"What about your brother?" Dev asked Zia, cutting into Gina's wild imaginings. "Do you know Dom's cell phone number?"

"Of course," she said wearily. "But the police ran a trace on that, too, with no results."

"With all due respect to our various law enforcement agencies, they don't yet have access to the kind of technology I'm talking about here. It's still in the developmental stage and… Well, damn! That's it!"

Dev's exclamation shot up the tension level among the others in the room. The women all sat up in their chairs. Vickers hunched closer as Dev whipped out his own cell phone.

"That's what?" Vickers asked.

Shaking his head in obvious self-disgust, Dev tapped a number on his speed dial. "Why the hell didn't I think of it before?"

"Think of what?"

"Hold on." He put the phone to his ear. "Pat, I need the MilSat access code for the gamma version of CSR-II. I've been trying to get on using the beta version but… Yeah, I know. I know. Just get me the damned code."

"Ooooh," Sarah murmured, her green eyes dancing, "that's going to cost him."

"Pat Donovan is Dev's right-hand man," Gina explained to a bewildered Zia. "He's a wizard. Really, I think the man has magical powers. He can move mountains with a single phone call."

"If not mountains, at least the occupants of an entire Parisian hotel," Sarah recalled. "I don't know what kind of a bonus Dev paid him for that particular trick but I have a feeling it ran to big bucks."

"Say again," Dev barked into the phone, his brows knit. "Right. Right. Okay, got it. What? Yeah, we'll talk about that later."

He disconnected and switched to his handheld device. The thing looked so innocuous. Just a small, wafer-thin box with a greenish-colored digital screen and a set of icons that appeared with the tap of a finger. It fit in the palm of Dev's hand and could easily be mistaken for a smart phone, except this little gadget could evidently bounce signals off the moon or something.

He was entering a long involved code when the sliding doors to the study slammed back. Every head turned in surprise as Driskell's partner raced out and made a beeline for the foyer. Driskell herself was right on his heels, with Jack's dad staggering white-faced behind them.

The FBI agent paused only long enough to throw out a terse explanation. "We've got a report of shots fired. Initial indications are the situation may involve the ambassador."

"Involve *how?*" Gina jumped up. The violent movement sent her chair crashing to the floor. "Agent Driskell, wait! Is Jack hurt?"

"Or my brother?" Zia demanded as she, too, surged to her feet.

"I don't know," the FBI agent replied on the run. "I'll contact y'all as soon as I do."

"I'm coming with you!"

Gina shouted to an empty space. Driskell was already out the front door, leaving a frozen tableau of tension and fear in her wake. Dev shattered the silence with an abrupt command.

"Gina, do you have Driskell's cell phone number?"

She could hardly speak past the terror lodged like a spiked ball in her throat. "Yes."

Wedging a hand into the pocket of her jeans, she extracted

the business card Driskell had given her earlier. Dev snatched it from her fingers and entered the number on his device. Mere seconds later, his blue eyes lit with fierce satisfaction.

"Okay, I've got her." He swung toward the foyer. "Let's go."

Gina, Zia, Jack's dad and Dale Vickers all wheeled in a swift formation that would have done a platoon of marines proud. Their syncopated turn didn't impress Dev.

"Whoa! We can't all—"

"Do not say it!" Zia interrupted. Her dark eyes blazed and her accent went thick with passion. "I am a doctor. If Dom... If anyone is hurt, I can help."

"I'm going, too," Jack's dad growled.

Dale Vickers didn't say a thing but his pugnacious expression dared anyone, Dev included, to try and stop him.

Sarah was the only who exhibited any restraint. "I'll stay with Grandmama." Her gaze drilled into her husband. "But please, please, be careful."

"I will." Dev strode for the foyer. "We'll have to take two cabs."

"Sarah!" Gina called over her shoulder. "Buzz down and tell Jerome to get on his whistle. We need two taxis, like pronto!"

The doorman had them lined up and waiting at the curb when they all poured out of the elevators. Dev aimed for the lead vehicle and issued orders in a voice that said he wasn't allowing vetoes this time.

"Gina, you and Zia with me. Vickers, you follow with Mr. Mason."

They scrambled into their assigned cabs. Gina and Zia took the backseat of the first, Dev folded his tall frame into the front.

"Hey, mon," the cabbie said in a lilting Caribbean accent that matched his shoulder-length dreadlocks and colorful orange, green, yellow and black knit cap. "Where ya goin'?"

"Straight down Central Park West until I tell you to turn."

The cabbie shrugged and activated his meter. As the leafy green of the park zipped by, Dev kept his narrowed gaze on the street grid filling his screen.

Gina edged forward on her seat and looked over his shoulder. All she could see was a tiny red dot racing along the grid.

"Is that Driskell?"

"It is."

"What happens if she gets or makes a call? You won't lose the track, will you?"

"Heads in my R-and-D division will roll if I do."

Not quite reassured by that grim prediction, Gina groped for her cousin's hand. Zia threw her a glance filled with equal parts hope and determination.

"They will be okay, your man and my brother. But to make sure…" She squeezed Gina's fingers. "I shall say a special prayer to Saint Stephen. He is the patron saint of your grandmother's homeland, you know."

No, Gina didn't know. At this point, though, she would pray to any celestial being who might intercede on Jack and Dom's behalf.

As if sensing how close her cousin was to a total meltdown, Zia tried to distract her with details about the saint. "He is Istvan in our language. He was born in 965 or '67 or '75. No one knows for sure. His father was Grand Prince Géza of Hungary. His mother, the daughter of Gylua of Transylvania."

The mention of Transylvania diverted Gina long enough for all-too-vivid images of werewolves springing out of coffins to flash into her mind. Or was it vampires who rose from the dead? For God's sake! Who cared?

Zia refused to let her cousin's wildly careening thoughts and emotions overwhelm her. Speaking calmly, slowly, soothingly, she related how the eventual Saint Istvan married Giselle of Bavaria and ascended to the throne of the Magyars on the death of his father. How he discouraged pagan customs and strengthened Christianity by a series of strict laws. How he was devastated by the death of his oldest son, Emeric, in a hunting accident, after which his cousin, Duke Vazul, took part in an assassination conspiracy.

"The attempt failed," Zia related as Dev issued a sharp order to the cabbie to cut across town. "Vazul had his eyes gouged out and molten lead poured in his ears."

"Umm," Gina murmured.

Her eyes were on that blinking red dot, her thoughts anywhere but with some long dead saint.

"Without a living heir, King St. Istvan asked the Blessed Virgin Mary to take the Hungarian people as her subjects and become their queen. He died on the same feast day that commemorates the assumption into heaven of the Blessed Virgin Mary, yes?"

"What? Oh. Right."

Gina had no idea what her cousin had been talking about. Her focus was on the bridge ahead. As a native New Yorker, she understood why the cabbie balked.

"I don't do runs to that part of Brooklyn," he said with a head shake that set his dreadlocks swinging.

"There's an extra five hundred in it for you," Dev countered.

"Say no more, mon."

As they cruised onto the bridge, Gina twisted around. The second cab was still following. She dropped back in her seat, wondering how much Jack's dad had offered his driver.

Once across the bridge they entered a twilight zone of abandoned warehouses and crumbling industrial facilities. The area had formerly been home to the Brooklyn Navy Yard and had died a painful death in the '60s or '70s. Gina knew a comeback was planned, but it was still a ways off.

Artists and commercial activities rented space in the cavernous building that hadn't collapsed under the weight of time and disuse. She saw a bright pink neon sign indicating a movie studio. Another, slightly less attention-grabbing bill-board advertised Brooklyn Grange Farm. The farm suppos-edly utilized 45,000 square feet on the roof of Building 3, wherever that was. Sadly, all too many of the structures showed an endless vista of graffiti-covered walls, trash-strewn yards fenced off with razor wire, and row after row of broken windows.

With every deserted block the cab skimmed past, Gina's hopes dipped lower and lower. They hit rock-bottom when the taxi turned a corner and she spotted what looked like twenty or more emergency vehicles dead ahead.

The cabbie screeched to a halt a half block away. "Hey, mon, I can't cruise close to no cop cars. They might have dogs with 'em."

"Christ," Dev muttered, "what are you hauling in… Oh, hell, never mind."

He shoved a wad of bills at the driver and shouldered open the door. Gina and Zia scrambled out at the same time.

"Stay here until I scope out the situation," Dev ordered brusquely.

"No way," Gina said, her frantic gaze locked on the two ambulances parked side by side amid the other vehicles.

She took off after Zia, who'd already broken into a dead run. All Dev could do at that point was curse and charge after her. If shots were fired from any of the broken windows star-ing sightlessly down at them, he'd damned well better get in front of Gina and shield her body with his. Sarah would never forgive him if her sister got hurt. Zia would just have to take her chances.

The cabbie barely waited for them to clear his vehicle be-fore screeching into a three-point turn. He almost swiped the second cab's fender when he peeled off. Dev heard the shriek of brakes, the thud of doors slamming, the slam of footsteps on pavement as Vickers and Jack's father raced down the street.

Luckily, they all reached the protective screen of emer-

gency vehicles without shots erupting from the warehouse.
The uniformed officer on the perimeter looked as if he might
draw his weapon, though, when the two women leading the
charge ignored his command to stop. Parting like the pro-
verbial Red Sea, they started to go around him.

"Hey! Hold it right there."

He made a grab for the closest, which happened to be Zia,
and got a face full of raging female.

"*Vagyok orvos!* Ach! I am doctor! Doctor!"

Her unleashed emotions made her accent so heavy that
the English was almost indistinguishable from the Hungarian. Neither made an impression on the uniformed officer.

"Look, lady, you...all of you...better not take another
friggin' step until I see some ID, log you in and get clear-
ance to..."

"*Ide,* Anastazia!"

The shout came from an unmarked vehicle parked inside the cordon. Zia whirled and gave a glad cry. The rest
of the group spun around, as well. Gina registered a half-
dozen wildly careening thoughts as she watched Dominic
stride toward them.

Blood seeped from a slash high on one cheek. One eye
was swollen shut. He wasn't in handcuffs. And he was alone.

Dear God! He was alone.

With a sob of sheer terror, she dodged the uniformed officer and broke into another run. He gave a shout, but in-
terpreted a short air-chop from Dominic as a signal that his
duty lay in keeping the rest of the crowd corralled.

Ten steps later, Gina flung herself at Dominic. Her fists
hammered a frantic drumbeat on his chest. "Where's Jack?
What did you do with him? If you or those thugs you were
with hurt him, I'll carve out your heart and shove it down
your throat."

Dom's eyes widened, and Gina shocked even herself with
the viciousness of the threat. A distant corner of her mind
registered a flicker of surprise that she hadn't burst into her

by-now-usual flood of tears. Her otherwise volatile hormones seemed to have narrowed to a single, deadly and completely primal urge.

If this man—if any man—had harmed her mate, she'd make that Italian crime organization Jack's dad mentioned seem like a bunch of playful kindergarteners.

"Tell me, dammit. Where's Jack?"

Dom caught her pounding fists before they did serious damage to his chest wall. "He's there, Gina." Keeping a careful grip on her wrists, he angled her around. "Talking with some agents from the FBI."

She spotted him the same moment he followed Agent Driskell's nod and glanced over his shoulder. In the ten seconds it took for Gina to wrestle out of Dom's hold and Jack to sprint the fifty or so yards separating them, she saw that he was as bruised as her cousin.

But it was his eyes that lit her heart up like the Fourth of July. His fierce, unguarded expression. The raw, male pheromones shooting off him like live sparks when he caught her in his arms. Her blood singing with joy, she returned his kiss with every ounce of relief, of desire, of love that was in her.

Swift, frightening sanity came in the form of a sticky residue that transferred from the sleeve of his dark charcoal suit coat to Gina's palm. In her mad rush to his arms, she hadn't noticed the stain.

She couldn't miss it now. It left her palm a rusty red and a lump of dismay the size of a basketball bouncing around in her stomach. Gently, gingerly, she tried to ease away from the injured arm.

"You're hurt."

"So are you."

He curled a knuckle under her chin and angled her chin to survey the ugly bruise.

"I thought slamming my fist into your cousin's eye made up for this," he said, murder in his voice. "Looks like he still has some payment coming."

"You gave Dom his black eye?" Gina couldn't make sense of any of this. "If he was part of the plot to kidnap you, why isn't he under arrest?"

"Long story. Why don't we…?" He broke off, his gaze going to the men who now approached. "Hello, Dad. Dale."

Jack didn't seem the least surprised to see his father or chief of staff. Gina backed away to give them access to the man they all loved. She could share him with his family. With his obnoxious assistant. With his memories of Catherine.

And with the child they would welcome to the world in just a few short months. Lost in a love undiminished by the past or constrained by the present, Gina acknowledged there was more than enough of Jack Mason to go around.

Fifteen

Once again the duchess's spacious apartment served as command central. Most of the key players in the day's drama sat elbow-to-elbow at the dining table, relieving their tension with their choice of coffee, iced tea, fruit juice, *žuta osa* or the last of the double-distilled *pálinka*.

The duchess and Jack's father had opted for the brandy. Jack, Dev, Zia and Dom braved the throat-searing kick of the liqueur. Dale Vickers went with coffee, while Gina and Sarah chose juice. The duchess insisted Maria fill her own glass rather than trying to keep everyone's topped off and just sit down.

Pam Driskell put in a brief appearance, as did Jerome. The doorman had delegated his post to a subordinate to accompany the FBI agent upstairs. He'd abandoned his dignity long enough to wrap Gina in a fierce hug. He then shook Jack's hand, told him how happy he was to see him safe and went back to work.

The only major players who failed to put in an appearance were Antonio Cordi and his two thugs. Cordi because he was dead, shot through the heart during the violence that erupted inside the warehouse just moments before the police arrived. One of his hired hands was also deceased, the big one Jack bitingly referred to as Goliath. He'd had his jugular sliced by the lid of a rusty tin can and had bled out before the EMTs arrived. The second thug was now a guest of the U.S. government and likely to remain so for a long, long time.

Even now, huddled at the table that could seat twenty comfortably with the leaves in, Gina felt sick at the thought of how close both Jack and Dom had been to being on the receiving end of a bullet.

"Cordi must have wondered if my well-publicized departure from Interpol was a blind," Dom related after tossing back another restorative shot of *pálinka*. "He allowed me into the outer fringe of 'Ndrangheta but never let me get close enough to gather the evidence we needed to nail him."

"So to get close to the capo," Jack drawled, "you suggested using your kinship to Gina as a means to get to me."

"Cordi had sworn a blood oath to avenge his brother," Dom said with an unrepentant shrug. "He would have gotten to you eventually. I merely proved my loyalty by offering to set up the hit."

Gina still couldn't believe the tangled web of lies and deceit Dom had lived for almost a year. Danger had stalked him with every breath, every step.

Zia was even more appalled. She'd had no idea her brother had infiltrated one of Europe's most vicious crime organizations. Or that he'd arranged this "business" trip to New York City for a specific, and very deadly, purpose.

"No wonder you balked at my decision to accompany you," she said, scowling.

"You would not have accompanied me, had I not been sure I could keep you safe from danger."

"Not to mention," Dev guessed shrewdly, "the fact that she added to your credibility with the duchess."

"Yes, there was that consideration." A wry smile curved Dom's lips. "You don't know my sister very well, however, if you think my objections carried any weight with her. If I hadn't been certain I could keep her safe, I would have been forced to chain her to a wall in the dungeon of the crumbling castle the Duchess Charlotte once called home."

Jack's voice cut across the table like a serrated knife blade. "Too bad you couldn't offer the same guarantees for Gina."

"Ah, yes."

Dom's glance went to the bruise on Gina's chin. His one eye was still swollen shut, but the other showed real chagrin. "I very much regret having to hurt you, cousin. My associates had become impatient, you see, and I had to act or risk blowing my cover."

His glance slewed to Jack, then back to Gina. A rakish glint replaced the regret in his good eye. "If you would but let me," he murmured, "I would kiss away the hurt."

Jack answered that. This time his tone was slow and lazy but even more lethal. "You really do like living on the edge, don't you, St. Sebastian?"

"That's enough!"

The sharp reprimand turned every head to the duchess. Her chin had tilted to a degree that both Gina and Sarah recognized instantly, and her faded blue eyes shot daggers at the two combatants.

"May I remind you that you're guests in my home? Dominic, you will cease making such deliberately provocative comments. Jack, you will stop responding like a Neanderthal ready to club all rivals. Gina…"

When her gimlet gaze zinged to her youngest granddaughter, Gina jerked upright in her chair. She'd been on the receiving end of that stare too many times to take it lightly.

"What did I do?"

"It's what you haven't done," the duchess informed her. "For pity's sake, tell Jack you love him as much as he so obviously loves you and get on with planning your wedding."

A few moments of stark silence greeted the acerbic pronouncement. Jack broke it with a cool reply. "With all due respect, Duchess, that's something Gina and I should discuss in private."

His father joined the fray with a sudden and explosive exclamation. "Bull hockey!"

"Dad…"

John II ignored his son's warning glance. The face he turned to Gina wore a mix of regret and resolution. "I know I acted like an ass when you came to visit us at Five Oaks."

"Pretty much," she agreed politely.

"I need to apologize for that. And for the ugly name I called you earlier this morning," he added with a wince.

"Christ, Dad, what the hell did you…?"

"Be quiet, Jack. This is between Gina and me."

John Harris Mason II hadn't lost his bite. His son matched him glower for glower but yielded the floor. Once again, the older man addressed Gina.

"That was unforgivable. I hope you'll chalk it up to a father sick to death with worry over his son."

"Consider it chalked," she said with a shaky smile.

Oh, boy! Her emotions were starting one of their wild swings. Now that the danger to Jack had passed and she was surrounded by everyone she loved most in the world, she wasn't sure how long she could hold out before dissolving into wet, sloppy tears.

Jack's father didn't help matters. He leaned forward, his gaze holding hers. "I've never seen anyone turn Jack on his head the way you have, Gina."

"Is that…?" She gulped. "Is that good?"

"Oh, yes. More than I can say. You've shaken him out of the mold I tried… We all tried," he said with a glance at Dale Vickers, "to force him into."

He paused. His throat worked, sending his Adam's apple up and down a few times. When he could speak again, his voice was raw with emotion.

"Jack's mother would be proud to call you daughter. So would I."

That did it. Gina could feel her face getting all blotchy with the effort of holding back tears. "I…I…"

Shoving back her chair, she resorted to her most trust-worthy excuse for beating an instant retreat.

"I have to pee."

Sarah had followed her when she'd retreated to the bath-room earlier in the afternoon. This time it was Jack. Except he didn't knock, as her sister had. Nor did he ask for per-mission to enter. He just barged in and kicked the door shut behind him.

Luckily, Gina hadn't really needed to go. Her panties weren't around her ankles. The skinny jeans she'd been wear-ing for what now felt like two lifetimes were still zipped up. She was on the pot, though, and the tears she'd tried so hard to stem streamed down her cheeks. Like Sarah, Jack sank to his knees beside the stool. Unlike Sarah, he didn't hesitate to drag Gina off the throne and into his arms.

"Don't cry, sweetheart. Please, don't cry."

He held her, rocking back and forth, while the residual stress and tension and fear poured out via her tear ducts.

"It's…it's the hormones," she said through hiccuping sobs. "I never cry. Never! Ask Sarah. Ask…ask Grandmama. They'll tell you."

"It's okay."

"Noooo," she wailed, "it's not."

She grabbed the front of his shirt. His bloodied shirt. He hadn't had time to change, either.

"I didn't get a chance to tell you this morning, Jack. I…I didn't think I'd ever get a chance to tell you. I love you."

"I know, darling."

"No, you don't!"

The tears evaporated, replaced by an urgency that reached deep into her core.

"I think…" She shook her head. "Scratch that! I know I fell a little bit in love with you our first weekend together. I'm not sure when I tumbled all the rest of the way, but I'm all the way there."

"Me, too, my darling."

His smile was all Jack. Charming, roguish and so damned sexy Gina could feel her tears drying and another part of her starting to get wet.

"So what do you think?" he said, dropping a kiss on her nose. "Want get off the floor, go back into the dining room and tell your grandmother to start planning a wedding?"

"No."

His confidence took a hit, but he recovered fast. Shaking his head, he acknowledged his gaffe. "I'm such a jackass. How could I forget you're the world's greatest event coordinator?"

"Yeah, right."

Those damned hormones! Gina could for the sneer curled her lip and the sulky response she couldn't hold back.

"I can't be that great if you had to send Washington business TTG's way."

"What are you talking about?"

"Dale told me you steered business to TTG." She made a heroic effort to keep the hurt out of her voice. "I appreciate it, Jack. I really do. It's just that I wanted to… I was trying to… Oh, crap!"

The hand that took her chin and tilted it up was anything but gentle.

"Listen to me, Eugenia Amalia Thérése St. Sebastian. I'm going to say this once, and once only. If Dale Vickers or anyone else in my office steered business to TTG, they did it without my knowledge or consent. You got that?"

The fire in his blue eyes convinced her as much as the uncomfortable grip on her still sore chin.

"I've got it."

"You'd better," he said, the anger still hot. "Now, do you want to work the wedding arrangements yourself or not?"

"Not."

"Dammit all to hell! I'm past being civilized and modern and reasonable about this. If I have to lock you in those chains your cousin talked about and drag you to the altar, I will. One way or another, you're going to marry me."

"Oooooh."

Gina batted her eyes and thought about leading him on a little longer. She decided against it, primarily because she wasn't quite sure he wouldn't follow through with that bit about the chains.

"As much as I might enjoy the kinky aspects of your proposal," she breathed, "I think we should go for something a little more traditional."

"Then for God's sake," he bellowed, "tell me what the hell you want."

Whoa! What happened to the smooth, polished diplomat who'd seduced her with his charm and sophisticated wit? This glimpse of the angry male under Jack's urbane shell thrilled and made her just a tad nervous. Yielding to the age-old feminine instinct to soothe and soften and placate her mate, Gina stroked his cheek.

"What I want," she said, "is for us to get off the bathroom floor. Then we'll make a call to your mom and get her up here on the next flight. After which, we'll haul ass to a lab and have our blood drawn so we can stand up before the nearest justice of the peace."

Jack agreed with the last portion of her agenda, if not the first. Instead of pushing to his feet and pulling her up with him, he kept her anchored to the fluffy bath mat. The fire went out of his eyes, the irritation out of his voice.

"Are you sure that's what you want?" he asked in a much subdued tone.

"That's what I want."

"No big fancy wedding? No exotic theme?"

"No big fancy wedding." With silent apologies to Nikki and Samuel and Kallie, she lied her heart out. "No exotic theme. Just you and me and our immediate families in front of a JP."

* * *

Gina should have known that plan wouldn't hold up against the combined assault of her sister, her grandmother and Jack's mom, Ellen. All right, maybe she didn't really want it to. She'd given too much of herself and her energy to the party-planning business. In her heart of hearts, she secretly wished for at least a little splash.

Still, she had to work to overcome her irritation when her boss called less than an hour after Gina and Jack had emerged from the bathroom and announced their intentions to the assembled entourage. Vickers, Gina thought immediately. The little toad probably had TTG on his speed dial.

"Gina," Nikki gushed in her rapid-fire way, "I just heard! You've finally come to your senses."

"I…"

"I'm so, so glad you've agreed to marry your sexy ambassador."

"I have, but…"

"Listen, kiddo, I know Jack is hot to get you to the altar before you change your mind. I also know you want to keep the wedding small and intimate, but the midtown venue's available Thursday evening."

"Nikki…"

"My office, ten tomorrow morning. We'll hammer out the details. Oh, and bring your grandmother. I've been wanting to meet her since the day my father announced he was leaving my mother for her. God, I wish he had! Might have saved me thousands of dollars in shrink fees. *Ciao,* my darling. And don't worry. TTG will send you off in grand style."

Send you off in grand style.

The blithe promise had been intended to reassure. It acted instead like a bucket of frigid water. Every spark of Gina's newfound joy got a thorough dousing.

Grandmama, she thought on a wave of dismay. How could she move to D.C. and live with Jack? Not that he'd remain in

D.C. much longer. Vickers had hinted he was being considered for a major diplomatic posting. London was a definite possibility. So was Athens.

Heartsick, she caught Sarah's eye and telegraphed a silent signal. Her sister's hidden antenna were obviously in full receive mode. She nodded and moments later pushed through the swinging door to the kitchen. As soon as she saw Gina's face, concern clouded her green eyes.

"What's the matter?"

"Nothing out of the ordinary," Gina said bitterly. "I'm just being my usual, selfish self."

"Selfish how?"

"I didn't even think about Grandmama when I agreed to marry Jack. She's so looking forward to the baby. She's already talking about converting the study to a nursery. How can I just flit off and leave her alone?"

"She wants you to be happy. She wants both of us to be happy. You know she does."

Gina might have believed her if not for the guilt clouding Sarah's forest-green eyes. She'd experienced the same wrenching pangs before her wedding to Dev. They hadn't eased until Gina posed the possibility of moving back into the Dakota.

"Dev said he could set up a temporary headquarters here in New York," Sarah reminded her sister. "We could still do that. Or…"

The swish of the swinging door cut off whatever alternate Sarah had intended to propose. She and Gina both turned to face Zia.

"I'm sorry to intrude," she said. "But I wished to speak to you both, and this may be my only chance before Dom and I move to a hotel."

The heavy, stress-induced accent had disappeared. Zia was once again their gorgeous, self-assured cousin.

Or a third sister. One demanding to be included in this

girls-only enclave. The thought struck Gina all of two seconds before Zia gave it flesh and blood.

"As Gina knows," she said to Sarah, "I've just finished my last year of medical school at Semmelweis University in Budapest. It's a very prestigious institution and...well..."

She shrugged, as if to downplay what both sisters knew had to be a major accomplishment. "I've been offered a number of residencies in pediatric medicine," she continued after a moment. "One of them is at Kravis Children's Hospital. That's why I insisted on accompanying Dom on this visit. I...I have an interview with the head of the residency program tomorrow," she finished on a note of uncharacteristic hesitation.

"That's wonderful," Sarah said with unfeigned delight. "You and Grandmama will be able to visit and get to know each other better."

"Yes, well..." Zia's glance shifted from one sister to the other. "The duchess has invited me to live with her, should I do my three-year residency here in New York City. I'm overwhelmed by her generosity but I don't wish to impose on her. If the idea concerns you...either of you...or in any way makes you think I'm taking advantage of her, please tell me."

Gina wished she were a better person. She really did! Here she was, wracked with guilt one moment at the prospect of leaving her grandmother alone. In the next, she was battling a toxic niggle of jealousy at the idea of this ultra-smart, ultra-achieving woman taking her place in the duchess's heart.

And of course, because Zia *was* so damned smart, she read every emotion that flitted across Gina's face.

"I will not live here if you don't wish it," she said quietly. "Or you, Sarah. I know how much you love the duchess. How much she loves you. If it will cause you or her heartache, I'll turn down the offer from Kravis. None of you will ever hear from me again."

Gina knew the speech came straight from the heart. But it was the mist that sheened her cousin's dark eyes that obliterated any and every doubt. Somehow, someway, the knowledge that brilliant, self-assured Anastazia St. Sebastian was susceptible to human emotion made everything all right.

The jealousy fell away, leaving only a profound thankfulness. Smiling, she reached out and squeezed Zia's hand.

"I think it would be wonderful for Grandmama to have your company."

Sixteen

Nicole Tremayne came through as promised. TTG sent Gina and Jack off in grand style.

The balmy June evening was perfect for an outdoor ceremony. Thousands of tiny white lights gleamed in the topiary trees outlining the terrace of TTG's midtown venue. More lights sheathed in filmy white netting were hung in graceful loops to form an archway from the reception room to the dais. The platform itself was framed by antique wrought-iron. The intricate iron work was painted pearl-white and intertwined with netting, lights, ivy and fragrant yellow honeysuckle.

Gina and Jack had kept the guest list small. Relatively small, that is, compared to the hundreds who usually attended TTG's functions. Still, the attendees filled eight rows of white chairs arranged in a semicircle on the terrace overlooking the East River.

Gina's coworkers at TTG came as guests for a change instead of employees. Jerome and his wife had been invited, of course, and Maria beamed from her seat in the front row. Dominic sat beside her, his black eye still noticeable but considerably reduced in size and discoloration.

Jack's guests filled the seats on the other side of the aisle.

Following her son's wishes, Ellen had been ruthless. She'd axed every one of the political cronies her husband had tried to add to the list. Only Jack's family, close personal friends and associates survived the hatchet. In his case, though, "close" included the Secretary of State, the current U.S. Ambassador to the U.N. and Virginia's lieutenant governor.

"You ready, Gina?"

Kallie was the only of her fellow employees not seated out front. She'd volunteered to get the major players in place and cue the music. The wings in her red hair were yellow tonight in keeping with the yellow roses that wreathed the hair of the bride and her attendants.

The event coordinator in Gina had her taking a quick peek through the gauze curtains to make sure everyone was where they were supposed to be. Sure enough, Jack waited under the wrought-iron arch with his groomsmen. Dev stood tall and handsome beside him. Dale Vickers was arranged next to Dev. Gina grimaced inwardly but reminded herself of her resolution to *try* to build a better relationship with the little toad.

She let the curtain drop and sent a smile to the other three women clustered with her in the small anteroom. Her grandmother, regal in royal blue silk and lace, looked like the grand duchess she was. Gina had asked Zia to be one of her attendants. And Sarah, of course. They were each wearing the dress of her choice. Zia had hit the shops on 5th Avenue and found a body-hugging gold silk sheath that dipped to her waist in the back. With her black hair piled loosely on top of her head, the rear view was sure to drop most of the male jaws in the house when she glided down the aisle.

Sarah's dress was one of the retro classics she still favored despite Dev's repeated attempts to get her to buy out Rodeo Drive. This one was a Balenciaga that fell in soft, shimmering folds in the same vivid green hue as the Russian emerald Dev had slipped on her finger when they'd become engaged.

Gina's choice of rings was more traditional, if you could

call a three-carat marquise traditional. Particularly since Jack had upped the weight from her original choice and had the stone set in a band studded with another three carats of baguettes.

The diamonds' glitter didn't compare to the sparkle in Gina's smile as she gave Kallie the go-ahead. "I am so ready."

She wasn't sure, but she thought Sarah and the duchess let out a collective sigh of relief. Even Zia perked up as the music swelled and she led the way down the aisle. Sarah gave her sister a quick kiss and went next. Then Gina slipped her arm through her grandmother's.

As they made their slow progress under the arch of netting and tiny white lights, Gina couldn't believe how her world had changed so drastically in such a short time. Was it only two months since Grandmama had made this same, slow walk with Sarah? Two and a half months since Gina had peed on a little purple stick and felt her world tilt off its axis? Those frantic days might have happened in another life, to another person. Everything in Gina's world now was right and bright and perfect.

The duchess seemed to agree. When she and her youngest granddaughter reached the dais, her faded blue eyes shone with love. "My dearest Eugenia. I'm so very proud of you."

Gina wouldn't cry! She wouldn't! She wanted to, though. Big, fat, wet, sloppy tears that would streak her entire face with mascara.

Uh-oh! Jack must have sensed how close she was to a meltdown. He took a hasty step forward, smiling as he relieved the duchess of escort duty.

"I'll take it from here."

Bending, he dropped a kiss on his soon-to-be-grandmother-in-law's cheek. She murmured something for his ears only. Probably the same death threat she'd issued to Dev, Gina guessed, threatening him with unspeakable agony if he hurt so much as a single hair on her head.

Jack acknowledged the warning with a solemn nod. Then

his eyes were on Gina. Only on Gina. Her glorious smile, her tumble of silvery blond curls, her laughing blue eyes. He tucked her arm in his, amazed and humbled by the fact he'd been given the precious gift of love twice in one lifetime.

In all the excitement of the past week, he and Gina had almost missed their second appointment with their OB doc. They'd gone in yesterday and had the first ultrasound done. Jack carried a copy of the scan in his tux pocket now, right next to his heart. As far as his parents knew, he and Gina would welcome the Mason family's first set of twins.

First things first, though! Jack's number one priority at the moment was getting a wedding band on Gina St. Sebastian's finger. He practically dragged her into position on the dais and issued a swift instruction to the senior judge of the U.S. Court of Appeals for the Second Circuit, who also happened to be his former college roommate.

"Let's do this!"

Epilogue

What an exciting, frightening, wonderful week this has been! Eugenia, my darling Eugenia, finally admitted what I've known since the day she returned from Switzerland. She's in love, so very much in love, with the father of her babies. Babies! I can't wait to cradle them in my arms, as I once held Gina.

Then there's Sarah, my lovely Sarah. It makes my heart sing to see her so happy, too. I suspect it won't be long before she and Dev start their family, as well.

I thought my life's work would be complete when I escorted those two precious girls down the aisle. How odd, and how wonderful, that another young and vibrant twosome has helped fill the void of losing them. Dominic goes back to Hungary in a few days and is pressing me to return to my homeland for a visit. I shall have to think about that. In the meantime, I'll share Anastazia's trials and tribulations as she begins what I know will be a grueling residency.

Who would have imagined my plate would be so full at this late stage in my life?

From the diary of Charlotte,
Grand Duchess of Karlenburgh

* * * * *

Merry Christmas
& A Happy New Year!

Thank you for a wonderful
2013...

A sneaky peek at next month…

Desire™

PASSIONATE AND DRAMATIC LOVE STORIES

My wish list for next month's titles…

In stores from 20th December 2013:

☐ Beneath the Stetson – Janice Maynard

& For the Sake of Their Son – Catherine Mann

☐ Pregnant by Morning – Kat Cantrell

& The Nanny's Secret – Elizabeth Lane

☐ At Odds with the Heiress – Cat Schield

& Project: Runaway Bride – Heidi Betts

2 stories in each book - only £5.49!

Available at WHSmith, Tesco, Asda, Eason, Amazon and Apple

Just can't wait?

Visit us Online

You can buy our books online a month before they hit the shops!

Come in from the cold this Christmas with two of our favourite authors. Whether you're jetting off to Vermont with Sarah Morgan or settling down for Christmas dinner with Fiona Harper, the smiles won't stop this festive season.

Visit:
www.millsandboon.co.uk

MILLS & BOON®
Book Club

Join the Mills & Boon Book Club

Want to read more **Desire**™ books?
We're offering you **2 more** absolutely **FREE!**

We'll also treat you to these fabulous extras:

 Exclusive offers and
much more!

🌹 FREE home delivery

🌹 FREE books and gifts with our
special rewards scheme

Get your free books now!

visit **www.millsandboon.co.uk/bookclub**
or call Customer Relations on **020 8288 2888**

Mills & Boon® Online

Discover more romance at
www.millsandboon.co.uk

- **FREE** online reads
- **Books** up to one
  month before shops
- **Browse our books**
  before you buy

...and much more!

For exclusive competitions and instant updates:

 Like us on **facebook.com/millsandboon**

 Follow us on **twitter.com/millsandboon**

 Join us on **community.millsandboon.co.uk**

Visit us Online Sign up for our FREE eNewsletter at
www.millsandboon.co.uk

WEB/M&B/RTL5